The Bene

Assumed identity

By Allan Jonas

ISBN: 9798354467143

Acknowledgements:

Many thanks to the various friends and family members who helped me through proof reading and giving feedback on my book series. This is the fifth one. My books are much better for your input.

Prologue

Caves near Avignon, September 1378

His monk's habit was dirty and dusty and he felt tired.

Matty Cutler sat in the mouth of a cave, watching dozens of rooks in the nearby trees, listening to their constant calling, the 'kaah' sound filling the air.

There was little more he could do but wait. He had stopped running. He used his time to sharpen his sword, finding a smooth rock and spitting on it, then running it along the blade. He checked the tension on his bow and sharpened the points of his arrows. It was like the night before a major battle, the calm before the storm, the time to pray for delivery and, failing that, a good death.

He knew the soldiers would find him eventually. He had already seen them in the distance, maybe two or three miles away, threshing through the valley below. They were close enough that he even heard shouted commands, voices carrying upwards on the breeze to his position high amongst the rocks.

There were two groups of soldiers. He did not know if they were together or were two sets of enemies, but they had a common goal, to find him, the English Benedictine, and take him back. Or were their orders simply to keep him from falling into the hands of others, even if that meant killing him?

Darkness was closing in. He set his sword in the soft, wet ground of the cave. He had one candle left, enough for this final night before the soldiers reached him. He needed to rest, to regain strength through sleep. But it was impossible. There were too many things on his mind. Thoughts of home and family. Thoughts of what was to come the next day.

He stared at the candle. In it he saw things, shapes, figures of people dancing with the movement of the flame. He knew he was imagining them, but the sight triggered a thought out of nowhere. A realisation. It was something someone had said. It offered him a possible connection to his past life. And he knew he had to go to the place he had been escaping from; the same place his pursuers wanted to take him back to. A place that held danger for him.

He had to return to Avignon. But he would not go as a prisoner. He would go back on his own terms.

Part One

Clouds of the mind

Chapter One

Somewhere off the coast of Brittany, January 1378

Matty Cutler hated the sea.

He had no point of reference for his foreboding. His memory had still not fully returned. But as the ship rolled and his stomach churned, he knew that somewhere in his past he had encountered the sea at its most terrifying.

It was two weeks since he regained consciousness. He had woken in a small room, laying on a straw bed. When he had tried to get up his head pounded and he fell with a thump on the wooden floorboards.

A girl had responded, helping him back on to the bed, where he drifted once again into deep sleep. It was another full day before he woke for a second time.

Mireille was twelve years old and his main carer, simply because she spoke English. She asked him his name.

At first, no name would come to him. Then there was a name, vaguely etched on his mind. Stephen. With the name came an image of a monk, tonsured and dressed in black. He described what he saw, and the girl said it sounded like the garb of a Benedictine. She told him they were known as black monks because of what they wore. The word was familiar to him. *Benedictine.* Beyond that it had no meaning.

For a week Mireille helped him regain some strength. He was not a tall man but Mireille commented that he was muscular, and although his strength was reduced by his fever it was still clear that he had known manual labour, not a softer life. But his muscles could have come from any one of many occupations. Maybe he was a farmer or ironworker. Nothing emerged from the depths of his mind to explain his physique.

Mireille was wise beyond her years. She calmed him, telling him his memory would return in time. He knew she was being kind, because how could she know? What if it never came back, leaving him without a past?

She told him where he was, at St Malo, on the northern coast of France. She asked him questions she hoped would help him remember something, anything, about himself. She mentioned places she knew in England. Was he from London, or Portsmouth? Perhaps he could recall the monastery he lived in, because now it was accepted fact that he was Stephen, a Benedictine monk. But all he had was one name and the memory of a figure who might be a monk. With the passing days, his frustration grew.

She tried to help by telling him how he came to be in St Malo. She explained that he had been found in the shallow waters of a beach on England's south coast. There had been a battle and the crew were looking for survivors. When they saw him face down and about to drown, they rescued him, thinking he was one of their men. And when the ship sailed for France, so did he.

Mireille explained that, on the crossing, he had been delirious, talking nonsense and shouting in his sleep. His words were English, and there were few English mercenaries with the fleet. The captain needed someone who spoke the language to find out who he was. Maybe he was a spy and should be killed, but he might be an important nobleman who would command a ransom. The captain needed to know.

It was Mireille's brother, a senior crewman, who stepped forward, sensing an opportunity to earn a little money and win the captain's favour. He offered Mireille's services as nurse and interpreter once they reached St Malo.

Matty listened, but none of what Mireille said triggered any new memories. Nothing was familiar. He shook his head. He had no recollection of a beach, no recollection of a battle. His life story was empty.

So Mireille passed time telling him more about herself. She lived at the port with her brother and two younger sisters, but rarely saw her brother, who spent most of his life at sea. With her brother away, she was the head of her household. Her parents were dead. Her father had died first, soon after the arrival of the fourth child. It left the family without an income, and her mother started making and selling souvenirs to the sailors and sundry traders who came to St Malo. All three girls helped with the work.

Mireille's mother passed on her craft skills to her children. She also became fluent in English as she dealt daily with merchants and sailors from England. She taught Mireille what she learned of the language. "You can provide for your sisters when I'm gone," she told her. And when her mother followed her father to the grave, Mireille did just that, assuming the role as head of household and main breadwinner.

She showed Matty some examples of the souvenirs she and her sisters had made. They were fashioned from any materials that were freely available. There were bracelets and necklaces made from shells, as well as dolls and small boats carved from driftwood. There were also scavenged pieces, such as pocket-knives that had washed up on the shore and which she had worked on, scraping off the rust and sharpening the points.

Matty said he was impressed, to which she laughed. "The jewellery is crude and worthless," she told him. "But many of the sailors' wives live in villages far from the sea and have never seen it. The sailors convince them that the shells are rare or that the dolls have been made by skilled craftsmen. They make up exotic stories about how they got them. One sailor told me he had convinced his wife that her necklace was made by a mermaid." She laughed again. "Because of these trinkets my family gets to eat. And now, I earn a bit more by caring for an elderly monk."

Matty thanked her for sharing her story with him. It had lifted his spirits. As he lay awake that night, thinking of the things Mireille had made, an image came to him. It was a child's toy.

The image was of a horse carved in wood. It had no context. There was no clue to its story, and nothing to tell him about the child whose

7

hand held it. It felt significant, an important part of his life, but the reason for its importance would not come to him.

Mireille and an older woman nursed him for several more days, simply making him comfortable and using a weak potion to soothe the cuts and bruises on his skin. At one point, Matty sniffed at the potion. "Marigolds," he declared.

Mireille became excited. "You know of remedies," she said. "Surely learned at your monastery. Perhaps you were the Apothecary." She sighed. "What is your story, monk Stephen? I would love to know it."

"So would I," he replied.

Over the following days Matty gained a little strength and ventured outside, a little further each day. Mireille's cottage was at the top of a cobbled street overlooking the port. There were boats everywhere, a sea of masts and rigging.

One such morning, he felt dizzy and sat down with his back to the cottage wall. Two men arrived.

Mireille heard them and came to see who was there. One of the men was a priest and was carrying a large sack. It was the other who did the talking. He spoke in Spanish to Mireille, another language she had learned from her mother and then working in the port. Matty could not understand what was being said but could tell what was happening. Mireille was being interrogated.

She interpreted for him. "They want to know what I have discovered about you." From the Spaniard's gesticulations, it was clear he was not happy with her answers. Mireille confirmed it. "I have learned so very little about you," she told Matty, as the man stormed off angrily.

The priest stayed and spoke to Matty. His English was good. Not as good as Mireille's, but good enough to hold a conversation. "You are lucky to be alive," he said.

"I know. Mireille has told me. I could have drowned."

"Mireille says you are a monk, a Benedictine. And that your name is Stephen."

Matty shrugged. "Seems so. But in truth, my mind is a mass of fog, like I'm passing through thick clouds. Even when I see a gap through them, I'm not sure what I'm looking at." He told the priest about the toy horse he had seen.

The priest nodded. "Have you looked in a mirror, I wonder?" Matty shook his head. "I thought so. If you had, you would see why you are in such a state." He pulled a silvered mirror from a large bag he carried. "Take a look."

Matty took the mirror and gazed at his reflection. He knew he had a large bump on his head, because he could feel it protruding. But when he saw the size of it, he gasped. On the same side of his head his face was a mix of purples and blues, and his eye was swollen. He was more than forty-five years of age but looked much older. His hair was long and matted from dried blood, while stubble on his chin added to the general sense of neglect and decay. He looked like a vagrant, a beggar. Mireille had done her best to improve his appearance, but he was still quite a sight.

"Somebody took a dislike to you," suggested the priest.

"Mireille told me there was a battle."

"You remember nothing of it?"

"No."

"Well, whatever happened, you lived." The priest pointed towards the receding figure of the man who had stormed off. "He is the captain of the ship you came on. And now he must decide what to do with you. I don't suppose you are important in England and worth a ransom, are you?"

"I shouldn't think so. Look at my clothes." He wore the basic shirt and breeches of a countryman. He had no finery, no rings or adornments.

The priest nodded. "The captain thinks the same but has wondered whether his crew might have stolen your possessions while you were unconscious." He took something else from his sack and tossed it to Matty. "Take off those disgusting clothes," he said, and Matty obeyed.

9

"Let's see if we can make you more presentable. Try this on." It was a cloak. "It's a Benedictine's garb, as you probably know. It belonged to a friend of mine, but he has no use for it now. Last winter took him." A sad expression came over the priest.

Matty held the habit. It was a simple cloak with a hood, a scapula. He hoped it would awaken memories of an abbey and give him some inspiration, a link to his past life. Instead, he felt nothing. There was no connection, no moment of new awareness. He felt no emotion.

The cloak seemed clean, but he wanted to be sure. "Did the last owner die of plague, by any chance?" he asked.

The priest frowned. "No. He was over eighty years old. It was simply his time to go to his maker. There are some underclothes as well, braies, socks and a shirt. They aren't from the same man. I prevailed on the ship's captain to let me buy them for you, though they are not new and the trader could tell me nothing of their previous owner. You'll have to wear your own shoes, but they don't look to be in as bad a state as the rest of your clothing."

Matty tried on the cloak. "There's no belt, I'm afraid," said the priest. "That was lost. Perhaps that's why you look so awkward in it. It's a bit loose and wears you instead of you wearing it. But maybe that's to be expected in the circumstances. You have lost weight, I think."

"Mireille feeds me well, but my stomach doesn't always let me keep the food down." He paused, then frowned. "If I look awkward in it, what if it's because I have never worn such as this and am no monk?"

"Then you will have to explain to God why you are dressed like one when you see Him."

Mireille now joined the conversation. She told them what the captain had said to her. "Tomorrow you will be going back to the ship," she said.

The priest turned and started to go. "Good luck, Stephen the monk," he said. "You will need it."

Mireille stared at Matty in his black habit, shaking her head. "Forgive me," she said. "I have seen many holy men. You do not look the part. Let me at least cut your hair as a monk would before you leave."

****

The following day, two sailors came to fetch Matty. Mireille asked where they were taking him, and was told they would be sailing south, to La Rochelle as their next port of call.

Matty thanked Mireille for what she had done for him. "I wish I could give you something by way of thanks," he said, his arms outstretched in a gesture of poverty, because he had nothing to give her. All he had in the world was the habit the priest had given him.

She smiled and produced a gift of her own. It was a necklace made from shells, with a small wooden cross attached. "A man of God should not be naked at the neck," she said as she gave it to him.

He had no chance to say more, as the sailors pulled him away. He went willingly, not knowing what else to do, but still they chose to manhandle him out from the house and down the cobbles to the quayside.

Mireille watched him go. She sighed. The future looked bleak for the Englishman, but at least he now looked like he should, with his monk's habit, newly tonsured hair and wearing a cross. She would pray for him.

The ship was huge, as big as any Matty had ever seen. It was a twin-sailed carrack, fitted for war but currently employed as a merchant vessel. Guns still protruded from holes all along its side, from bow to stern.

One of the Spanish sailors barked out orders to him and, as before, he understood the meaning without knowing the words. He mounted the gangplank and reached the deck, then obeyed an order to settle down amongst a row of sacks.

11

There was a great deal of activity. Preparations were being made to cast off. And for a while, Matty was left alone, ignored. He was given neither food nor water and was told nothing about the plans for him.

It was afternoon before the ship sailed, leaving the calm, sheltered waters of the bay then turning westwards against the prevailing winds, hitting their force full on and fighting the wind and waves as the English Channel met the Atlantic Ocean.

The clouds in Matty's mind opened a little and another memory came. He had been at sea before, but not here. And he had faced peril on the seas. He knew it. But, as with his memory of the wooden toy, it was no more than a glimpse into something, a feeling without detail, without certainty of its truth. But it gave him a sudden foreboding, a feeling that sea travel was anything but safe.

He took refuge from the sea spray and watched in admiration as the crew went about their business. He saw terror in the eyes of some, and remembered watching another crew fighting the same feelings, the same trepidations.

The day passed into night, and he slept fitfully.

****

Around midnight he was awake, kept so by the constant clattering of the rigging in the whistling winds. It was raining and he was soaked to the skin.

The saving grace was that he had not eaten and neither had he drank much for hours, so had no need to make the journey to the ship's bows in order to relieve himself. Given a choice, the pangs of hunger and thirst he had were a much more attractive option than that. He was happy to stay where he was.

He dozed again and awoke to a different world. The sun shone and the sea was calmed. The sailors who had seemed terrified in the night now wore cheerful smiles and some were singing, or rather chanting a repetitive chorus. One sailor set up a chant that had his shipmates responding, as if answering some question or plea.

Matty understood. The crew were as relieved as he was that the weather had turned and they were releasing the tension that had built during the fearful night.

A cup and plate appeared in front of him. "Eat, drink," said one of the crew, and he accepted greedily, his over-enthusiastic eating bringing guffaws of laughter from the sailor.

But his stomach was still refusing to accept food and he was soon rushing to the side of the ship to vomit overboard. There he looked up at the endless vista of the ocean, the horizon rising and falling with the ship's roll. And he vomited again, but with nothing in his stomach it was more of a retch, a gag in his throat. And he wanted to die.

It was late in the evening before further attention was paid to him. A sailor gestured for him to get up and follow. And he found himself in the captain's cabin.

The captain was studying charts. Matty was surprised to see the priest he had met the day before, seated in a corner.

The captain pointed to an area in the charts. "Here is us," he said in a basic, awkward English. "Bay of Biscay. We go here." He pointed to a port and Matty read the name of La Rochelle. It was where Mireille had already told him he was going.

"There you leave," added the captain.

"And go where?" replied Matty.

The captain spread his hands and shrugged. "How should I care?"

Matty was taken back on deck.

The priest joined him. "You are of no value to him," he said. "On many ships you would be thrown overboard. But our captain is a pious man, and superstitious. That's why he has a priest accompany him whenever he sails. I say prayers with him several times each day. Mostly I ask God to quell the fury of the seas."

"And does God answer your prayers?"

The priest shrugged. "We have not yet sunk."

13

"So why does the captain let me live? He knows I have no value."

"In case you are what you say you are. He does not want to anger God by killing a holy man."

"Then I am fortunate indeed to be a monk."

****

The going was slow against the winds and it was several more days before they reached La Rochelle. As they approached the harbour, Matty stood near to the starboard bow and watched as the land grew nearer.

The captain joined him. He was grinning. "The port for long time belonged England," he said. "Not long ago, sea battle here. French and Spanish ships. English fleet beaten." His grin widened and he made downward, wavy gesture with his arm, mimicking the sinking of an English ship. "French and Spanish hate English." He laughed.

Matty could see defensive towers and there was building work being done in the port. "English castle destroyed," said the captain. "Stone used for new town walls."

The ship pulled in and the crew wasted no time in readying to disembark. The captain pointed to the quayside. "Go," he said to Matty. Matty looked round for any sign of the priest. It had comforted him to have the company of someone who could speak English. But there was no sign of him.

Matty took the few steps on to dry land, sighing with relief to leave the sea behind. He looked around. He felt alone. A man without an identity in a land where his countrymen were hated and where he could not speak the local language. He lacked a past and his future was uncertain.

He sat on a wall to consider what to do. Mireille was uppermost in his thoughts. He had no memory of anything before he met her, other than the name Stephen and a child's toy. So Mireille was the full story of his life. She was just a child scraping a living to support her younger sisters. It was a harsh world. He hoped she would survive it.

14

He looked at the clothes he wore. *'It seems I am a monk,'* he thought to himself. *'And what monks do is pray.'* So that is what he did, bowing and silently asking God for some direction, and asking Him to take care of the good child who had nursed him in St Malo.

When he finished, he stood and sighed. Then walked, to whatever God or fate had in store next for him.

Chapter Two

Lucan House Manor, Nottinghamshire, January 1378

Mary was quietly threading a needle through cloth, working on a table linen for the hall. A fire had been blazing in the hearth but was now reduced to embers, left to diminish as the evening drew in.

A knock came at the door, but the visitor did not wait to be called into the room.

It was the third evening in a row that Edwina had appeared at this time of day. Because the evenings were her worst times.

"It's coming on," said Edwina, nodding towards the cloth.

"Another day or two and it'll be finished. But the candlelight isn't good enough to work in now, so I can do no more today."

Mary welcomed the intrusion, the company, even though there was always more to Edwina's visits than was immediately apparent. Edwina looked tired. At first, she did not say what was troubling her. But Mary knew not to ask questions. That was not how to deal with Edwina. It only made her clam up and say less, unwilling to bare her soul, even to her best friend. So Mary waited, ever patient, and quietly made Edwina a warm cup of chamomile and honey. They sat and sipped, saying nothing.

Finally, Edwina began. "It feels strange being back," she said.

"Have things changed?"

Edwina laughed. "Well, there's you and Sam, for a start."

Mary shrugged. "We haven't changed."

"No, but you are married now. That feels different."

Sam was the local cobbler. He and Mary had been in a relationship for many years, living together in the room above Sam's workshop. They had three children. Sam had proposed many times but Mary had always rejected his proposals, worried that marriage would somehow spoil what she had with him.

16

Then, a year ago, Mary was instrumental in persuading Edwina to take a chance in her life, to attend a royal wedding at Windsor. Edwina had not wanted to go. She wanted to stay where she felt safe and comfortable.

It made Mary re-evaluate her own life. She realised she should take her own advice and, for once take a chance, a risk. She surprised Sam by suggesting they should wed, and within a couple of weeks they had made their vows in the local church.

"Perhaps it's me that has changed," suggested Edwina.

Mary leaned forward very slightly. "You worry about your father. That's natural. But I think there are other things on your mind also," she said. It was an invitation to Edwina to express whatever worries were on her mind.

Edwina sighed and rubbed the stump where her arm used to be. She had lost it after being savaged by a dog when she was a child. "Is your arm sore?" asked Mary.

"No more than usual." Edwina frowned. "But I can't sleep for it."

"Of course. Is that the only reason?"

Edwina turned sharply and looked into Mary's quizzical eyes. Mary had expected a response. It was like a game they played that always went through the same stages. For once, Edwina did not anger, and Mary felt encouraged enough to probe further. "Is it Michel?" she asked.

Edwina laughed, a mocking laugh. Michel was a merchant who she had met in Rye. He had fallen for her and wanted her to stay there and marry him, but Edwina turned him down and came home to Nottinghamshire. Mary suspected Edwina regretted that decision.

"No, not him."

Mary tried again. "You went through such an ordeal at the hands of the smugglers. It can't have been easy."

Mary knew some of what had happened to Edwina. She knew that, after the royal wedding Edwina had gone to be a maid to Princess

17

Phillipa, the king's granddaughter, at Hedingham Castle in Essex. There, she had fallen foul of an evil man, a local smuggler. For months he held her captive, planning to sell her, but she escaped, only to end up in the middle of a battle as French and Spanish ships raided England's south coast.

"You don't understand."

Mary leaned further forward. "Then tell me," she said, her voice kind and gentle. Caring. Softly pleading. Sincere.

Tears welled in Edwina's eyes. She sobbed. "I see the bodies," she said. "Lying in the streets and on the beach. I see the blood, and hear the voices, crying *help me!*' and I see the women and children weeping for their husbands and fathers."

Mary took Edwina and hugged her. It was better than words. And Edwina's sobbing increased as she gave herself to her friend's compassion.

"I cannot imagine the things you saw," said Mary. "War is a terrible thing. But you are safe now."

Mary pulled away from the hug. "You don't understand," she said. "I *am* safe here, while my father is somewhere out there still."

"You think he's alive?"

"I know it."

"Your Moses Tree tells you?"

It was not said unkindly. For years Edwina had taken comfort and strength from an old tree at the edge of the village. She felt it gave her a connection to family who were long dead. It was also her source of inspiration. And Mary took it seriously. She was not mocking Edwina. She did not doubt the power of such things.

"I saw him. I was by the tree and looked up at the clouds. There he was. He was with some people I didn't recognise. One was a young girl. He's alive, I know it, and I have to find him."

Mary sighed. "Less than a year ago I told you to make a journey to a wedding. It would change your life, I said. Little did I know how right

18

I was or how much pain it would lead you to. And if I hadn't advised you so, your father would never have gone to that battle at Rottingdean and disappeared. So this time I have different advice. I say, don't go. Stay here and live a full life in the place you have always known, with your friends and family. Find a man to marry."

Edwina was angered. There was always someone telling her she should be wed. Usually it was her mother, but now it was Mary. She picked up the cup of chamomile and threw it into the fireplace. "I'm going back," she said. "With or without your blessing."

Edwina was head strung but Mary admired her spirit and knew it would be pointless trying to change her mind. "You have decided," she said, her voice still calm.

Edwina calmed in response. "Yes. And I know you mean well. But I must go. It's what I must do. That's all there is to it."

"But to do what? You searched twice but nobody could tell you what happened. No-one saw your father after he joined the battle in the town square."

Edwina shook her head. "I don't know. I did speak to everyone I could. I must have missed something important. I must go back."

Mary took a deep breath. Something had occurred to her a while before, but she had kept it to herself. Now she realised she had to say it. "You didn't speak to everyone," she said, almost in a whisper.

"I did. Michel was with me."

"You spoke to everyone from the English side of the battle. But others were there. The French or Spanish soldiers and sailors. They were there. Perhaps…"

Edwina's eyes widened. "You're right. Perhaps they will know. They must have seen him, they must!"

Mary had given Edwina new hope, a new idea to take forward. Maybe somebody from the invading army had seen what happened to her father. But how could she find out?

19

Mary had read her mind. "Start with Michel," she said. "He trades with the French and Spanish. If anyone can help you, he can. Go with strength of purpose, and, yes, go with my blessing, whether you want it or not. Oh, and I do not expect you to marry him."

They laughed together and enjoyed some more relaxed time, as they always did.

Chapter Three

La Rochelle, France, January 1378

The old port was busy. It was overwhelming.

Matty felt dizzy. He was still suffering the effects from his head injuries, but also the confusion that came with feeling lost. He walked without making progress, turning this way and that. He could not concentrate, which nearly cost him dearly when he stepped into the path of a horse. The rider shouted obscenities in French, fist raised in a gesture of threat, angered more because his valuable mount might have been hurt than for any concern about injury to Matty or himself.

Matty needed to get away from the crowds. He found a quiet alleyway and went down it. In the shadows, he disturbed a couple making love. The man was angry, his moment of ecstasy spoiled, and he became abusive. By contrast, the woman did not seem to notice the intrusion. She looked vacant, as if thinking about anything other than the sexual act. A prostitute, thought Matty, one who had developed a way to dissociate herself from an act that repulsed her, but that was necessary for her survival.

At the end of the alleyway was a small square. Matty found a place to sit down. His head was pounding and he felt physically and mentally exhausted. He had probably been on land less than an hour, but it felt a lot longer. He needed to rest and regain some strength before moving on.

A door opened behind him and a figure emerged, then barked out some abuse in French. The man was clearly angry about Matty being there, sitting outside his house. Perhaps he thought Matty was begging. Despite now looking more like a monk, Matty still looked like a vagrant. In response, he managed a single word. "English."

It earned him a look of disgust. The captain had warned him. The English were hated here.

The Frenchman kicked him hard in the back, shouting more obscenities, then disappeared down a street that ran off the square.

Matty knew he could not dwell there, but where to go? And he lacked the energy to think, to decide what direction to take. It was so much easier just to stay there.

Then he heard voices. At first there was a single voice, then there were more. He looked up. Men were emerging from the alleyway that he had come through. And he recognised one of the men.

It was the man he had disturbed with the prostitute. And he had brought friends. They all carried thick wooden sticks.

Matty knew that there was violence coming. He silently laughed to himself as a thought occurred. Had he ever fought and, if so, was he any good at it? He would soon find out.

He tensed in anticipation, and another image came to him, another hazy memory. It was of a man so close to his face that he could see deep into the man's eyes. He heard the man growl and tasted stale breath as the man's face filled with murderous intent.

But then the image was gone, because the Frenchmen were upon him. Instinct kicked in. He felt that he knew what to do faced with such odds. So he *had* fought before. But he lacked the strength to do what he knew he should.

He was unconscious long before the final blows were made. He did not hear the shouts of jubilation from his assailants. They had beaten an old vagrant monk and felt proud of themselves despite the overwhelming odds in their favour.

Not long afterwards, the houseowner returned, in the company of a town official. All he had wanted was to move the monk on, but now he sighed at the sight of the bruised, bloodied, pathetic figure that lay there outside his house, and felt only compassion.

Matty was barely conscious, and the houseowner realised he could not leave him unattended, so he spoke quietly to the official, then they took Matty inside.

Matty was taken to a large kitchen area and placed in a chair. He felt the arms of the chair and realised they were ornately carved. He looked round, struggling to focus through the blood in his eyes. The room felt quite grand. Shelves lined the walls, with pans hanging beneath. An array of metal containers stood on top. Across the room was a door leading to a walk-in larder cupboard. A fire was lit in the huge stone hearth, and a maid was preparing food on a large wooden table.

Staring into the dancing flames of the fire, Matty had his next glimpse back in time, deep into his own past.

He was in a simple room, with a hearth that was no more than a slab of stone. There were no shelves, no larders. There were a few pans filled with vegetables, and there were beds in every corner of the room. It was a room for all purposes. There were people. Merely shapes. Featureless, with blank faces. He heard a baby cry.

Then the memory was gone.

He was given a cup of weak wine. A woman came into the kitchen and Matty listened as she and the householder argued. It was clear she was the householder's wife and that she was calmly but firmly telling her husband she was not happy that he had brought a vagrant, a tramp into her home. The argument was in French, but from the householder's gestures Matty could guess what the man was saying. It amounted to, *'but what else was I to do? Look at him!'*

For the first time Matty noticed religious adornments to the room. Crucifixes abounded, on the walls and the shelves. He remembered the priest on the ship and the pious captain. He was in a world where faith played a strong part in everyone's daily life, yet he still did not quite accept his given role, as the Benedictine monk.

And then the argument escalated. Because a young man entered the room. Their son, presumably. And Matty recognised him. He was one of those who had beaten him earlier the same day.

The young man joined with his mother in berating his father. But whereas the mother had been calm, he was anything but. More than once he lunged towards Matty and had to be restrained by his father.

23

Eventually, the father asserted his authority. The old monk would stay. And the mother, accepting her husband's decision, dutifully went to examine Matty's injuries.

She softly sighed. "Mon dieu!" she exclaimed. All over his face there were new bruises covering old ones, fresh upon scabbed. When she lifted his habit, she saw more on his body.

"Nom?" she asked.

It was one of the few French words Matty understood. "Stephen," he replied. He was still unsure whether that was his name, but it was all he had.

The woman examined the shell chain round his neck, then turned and said something to her husband. She was shaking her head. Matty recognised another word. *'Argent'*. The woman was pointing out that there was going to be no money earned from caring for this monk.

And Matty's eyes started to close.

Chapter Four

La Rochelle, January 1378

Matty woke to find himself in a small, but quite grand bedroom. The bed was comfortable, with a thick mattress and feather pillow. He wore a fresh linen nightgown. It smelled of winter jasmine.

He got up and looked out through a glazed window that offered a view across the harbour.

A maid heard him moving around and came into the room. It was not the same maid as had been in the kitchen. This one had black skin.

She spoke to him in French but at no point did she look directly at him. He was not dressed immodestly. His nightshirt was full-length but moved loosely round his thin frame. She was clearly nervous of being alone with him.

He wanted to re-assure her that he would do her no harm, but the language barrier prevented conversation. Instinctively, he started using his hands to create words in the form of signs.

It was unnerving the maid, who could not understand what he was doing, waving his hands about. So he stopped, then wondered how he knew this language of the hands. It came easily to him. He had done it before.

Communication. Without it, so many things were impossible. He felt frustrated. Since waking in St Malo, he had not been able to communicate at more than the simplest of levels with anyone other than Mireille and the priest. It was a lonely feeling.

The maid left the room briefly, and while she was gone, he sat and thought, putting together the pieces of information he had gained about himself. He had faced violence before, that was clear. The image of the close-up man told him so. He knew how to fight and somehow knew a sign language that came easily for him. He had some connection to a house so small that a single room was kitchen, living area and bedroom all in one. And a child's toy meant something to him. A few things that seemed unrelated, but that might knit together when other memories were added. He needed more memories, and to find the glue connecting them all.

The maid came back with a bowl of shellfish in oil and a cup of wine. He was familiar with the seafood but not comfortable eating it, struggling to prise food from the shells. He thought that wherever he came from, it was somewhere distant from the sea. That fit with the fear he had felt on board the Spanish ship. It was another piece of the puzzle, but of little use. There was a vast amount of land that was not near the sea.

As he ate, he heard footsteps on the wooden stairs, and a figure appeared in the doorway. It was the son, the young man who had been one of his assailants. Behind him was a taller man, who Matty recognised as another of his attackers.

The maid sensed trouble and rushed out, then the two men stepped forward, exchanging a look while closing the door behind.

Matty was lying in bed and realised how vulnerable that made him, so swung his legs round into a sitting position. There was no point trying to talk to the men. He lacked the language, but in any event knew they had not come for idle chat.

It was the taller man who made the first move, circling the bed so that Matty was between him and the householder's son, his eyes narrowed and his body angled in readiness. It was a mistake.

With his opponents split, Matty saw an opening and made a pre-emptive attack.

In his sitting position, he was much lower than the taller man. He drove upwards, using his whole body and every ounce of his remaining strength to pin the man against a wall, grabbing the man's long arms and pushing them wide, then delivering an upward blow with his head into the young man's chin. The smaller man, the houseowner's son, was shocked and froze.

Matty delivered a second blow to the taller man, a fist to his nose. Then he rounded on the smaller man, who was staring in disbelief. This was not supposed to be happening. An old monk, weak and frail,

26

should not be capable of such a thing. And Matty capitalised on the hesitation.

Everything Matty was doing was instinctive, as if he knew how vital it was to act quickly, decisively. He stepped to one side and swung a blow with his elbow into the man's midriff, causing him to double over. He quickly checked on the taller man, who was holding his nose and in pain. That one posed no threat. So he fell again upon the householder's son, pinning him down and pulling back his arm to land a blow to the face. And a new image came to him.

He was holding a man down in water, about to drown the man. Until someone intervened, making him realise he was going too far, causing him to release his hold on the drowning man.

He let go.

The commotion brought the householder to investigate. He gasped at the sight of his son being held down by the English monk. "Leo," he shouted.

Matty looked up. "Please, find me someone who can speak English," he begged. Then he collapsed, his reserves of energy spent.

****

When Matty woke he was no longer in the comfortable bedroom. Instead, he was in a dimly lit cellar, lying on a dirt floor. There was only one way out, up a set of stairs, and two burly men stood at the top, barring that exit.

A voice came from one side. "We meet again, Englishman." It was the priest from the ship.

The priest helped Matty to his feet. "Will the guards be necessary?" he asked. Matty shook his head, and the priest took him on trust, nodding to the guards, who relaxed visibly and retreated up the steps.

"You asked for someone who could speak English. They found me. Do you know whose house you are in?" asked the priest.

"No."

"Does the name du Guesclin mean anything to you?"

27

"No. Should it?"

"Probably not. It's unlikely that in England the name of a French hero is widely known, especially when some of his victories were against the English, including the sea battle here at la Rochelle. But to Frenchmen, the name is filled with honour."

"And he lives here?"

The priest laughed. "No. Bertrand du Guesclin is Constable of all France now. This house is far too modest for one such as he. But his cousin lives here and is a *seigneur,* like the lords you have in England. He is a very important man in the region."

"And I nearly killed his son."

"Precisely."

"So what is my fate?"

"Come," said the priest.

They climbed the cellar steps and the priest led the way, with the guards watching every movement Matty made. They went into a hall. The room was too small to be in a castle or even manor house but the quality of the room, including a marble fireplace and silk rugs, echoed the level of comfort and wealth that had been apparent in the kitchen and bedroom. The priest had been right. The seigneur was an important person.

The seigneur was there, lounging on a couch. His wife sat opposite him. Matty looked round for the son, but he was not there.

The priest and seigneur spoke in French. Then the priest turned to Matty. "He has made a decision," he said. "And you are a lucky man. You are to live."

"For what purpose?"

"You are to accompany the seigneur's son on a journey he has to make. The seigneur has decided you will be a companion and bodyguard."

It seemed a strange decision. Matty had lots of questions. His first was a practical one. "Where is the journey to?"

"Avignon." The priest beamed. "The lad has an audience with God's representative on Earth, the head of the Christian church, his holiness the pope. Prepare yourself for an unforgettable experience."

Chapter Five

Windsor Great Forest, February 1378

It was the second time Edwina had made the long journey south.

On the first occasion, her mother had been the one who wanted her to go, and Edwina had initially resisted. Why would she want to go to a royal wedding, halfway across England, with people she had never met. Whereas to her mother, the invitation was a great honour, an opportunity she should surely not turn down.

In the end, she was persuaded in part by her friend Mary but then also by an omen. As she sat under her Moses Tree and asked for guidance, she saw a flock of swallows flying south and took that as a sign she should follow them and go to the wedding.

This time was different. Her mother did not want her to go. *'After what happened last time, I forbid it,'* she had said. Which simply made Edwina more determined to go.

The journeys were also different. The wedding was at Windsor castle, and Edwina was accompanied by Tom Watt, the steward at Hainsby Manor in Lincolnshire. He went as her friend but also protector, because travelling England's roads was a dangerous thing to do.

This time Edwina was heading for an old hunting lodge in the forest, just south of Windsor town. Tom was ill, suffering one of the usual afflictions the harsh Lincolnshire winters always brought. Edwina could not go alone. Even she understood that. But she discovered that a party of merchants was heading south, and they were happy to take her along with them.

Edwina's mother, Lady Alice made enquiries about the merchants. They were making their way from Lincoln to London, accompanied by several armed guards. They traded in the livestock markets of Lincoln and Nottingham and wanted to expand their business. The capital would be an obvious place to do so. They had learned of a thriving new market in central London, called Leadenhall. It was known especially as a poultry market. They were going there to find out whether there was money to be made.

Lady Alice arranged for her own guards to take Edwina as far as Lincoln to join the group and paid the merchants to take a different route from the one they had intended. They would now go via Windsor. It was not a huge diversion for them, because from Windsor they could take a barge the rest of the way, along the Thames. And Alice was satisfied she had done everything she could to ensure her daughter's safety.

What Lady Alice did not know was that Edwina would only have the protection of the merchant group until Windsor town. From there she would still have several miles to go to reach the lodge.

Edwina kept it a secret. She knew the forest, because she had lived there for a while with her father. But if her mother knew she would be riding alone there, she would have forbidden the whole journey.

The journey as far as the forest edge had gone without incident, no doubt due to the presence of the armed guards. Now, Edwina was alone, riding her bay mare.

The forest started immediately at Windsor town. There were no villages or other towns in between. The forest had been owned by English kings for centuries and maintained as wilderness for their private use as hunting grounds.

She felt no fear riding alone in a place that was so familiar to her. Her father had been given the tenancy of an old hunting lodge there, and when plague returned, he took her to live with him, to keep here away from the towns and villages where plague was devastating whole families and communities.

She was just a child then. At first, the forest sounds frightened her, especially at night. The darkness was so absolute. But with her father's help and encouragement, she grew to love the place.

There was about half a mile to go to the lodge and she had seen no-one. She stopped, taking in the shapes of trees, barren of leaves at this time of year. As well as the good memories, the forest held some bad ones that now came back to her. She remembered men coming here with the intention of harming her father. At one point she had to hide from the evil men, alone and afraid. She shuddered as she recalled the fear she had felt.

She urged her horse forwards, searching for the narrow track off the main thoroughfare that took her to the lodge.

She stopped again as she saw the buildings loom out of the density of the forest. She had quite forgotten how grand a place this was. Her father had put his heart and soul into renovating the lodge, bringing the disused buildings back to life, recreating the grandeur they had known when they were used regularly by successive kings to entertain important guests.

She had expected to find some activity. Instead, there was an eerie quiet, broken only by a scurrying noise under the leaves. A squirrel perhaps. Or a stoat.

She approached the gates, and as she did so she heard voices, and figures appeared.

There were three children. Edwina recognised them all. They were her half-siblings. Gylda was the eldest at nearly twelve years. Then there was Maude, who was nine, and Edward, five. They were all much smaller last time she saw them. Gylda especially seemed almost fully grown now, a young woman even.

They greeted her joyfully. She dismounted and hugged each one in turn. Then looked round. "Where is your mother?" she asked.

Gylda said nothing but led Edwina towards the kitchens. There, sitting disconsolately at a table, was Charlotte, the wife of Edwina's father.

At the sight of Edwina, Charlotte managed to stir herself, as any dutiful host should, welcoming the visitor with a smile and offering refreshments after the journey. But Edwina noticed there was a flatness to Charlotte's tone and Charlotte did not ask why Edwina had come. Something was wrong. Charlotte was pre-occupied, worried.

Edwina also noticed an air of neglect. It was surprising. Charlotte was a diligent housewife, a hard worker, but clearly had let her standards slip. And Edwina thought she knew the reason.

It had always been Charlotte's biggest fear, that she might lose her husband and be left here, in the middle of nowhere with only her children for company. She loved her children. But the lodge was so remote. It would be a hard and lonely existence without adult company, so far from the rest of the world. There were no local markets, no fairs, no taverns for miles around, only scattered farms where people were too busy to be good neighbours.

Later in the evening, when the children were in bed, the two women shared wine by the fire. Edwina voiced her thoughts. "It must be hard for you now," she said.

Charlotte scowled. "You don't know the half of it."

The scowl spoke volumes. It was unlike Charlotte.

Edwina knew that Charlotte blamed her for what happened. Mary's words came back to her. '...if I hadn't advised you to go, your father would never have gone to that battle at Rottingdean and disappeared.' But she turned the words inwards on herself. 'If I hadn't come south my father would still be here with his wife and children.'

For a moment Edwina felt guilty. But not for long. She stood up suddenly, her feelings turning quickly from guilt to rage. "You aren't the only one grieving," she said, her voice rising with each word. "Don't you think I would change everything if I could?" And tears began to flow as a year's repressed emotions surfaced.

Charlotte calmed, then sighed. "Sit down," she said, kinder now in her manner. And Edwina sat back down.

Charlotte took a deep breath. "I'm sorry," she said. "I'm not myself. I had a visitor yesterday from Windsor. I've been told I must leave the lodge."

Edwina's eyes widened. "Why? Who?"

"We have a new king, as you know. It was his grandfather, King Edward, and his aunt, Princess Isabella who gave Matty and me this place to live in and bring back to life. And sometimes I have hated the place, especially now with Matty gone. But it's my home and the only home my children have known. Mostly, I love it here. I don't want to leave it. Where would I go? But our new king has designs on the lodge now it's restored. And I have to go by the end of the year." She laughed. "Some might say I'm fortunate to be given even those few months."

"The old king gave you deeds. Surely they are still legal."

"The lodge was given to my husband. The deeds say that if he dies, his wife and children can stay here *'subject to the king's pleasure'* and we have a new king, a child who undoubtedly will want to take advantage of the pleasures of a playground like this on his doorstep, somewhere to bring his friends to play, to show off, feast and hunt.

"Not only that, but if Matty is declared dead I will have death tax to pay. How stupid is a country that makes laws penalising women for the supposed fortune of inheriting their dead husbands' wealth? And what wealth? We live hand to mouth. So I not only have lost my husband but I will have to sell our best horse to pay the tax, and even that might not be enough. What have I left? No man, no home, no possessions, and three children to feed. After all the work we have done here. The place was a ruin before we came."

"Have you spoken with Isabella? She has always been fond of my father."

"She lives in France and rarely comes to England. And anyway, I'm told she now has little influence at court. Her brother, John of Gaunt, rules the country until the king is an adult, and the old king's mistress is in charge at Windsor."

"What about Parker? He would help you." Parker was King Edward's steward of the forest and had been the go-between for Matty and Charlotte to the king.

Charlotte shook her head. "He lives in a hospital now, the hospital of St John the Baptist in Oxford. They say he has no mind left and just sits staring all day. It's very sad."

Edwina sipped at her wine, giving her time to consider whether to say what was on her mind. Then Charlotte spoke again, and in a way made the decision for her. "You haven't yet told me why you are here."

Edwina had only one answer; the truth.

"I think he's alive," she said, leaning forward in her enthusiasm. "I have an idea how to find him."

If she thought this would cheer Charlotte, she was sadly mistaken. The scowl Charlotte had worn earlier was there again. And Charlotte flew at her, grabbing for her hair.

Edwina was shocked but did not react. It was the right thing to do. Charlotte quickly let go and sat back down. "I'm sorry. I shouldn't have done that," she said. "I'm sure you mean well, but false hope is not what I need just now."

Edwina understood but stayed firm. "If I thought that was what I was bringing you I would not have come."

Charlotte sighed. "So, tell me what you know that I do not."

Edwina hesitated. She had learned to trust her feelings, her instincts; and she had been proved right before. A year earlier she had been imprisoned in a cottage by the sea, her situation hopeless, when she sensed something. She had a feeling her father was nearby, and when she looked out from her barred window, there he was. It had given her new energy and the will to fight back. But explaining her gift, her ability to sense things, was never easy.

She lived in a world where visions and prophecies were accepted as reality, but where many charlatans took advantage of people's beliefs. Many had a healthy scepticism of claims that were made. And she never had concrete evidence to back up what she felt. She could never claim to see things, pictures in her mind. All she had were feelings, sensations. She did not understand it herself, so how could she expect others to do so?

She knew that Charlotte was asking for a piece of proof, however small. She had none, so avoided giving a straight answer. "I know he is alive," she said. "I know it."

Charlotte scoffed, not attempting to hide her irritation. "If you feel it, then of course it must be true." She grimaced, knowing she was being too harsh. She changed tack. "Does Daniel know you are here?"

Edwina instinctively felt at the chain around her neck, the wooden amulet her half-brother Daniel had given to her as a lucky charm.

As children, Edwina and Daniel were not the closest of siblings, but they had grown closer as they became adults and shared experiences that tightened the bond. She had considered contacting him and telling him she had decided to try once more to find her father. He would have offered to go with her. But she chose not to tell him. For one thing, he had a new life. Why upset it? And for another, Edwina's father was not Daniel's father. This quest was hers, not his to fulfil.

"No," she replied. "He is happy with his wife in Essex and I would not disturb him. This is something I must do alone." She paused. "My father never gave up looking when I was missing and I must do the same for him. I have one last thing to try. I am going to France to seek witnesses to what happened at Rottingdean. I will ask Michel to help me get there. If there is nothing, only then will I give up my search."

"I think you are wasting your time," said Charlotte. "But I pray you are not. And you do give me hope, just a little." She gave Edwina a hug.

"What of you?" asked Edwina "What will you do?"

"My family is in Kent. I have not seen them for a long time. It will be good to see them again. I'm sure one of my nieces or nephews will take us in, at least for a while."

Edwina looked her in the eyes. "Please wait for as long as you are able. You have nearly a year to run. Stay, until you get word from me. If I can't find my father, *then* you can make your other plans."

Just then, Charlotte's youngest child, Edward, came into the room, rubbing his eyes. "Can't sleep," he mumbled softly. She smiled to see him, then took him and hugged him, and as she did so she whispered to Edwina. "All right. For the sake of my children I will stay longer, but if you aren't back with good news before next winter, we will have no choice but to go."

Chapter Six

South of Limoges, France, March 1378

There were six in the party, including Matty. Leo du Guesclin was the leader, naturally and despite his youth. This was his trip. It was a chance to shine as a businessman and ambassador for the family. It was also a pilgrimage of sorts, a religious experience, a meeting with the pope.

Leo had a squire, a lad of nine or ten years, named Louis. The lad had many sundry duties, including being responsible for the needs of the horses. There was also a young girl of about the same age, a slave girl. Her name ironically was Francesca, meaning *'free'*. Her job was to see to Leo's personal needs, including washing his clothing, heating water for his bathing and keeping his hair and beard in order along the way.

Another member of the group was the priest Matty had already met. Matty now knew the priest's name was Jean.

The final member of the group was a tall youth; the same one who had attacked Matty with Leo. His name was Roland.

Leo and Roland wore long swords while Matty was lightly armed with only a short sword, even though his role was supposed to be as a bodyguard.

Matty had a few days to recover in La Rochelle before they set off. He spent some time with Pere Jean, finding out more about what was in store for him.

The priest explained. "This will be an important journey for Leo. It's a pilgrimage, as you are aware, but also a rite of passage, a coming-of-age ritual. It should have happened when he was a little younger, but the La Rochelle region has not been stable and Leo's father decided to wait. Even now it will be risky. It will be a trek of five hundred miles with no men-at-arms for protection, other than yourself."

"So why me? Why choose me to go?" asked Matty.

The priest grinned. "Leo's father is a clever man. He saw how easily you bested his son and friend. You displayed the skills of a seasoned fighter. And you are a monk. A fighting monk is a good combination for a religious journey such as this. Having a monk along as well as a priest will add to the sense of sincerity of the pilgrimage. The pope will be impressed."

"You believe the seigneur is a clever man. Couldn't he have dressed one of his trained guards as a monk?"

"Perhaps. But what do you know of the politics of nobility?"

Matty shook his head. "Nothing."

"Then let me enlighten you. The life of a nobleman here in France is a life always on the edge. The du Guesclins have rivals and enemies everywhere. There are many petty disputes but also local wars. And the seigneur is constantly watching his back. Yes, he has guards, but which of them can he trust to say 'no' to the offer of a handsome reward for putting a dagger into his back or kidnapping his son for ransom? He can never be sure."

"So he puts his trust in a monk who cannot even remember where he is from. An Englishman at that. An enemy of France. Maybe I'm the one who will wield the dagger."

"Maybe. But he thinks not. If you wanted to kill his son you had the chance and did not take it."

"Well, one thing is for sure. Leo and Roland need all the help they can get. Between them, they have the fighting skills of a distressed ewe."

The priest nodded. "Which is plain for all to see. In fact, our whole band lacks any appearance of strength. But sometimes when you look threatening you draw interest from those who would seek conflict. Better to pass through unnoticed. And if the plan fails, we have you, and the seigneur thinks you are a wolf in sheep's clothing."

Jean could see that Matty was thinking about what he had said, taking it all in. Then he spoke again. "The trip isn't just a youth's pilgrimage," he said. "There is purpose. Leo has been given a job to do by his

39

father. There are alliances and trade deals to be struck at Avignon. It is a test of his ability as heir to the family business."

"What kind of trade deals?"

"Avignon is one of the richest cities in the world. La Rochelle trades in fish, of course, but more importantly it exports a great deal of salt. The pope is an important client, as are his many cardinals in the city, but also Avignon attracts very special visitors, kings and queens, the Holy Roman Emperor. You name them, they go there. So there's a great deal of money to be made. But the alliances are as important as the trade deals. It is good to have powerful friends when the world is ever dangerous, and a man's name must be known for him to progress and gain power. The name du Guesclin is well known, but Leo is not. This is his chance to change that."

****

After more than a month travelling from La Rochelle, they were one-third the way to their destination. They could have made swifter progress, but for the first two weeks they were still within an area that was familiar to Leo, and he kept stopping to take advantage of the hospitality of friends of his father. They should have stayed no more than one night at each place but Leo enjoyed the company too much and they stayed longer.

Now, beyond that comfort zone, they stayed wherever they could. Matty was discovering that Leo and Roland were used to a high level of luxury, but the opportunities for a feather bed were becoming limited in the sparsely populated countryside. Most pilgrims found rooms in cheap inns, but this pair of travellers wanted the best, and when they did come across somewhere they liked, it tempted them once again to stay too long, enjoying the warm beds, better quality food and wine, and sometimes female company.

Matty and the others did not share in such luxury. They had to make do with the humblest rooms each establishment had to offer. At one inn, the rooms were particularly awful. Leo joked to Frere John, who interpreted for Matty. "Leo says priests and monks have a duty of poverty, to cast aside the comforts of the world. He thinks he is doing us a favour by renting this place for us."

"While he enjoys the comforts of the world to the full," replied Matty.

The conversation led Matty to ask Frere Jean a question. "Forgive me, but I cannot remember what it means to be a Benedictine. I don't know what to do."

"The rules of St Benedict are many and complex but can be simplified quite easily. Pray long and work hard."

"And do they tell you *how* to pray? It's another of the skills I seem to have forgotten."

"Indeed they do. But until you get a chance to read the rules, or your memory returns, my advice is to consider what is the most time you can spend in prayer and the hardest you can work. Then double both."

In other respects, the journey had so far proved uneventful, the days a tiresome repetition one of another. Moreso for Matty, because he could only communicate with Frere Jean.

So he spent his time observing, learning more about each of his companions. He found it hard to build any respect for Leo or Roland, who he thought were too soft and pampered for a venture such as this. He said as much to Frere Jean, who gave him a word to describe the two. They were *'papegais,'* or parrots. Jean said he thought the equivalent English word was *'popinjays'*.

The young squire and slave girl kept themselves apart from the others whenever they could. They rarely spoke around Leo, but Matty sensed a kind of bond between them, forged no doubt from what they had in common, a life of servitude. Although Louis had a potential future if he squired well, Francesca's future would undoubtedly be permanently as a slave.

Matty tried to communicate with them, using the sign language he knew. They showed little interest, but when they were together, they shone, filled with the laughter of innocent children. Watching them play gave him some of his brightest moments in the endless repetitive days of travelling.

As for Frere Jean, he was an enigma. Matty had first met him on a Spanish ship, then encountered him at the seigneur's house, and now on this journey to see the pope. The priest was clearly more than the average cleric.

They reached Limoges and stayed at the Abbey of St Martial. While there, a thought came to Matty, and once again he sought help from Jean. "Forgive me again, but it has just occurred to me. What's left of my mind tells me that the pope's home has always been in Rome, not Avignon."

Jean nodded. "It was, until about sixty years ago, when there was turmoil in Italy, civil wars and such. The cardinals wanted change and a Frenchman was made pope, but it didn't take long for the new pope to realise Rome was not stable, not a safe place. He got tired of all the infighting between factions in Rome, all trying to improve their positions. It didn't help that some of the Italian cardinals never wanted a French pope in the first place. So the pope appointed French cardinals to balance things in his favour, then decided to move the Holy See to Avignon. One reason he gave was that by moving north he would be better positioned to help end the war between France and England, which was bankrupting both nations and therefore preventing them from supporting his own ambition, a new crusade to the Holy Land. Whatever his reasons, Avignon became the new Rome, though in the past few years there have been moves for a return to Rome. It is a time of much uncertainty for the papacy."

****

They journeyed on, following the course of the River Vienne, heading north-east then turning south, winding their way through the valleys rather than taking the harder up-and-down route over the many hills. There had been a period of rain and the river was quite high. On the horizon, storm clouds were building.

42

The area was heavily forested and was deserted, apart from the occasional farm. There was peacefulness in the environment.

Their destination was the monastery at Saint-Leonard-le-Noblat, a grand Romanesque building next to the river, and one of the few resting places available on this part of the route.

The group refreshed themselves in the river, beneath a stone bridge, then made their way to the monastery.

They were not the only pilgrims there. The monastery was a crossroads, a stopping off place for pilgrims who, like Matty's group, were heading south-east, but also for those heading south-west towards another pilgrims' route, the Camino de Santiago.

It meant that the monks were well prepared for the flow of visitors. As well as providing the usual basic food, they made a variety of products for sale, such as almond biscuits the pilgrims could take with them as a nourishing supplement for their onward journey.

There was a hospital to aid those pilgrims for whom the journey had taken a toll. Many ageing pilgrims forced themselves to go on despite suffering greatly from the hardships of the road. The monastery gave them care to help them continue their way.

Matty asked Frere Jean about the saint the monastery was named for. "He is the patron saint of prisoners," said Jean. "He was given authority to free many who he believed deserved it. Later in life, he lived as a hermit in the forests we have just passed through. People would travel for miles to see him and the sick would ask him to heal them."

"A worthy man," said Matty. As he said it, he found himself distracted, looking back along the river valley the way they had come.

"What is it?" asked the priest.

Matty said nothing but strode purposefully back to the river, stopping and looking up and down its course. There were some cottages along the banks. He approached one and knocked on the door.

An old woman answered the door. Matty realised he lacked the words to say what was on his mind. He turned to Jean. "Tell her she must leave the cottage," he said. "Without delay. It is a matter of life and death."

Jean looked quizzically at Matty, but did what was asked, earning himself a scolding from the woman, who closed the door in his face.

"Thank you for that," said Jean. "What reason had you for giving me such a task?"

Matty again said nothing but went to the next door. This time it was a younger woman who answered. She had a boy at her side, aged about ten years. Matty took the boy to be her son. He tried a more tactful approach this time. "Tell her I mean her no harm, but she must follow us," he said. "For the boy's sake."

Jean sighed, unsure what to do, but once again did as Matty suggested.

The woman hesitated. Matty gestured to the bridge, then walked along the bank and on to it. The woman looked at Jean, who nodded. They both followed Matty.

Matty was looking upriver from the bridge. "Listen," he said. At first, Jena heard nothing. Then, in the distance there was a low rumbling noise. "The banks are about to burst," added Matty. "All the cottages will flood. It will be here in minutes."

Jean hurriedly explained to the woman. She could also hear the rumbling and strained her eyes looking for visual evidence of what Matty said. And sure enough, the water level had risen and was rising by the minute.

She turned and ran back to the cottages, collecting her son then alerting her neighbours, including the old woman. They grabbed their most precious possessions and, with Matty and Jean's help, made their way to higher ground. Then the old woman spoke to Jean.

He told Matty what she said. "She has lived here all her life and has known occasional flooding, but never too bad. She is following your advice but thinks it will prove unnecessary."

44

They watched as the water level continued steadily to rise, then suddenly a deluge came, a wall of water surging towards the cottages. There would have been no warning for the residents. First, the bridge buckled and its timbers were taken by the force of the river. Then, chunks of the riverbank disappeared, and finally the buildings' meagre foundations gave way. The cottage dwellers watched as their homes collapsed and tables, chairs, beds and other items were carried rapidly downriver. There were personal possessions amongst the debris. Within an hour there was nothing left standing where the cottages had been, and the bridge was gone.

The residents of the cottages stood like statues, some open-mouthed, contemplating what they had just witnessed and what might have been had they been inside their homes. As they did so, Jean took Matty to one side. "How did you know?" he asked.

"When we were coming down the valley, I saw that the river was blocked and there was a small lake building up behind the blockage. It was like a dam. When we came here, I saw the river level rising and heard the rumbling noise. I realised the blockage was breaching."

"Well, you have saved lives today. You should be proud of yourself."

Matty thought what he had done was nothing to fuss about. By the time the cottage residents had come out from the initial shock and wanted to thank him, he was on his own, walking round the outside of the monastery examining the structure.

But the young woman he had warned, the mother of the boy, sought him out and found him.

She went up to him and took his hands in hers. "Merci," she said. She knelt and kissed his hands. Matty quickly took his hand away, embarrassed. He wanted to say that he had done very little but without the French words he spread his arms hoping the gesture would be understood.

The woman's son was behind her. His view was of Matty, arms stretched, standing in front of the blue sky and with the sun behind him, his black robes creating a silhouette. "Corbeau! Corbeau!"

shouted the boy. His mother stepped back to where her son stood. "Oui, c'est vrai," she replied. Then she got up and together they ran back to the riverbank, the woman to start the process of picking up the pieces of her shattered life, and the boy to tell everyone what he had seen.

Matty felt strange. He could understand her gratitude but why had she kissed his hands? And what had the boy meant? It wasn't important. He went back to what he had been doing. There was something drawing him to the stonework. And he had another flashback into his past.

He remembered working, chisel in hand, chipping away at a huge piece of stone, carving it into the shape of a gargoyle. Men all around were also working on stone. One pointed to the sky above and Matty looked up. There he saw the building he was working on, with a spire that stretched high above. It was a church. No, it was bigger than a church. It was a cathedral.

It puzzled him. Did monks work with stone? Perhaps they did. Or maybe he had been a stonemason before becoming a monk. It was another piece to his puzzle, and another mystery. He was building a picture of his life but it remained an unsolved puzzle, because the pieces did not easily fit together. His life story remained as inaccessible as before.

He made his way to the communal sleeping area where he and Jean would be spending a few nights. Leo and Roland would be elsewhere, in greater comfort of course, while Louis and Francesca had the worst accommodation, a dusty, cold area in the stable block. They would have to find a way to sleep against the stench of the horses.

The routine of the resident monks in the monastery included prayers and chants throughout the day and night. Matty thought that if he was indeed a monk, he should try to be part of that, so allowed his sleep to be punctuated by attendance at Mass. He mimed to the prayers and chants, imagining the eyes of the other monks on him as he did. He was sure they were not fooled. In fact, they were all focused on their own meditations and his clumsy attempts to do what they did went unnoticed.

The next day, one of the monks approached him and Frere Jean, and spoke in English. "We have heard about what you did to save the villagers," he said. "Though I think you had some help." He looked to the heavens, smiling.

The monk held up a length of thick iron chain. One of the links was broken. "This is one of the chains our patron saint caused to break to free some penitent prisoners. I was cleaning it at the precise time you arrived at the cottages. I think it no coincidence. Saint Leonard saved those wretched souls, with your help of course."

Matty could not help himself. He scoffed. "As you say," he whispered. It was just loud enough that the monk heard it, and it was clearly a moment of disrespect. The monk scowled and Jean drew Matty away.

"That was not wise," said Jean.

"I cannot abide such men, full of their own importance."

"When we get to Avignon you will be in the city of the popes. Say such things there and you will be declared a heretic."

"I will be careful, but I cannot help questioning."

He left Jean and wandered, drawn again to the architecture of the monastery, this time the rooms and corridors.

He came across the reliquary housing the relics of St Leonard, including more broken chains but also the saint's skull. As he looked at it, just idly curious, a voice came from behind and he turned to see who was there.

But it was not just one person. There were several. And they were not monks, but ordinary folk. Some got down on their knees while others touched him gently, on any part of him they could reach. It unnerved him.

Pere Jean appeared, blessed the people then ushered them away. When they were gone, he stared at Matty for a while, then spoke.

"Word has spread," he said. "About the humble, silent Benedictine, who has the gift of foresight, who predicted a great flood and saved many people. And now they find you at the altar of their saint and will tell everyone they know that you are something special, maybe even a reincarnation of St Leonard himself."

"Superstitious nonsense," replied Matty. "They think I'm silent but it's only that I have no-one to talk with other than yourself. And I have done nothing to warrant their attention."

Jean laughed. "The people are certainly superstitious, as you say. But I have to say, Frere Stephen, there's something about you that makes even me wonder. So perhaps they are right to follow you."

"The young woman's son said something yesterday."

"I know. He saw you with your arms out and thought you looked like a big bird with its wings spread. He told his mother you looked like a big black bird. Did you know that St Benedict was tempted by the Devil in the form of a black bird?"

"What does that make me? A holy man or a devil?"

"All I know is that life is not dull in your company, my friend." He patted Matty on the back affectionately.

When they stepped outside the monastery there was no large crowd, but a young boy had been waiting for them. He was crying. Frere Jean asked why, then explained to Matty. "His mother is ill and he came to ask you to heal her."

To his surprise, Matty made no attempt to refuse. He found himself wanting to know more. "What ails her?" he asked.

Jean asked the boy, then interpreted the reply. "She is a widow and feeds her family from what she grows on a patch of land they have, but she has hurt her shoulder and can't do the work. She sent him to see the holy man because she is worried her children will starve."

"Tell him to take me to her," said Matty.

Now it was Jean's turn to be surprised. "Have you decided you really are what these people believe you to be?"

"No. But something tells me I may be of help to the boy's mother. And if that is so, what kind of man would I be to walk away?"

Jean smiled. "This will be very interesting, my friend. Let us go." He motioned the boy to lead them and within a few minutes they were at another row of cottages. The boy's family's cottage was in the middle. Patches of worked land, each allocated to one of the cottages, could be seen nearby.

Once inside, they saw a woman in her mid-twenties, sitting by a fire and with a pained expression on her face. Two children, younger than the boy who had fetched Matty stood beside her, their anxiety for their mother plain to see.

Matty knew what to do but had no idea how he knew. He examined the woman's shoulder, then asked Jean to tell her to relax her arm down by her side. While she did so he searched for something to use as a weight, then placed it into the hand that was hung loose. Then he waited. And before long, the weight pulled the woman's arm sufficiently to relocate her shoulder. The click disturbed her, and she feared the monk had made the damage to her shoulder worse, but then she beamed as her arm moved freely and without pain.

Matty needed no help to understand the word that the woman said repeatedly. It was the same in French as in English. "Miracle!" she declared. "Miracle!"

Matty turned to go, but she would not let him. She took him by the hand and led him to another cottage. Inside was a child with a cut hand. He had picked up a blade and his mother had been unable to stem the bleeding. Matty wrapped the hand in cloth expertly.

By the time he left the row of cottages, Matty had provided basic medical aid to four households.

"You wanted people to stop following you, but now I think they will never leave you alone," commented Frere Jean.

****

Two days later Matty and Frere Jean set off from the monastery early in the morning. Leo and Roland were still asleep but had faster mounts and would catch them up later in the day. Matty had been trying to avoid the unwanted attention his new fame had created and he was glad to be leaving.

But before long, he was again the centre of attention.

They came across a procession of people, at the heart of which was a cart drawn by an emasculated mule. A simple coffin lay on the cart. A woman was wailing in her grief. But it was another woman who caused the procession to stop. "Le corbeau; le moine!" she cried, pointing at Matty. The words were now familiar to Matty. The black bird; the monk.

The grieving woman responded, approaching Matty and falling at his feet. Matty offered his hand, trying to encourage her up, but she clung to him. Frere Jean bent and spoke to her, then told Matty what was happening. "She wants you to bless her dead husband," he said.

Matty was looking round. "Where is the church?" he asked. "Surely it is nearby, with a priest somewhere."

Jean pointed to a hill some distance away, above which the top of a tower was just visible. "He waits there," he said.

"That's miles from here," said Matty.

"It's their nearest church. This area is farmland. There are few villages. And all the woman's family are buried there."

Matty was incredulous. "They have to take the coffin up and over that hill?"

"Yes. They are in for a long day. They will need to carry the coffin most of the way up the hill. The mule isn't strong enough."

The woman continued her wailing. Matty could see expectancy in the eyes of others in the procession. They also wanted him to give his blessing to the deceased. "I wouldn't know what to say," said Matty. "And if I am not the holy man that they think I am, what will God think of me bestowing such a blessing?"

Jean shrugged. "These people need comfort. They need to know their loved one is supported into the next life. If you deny them this simple request, they will believe you are damning him, and no matter how hard you try to convince them you are not a monk it will make no difference."

Matty sighed. "Very well but can we do it together?" he asked. Jean nodded. "Please tell them we will do a double blessing. Then I will follow your lead."

Jean agreed and began the process. When they had finished, the grieving woman thanked Matty vigorously but ignored the priest, whose contribution was of less value to her.

As the procession moved away, Matty realised that Leo and Roland had arrived and were watching the spectacle. As the full group set off again, following a dirt track, Matty cast a glance at Leo, who was looking at him intensely but then looked away to avoid Matty's gaze.

Mid-morning they stopped by a stream to let the horses drink, and Leo approached Matty, looking him up and down then shaking his head. Under his breath he quietly said one word. "Imposteur." It was another word so near to the English equivalent. Leo thought him a fake, a charlatan. Matty did not argue the point. Because he believed that he was just that, albeit unintentionally.

"Do you think God knows you?" asked Jean.

"I don't even know myself."

"That is different. God knows all. I think Leo is wrong. You are no imposter. Have faith."

When the horses had drunk their fill, the group readied to resume the journey.

It was then they had their first encounter with trouble since they left La Rochelle.

Chapter Seven

Winchelsea, March 1378

Edwina's arrival took Michel by surprise. He had resigned himself to having lost her, and here she was.

When he first saw her, he managed to suppress elation, welcoming her warmly but staying cautious, both physically and emotionally.

She was tired after her long ride from Windsor. He was angry with her for making the journey alone, but his rebuke was muted. He admired her spirit, and she had made it safely, which was all that mattered.

He had a bed made up for her and let her go almost immediately to it. Questions could wait until the morning.

And Edwina slept long. At one point in the early morning, Michel could not resist looking into her room and watching her sleep, her body rising and falling under the blankets. As he did so he knew that he loved her still.

When finally she rose, a maid helped her wash and dress, then she joined Michel in the main room of his house.

Michel was a successful merchant and was quite wealthy. He was not titled or a landowner but had means sufficient to own one of the grander houses in the town. It had more rooms than most, including a small second floor room he used for reading, writing letters and general accounting. She found him there, working at his desk. Everything was ordered, tidy, efficient. That was his character. Organised. It was one of the reasons she had rejected him. He was kind and she felt safe with him, but not excited by him.

There was a leather chair. She sat in it. And smiled nervously.

"Never thought I would see you again," offered Michel, just as nervous.

Edwina did not know what to say. She wanted his friendship and needed his help but was cautious, needing to avoid giving any signals that might be misinterpreted. She knew he still wanted a relationship beyond friendship, one she could not give him. It was she who ended the beginnings of a relationship before. He had been devastated then, and she did not want to repeat the experience by re-igniting his hope for more.

"It's good to see you again," she managed.

"I've missed you."

She sighed and straightened. "I need your help."

"I guessed that. Anything you ask, I will do my best."

She felt awkward but had to carry on. "I need to go to France."

His eyes widened. There were plenty of ways to get to France without his help.

She continued. "I want to find soldiers or sailors who were at Rottingdean, where my father went missing. I want to ask if anyone knows what happened to him. My French is not good enough. Will you help me?"

He nodded slowly, then his mouth curled in a look of uncertainty. "I have crossed the Channel several times since last I saw you and had the same idea. I already made some discreet enquiries, but I'm afraid there was no new information to be had. Nobody I spoke to knew anything about your father's disappearance."

Edwina sat open-mouthed. It had never occurred to her that Michel might already have tried the one avenue she had left. Moments earlier, she had worried about rekindling Michel's hope for a relationship with her. Now, at a stroke, he had just destroyed any hope she had of finding her father. Suddenly she felt despair rising through her body. The stump of her arm started to ache. And for the first time in a while she had a seizure.

When she came round from her seizures, Edwina never knew how long the episode had lasted. Sometimes she was unaware that it had even taken place.

This time, when she looked round, she realised she was still in Michel's study, still in the same leather chair. "How long?" she asked him.

"Not long. A few minutes." There was tenderness in his voice. Compassion. He had watched her have seizures before and knew what to do, putting cushions at her side so she would not harm herself on anything hard or sharp as she thrashed about. She thanked him with a thin smile.

For years Edwina had felt embarrassed by her seizures. She had listened to those who believed they were evidence of demonic possession, but her father had assured her otherwise and she no longer felt ashamed. But the episodes did make her tired, and Michel knew that what he had told her had affected her and caused this one.

He called a maid and Edwina retired to her room, where she washed and changed. Edwina had met the maid before and this was an opportunity to speak with her. Maids were always a good source of information. She asked what Michel had been doing since last she saw him. But the maid had a surprise for her. Without any thoughts of discretion, the maid told Edwina that Michel had a new woman in his life.

When she re-joined Michel, he made an apology. "I'm sorry," he said. "That was my fault. I took away your last hope."

"My affliction is nobody's fault, least of all yours. But you are right that what you said hit me like a runaway horse. In my room, I thought some more. It changes nothing. I will still go to France and ask the questions myself. That is all there is to say."

He gave her no argument. "Then I will go with you, of course."

She had expected it and welcomed it. She needed him. But also, she was beginning to remember why she had fallen for him in the first place. He never got cross with her. He had wisdom. And he was good looking, tall and upright. His devotion to her was absolute, and that was something special to cherish rather than throw away. Perhaps the torch she once held for him was not quite extinguished.

54

Edwina could hear preparations being made in the next room for the evening meal. She had to ask. "Will anyone else be joining us tonight?"

He looked uncomfortable. "Yes. There's someone I want to introduce you to."

And she knew she had a rival.

Chapter Eight

The French countryside, March 1378

There were three of them. And they had been waiting. It was an ambush.

The three men blocked the road, astride their horses, weapons visible but not drawn. Each carried a long sword on one hip and a dagger on the other.

They wore padded jerkins, the quality of which would not have been out of place on Leo or Roland. These were not the usual rough highwaymen who lived in the shadows and scratched a living. They were men of means.

Why here, thought Matty? He had seen no other pilgrims on this road for two days or more. It was not an obvious place to wait for passing victims to appear. Highwaymen needed regular work just like anyone else. They would not get it here.

He observed the two youngest members of his party, Louis and Francesca, who looked terrified. With good reason. Their lives were completely submissive. Whatever the outcome might be, they would have no say in it.

By contrast, there was one who radiated calm. Roland. It seemed strange, but he dismissed the thought, because he had to focus on the immediate threat he and the group faced.

There was an exchange between the robbers and Leo. Their leader was a man a little older than Leo, but with the same kind of self-confidence. Matty cursed the fact he could not understand what was being said. Then the first sword was drawn. Roland responded, making for his sword, but his lack of skill showed. He was not quick enough, and the robber leader put his sword point to Roland's neck.

It was too easy. And when he looked at the other two robbers, Matty knew why.

He spurred his horse forwards at the two men, leaving Roland to the mercy of the leader. Leo gasped at the stupidity of the charge, because surely Roland would pay for it with his life.

Matty's move took his quarry by surprise. Before they had drawn swords, he was upon them, driving his horse between theirs. The robbers' horses panicked and reared up enough to turn their riders sideways, offering Matty a choice between two unguarded targets. With a sweep of his short sword he had sliced through one man's arm, enough to draw blood but not to kill. The man yelped with pain.

The second rider looked stunned. He froze, keeping his sword sheathed. This was not part of the plan.

Matty looked back. It confirmed his suspicions. No harm had come to Roland. The robber leader still held his sword to Roland's neck, but loosely, nervously, and in a way which Roland could have parried if he had the mind to do so.

Leo now had his sword drawn. Matty pointed to his eyes and then the two robbers he had just challenged. Leo understood. *'Watch them'.*

Matty made his way towards the leader and Roland, beckoning Pere Jean to go with him. "Tell Roland there's no need to keep up the pretence," he said. Jean hesitated, unsure what was happening, then interpreted.

It seemed Matty was still gambling with Roland's life. The leader still had his long sword drawn. But Matty knew what he was doing, and oused self-confidence. The robber leader exchanged a look with Roland. He knew he was defeated and pulled at the reins to gallop away from the scene. Roland's head dipped, knowing his scheme had failed.

Leo still watched the other two robbers. They probably had more skill than he had and could have overpowered him, but there was no attempt made. Understanding came to him at last. He spoke to Jean. "He wants to know what we should do with these two," said Jean to Matty.

"Tell him to let them go."

Once again Jean was uncertain, but said the words and Leo, equally uncertain, did what Matty suggested.

The two men rode away, thankful to be spared. Matty dismounted and gestured for Roland to do the same. Leo and Jean followed. And to Matty's surprise, Roland spoke in English. "So, warrior monk, what will you do with me?"

"That will be up to Leo."

****

An hour later the party was on the move again, but without Roland.

With Jean interpreting, Leo had told Matty more about Roland, who was from a poor family but had grown up with Leo as a close friend, gradually earning a place at the du Guesclin table despite his low birth.

That triggered a new memory for Matty, a memory of childhood friendship.

He was playing a game, pretending to be a brave knight, fighting with his best friend. He saw more than just a blank face. He saw his friend clearly. And remembered his friend's name. Edmund.

He was elated. His memories were beginning to take form, with greater detail. He was recovering.

As they rode on, Jean asked how Matty had known Roland was false. Matty explained his feeling that a robbery at that point in the road seemed wrong. Then he saw how easy it was for the robber leader to put his sword to Roland's neck, with no hint of response from Roland, no sense that Roland was afraid and no attempt by Roland even to move away to safety. But the final proof came when he saw the glance from one of the other robbers to Roland. It was hardly noticeable, but it was the final piece of evidence It was the look one friend would give to another, not the look a robber would give his victim. It was all Matty needed to confirm his suspicions.

They had questioned Roland and he told all. He had known what Leo had in a leather bag he carried. The bag had the family coat of arms on it, a two headed eagle under a red diagonal stripe. When they set out on their journey, Matty had commented that the emblem was an advertisement to thieves. It said, *'in this bag is something of value'*. The only surprise was that the danger had come from within the family circle rather than any opportunistic robbers.

Leo showed Matty what was in the bag. A small bag of gems was sewn into the lining. He explained that the gems were to be a tribute to give to the pope.

"A bribe," said Matty.

"No. Not that," replied Leo. "It is to support the work of the church. How else would there be funds for helping the poor, or for crusades to the Holy Land."

Matty was unconvinced, but either way, the gems were a valuable prize, one that Roland had been unable to resist. Roland hatched the plan with some gambling associates, to steal the gems but make it look like the work of highway robbers. The robbers would pretend not to know the gems were in the bag. Leo would think they had just been lucky. Roland would not be implicated and would remain in Leo's favour.

Leo wanted to take Roland to the authorities and have him punished. Matty dissuaded him. It would mean a significant detour to the nearest town with a sheriff. Besides which, Roland's loss of his place at the table of a wealthy household was punishment enough. And when Leo returned home, he would blacken the reputation of his former friend, causing Roland to be an outcast. He would have to move away from La Rochelle. His life had been privileged and he most probably had learned none of the skills needed to make a living. He would be reduced to general labouring, getting his hands dirty working for scraps. It would be a struggle. Roland did not need to be whipped or imprisoned to suffer for what he had done. It would happen automatically.

With Roland gone, there was one less in the pilgrim group, and as they continued towards their destination, it was evident that the incident had affected Louis and Francesca. They had watched as Matty tackled not one but two armed robbers. They had a new hero and wanted him close. They were suddenly keen to learn the sign language he had tried previously to teach them. They wanted to communicate with Frere Stephen, the ageing monk.

In the villages where they rested along the way, Louis and Francesca told anyone who would listen about their friend, their protector, the monk who foresaw floods, saved lives, and was such a great warrior, a hero. And their story was embellished with every telling. It became a whole town he had saved from flood and a group of five, six, seven highwaymen he had defeated, seven feet tall and armed with axes.

Which all drew attention to Matty. He did not want the notoriety. He was still trying to work out who he was. Part of him quite liked the fame, but mostly he just felt false. He did not feel like a gifted hero. And just what was his true story? What if it was altogether less interesting? Or worse, what if his past life had been one long history of bad deeds? Perhaps that was why his mind had chosen to forget the past, to erase memories it was ashamed of.

And then there was Leo. He was a du Guesclin, the heir in a proud family. Roland, his friend, had been revealed to be a scoundrel, and that reflected badly on him. In his world, there would be those who would call into question his judgement for choosing such a man as his closest confidante; and others might even suspect he had planned the robbery with Leo.

So Matty's discovery of Leo's part in the robbery did not result in Leo treating him any better. Leo continued to treat Matty poorly, with no improvements in the accommodation he arranged for him. If anything, things got worse. By uncovering Roland's real self, Matty was the one who had turned Leo's world upside down. Leo believed he would have been better off not knowing.

Frere Jean saw what was happening and tried to counsel Leo to treat Matty better, but the priest was ultimately powerless. At first Leo abused Matty only with a sharp tongue, but as the days went by, he added more deprivations and gave Matty unpleasant and unnecessary duties. Matty was always given the worst accommodation, worse even than Louis and Francesca; his horse was burdened with more than it could carry, making him walk to ease the beast's burden; and when they stopped to eat, Leo bought meals for Matty that were smaller than before. The food was insufficient to meet Matty's needs.

Matty did not complain. His mood was passive. He was still wrestling with the idea of being a monk with vows of poverty. He was trying to accept what he thought he was and fulfil those vows. But after several weeks he was growing weak.

Then a strange thing happened. News about Matty began somehow to get ahead of the group and crowds began to greet them as they entered larger towns. And the people saw a man who was emaciated. He was the physical embodiment of all they imagined a holy man of God to look like.

Central to their religion was a man who sacrificed himself for the greater good. If Matty had arrived with a beer-belly and double chin they would have doubted him. Instead, he possessed the right kind of aura. It was what they imagined a saintly person to look like. His reputation grew even more.

People wanted to touch him, hoping his spirituality would somehow rub off and they would become better people, kinder, wiser, healthier. In one of the larger villages Matty found himself engulfed by the crowd. It felt stifling, claustrophobic, and wrong.

He confided in Jean. "This must stop. These people should be told that I am not what they think, that I am just a man."

But Jean's response surprised him. "I've been on the road with you for many weeks, my friend. I don't know who you are, but I see something in you that *is* different. And if these poor folk need to draw hope from being near you, who am I to take that away from them?"

The villagers and towns' people began to bring food for Matty. At first, he waved them away, refusing to take their charity, knowing they were depriving themselves. But they were persistent, and his hunger got the better of him. He found himself taking from those who

61

were most offended by his initial refusals. It was easier than protesting. So whatever Leo hoped to achieve by virtually starving Matty, it was thereby undermined. Matty grew stronger, and Leo's anger grew greater.

Chapter Nine

The English Channel, April 1378

At last, they had found a ship heading for St Malo. For a month there had been none, the weather too bad for even the most hardened captain to risk the crossing.

So Edwina kicked her heels in Winchelsea, filling time as best she could. Mostly, she was bored. The one notable exception was that she was able to visit Alexander.

Alexander was seven years old. When French and Spanish raiders ravaged the ports of southern England the year before, they took him with the intention of enslavement. His family had no idea where he had gone and whether he was still alive.

By some miracle he turned up on the beach at Rottingdean after the battle there and was eventually re-united with his family. It was one of the few things that gladdened Edwina's heart at the time, and she now delighted at the chance to spend time with him.

She was not disappointed. In the bosom of his family he was healthy, lively, happy again.

There was another reason why Edwina wanted to see him. Alexander had been in hiding on the beach behind some rocks and had seen a man in the sea, face down with a bow and quiver alongside. When the boy looked away, then looked back again, the man had disappeared.

Edwina's father had been amongst the English archers that day, fighting the raiders. Could the man with the bow and quiver be her father? It was a possibility she had often wondered about, but Alexander never remembered more.

When she spent time with him, it was because of genuine affection for him. But one day they were wading in the rock pools near Winchelsea beach, looking for any lifeforms they could find. Alexander found a small crab and they examined it together, then started to talk for the first time in a while about the archer he had seen in the water.

Edwina encouraged him to talk, asking him questions. Was the man old? What colour hair did he have? Did he say anything? Her questioning was not rough but was more persistent than she intended.

He still remembered nothing new. So she stopped asking him and just played with him. They ran on the beach. It was fun. But when he got home, he told his parents about the questions, and Edwina's visits were curtailed, her welcome withdrawn, and she was angry with herself. She should not have pressed the child so much.

Now, she watched the English coastline recede. There were blue skies and the day was unseasonably warm. Michel was also on deck. She watched his profile as he looked out to sea. He was not handsome as such, but neither was he ugly. He was just Michel, dependable Michel. Many women would see him as quite a catch.

The new woman in his life was a young widow in her late twenties. Her name was Wenna and she was originally from Cornwall. When Michel introduced her to Edwina, he joyfully declared that her name meant 'blessed'.

Edwina thought Wenna pretty, in a homely kind of way, but did not like her and could not work out why. Except, of course, that she was a rival. Or was she? Because for anyone to be a rival, 'blessed' or otherwise, Edwina had to want more than just friendship with Michel. And she still did not know if she did.

Perhaps it was Wenna's perfection. Edwina had a missing hand and scarred face following a childhood incident with a hound. Wenna had perfect skin and eyes like emeralds. Edwina had a temper. Wenna was mild mannered, as a lady should be. Edwina had never been able to learn how to sew, make conversation, act in a refined ladylike way. Wenna could do all those things. Whether or not Edwina wanted Michel for herself, she found she was jealous of Wenna.

Michel had said very little about his feelings regarding Wenna, one way or the other. Which infuriated Edwina. Because she needed to know.

Hours later, Edwina was again on deck, this time watching the French coast as it came into view. Michel found her. "Nervous?" he asked.

"Frightened," she replied. "Afraid of disappointment. Am I wasting my time and yours?"

He gave her a smile of re-assurance. "Trust yourself," he said. "Have faith." He wanted to give her a re-assuring hug but feared it would not be well accepted. She would feel awkward, seeing it as his attempt at more than just friendship.

His words surprised her. She had been sure he believed she was doing the wrong thing by going to France.

Although they could see land, it would be next morning before they were in port. It gave Edwina time to think. She retired early. As she lay in her bed, she once again clasped her amulet in her hand and said a silent prayer. And a thought came to her. Something she had forgotten.

When she was a small child, her mother, Lady Alice found a new love, a man named Luke. Edwina's aunt Marianne thought Luke was bad for her and tried to warn Alice against him, but Alice would not listen. As more evidence of Luke's falseness grew, Marianne decided her brother should be told, because he was Edwina's father. She had to find him but knew he was in exile. In France. And after weeks searching, she found him.

History was repeating itself. France seemed vast and Edwina's task daunting, but it was not impossible. She really could find her father, just as her aunt once did. In her heart, she had always believed he was alive, never doubting. That was the easy part. Turning belief into reality was the hard part. Thinking of Marianne's success changed things, giving her new hope. She felt renewed, better than she had felt in a long time.

Part Two

Avignon

Chapter Ten

Avignon, April 1378

They arrived from the north, passing a huge castle. "Fort St Andre," said Jean. "We are still in France. Avignon is over the river and is a separate state. French kings have not always been comfortable having the power of the papal city so near. So they built the fort to watch over the city."

Matty noticed grand mansions all around. "Homes of the cardinals," said Jean.

Jean pointed to the south. "We cross a bridge on to an island that divides the water channel. Then we cross a second bridge and are in the city," he said. "There is no other crossing point on the river for twenty-five miles."

The second bridge was three hundred years old. It was the Pont Saint-Bénézet. It had twenty-two arches and was the main route for trade, pilgrimage and general travel between Italy and southern France. As Jean had said, there was no other crossing point for miles, so it was heaving with people, horses and carts. "We have left France," said Jean as they crossed it. "We are now on land belonging to the church."

The bridge was narrow. To Matty it seemed the whole world had decided to cross at the same time and from both directions. All varieties of human life were there. Traders had set themselves up to sell all kind of things to the pilgrims, including souvenirs to mark the end of the pilgrims' journey.

More than once, Matty was jostled by men hurrying to get wherever they were heading. He saw a girl he thought might get trampled, and went to help the child, but the girl's mother stepped in his way and gave him an angry look. She was suspicious of his motives and dragged the child away from him, every protective instinct she had kicking in. He opened his mouth to say he meant the child no harm, then realised he probably would have acted just as the mother did in this throng of people. No doubt there were men and women within the crowd who would indeed pose risk to any child who lacked a caring parent such as her.

Underneath the bridge, on the island in the river, an inn prospered. Leo made straight for it. Matty would have done the same if he had the means. His own throat felt as dry as a bone, but he had no money.

He found a yard of space standing at the bridge's edge and looked across to the city. He could see huge ramparts, protected by a moat and a series of towers. It looked as though the ramparts extended round, encircling the central area like some massive motte and bailey castle. Some of the towers also served as entrances protected by drawbridges and portcullises.

Beyond the ramparts, in the central area, the tops of a series of grand stone buildings were visible. Jean smiled as he saw Matty's look of wonder. "The magnificent Cathédrale Notre-Dame des Doms d'Avignon and the pope's palace, the Palais des Papes. Together, they form the main part of the papal city," he explained. "It is all built on a huge rock, the Rocher des Doms. I have been here before but am still amazed at the sight. It is worthy of our god. But you must excuse me. Much as I would love to show you the sights, or join Leo to wash away the dust, I have a duty to perform first."

The priest made straight for the great cathedral, to give thanks for arriving safely in the city.

Matty crossed one of the drawbridges into the heart of the city. He was fascinated by it, but his interest was not a religious one. Instead, he had a feeling like the one he had felt at the monastery near Limoges. There he had remembered working with men, masons under a great church spire. And now, in the face of such an imposing structure, the same feeling returned. He was sure he had once worked on a grand building like this.

It was the Palais that caught his attention most. It had an entrance ramp, where he stood looking up at yet more towers. There was something not quite right. And then he realised. The windows were small, the stonework less ornate than the cathedral and the corner towers were crenelated. The city was fortified by its ramparts and the Palais was constructed as another layer of defence as much as it was a place of worship.

Yet this was where the pope lived. It was the religious and administrative centre of the Christian church. Clearly, the succession of popes here had felt the need for an awesome level of protection. On the journey, Jean had explained it. France was to the north. The Holy Roman Empire was north-east. Hostile Italian city states lay to the south-east. Moorish Spain was to the west. And raiding bands of unemployed mercenaries were everywhere. The city was like the fort across the river, built because of insecurity and fear.

He sat down by the walls and rested. He thought again about the puzzle that was his past life. So far, he had been collecting memories spasmodically with no control over their appearance. With the clues he had, perhaps he could find a way to make them come to him.

He closed his eyes and tried to shut out everything that was happening around him. He willed himself to bring back and add to the memories he had regained, of a mason's chisel and a cathedral spire. For a while nothing new came, but then he began to see tall windows, leaded and stained in bright colours, and strange stone figures. The ornamentation of the building came slowly into focus.

One image sharpened. It was not a gargoyle, but the stone carving of a small creature, a fairy, a demon, an elf. It was a clue to a place he had been. But where?

He opened his eyes and saw that a small crowd had gathered and was watching him. In the middle was young Louis, who was pointing in his direction. In return, people were giving Louis coins.

Matty stood up and narrowed his eyes, giving Louis a look of reproach, and the boy took the hint, stepping back. But it was too late. The crowd had already built, surrounding Matty and, as before touching at his clothes, his beard, his hands. They had been told about the holy man, the miracle worker, and had found him outside the cathedral with his eyes closed, so assumed he was meditating as all good holy men should. They wanted to be near him, but he wanted just to escape from them.

It was Leo who rescued him, barging his way through and dragging Matty away.

Leo looked round. "Frere Jean?" he asked. Matty pointed towards the cathedral. Leo nodded. "Come."

They went inside the cathedral. It took a while for them to find Frere Jean. He was praying in a beautiful chapel, ornately decorated with images of the Virgin Mary. The roof was painted as a night sky filled with a host of angels. Leo did not wait for the priest to finish his period of contemplation, rousing the priest up and beckoning him and Matty outside.

Jean was furious. "This is the Chapel of Our Lady of Miracles," he yelled. "Your lack of respect is a matter of shame for you. Your father would be astounded." But Leo ignored the protests, shouting in turn and gesticulating wildly. They exchanged words in French, then Leo left.

It took Jean a while to regain his composure. When he did, Matty asked what was happening. "That outburst was unlike you," he said.

"I'm sorry, but sometimes he tries my patience," replied Jean. He calmed down. "He wanted to tell me the pope is dead."

"How does he know? We've only just got here."

"The inn, of course. I also knew. I found out as soon as I walked in here. There's talk of nothing else. The city is in turmoil. And for Leo, it is bad news. His audience with the pope will not happen, so he is angry at having made such a long journey for nothing. It's all made worse because of who has been chosen as the new pope."

Matty shrugged, not understanding.

"They have chosen an Italian. It is a death sentence for Avignon. I told you before there have been thoughts of taking the Holy See back to Rome. With an Italian pope, that is what will now happen. The French cardinals will not take kindly to it. Indeed, the French king will not like it, and for the people of Avignon, their city will lose much of its importance. It will be less bountiful a marketplace, and that angers Leo. His chance to make a lucrative trade deal has gone."

Jean led Matty back outside. "Look," he said, pointing towards the bridge. "The exodus from the city has already begun." It was true. More were leaving the city than entering it. Matty had not noticed when he was in the chaos on the bridge.

"This is a place that looks after itself," added Jean. "Indeed, many call it the city of thieves. But it is the papacy that lifts it to another level. Without it, the city could face ruin. Who knows what the consequences might be?"

Matty shrugged. "What of us? Do we return to La Rochelle?"

Jean laughed. "Leo won't just turn round and go home. He must save face. It is what we were arguing about. He has gone to ask for an audience with the Archbishop of Cambrai. He hopes the archbishop will be able to do for him what the old pope would have done. I said it was a foolish thing to do. Anyway, he says he will find a small house for us all to stay until the audience is granted."

"Why would that be foolish?"

"You do not know the archbishop."

"Will Leo get an audience at such short notice?"

"Probably. The du Guesclin name counts for much. Oh, and he says he wants you to be there with him."

"Why?"

Jean shook his head. "I don't know. All I know is that he is a headstrong young man. No good will come of it."

Chapter Eleven

Avignon, April 1378

Despite the du Guesclin name, it was two weeks before Leo got his audience with the archbishop. It was frustrating for him and he spent most of his time gambling at the inn on the river. He was not a good gambler, so he lost money and his mood worsened.

In the meantime, Matty spent his days on the rocks that lined the riverbank, trying to recover more of his memory. He needed to know where his home was. He knew it was somewhere in England, but England was a big place. He had to remember more, a village, a town, any detail that would connect him further with his former life. He kept having thoughts of a canal and some sights, sounds and smells of streets and lanes, but where was it? It was elusive. Then the image of the little demon came to him again. Was that connected to his home village, or a place he had worked or somewhere he had simply visited?

He was feeling stronger. Leo had given up on denying him decent food, though Matty was not sure why. With renewed energy. he was able to take longer walks into the Avignon countryside.

One day he came across some youths practising their archery in a field. He watched for a while and the spectacle triggered his next significant memory.

He was a young person again, and his friend Edmund was with him. They were practising archery on a long field, just as these youths were doing. But there was somebody else there, watching. At first the face was a blur. He cursed his strained memory. But then the features appeared. It was a girl. As her face took form, he remembered her name. Her name was Meg.

And with one name came another, the most important of all, his own name. He smiled to himself. His name was Matty, and he was the eldest son of Joseph, a farmer and part-time cutler.

It was still like seeing into the life of somebody else, watching from afar. But it was his life, he had been transported there, and he knew the place was his home.

He remembered something important about Meg. He and Meg were expected to wed.

The suddenness of the thought hit him like a hammer. She had been his sweetheart, his first love. He strove to recall what happened to them. Did they marry? Where was she now? Was she sitting in some lonely cottage wondering where he was? His head pounded. He felt so close now to the answers he craved, yet also so far from them.

He fell to his knees. He was in agony, physically as well as emotionally. The young archers saw and came to his aid. They led him back towards the city. A woman was with them. Their mother.

The woman had seen Matty before. He was hard to miss with all the attention he drew, and while there were many black monks in the city, none wore such a simple wooden cross with its chain of shells. It was one of the things that made him stand out. So she knew who he was. She spoke to him in accented English. "Where should I take you?" she asked.

Matty took a deep breath. The woman's calm kindness soothed him and brought him back to his senses. "I'm with a priest," he replied. "He will be in the cathedral. He goes there every day."

They walked together, leaving the woman's sons to resume their practice. "You are the holy man," she said. "Frere Stephen."

He shook his head. "No. Not me. My name is Matty, son of Joseph, an English cutler." He looked back to where her sons were. "I have been an archer," he said.

"Whatever your name, the people revere you. The say you are a prophet come to rid this town of its wickedness. God knows it is needed."

"They are wrong. I must find a way to convince them."

The woman's eyes widened. "But they love you. You give them hope for a better world. Do not betray them, I beg of you." She hesitated. "And I fear that if you do, there are those amongst them who would do you harm. Maybe even kill you."

"The truth is the truth. I cannot change that."

"There are many truths in the world. Some must be shouted from the rooftops. Others are best kept hidden."

They were now approaching the cathedral entrance. Once again, Matty attracted a crowd. "Say nothing yet," said the woman. "Think hard before you decide."

He nodded. "What is your name?" he asked.

"Cornelia."

It was a name Matty had not heard before. "Where are you from?" he asked.

"I was born in Florence," she replied.

"Thank you for helping me."

He walked on towards the entrance, leaving her, but she rushed to catch him up. "Come for supper," she said. "My husband is an important man in Avignon. Perhaps he can help you make your decision."

He hesitated but knew he did need help, someone with wisdom and knowledge of the holy city. "Yes," he replied. "I will come."

"Good. I will tell you where we live."

****

Matty found Jean where he usually was and told him what had happened. "Things are coming back to me like a flood," he said. "I remember my family, my village, my childhood. I can't recall much about my life as an adult, but I think those memories also will return."

"I am glad for you," replied the priest. "But I agree with this woman you met. Do not be hasty to renounce yourself here. You are Stephen the Benedictine. For your own safety, stay that way. Be who the people want you to be, until God shows His purpose for you."

Matty returned to the rented house. Louis and Francesca were there, busy making clay models in the room that served as their workplace, bedroom, kitchen, living area and sleeping place. Matty watched for

74

a while, intrigued. Then he smiled to himself as realisation dawned. They were making tourist pieces to sell to pilgrims. Louis was carving a figure, a copy of one of the statues of the Virgin Mary he had seen in the cathedral. He asked to see it. The likeness was good and Matty was impressed. Francesca was applying beeswax to a similar piece Louis had made earlier. Matty wondered where she had got the wax from but decided not to ask her. He admired their enterprise.

In a corner of the room he saw more figurines. They were monks with the distinct black robes of the Benedictine order. His robes. They wore shell chains. Louis and Francesca were selling images of him.

He picked up one of the figurines and threw it to the floor, breaking it, showing his displeasure. Then he climbed the stairs to where there were two bedrooms. Leo had the larger room while Matty and Jean shared the smaller one. He sat on the edge of his bed and thought of home. He needed to get there. Enough memories had come back for him to have a clear enough picture of his family's home, the one he had glimpsed several weeks earlier, with its one room for all purposes, just like the one Louis and Francesca were in.

But this time there was more.

He saw people. As before, it started with faceless shapes, but gradually the faces appeared. He gasped as he saw his mother, his father and two younger brothers. But they were coughing. And he saw why. They had the tell-tale signs. Buboes. The plague was upon them. But he was not there. Where was he while they suffered? Then he remembered. He had been away, at a nearby market town. When he came back, he went straight to a feast at the local manor house, more interested to see Meg, his sweetheart, than his family. He had not known they were dying.

The memories were painful, He felt guilty for not going home and finding and helping his family. It was almost too much to bear. But then there was something else. He sat up. Someone had survived. He saw the face of his sister, Marianne. She wore the clothing of a novice. She was living in a convent. And with her was Meg.

His mind raced. He remembered good times. His childhood was happy, with a loving family, friends and a sweetheart. There was joy when he was reunited with Marianne when he thought she was dead. But alongside those good memories was such darkness. The loss of his parents and brothers. Meg's suffering. And Marianne's.

The daylight was fading. He broke off from his memories and went to Cornelia's home. On the street he passed Louis and Francesca. They were selling some of the souvenirs they made, but thankfully there were no more Benedictine monks amongst the souvenirs.

He found the house where Cornelia, her husband and sons lived. It was a rented house, near the artisanal zone of the city. The design of the house was like the one he was staying in, though Cornelia's was slightly bigger.

One of Cornelia's sons ushered Matty into a dining area and he joined the family at a long table. The food was plentiful, with several dishes Matty did not recognise. Cornelia saw his puzzled expression and explained what the dishes were. "The first one we have is a pie we eat in Italy," she said. "Our name for it is 'pizza'. It has a topping of chicken, but if you look over there, we have another topped with marzipan. We eat that one afterwards."

The food looked strange but appetising, and Matty sat down to eat. The meal was like nothing he had eaten before and was delicious.

"Welcome to the food of Italy," said Cornelia's husband.

"Are you well now?" asked the son who had ushered Matty in. It seemed the whole family spoke English, with varying degrees of fluency.

"Yes, thank you. It was good of you all to help me this afternoon."

The other son spoke. "We did not know what was happening to you. We thought a demon might have got into your head. Your calling must make you a target for bad spirits."

"My demons are in my past," replied Matty. "I remember things only hazily. When you saw me, I had just remembered something I had forgotten. A person who was very dear to me. It came as a shock."

"The past can be a terrible place." It was Cornelia's husband speaking now. "Did my wife tell you why we are here in Avignon?"

Matty shook his head.

"Forgive me," said the man. "I haven't yet made introductions. I am Alessandro." He made a sweeping gesture with his hand. "You already met my wife and sons."

Matty nodded in polite acknowledgement.

Alessandro continued. "We are Florentine, but our home city has been in turmoil for years. First, there was a war with Pisa. Then the ancient guilds and the newer guilds started to fight with each other, because the new think they deserve the wealth and power of the old, while the old resist change. It means Florence is a dangerous place just now. Not only that, but the people are not respectful of our pope, here in Avignon. That creates more trouble. I was in the guild of silversmiths. It was getting harder and harder to make a living, so we decided to escape the turmoil. We came here because Avignon is a place of great opportunity for craftsmen. There are a lot of wealthy clients here, eager to part with their money."

"I'm sorry to hear you had to leave your home," said Matty. "It sounds like you had no choice. But I'm told we are to have an Italian pope. How will that affect you? Will you go back to Florence?"

Alessandro grimaced. "We don't yet know. At least, though the Archbishop of Cambrai will not now become pope."

Cornelia gave her husband a sharp look and a kick under the table. She thought he was saying too much in the presence of a man they had only just met.

"I am here with a merchant, Leo du Guesclin," said Matty. "We are to meet the archbishop. Is there something we should know?"

Cornelia's look hardened, but her husband was not to be silenced. "Florence is not the only place in Tuscany that has disliked the French popes. A year ago the old pope, Pope Gregory decided to do something about it, to bring them to heel. He chose a man to deal with it, and that man was Robert of Geneva, the Archbishop of Cambrai. He is cruel. At Cesena, he laid siege to the town. The people were told that Pope Gregory would be lenient if they opened their gates. On 3rd February they did so, but there was no leniency. The Archbishop of Cambrai ordered a slaughter. Three days later there were 5,000 dead. Many women and girls were raped. Some of the dead drowned in the city moat trying to get away, all at the command of one who would be pope if he had his way. My wife and I are devout Christians. Thank God another has been chosen to lead our faith. So, yes, there are things you should know about the man you will be meeting."

Matty's response was instant. His eyes glazed over and he stared, as in a trance, through and beyond Alessandro, who watched in stunned amazement. Matty felt the force of something invisible hitting him. It was not the idea of having to meet the archbishop. It was a new memory, vividly there for him to watch as if he was merely an observer of his own life. He was witnessing the devastation of a small town, just as Alessandro had described, but not in Italy.

He was in Normandy. And he was part of an English army that carried out the slaughter. The army was led by an English duke. They were carrying out a systematic ravaging of the towns and countryside, denying food and shelter to the French army. It was a chevauchee.

This was too much. Matty was struggling to cope with the new memories. They were now coming thick and fast, layer upon layer, each one filled with more trauma and emotion than the last. For the second time in a single day he lost his place in the present as the past consumed him. He felt as though his head would burst. He held it as if trying to keep everything in. He wept. And for the second time it was Cornelia who comforted him.

Chapter Twelve

Avignon, April 1378

Cornelia's voice was soothing. She held his hand. Her caring manner helped Matty return to the here and now.

"I'm sorry," he said. "It's as though I'm watching a group of players telling a story, except it's one where I am the main character."

He described his latest memory to the family sitting round the table. As he did so, Alessandro nodded constantly.

When he finished, Alessandro spoke. "It's the same problem as in Florence," he said. "Mercenaries given money to do as they please. Innocent people their victims. Were you one, a mercenary?"

"No. I was a soldier. I went to France looking for a friend and ended up in King Edward's army. I think I was an archer. But I also knew things about medicines." He paused, taking a sip of wine before carrying on. "Ever since St Malo I have had a name in my head. Stephen. And I could see the figure of a monk in black robes. So I assumed that's who I was, Stephen, the black monk, a Benedictine. Now I know that's not who I am. Stephen was a friend who taught me how to heal people. And in Normandy during the chevauchees that's what I did. I was able to tend wounds. I was fortunate. I no longer had to be part of the killing.

"I felt guilty at what I was part of, so after the English army went home, I stayed and tried my best to make amends for the slaughter. Innocent people, simple farmers doing no harm to anyone. Women and children." He was shaking his head with disbelief.

"Did you ever go back to England?" asked Cornelia.

"I think so, but so far all the details of my life end in Normandy." He took another sip of the wine. "It frightens me. What else is to come? Have I been a murderer or a rapist? Part of me wants to remember, of course, but maybe it would be better if I didn't."

Cornelia leaned across the table and put her hand on Matty's arm. "You were caught up in somebody else's war," she said. "But you found a way to be yourself, to be good. Whatever else there is to learn about your life I'm sure you have done no evil."

"Maybe I have not meant to. But even now, I live as two people, the son of an English cutler and the mysterious monk who folk think has magic powers."

One of the sons now spoke. "What does it matter? If they want to think of you that way, that is their problem, not yours."

"And you have helped those who have come to you. What harm can there be in that?" added the other son.

There was a pause, then Alessandro spoke again. "Let me give you some advice, cutler's son. Forget about your past, at least for now. Because your future is round the corner. You are to meet Robert of Geneva, the Archbishop of Cambrai. If I were you, I would put all my attention into that meeting, because it will be dangerous for you if it does not go well. Be on your guard. Be careful."

They talked more, until finally Matty rose and thanked his hosts for their hospitality, warmth and advice. "I hope we meet again," he said.

"You are welcome here at any time," replied Cornelia.

Matty returned to the rented house, to be met at the door by Frere Jean, who was waiting for him. "It is tomorrow," said the priest. "The appointment with the archbishop is set for one hour after dawn."

****

Matty slept unevenly that night, partly in anticipation of meeting the infamous archbishop, but also because of those things that had returned to his mind about his time in Normandy.

He was now close to having a sense of who he was, the son of a cutler who had lived a humble life until some extraordinary events took hold of his destiny. He now knew he had been a soldier. He had killed men by the bow but also up so close he could smell their breath and taste their fear. But the things he had been taught by a monk named Stephen rescued him, fitting him for work tending the wounded, allowing him to escape from the cruelty that was the soldier's job every day.

And he now remembered what happened to the real Stephen, his friend and mentor. Stephen had died doing the selfless things he always did, tending the poor and sick.

Of all the twists and turns in Matty's life, his present circumstances seemed strangest. The world had declared him to be important, a man of God, the Benedictine. He wondered where this new life would take him next.

As the dawn came, he started to prepare. He said prayers by his bed then washed and ate a chunk of leftover pizza Cornelia had given him the night before.

Frere Jean and Leo were waiting for him outside the rented house. Together they walked in silence towards the papal residence, the Palais. Matty sensed his companions were as nervous as he was.

As they crossed over one of the drawbridges, he paused. He now knew there were twelve circling the papal city. Would he be coming back out across one of them, he wondered?

The Palais was to the south of the cathedral. From its gates, Matty could see the huge French castle dominating the horizon, strategically placed as a defence against the power of the city, whether real or imagined.

One of the Palais officials met and escorted them. Jean pointed to a fortified tower. "The papal apartments are at the top," he said. "But we are going to the Hall of the Consistory. It's where the Avignon popes have always received their most important visitors, the kings and queens and so on."

"We are not kings or queens," said Matty.

"Some would say you are more important because you are closer to God."

The official heard the conversation. "Excuse me," he said. "The archbishop has decided not to receive you in the Consistory. I am taking you to the papal study."

Inside the palatial building they passed people going in every direction, all seemingly in a hurry to get wherever they needed to be.

They came to a cloister, the sound of chanting echoing around the vaulted ceilings. "There are four wings," said Jean. "There's a hall that seems to go on forever." He pointed out beautiful chapels and grand staircases. He was beaming, like a guide showing off a wonder of the world, trying to convey just some of the awe-inspiring brilliance of a place made by men to reflect their god's greatness.

Matty saw it differently. "So much money must have been spent on this place. A single fresco would have paid for food for a thousand starving families, and each statue even more."

Jean scowled. "On the road, I warned you to be careful with your tongue when we got here, and now you disrespect this house of God. Would you have the pope live in a hovel, a pigsty? And there are plenty of charities the popes have all supported. Some they set up themselves. The poor are not forgotten here."

"I'm sure the popes have made great sacrifices for the people," replied Matty sarcastically. "I'll bet some had only seven courses at their meals rather than eight or nine."

"Mocking comes easily to you, it seems. But some have lived frugal lives. Indeed, most of the Avignon popes were Benedictine monks, just like you are…or are not. Others have been more extravagant, yes, but who should deny God's most important representative here on earth of the bounty created for us all?"

"Who indeed?" Again, the words were loaded with sarcasm.

They reached the papal study. It was surprisingly small, an intimate room decorated with frescoes of hunting scenes rather than the religious images elsewhere in the Palais.

Although the room was small, two officials stood behind the archbishop, wearing swords along with the garments of cardinals.

And the archbishop himself was not what Matty had expected. Matty had an image in his mind of an ageing man, barely still alive,

82

chairbound and incoherent. Robert of Geneva was none of those things. He was still in his thirties, a picture of health with sharp eyes, a prominent nose and fulsome beard. He oozed authority and more than a little menace.

The archbishop greeted his visitors with an apology. "Welcome," he said. "I'm sorry I had to change the venue for our meeting. Now we have a new pope I have taken a step back. It would not be well viewed in Rome if I was seen to be receiving guests in those rooms used by the popes, even though it is I who have administered the affairs of Christendom since Gregory's demise. It is quite a burden. But please, sit and take food and wine."

A silver tray of sweetmeats was brought in, along with fine Etruscan wine. *Such frugality* thought Matty to himself.

Matty sat uneasily on a framed oak chair that was upholstered in leather. Jean did the same. The seats made sounds with every movement of the body.

Leo remained standing and said some words in French to their host, gushing appreciation for the invitation they had received. Jean made to interpret but Matty held up a hand as there was no need. It was clear what Leo was doing.

Whatever Leo was saying, it seemed to bounce off the archbishop, who was used to sycophancy of a much higher level of eloquence and grovelling. Leo moved on to raise issues of commerce and trade, but it was a misjudgement, coming too early in the meeting. The archbishop listened for a while, and showed some interest when Leo produced the gems he had secreted on the journey, receiving them with grace but still looking bored. Perhaps he had expected more. There was nothing given in return, no token of welcome. Now and then the archbishop gave the faintest of nods, as if acknowledging some point Leo had made, but Matty saw no evidence that the archbishop gave Leo any commitments in return.

Leo continued to argue his case and seemed pleased with himself in how he was doing, until the archbishop held up a hand, halting Leo in full flow. And turned his attention to Matty.

Matty now did ask Frere Jean to interpret for him. It was why the priest was there. Matty had asked for his presence, so he could know what was being said. Leo had agreed only grudgingly, because in truth he saw no need for Matty to be there. Leo had no expectation that Matty would take part in any of the discussions.

But Leo was wrong. The archbishop beckoned Matty forward and spoke. It turned out that his English was quite good. "So you are the famous English Benedictine."

Matty searched for an honest answer and found one. "Some call me that, amongst other things."

The archbishop smiled to himself. Matty's response was oblique, a politician's response. It suggested wisdom, or cunning, both qualities the archbishop admired. He was intrigued. "You have many followers. More, perhaps than even I." He laughed, and his officials laughed with him. It seemed that was the norm, part of their duties.

"We both know that's not the case," replied Matty, giving another simple, truthful, factual answer.

There was a brief frown from the archbishop. He was weighing Matty up. Then he smiled again and his tone changed as he decided he liked Matty's straightforward manner. "My name is Robert," he said. "I welcome you to my palace, Frere Stephen."

Matty did nothing to correct him on the name. He had stopped doing it. There no longer seemed any point, because whenever he tried to correct anyone, they ignored it.

Leo suddenly became animated, putting his arm on Matty's shoulder. He was beaming and started talking again, his words arriving too quickly and tripping over one another. Matty smelled alcohol on Leo's breath, no doubt taken before they came to the meeting, to give him courage.

Matty could tell what Leo was doing, trying to gain favour with the archbishop through close association with the one known as the Benedictine. In fact, it was why Leo had brought Matty with him. Leo had understood he could use Matty in that way, though he had not prepared himself for the possibility the archbishop would *talk* with Matty.

What happened next took Matty, Leo and Jean completely by surprise. The archbishop told Leo to shut up and sit down. Leo was stunned. The archbishop then signalled to one of his officials, and the official briefly left the room, returning with a young boy in tow.

The boy was maybe six years of age. He was dressed in expensive velvets but did not walk into the room. He was sitting in a chair that had three wheels attached. Matty had never seen anything like it. The official pushed the boy to where the archbishop stood.

The archbishop saw Matty's interest in the chair. "I learned of this contraption from a merchant who had been to the east," he said. "It's a simple but brilliant invention, the likes of which I have never seen in Europe. The boy is the son of a bishop, who happens also to be my brother. So he is my nephew. He has been like this for two years. I want you to heal him."

Matty looked at Frere Jean for some kind of indication what he should do. The priest simply shrugged. There was no choice in this.

So Matty duly examined the boy. The first thing he noticed was the boy's pallor and apparent lack of energy. He guessed why that was. "Your physicians have been letting his blood, I think."

The archbishop nodded, slightly impressed. "It is the treatment they favour."

"They must stop, because it is not helping him, only adding to the problems he has."

This time, the archbishop looked at Frere Jean, somewhat shocked at Matty's forthright manner. Matty noticed the look. "Trust me on this," he said. "I have seen the effects of bloodletting many times. I have never seen it cure anyone but it can cause weakness for some."

The archbishop said nothing, but watched as Matty proceeded to examine the boy, starting with the feet and legs. The boy had no reaction to Matty's touch. Matty increased the intensity of touching but it made no difference. The legs seemed floppy and unresponsive. As the examination moved to the boy's waist some feeling came, increasing as Matty moved higher up the body.

One of the officials spoke, and Jean interpreted. "The official is protesting about what you are doing. He says the papal physicians have done all the right things. They all agree that the imbalance in the boy's humours is great, but say the astrological signs are unfavourable for any intervention just now beyond the bloodletting and prayers."

Matty had heard this before. It was a blame game. The physicians were shifting responsibility to the stars, taking it away from themselves. "Of course," he said. "I hope you all check the night sky before you take your daily walk to the cathedral," he added in his best sarcastic voice. He gave the official a look of reproach. "The boy's condition has nothing to do with the stars." It was an unusual and controversial thing to say.

He continued the examination. "Is the boy in pain?" he asked.

Jean asked the boy and interpreted his response. "Only soreness around the top of his legs," he said.

Matty turned to the archbishop. "You told me he has been like this for two years. Could he walk normally before that?"

"Yes."

"Did he have an accident, a fall maybe?"

The archbishop thought. "Yes, he did. He fell from a pony."

Matty sighed and nodded. "In Normandy, I saw men who could walk well until they suffered blows to the head or upper body in battle. For some reason no-one understands, a blow like that can affect the ability to walk. I think there is something inside the body, some connection that breaks, though it's only my best guess."

"Did the men walk again?"

86

"Some did. We helped them learn again how to walk, like with children. We would walk with them until they got strong enough to stand alone. It took a long time and most still had difficulties, but the boy is young, so time is on his side. Beyond that, all I can do is recommend ointments for the soreness he feels."

"Thank you for your honesty," said the archbishop. He spoke to the boy, who burst into tears. "You were his last hope," he said to Matty.

"You will try what I suggest, and stop the bloodletting?"

"No. You have not convinced me of anything you have said."

The archbishop dismissed the boy, then rounded on Matty. "You are an arrogant man to dismiss the knowledge of my finest physicians when you have little else to offer the boy yourself. It seems all the stories about you are false. You are a charlatan, and I will see you punished for it," he said.

"You are afraid of the truth. If I told him he would be cured, I would be lying to him. It would have done him no service, and your physicians are guilty of the same crime," replied Matty. "I have never claimed to be able to cure the lame. And by the way, my name is not Stephen the monk. I am Matty, son of Joseph. My father was a farmer and a cutler. I have some medical knowledge, gained at a monastery in England then on the battlefields of Normandy. If I can help people I do, but miracles are not within my means. I cannot be blamed if other men and women think otherwise."

"Have you studied medicine?"

"I was given a place at Oxford, but it did not work out for me."

Suddenly, Leo became agitated and asked for a word with the archbishop in private. When they returned, the mood had changed.

"I apologise," said the archbishop. "Perhaps I expected too much from you. I think you believe what you say, so I will not punish you, but in return you must promise to do something for me."

"If I can, I will."

"Good. All I ask is that you attend a service I will be giving next Sunday. There you must say your penance before the congregation."

Matty was inclined to refuse. Penance for what? He had done nothing wrong. But he caught a glance from Jean, the slightest of nods. And he nodded his agreement to the archbishop's proposal.

"Good," said the archbishop. "That is very good. But you cannot appear in my church with a cross such as that." He pointed to the simple cross Matty wore, with its shell chain.

"It was a gift to me, from a young woman who nursed me when I was very ill. It's important to me."

"And it serves you to wear it, a clever way to appear humble. It matches your clothing. It is all part of how you present yourself, I think. It conveys the image you want people to see. But it is not fit for my church."

The archbishop left the room briefly, returning with a large silver cross. It was the biggest personal cross Matty had ever seen. It would have sufficed as the main cross at the altar in many chapels he had visited.

The archbishop's manner offered no possibility for debate. So Matty took the cross and put it on. He would wear it to the church then revert to the one he preferred.

It seemed that, charlatan or not, the archbishop had decided he had a use for Matty, son of Joseph the cutler, amateur healer but no worker of miracles.

Chapter Thirteen

Avignon, April 1378

As Matty entered the cathedral, he felt there were eyes upon him. For once, the eyes were not those of an adoring crowd. Two magnificent frescoes above the entrance seemed to watch him. One was of the Christ, the other of the Virgin. They seemed to challenge him, to denounce him as false, a pretender.

He knew why he was there. Frere Jean had explained it.

When the archbishop raged at Matty's failure to cure the crippled boy, Leo persuaded him that Matty had value regardless. If the people believed in Frere Stephen, that was all that mattered. No matter what the archbishop thought of Matty, he could still benefit through association, just as Leo had sought to do. The archbishop had not yet given up hope of one day becoming pope. Being close to the Benedictine could make the difference in a campaign to sway the cardinals.

The archbishop was a practical man, pragmatic, and used to the politics of his position. He was willing to bend with the wind if doing so helped him achieve his high ambitions.

As for Matty, he felt he had no choice but to comply with the deception. He reasoned that nobody would come to harm because of it. But he did stipulate just one condition. He would not take the Eucharist, the bread and wine. He felt it would be wrong to do so as part of a sham, a piece of theatre. It would be taking liberties with the Eucharist ceremony, here in one of the most important churches in Christendom.

Asserting the condition cost Matty some scornful looks from the archbishop, but he stood firm and the archbishop agreed. But despite his resolve about the Eucharist, he still felt guilty as he passed under the frescoes and walked down the cathedral aisle.

The cross he had been given weighed him down, literally and metaphorically. He felt on show. He felt stupid wearing such a thing. He wished he had his chain of shells and simple cross.

The cathedral architecture was as masculine as it was in the Palais, with stone arches everywhere. Both buildings were beautiful in their own way, but like the Palais the cathedral architects had favoured strength over delicacy.

The service was like any other Matty had attended. There was a processional entrance of clergymen, though this time they were all bishops, plus the waving of incense burners and the chanting of a choir. And just like those other services, Matty could not understand a word that was being said. He had never mastered spoken Latin, though he had learned to read some.

As well as the bishops, another difference was the makeup of the congregation, a large proportion of whom were well-dressed and wealthy. He remembered church services at home having one or two dignitaries, the lords and ladies of the manors, but otherwise the people there were poor farmers and their families.

Matty endured rather than enjoyed the proceedings, drifting absently away into his own thoughts. He thought of home, all those things his memory had allowed him to recall. He also thought about his future. He longed to go home to England, to those loved ones he could recall, and any others he still needed to remember. His life as an adult remained full of gaps.

A noise at the back of the cathedral brought him out from his reflection. He turned and saw a man being led towards the front. Then he heard a name called from where the archbishop stood by the altar. "Frere Stephen." He was being summoned. He looked up. "Come forward," said the archbishop.

He obeyed. By now the man who had been led in was alongside the altar. The man fell at Matty's feet, weeping and wailing, then stood up and said something in the local dialect. His speech was impassioned and it brought gasps from the congregation.

The archbishop now called for something to be brought forward. A bishop took him a casket, which the archbishop blessed. Then he spoke, and the congregation gasped again, this time falling to their knees, heads bowed.

The Mass resumed. Matty was told to sit in a seat reserved for him, higher than the main body of the congregation, looking down on them. He felt uncomfortable, as though he was on display. He caught a glimpse of Leo in the congregation, grinning from ear to ear.

He looked up at the image of Christ above the altar and said a silent apology. Whatever was happening, it felt wrong.

When the service ended, he sought out Frere Jean and asked what had taken place. There was anger in his voice.

Jean recognised the emotion. He was sheepish. "The man told the people he had been a leper until he met you. He said you laid hands on him and cured him."

"And the casket?"

"It contains relics of Saint Benezet. He was a shepherd boy who received word from God to build the bridge over the river. The archbishop told the people that when you arrived in Avignon you saw a vision of the saint, tending his sheep on a hillside, and the saint told you to minister here, because this, not Rome, is the true home of God's chief priest on Earth, the head of the Christian church, the pope."

Matty's brow furrowed. "Why? What does he hope to achieve?"

"It is complicated. The old pope, Pope Gregory believed the papacy should return to Rome. His wish was for a new crusade to retake the Holy Land from the infidels and return it to Christendom. He thought that ever since the papacy came to Avignon the popes had been looking north, wanting to resolve the war between France and England. He thought they should have looked east to Jerusalem. Gregory's beliefs have been persuasive and so the new pope is Italian, but the return to Rome is not without risk. Most of the cardinals are still French, and Italy is a place of small states always at war with one another. The Archbishop of Cambrai has not given up on becoming pope, and you have just strengthened his position."

91

"Without knowing it. It seems it is not only Leo who hangs on my shirt tails."

Jean looked serious. "I fear bloodshed. It will not be a good time for the church."

Matty nodded slowly. "When powerful men come into conflict, it is the ordinary men, women and children who suffer most. And I have now been held up as a prophet who says God favours a man I know as a butcher. That is a torch I do not wish to carry."

"For one like me, ordained a priest, the Holy See is a precious thing, the most important point of contact between this world and the spiritual world. I don't like how the archbishop is using you, but I believe it is right for the pope to live here in Avignon. Sometimes it is necessary to stretch truth for the greater good."

"So you are happy that the people are told such lies."

"I pray every day for guidance. It is all I can do. I suggest you do the same."

"I need no guidance about right and wrong. And what he is doing, this man who would be pope, is wrong." With that, he stormed out of the cathedral, desperate for the fresher air that was outside.

Part Three

No longer a slave

Chapter Fourteen

St Malo, May 1378

The Spanish carrack eased its way into the shelter of the harbour. The ramparts of the town slid by as the ship passed through the sea entrance and found a mooring, the small peninsula on which the town stood offering protection from the elements.

A young man stood at the guard rail and watched the port as it became ever larger. Ishraq's jobs on board ship were done, the sails taken down as the Santa Lucia coasted the last yards to a berth. He saw dots grow on the quayside until they took form and became people. He smiled to himself as he watched the contrasts, some folk rushing about while others calmly and assuredly went about their daily business, routines repeated day after day since forever. It was a sight he never tired of.

He was no longer a lad of fourteen. He was a young man, almost sixteen and with experiences that others of his age would never know in a lifetime.

It was six months since he joined this ship, this crew, this captain. His goal then was to reach Cadiz, from where he would strike out towards the lands of his birth, at the far eastern end of the Mediterranean Sea.

He never got to Cadiz. The Santa Lucia was destined to plough a single trade route between St Malo and La Rochelle, backwards and forwards. If only he had known, he would have found another ship, one going further south, taking him where he wanted to go.

But at least his life had been easier than ever before, though a little monotonous at times. And he had achieved something. Because he was now a senior deck hand.

On the high seas age, skin colour and background counted for less than ability. And Ishraq felt as though he belonged. In England, his dark skin had singled him out as different. But his shipmates had all kinds of shades of skin colouring, some weather tanned from years of living and working in the sun but others naturally dark in tone. It was

94

the first time he had known such an environment. And he was at last a free man.

Sea captains needed men they could rely on, and Ishraq had proved his worth. So in a matter of months he had gone from being the lowly servant, doing the worst of the jobs on board, to being one of the captain's trusted hands. The work was hard but had turned his young body into that of a man. The year had seen him grow taller as well. He was now close to six foot and as strong as an ox.

He had earned the friendship and respect of the crew, most of whom were Spanish. With money in his pocket he was able to join them in port, share some ale and some fun, have a laugh and sing the bawdy songs sailors sang.

Ishraq also had enterprise. In the few months he had been at sea he had learned how to sew, a skill passed on from sailor to sailor over many generations.

Sewing helped pass the time on calm seas but was also a useful skill, and Ishraq utilised his new skills better than most. He developed more than the basic ability to patch sails and shirt sleeves. He had imagination and could fashion clothing suitable for the tasks on board but also for nights out in port.

A common practice was to cut along the sleeves of shirts, creating something looser, less likely to snag on the rigging and cause a fall. But they were crudely fashioned. Ishraq was able to go further. He foraged for spare pieces of material and discarded shirts, washing them and storing them. The crew wore blue, the traditional colour for mariners' clothing. He scavenged any pieces of blue cloth he could, but also looked for more colourful materials, and in the winter concentrated on thicker ones.

In his spare time, he worked on creating new garments.

The end products were practical, but better made, brighter, and warmer than his shipmates managed. So he sold them easily.

At first he made just a few coins. That encouraged him to branch out. Knee-length tunics were in fashion but too expensive for the sailors.

By adding pieces to shorter tunics and making them longer, he was able to offer for sale something the sailors wanted, something they felt good in, something that made them feel more confident when they went ashore seeking the company of women.

On board the ship, none of the sailors wore shoes. Barefoot, they were less likely to slip on the wet deck. But walking barefoot around towns was a different matter. Ishraq scavenged faded and worn leather shoes, discarded as useless, then re-stitched them and nourished the leather with tallow and beeswax from the ship's stores. He made a pair for himself and sold several other pairs, including pairs of pattens, overshoes with wooden bases that raised them above the mud created by horses' hooves in the streets of the ports.

He was doing well and was content. Perhaps he would have just stayed with the Santa Lucia, comfortable and secure. But as the ship docked, he caught sight of someone he knew, and his world was about to change once again.

He waited, unsure whether to make himself known. As he did, a shout came from behind, an order. He was being asked to lower the gangplank. He obeyed the order, and when he looked back to the quayside, she was gone.

His next task was one given to him by the Greek captain, a man of near fifty years whose whole life had been at sea. The captain had been on boats and ships since first he was able to walk.

The captain was superstitious in the extreme and attributed his longevity to a fastidious regard for the signs and omens of sea travel. He was heavily tattooed with assorted Christian, pagan and general good luck symbols. There was a cross tattooed on his neck, a black cat on his shoulder, Poseidon on his arm. He carried out rituals before, during and after each voyage and watched for shapes in the clouds or the behaviour of sea birds before making decisions on navigation.

Ishraq's task was to buy fresh flowers. They were the captain's gift to the Santa Lucia for giving him safe passage. So at each port of arrival Ishraq would be sent to buy them. The task today, with spring flowers in bloom, was an easy one. During the winter months it was not so easy. This day he had no trouble finding an old woman selling small bouquets of yellow and pink blooms. He took them as always straight to the captain, who tied them to the mast. The captain then said a silent prayer of thanks, sighing in relief to be safe on dry land. The crew watched the ritual and gave their own silent thanks as they did.

****

That evening, Ishraq enjoyed the company of his fellow sailors at a quayside tavern.

Theirs was a precarious existence, dependent upon the vagaries of the ocean for their livelihoods and their very lives. Each one had a religion. On Ishraq's ship there were Christians, Jews, Muslims and one or two who believed in ancient pagan gods. But they all had one thing in common, a belief in the power of the sea. In a way, the sea was their god, and was a vengeful god, taking lives just because it could, often with no warning, the wind its mocking voice as it watched sailors perish.

So the crew made merry whenever they hit port. This excursion was enlivened by an argument with a rival French crew they had met before. By the time Ishraq made his way back to the ship, he was drunk on ale and sported a few new bruises, but happy to have been part of the excitement of a 'friendly' tavern brawl.

The lights on the ship beckoned him to come on board and rest for the night. But this time he took a moment to sit on the pebble beach and think. He had seen her here. Lady Edwina. He had to know what she was doing so far from home. He silently cursed his own curiosity, because wherever Edwina was, trouble was never far away.

He laughed because he also felt a shiver of anticipation. Edwina was never far from trouble, it was true, but it meant new adventure. Ishraq was drawn to find her. It would undoubtedly prove much more entertaining than a mere tavern brawl.

****

97

Next day, Ishraq had finished his jobs and was able to take time wandering the narrow streets of the old port. He was hoping for a sight of Edwina.

As he did so, he was remembering the times they had shared a year before. Seeing her had ignited feelings in him, memories of England. He had walked with her on a journey from Windsor to Hedingham. She was a lady and he a servant, but they became friends.

At Hedingham, they both faced danger from smugglers. Their paths crossed more than once, each peril worse than the one before, the greatest danger coming from foreign raiders.

Last time he saw her, Edwina was hiding in Rye while the town was being ravaged by French and Spanish pirates. It was there that Ishraq was captured and set to work on one of the raiding ships, ultimately to end up on the Santa Lucia.

He liked her. She was different from the other ladies at Hedingham. She lacked their sense of supreme self-confidence and their belief that everyone was their subordinate. To an orphan boy with dark skin, that meant something.

And she was loyal. She searched for him when she thought he was in trouble. No-one else he knew would have done that, let alone a titled lady.

So now, knowing she was nearby, he needed to find her, to make sure all was well in her world, to renew their friendship and maybe have a new adventure with her.

Instead, he was met by a bunch of drunken sailors weaving their way through the back streets towards their ship. They were the same French sailors who had fought Ishraq's crewmates earlier that evening. And Ishraq was now on his own.

****

The following morning, he woke in an alleyway, dazed and bruised. His first thought was that he might have been robbed. He was right. His precious shoes had been stolen. They were the only things he had on his person of any worth. The money he had saved from making clothes was hidden on board the ship.

He scrambled to his feet but could not stand without holding on to a wall. Hand over hand, he made his way gingerly to his ship, trying to avoid any sharp stones wedged within the cobbles. A friend helped him the last few yards. "Meet a girl and find she already had a man?" laughed the sailor. It was the usual reason for a beating such as Ishraq had been given.

Ishraq smiled but said nothing. He had been stupid to wander alone in this place. But he was undaunted in his desire to find Edwina. So he hurriedly bathed his bruises and ate a makeshift breakfast before returning to the quayside.

Seafood was the staple food for the crew. It came in every form imaginable, from simple shoreline catches of cockles, whelks, crabs and shrimps, to the whiting and flatfish that was plentiful around the northwest shores of France. Very occasionally there would be something unusual, and therefore more expensive, such as turbot. That was a treat, but it was still fish.

Ishraq had mixed feelings about the diet. He was never deprived of food, never close to starvation but he did often pine for something, anything that was not from the sea.

This morning he had a small crab and a chunk of bread, washed down with ale, the stale remnants of a barrel that had been opened a week earlier and which was a day away from being thrown over the side.

After he had eaten, he decided to change tack in his search for Edwina. He thought about what he had seen. She had been walking away from the harbour. She must have just arrived. He needed to find the vessel that had given her passage from England.

It was easy. He knew sailors on most of the ships and boats, as well as the harbour personnel. Edwina was distinctive, easy to describe. She was pretty, but also had distinguishing features, her missing hand and facial scars.

Before noon he found someone who knew where she was. A deckhand on a French cog was able to confirm he had seen a girl fitting Edwina's description, and that she was with a well-known merchant named Michel. More importantly, the sailor was able to tell Ishraq where they were heading within the town. It was known that Michel had a business house he used for his work and slept there whenever he was in the town.

With clear directions, Ishraq easily found the place. It was nestled under the town walls, handy for the port but far enough away from the town's rougher quarter.

Ishraq approached the house, then stopped. The house was on a corner, and two men were there, down the side of the building. There was something about them, a furtiveness. They were talking, not arguing, but animated, discussing something of importance.

He would have ignored them, but then they parted, one heading towards the port while the other, a portly merchant with a full beard, went to the door of the house and, without knocking, went inside.

On instinct, Ishraq decided to wait and watch rather than knock at the door.

His life had been one of servitude. He had been raised by a man he understood to be his father. Then, one day he learned that the man was not his father but had bought him in a slave market. It explained why he had always been treated, not as a son, but as a possession.

So it was a childhood in which he learned how to stay in the shadows, out of the immediate notice of his *'father'*. It helped him survive, keeping down the number of beatings he was given, and it was a strategy he came to deploy generally in life. He observed people before acting, weighing them up. Were they honest, caring, or thugs like the *'father'* he came to hate?

He found a place where he could watch the house without being seen from it. It was a well. He could crouch down behind it and hide, while spying through gaps in the stonework.

Before long, two people emerged from the house. One was a tall man with a wispy beard, not the portly man Ishraq had seen enter earlier. He might be the merchant, Michel. The other was someone he recognised. Edwina.

It was his opportunity to reveal himself to her, but then the portly merchant appeared and joined the two. The three seemed at ease with one another. It made him question his judgement. Maybe he was mistaken about the portly man. Still he hesitated, trusting his sixth sense, his instinctive ability to judge personality. The man troubled him, and he needed to know more before deciding what to do.

He watched as the three made their way along the path that ran underneath the walls. He followed at a distance, keeping his head down. It proved unnecessary. They did not look back, having no reason to suspect they were being followed.

The three turned a corner and were nearing the port. They stopped and exchanged pleasantries, then Edwina and the taller man made their way to where some ships were loading and unloading cargo, while the portly man continued onwards towards another area of the quayside.

Ishraq followed the portly man. At first, there was no sign of anything untoward. Then the man turned his head, quickly and sharply, looking in the direction he had come from, checking whether he was out of sight of the pair he had just left. Ishraq's suspicions were raised further.

Satisfied he was not seen, the man changed direction, walking away from the water, striding off down a narrow, cobbled street into the central area of the town.

Ishraq knew the town well. He had no need to follow the man. Instead, he took a route down another, parallel street. The layout of the town was a simple grid. Every few yards he was able to spy down a side street and see that the portly man had not changed direction. The man was quite relaxed, still unaware of Ishraq's presence.

More than one pair of eyes studied Ishraq. His behaviour, peeking down the alleyways then stepping behind a wall, was odd. He passed women washing steps and doorways. The women watched him carefully, giving him sideways glances as they worked. Few people used these alleyways, and those who did were generally up to no good.

Ishraq understood why the women were wary. He tried to look as innocent as he could, but it was hard to present as non-threatening with such a tall, muscular frame.

He passed a group of old men sitting round a table, playing a game with dice while sharing memories of bygone days, sea voyages and lost loves. They also gave Ishraq their attention. He pressed quickly on and heard a sigh of relief when he passed by, leaving them to resume their game.

The portly man emerged into a small square with a church at its centre. He crossed the square and made for another street on the opposite side. Ishraq followed as before.

They were now in the north-west of the town, still within the walls. There were fewer people here. Most of the town's activity was in the main harbour to the south.

The portly man passed through a gate, now leaving the enclosed part of the town. Once again, he turned to see whether he had been followed. But Ishraq stayed in the shadows, keeping out of sight.

Ishraq waited for a minute or two before going to the gate. He looked through a gap and saw the back of the man he had been following, striding out now towards the first of two islands.

Ishraq recognised the islands, having passed them many times going in and out of the port. He had never paid them much attention. They were small, barren and deserted, with a causeway to the first. He wondered what drew the portly man to such a place.

Then he saw it, a small rowing boat tied to a rock. A man was waiting by the boat. It was a pre-arranged meeting. The portly man got into the boat and they cast off, heading east along the coast.

Ishraq's mind was filled with suspicion. The location had been chosen for privacy, and the man had taken a lot of trouble to ensure this encounter was kept secret.

There was no more he could do, so he made his way back towards the main port area. He came to a decision. He would make himself known to Edwina, but for now would tell her nothing about what he had just witnessed. Instead, he would maintain a watching brief and only tell her about the portly man if, and when he was sure it was the right thing to do.

Edwina was easy to find. She was still with the tall man, the one Ishraq assumed to be Michel, accompanying him while he went about his business. For a while, Ishraq observed the pair. The man she was with moved between warehouses, boats and offices, making agreements, buying and selling. A trader, a merchant. Michel. Ishraq saw him examining wine casks, tasting the contents. It seemed wine was the main commodity he traded. Edwina stayed outside, just taking in the air.

Ishraq waited for a good opportunity. Then the merchant went inside another warehouse and Edwina stood alone with no-one else near her. He approached and stood idly watching the sea, not looking in her direction, pretending he had not noticed her. He wanted her to believe she had seen him first, and it worked.

Edwina's mouth gaped at the sight of him. She blurted out his name, or rather all the names she had known him by. "Boy, I mean Ven, I mean Ishraq," she said, surprise mixed with excitement in her voice.

He raised his eyebrows as if he was just as surprised to see her. "Lady Edwina," he said, politely and without her level of high emotion. "How nice to see you."

Edwina sighed at the formality of his welcome, then took the initiative and pulled him to her, hugging him tightly. His physique came as a second surprise to her. She discovered how much he had filled out since last she saw him.

"Come," she said, taking his hand and leading him to a bench on the quayside. As they sat, she tripped over her words when too many came all at once.

She took a deep breath and started again. She decided to begin with the here and now then work backwards in time to the last time she saw him. "Why are you here?" she asked him.

He pointed to the ship that was his home. "I am a sailor on the high seas," he declared with a degree of genuine pride. "We trade between here and la Rochelle."

Her brow furrowed. "As I recall, you had plans to go east to Baghdad and find out about your family. It was the most important thing in the world for you. Did you give up on it?"

Before she had finished saying it, she knew it was an insensitive first thing to say. It sounded like a criticism, as if she was disappointed in him. She bit her lip. She did not know his story since they were separated at Rye. There were many possible reasons why he had not gone east. She shook her head, disgusted with herself. "I'm sorry," she said. "Forgive me."

"It seems we have much to talk about," he replied. "But believe me that I am doing well here. My life is good. I suppose the answer to your question is 'yes, I have given up on it'. I have no wish now to search for a family I will probably never find, or a past that perhaps I might wish I had not discovered."

She understood. There was a time when she avoided facing up to some realities in her own life. She was mauled by a dog. That was how she lost her hand and how she got her facial scars. For a long while afterwards, she hid from the world, her confidence shattered. Perhaps Ishraq was doing something similar, she thought, taking the less risky option, just as she had done. And how could she say whether he was right or wrong to do so?

"You're not doing so well as to afford shoes, it seems," she said, noticing he was barefoot. This time it was meant as a joke, and he took it as such. It broke the ice between them, and they laughed together.

He decided not to explain that he had a very nice pair of shoes only the night before.

With the mood now more relaxed, they could start going back in time. "How did you escape the raiders at Rye?" he asked.

"With luck and God's grace," she replied.

Michel emerged from the warehouse. Edwina pointed to him. "Ishraq, this is my friend Michel. Michel, this is Ishraq. Isn't it amazing he is here?" She had told Michel a lot about Ishraq, how they met on the road from Windsor to Hedingham and the horrors they shared in Rye.

"Delighted to finally meet you," said Michel, shaking Ishraq's hand. Ishraq's first impression was of a genuinely friendly man but, as ever, he stayed on his guard. He was still thinking of the portly man, an associate of Michel's. Because of that, he was wary of Michel.

"You will eat with us tonight," said Edwina, leaving no room for Ishraq to decline the offer. He accepted. He hoped it would not be fish.

****

There was a formality at the meal that Ishraq was not used to. The dining room was small compared with the grand hall at Hedingham where Ishraq had once worked, but to have a separate room in the home just to eat in was impressive enough.

The food was good and more varied than the fish diet he was used to. There was pork and several small game birds. Ishraq would normally have picked one up and eaten it from his hands but was not sure that was the done thing, so did his best using the fork Michel provided. After the main meal, there were bowls of grapes and pieces of melon.

He was not comfortable making polite conversation. He just wanted to be back with his shipmates, singing sea songs and quaffing ale in a tavern. Consequently, he was quieter than Edwina ever remembered.

Edwina and Michel understood and did their best to make him feel at ease but could see he would rather be elsewhere. Nevertheless, Edwina wanted to know more about Ishraq's life since last she saw him. "When you disappeared in Rye, I thought you had been killed," she said.

"I was taken prisoner, to work on a cog," he replied. "After the battle, I stole aboard another ship, the one I am on now. It was bigger and I hoped it would take me further away than the cog, to somewhere near the lands of my birth. My plan was to escape and find my family. Like you said, that was my dream then. I didn't know that the ship just goes backwards and forwards along the French coast as far as La Rochelle."

She frowned. She vaguely knew where La Rochelle was. It was south and west of St Malo, no nearer the place in the east he wanted to be. "Could you not have changed ship again?"

He shrugged. "Maybe, but I like the Santa Lucia. The captain is good to me. Besides, my dream is hopeless. I have spoken to sailors about wanting to get to Baghdad, but they laugh and say it is at the other side of the world, so far away I will never get there."

"Baghdad is your home?" asked Michel.

Ishraq took out the precious document that had once driven his quest to find his homeland. He only knew part of what it said. He had never found anyone who could read the whole text.

"It's written in Arabic," said Michel.

Ishraq's eyes lit up. "Can you read it?"

"Yes, I think so." Michel read the document. "It has a title. It is the bill of sale for a child."

Edwina gasped. Ishraq remained passive. It was what he had expected.

Michel continued. "The boy for sale is called Ishraq and he is blessed, the descendant of a Baghdadi Mamaluke."

106

There were signatures. There was the name of the buyer, the same man Ishraq had understood for many years to be his father. It confirmed what Ishraq knew. "There was no name for the seller," said Michel. "But there is the name of the marketplace. The sale took place in Florence."

Edwina felt sick. A bill of sale, but not for wine or wool. It was for a human being. Ishraq was bought and sold like a chattel, a horse or bale of cloth. But she saw that Ishraq was visibly lifted. At last he had a full translation of the document and although it was brief, it offered his first clue to his identity.

"What is a Mamaluke?" he asked.

"A kind of warrior," answered Michel. "For many years they have been the most trusted guards of the sultans in the east. They are not from a single dynasty or family, but rise and fall over generations, chosen for their strength and skill with a sword."

"Powerful men," exclaimed Edwina.

"Yes, but also ruthless," added Michel. "They have to be."

Ishraq recalled how his *'father'* had often called him *'Baghdad'* as a joke nickname. He was now sure of the connection, but also now had another place of interest to ask about. "Where is Florence?" he asked.

Michel thought for a moment how best to explain. "Not as far as Baghdad. But still a thousand miles from here."

Edwina saw the mixture of hope and despair written across Ishraq's face. A thousand miles was a vast distance to him. The new information he had did not help him greatly. She decided to change the subject. "As for me, I am looking for my father."

Ishraq showed interest. So she continued. "I believe he might have been taken by the raiders, just as you were. I'm here to find him, wherever he is."

"If he is still alive," added Michel, then apologised. "You know I worry that you build your hopes too high. I will not lie to you. I think your father is dead and I don't want you to be devastated when you find out."

Ishraq noted real emotion there. Michel cared about Edwina. He was in love with her.

Edwina was annoyed with Michel and about to protest, but before she could, a man entered the dining room.

The entrance drew everyone's attention as the entrant took centre stage, larger than life and full of self-confidence, filling the room. He sat down, announced himself to be ravenous and set about devouring a woodpigeon, not bothering with any of the table manners Ishraq had thought might be necessary here.

Michel introduced him. "This is my business partner," he said. "Jack, you know Edwina. This is Ishraq, her friend from England."

Jack nodded but did not look up from his meal. "Doesn't look English," he said.

Ishraq stared at the man he had followed earlier in the day. Meeting the portly man was not making him feel any easier. The man was rude and a slob, a strange bedfellow for a sophisticated merchant such as Michel. He looked at Edwina. She showed no sign of unease in Jack's company, so perhaps she knew him better and knew him to be trustworthy, a fine fellow.

Nevertheless, Ishraq watched Jack like a hawk, though all he witnessed was the man's ability to eat and drink. When the pigeon was gone, a partridge followed along with slices of the pork and chunks of bread, accompanied by a huge belch.

"What is your business, if I can ask?" said Ishraq politely.

"Import and export," replied Michel. "Anything and everything that is saleable. But mostly wool from England to France and wine the other way."

Jack finally entered the conversation, talking through a mouth full of marzipan sweetmeats. "He doesn't make enough profit, though. He is too generous by half," he said. "He's known as an easy touch."

108

"I believe that all of us fortunate to be without want have a duty to help those less fortunate than ourselves," replied Michel, earning a smile from Edwina.

Jack's lip curled at the edge. "You and I have worked hard and earned what we have, unlike those who would beg, steal and borrow their way through life," he said. "I, for one started off with not a penny to my name, and if charity such as yours had come my way perhaps I would still be in the gutter instead of being the man I have made myself to be."

Edwina sighed, and Ishraq was sure this was a conversation that had happened before. He thought to himself that Jack did not look like someone who had worked hard all his life. And Jack had shown another unpleasant side to his character, dismissing the hardships of those less fortunate than himself. Since he became free, Ishraq had learned more about the world and knew how unfair it could be. He thought most wealthy men had simply been born to the right parents and he felt nothing but disdain for the majority. His first impressions of Michel, however suggested the merchant might be an exception to that rule.

Ishraq decided to change the subject. "Can I do anything to help you find your father?" he asked Edwina. "Tomorrow, I have some jobs to do in the morning, but the rest of the day I'm free. The ship I'm on sails the day after tomorrow."

Edwina thought for a moment. "Michel and I will be talking with the people in the town, traders and some townsfolk, to see if anyone knows anything. Could you enquire of men on the ships? They might talk to you more than they would to us."

"Especially the Spanish," added Michel. "I am half French and can speak the language, but I only know a few words of Spanish, and they are a closed bunch."

Ishraq nodded. "On the Santa Lucia, I have learned to speak a bit of Spanish. What should I say?"

109

"That you are looking for an Englishman, of medium height and aged near fifty. He was an archer with the English army who fought at Rottingdean but he disappeared after the battle. His name is Matty Cutler. Oh, and he knows a lot about medicine."

"I will do what I can, my lady."

"Please, just call me Edwina. You are no longer a servant, no longer a slave. You are a free man and a friend."

He made to leave. "Wait a moment," she said, then went up some stairs. When she returned, she held a pair of fine leather shoes. "Michel has too many," she joked.

Ishraq took them gladly. He tried them on. They were a little tight for him, but he made no complaint. "They're just right," he said.

Jack also took his leave. "I have a house in the north of the town," he explained. "And I need my bed after that excellent meal."

****

The next day Ishraq found it hard to concentrate as he did his chores on the Santa Lucia. He thought about Edwina's quest, but also about what he had discovered. He needed to find out more about his Mamaluke ancestry. Both tasks seemed equally impossible.

He decided to set aside his own needs for the time being. They would have to wait. His immediate duty was to help Edwina. *Lady* Edwina. He could not think of her as she had told him to, simply as a friend. When he first met her, she was a lady-in-waiting to a royal princess. It was hard to think of himself as her equal. She was a refined lady and always would be in his mind. But perhaps he was able to help her. Perhaps his contacts in the world of sailors would produce the piece of information that Edwina needed. He would try his hardest.

His new shoes drew some sarcastic comments from his best friend, a fellow sailor called James.

They had met on the cog that had taken Ishraq the previous year. James too had been taken. They had worked together to help a younger boy escape the cog, and from that their friendship grew.

110

James had a more modest dream than Ishraq. He just wanted to go home to England. He was no nearer to achieving that simple goal than Ishraq was to reaching Baghdad.

While Ishraq had become important on the Santa Lucia, James remained a lowly deckhand, a servant at the beck and call of the senior sailors. The task he most hated was to skim rat droppings off the top of the ship's food stores. He would constantly moan to Ishraq about it. "I hate the buggers," he would say. "They sit and watch me. I swear they are laughing at me." He would take all sorts of weapon down with him in the hope of taking his revenge on one or two, but he was never quick enough.

At one point, the captain advised him that prevention was always better than cure. "Stop them coming on board and your problem will be solved," he said. So James tied various obstacles to the bottom of the rigging to stop the rats climbing the ropes in harbour. Nothing worked. James concluded the vermin enjoyed the challenges he posed them, so he stopped even trying.

The friendship was important to Ishraq. He and James were the only Englishmen on board. When the crew sang in the taverns, it was in French or Spanish. Ishraq had learned some of the refrains, but the highlight for him was always when James sang the one song they both knew.

Although the song was called *Summer is Coming,* it was sung to celebrate the arrival of spring in England. James only knew some of the verses, but when he got to each chorus his voice rose as he sang *Cuckoo, cuckoo, sing well cuckoo. Never stop now. Sing cuckoo, sing well, sing merrily.* And Ishraq always joined with him, to the amusement of the rest of the crew.

"Been stealing down the market?" asked James when he saw the shoes. As he did so, he grimaced and held his hand to his mouth, having bitten into a particularly hard walnut. He threw the nut away. "Where did you get them?" he asked, more seriously. He knew Ishraq would not have stolen the shoes, but they were of good quality.

111

"A lady gave them to me."

James' eyebrows were raised. He assumed Ishraq had made a conquest. "Is she pretty?" he asked, eager for details.

Ishraq shrugged. "I suppose so."

"And rich, obviously."

"She is a lady."

"Ah, the ladies like to feel a sailor's collar, don't they. You lucky swine."

"No. It isn't like that. She is a friend." James smiled knowingly. He was not to be convinced and continued to poke fun at Ishraq to the point of irritation, only stopping when the pain in his tooth became a more pressing concern.

Now it was Ishraq's turn to have some fun. "Shall I get a surgeon for you to yank it out?" he asked.

James shook his head vigorously. "No, no, don't do that. I'll be fine. It doesn't hurt that much."

Finally, with his work done, Ishraq set about the task he had promised to do for Edwina, starting with the crew of the ship he was on, then moving along the quay, boat by boat.

But no-one had any information about a man fitting the description of Edwina's father.

He tried all the favourite sailors' haunts, without any luck.

He was about to give up and was heading back to the Santa Lucia, when a young woman hailed him.

"I work in the tavern you just visited," she said. "I heard you asking the sailors about an Englishman," she said. "And a thought came to me. It was when you said he was someone who knows about healing."

She hesitated. Ishraq wondered whether she was waiting for a reward. He got a coin out, but she waved it away.

"It's probably nothing," she said. "But there are tales of an Englishman in the south. I hear more each day. He is about the same age as the one you seek and is a healer, a miracle worker." Her voice rose excitedly. "He even brings people back from the dead, so they say. He is a monk. They call him the Benedictine. They say he is going to Avignon. To see the pope, I'll bet."

Ishraq frowned. "He sounds like a pagan shaman," he said. "Or a trickster. The man I seek is a proper physician and is not a monk. I don't think it's the same man my friend seeks. Thank you anyway, for your trouble."

The woman looked disappointed. "I hope you find him," she said. There was an inviting sparkle in the blue of her eyes and Ishraq was tempted, but he had work to do. So he thanked her and moved on.

He had now exhausted all avenues and sought out Edwina. He found her in the old cathedral, praying for guidance. He asked whether she had made any progress in her quest.

"No," she replied. "Have you?"

"No," he said. "None." He thought to mention what the young woman had told him but decided against it. There was no point. The monk could not be Edwina's father.

She nodded. It was what she had expected. "What will you do now?" he asked.

"I have one more thing to do before I go back to England," she said.

"You will find your father, I know it."

"And you will get to Baghdad, or at least Florence."

Ishraq left her to her prayers. As he neared the port, he saw the portly man, Jack. This time, Jack was talking with two men, one of whom was the one Ishraq had seen Jack with the day before. Once again, there was an air of secretiveness about them.

They were outside the warehouse Michel had been in when Ishraq and Edwina first spoke. One of the three men glanced in Ishraq's direction, then nudged Jack.

Jack turned and stared at Ishraq for a while. He recognised Ishraq from the previous night and forced a smile.

113

Ishraq waved back casually, then walked away. Evening was drawing in and the sky was heavy. He decided to return to the Santa Lucia, where he found James in his hammock, groaning in pain, his mouth swollen and red.

"You cannot go on like this. You have no choice," Ishraq told him. "You will have to face the surgeon." And James groaned even more.

They found the barber surgeon's house. At first, he refused to treat James because of the lateness of the hour. It took money to change his mind, all Ishraq's earnings from making and mending clothes.

The surgeon bid James to sit on a bench, then produced the tool he planned to use to extract the broken tooth. James had his eyes closed but Ishraq gasped at the sight. James knew better than to open his eyes to see what made Ishraq react that way. He shifted uneasily as he imagined what the surgeon held.

"Le Pelican," said the surgeon, holding the tool up to show Ishraq. It had a mechanism, a claw that opened and shut. The claw resembled the beak of a pelican, hence the name.

Ishraq saw a spot of blood on the pelican and pointed it out. The surgeon wiped it away with a dirty rag, then wrapped the same bloodstained rag round the pelican, pushed James back on the bench and climbed on top of him. He yanked James' mouth open wide and placed the pelican's claw on the painful tooth, with the other part of the extraction mechanism held against James' gums. Then he pressed hard on the handle, trying to lever the tooth out.

The surgeon was twisting and pulling, but the tooth was stubborn. James writhed in agony. "Calme-toi!" shouted the surgeon, with little effect. Ishraq went to help by holding James' legs, keeping him as still as was possible under the circumstances.

The surgeon resumed his work and there was a crunching sound as he finally pulled the tooth away, beaming in satisfaction at his success. "Voila!" he declared.

The surgeon gave Ishraq a balm to soothe James' gums. "He will be in pain for an hour or two, then he will be well," he told Ishraq.

114

Ishraq paid the surgeon and led James away. James was in great pain and moaning, his mouth red with blood. He held the bloody piece of cloth to it trying to stem the flow.

As they neared the ship, Ishraq saw Jack again. The light was now poor, but he was sure it was Jack. "Go to your hammock and rest," he told James. "I will see you later."

He followed as before. Jack went to the warehouse. The other two men Ishraq had seen earlier were waiting there.

Jack produced a key and they went inside. Within minutes the three men emerged with a barrel of wine.

Jack locked the warehouse door. As he did so, one of his companions retrieved a small cart hidden in a side street. They loaded the barrel on the cart, then the three made their way through the narrow streets to the causeway where Ishraq had seen the rowing boat. There was some weak moonlight. A lantern attached to the cart provided some additional light, just enough to make a difference. They could make out the rough track they were following.

Ishraq thought they were clever. They had taken just enough wine for easy carriage but not so much to arouse suspicion. If anyone saw a large quantity of wine being moved at this time of night it would be obvious that smugglers were involved, but a single small barrel could be explained away as just being for personal use.

At this time of night, the streets were deserted and they went unnoticed. It was easy. The men put the barrel into the boat. Then Jack returned to the town, while his accomplices rowed away.

Ishraq had seen enough. He knew what was happening. He returned to the Santa Lucia.

James was sleeping, which Ishraq thought a mercy.

The following morning, Ishraq woke early. He checked on James, who was still asleep. The flow of blood from James' mouth had stopped. Relieved, Ishraq made his way to Michel's house and

115

workplace. Despite the early hour, Michel was already out, but Edwina was there.

"Where is Michel?" asked Ishraq.

"He has a shipment leaving this morning and has gone to make sure all is well with it. Why do you ask?"

Ishraq told her what he had seen the night before. "Jack is stealing from Michel," he concluded.

"But they've been partners for a long time. Michel says he trusts nobody more than Jack."

"Then he is being taken for a fool. You heard what Jack said. He sees Michel as an easy touch."

They waited, and mid-morning Michel returned. Edwina told him what Ishraq had witnessed. Michel listened in disbelief. "He is my friend," he said. "I've known him for years. You must be mistaken."

"I have been thinking," said Edwina. "Would you know if any of your wine was missing?"

Michel shrugged. "Jack takes care of all our business here, while I manage things in England. He does the wine, while I do the wool. It's a good arrangement, easy to manage. I suppose he could take wine for himself, but I've never had reason to question his honesty. We make good profits and his ledgers are always tidy."

"He is being careful," said Ishraq. "Taking just enough that you never notice. But I think it's a regular thing. If I'm right, the amount he takes will add up to a lot over time."

"Michel stroked his beard. "I need to be sure," he said. "Come with me," he added to Ishraq.

Michel was well connected, but also, as a wealthy merchant, well protected. He had hired muscle to call upon. He found them where he had left them earlier that morning, keeping watch on some of Michel's cargo as it was loaded on to a cog bound for England. He beckoned them to him. There were two men, an Englishman with a full beard

116

and a Frenchman with tattoos on his neck. They both stood a head taller than Ishraq, and were heavily armed.

"I have a job for you," Michel said to the Englishman. "Your wages will be doubled tonight."

The Englishman grinned. He knew what it meant. The chance for some fun.

Michel explained what he had in mind. They agreed a time, just after dusk.

"Will two be enough?" asked Edwina.

"Ishraq says there were three men including Jack. Even if the other two are fighting men, I would back my two men against any. They are veterans. As for Jack, he will be mine."

****

That afternoon, Michel's men completed the first task he had given them. They took a small boat and rowed to the islands. They were looking for any sign of a larger boat moored there, a vessel that Jack's men could be taking the wine to. There was none.

They continued eastwards along the coast. And then they saw it. A single-sailed cog, small enough to lie unnoticed in a cove but with the capacity to carry a decent cargo of wine.

They returned to St Malo and reported their find.

As dusk approached, Ishraq was in place for the next part of Michel's plan. He hid as he had the night before to watch Jack and his accomplices at the warehouse.

Sure enough, the three arrived and repeated their performance of the night before. It seemed it was a nightly routine.

Ishraq signalled to Michel, who was waiting in a nearby side street, positioned to be ahead of Jack and in the direction of the causeway. Michel acknowledged the signal and made his way towards a second vantage point, then hid again, this time simply using the shadows as his cover.

When the three men reached the rowing boat all seemed well. They loaded it with a barrel and as before two got in while Jack started to walk back through the town.

Jack's men in the boat were experienced smugglers, both in their thirties. The May night was warm and they wore thin shirts and breeches. They both had short swords, expecting no trouble.

They were relaxed, doing something they had done many times before without challenge. When they saw a light approach from the sea, they watched it out of interest rather than concern.

The light grew larger, until they were certain it was heading straight for them. They looked at one another and began to feel the first pangs of panic. "Customs men," said one to the other. They put their hands on their sword hilts but left the swords sheathed. They were likely to face questions only, but some customs men could be violent. It was wise to be prepared either way.

But still they were confident. They had a story prepared and it felt quite nice to finally get to use it. They would say they planned a surprise party on the island for a relative's wedding and were hiding the wine as part of the surprise. If that did not work, bribes would be paid.

But they had never seen customs officials quite like the two men who loomed large and came alongside them.

Jack's men were no strangers to a fight, but Michel's men were in a different league, professionals, standing bigger, clad in mail and carrying long swords.

It was the swagger of Michel's men that was their most powerful weapon. They had the air of confidence that came from knowing they were good at what they did for a living and enjoyed doing it. It added to their sense of menace.

Jack's men were terrified, and wise enough to want to avoid a fight. They tried to talk their way through the situation, nervously offering their made-up story, hoping to sound convincing about the fake wedding.

The conversation was in French, so the tattooed Frenchman took the lead as interrogator. At first, he was full of bonhomie. "Un mariage? Merveilleux!" he said jovially, patting one of the smugglers on the back just a little more forcefully than was necessary.

He then took the lid off the barrel and dipped a small cup into it, took a swig of the wine, nodded his approval, then wiped his mouth and smacked his lips.

Jack's men relaxed a little. It was obvious they were going to lose their evening's haul. The bigger men would undoubtedly steal it from them. But it was only one night's work, and if it meant they could get away unharmed, that was the main thing. The barrel of wine would be written off, a small loss. They smiled and gave a submissive gesture. "You like the wine?" one said. "Take it, with our compliments. We can get more."

The tattooed man smiled. "You can indeed," he replied. It seemed he was going to accept the wine as a payoff. He gestured for Jack's men to transfer the barrel from one boat to the other, which they did.

When they had finished making the transfer, the smugglers turned and saw that the situation had changed. The Englishman held an axe. He suddenly brought it down hard on the bottom of their boat. The timbers shattered, and he joyfully repeated the action until the boat had no bottom left, only splinters where the planks had been.

The tattooed Frenchman stepped forward and threw a punch at one of Jack's men, then the Englishman kicked hard into the ribs of the other. There was little resistance. The smugglers still thought these brutes who were spoiling their night were probably corrupt customs men taking their wine while meting out their own form of rough justice. For the smugglers, that was preferable to being hauled before the authorities. So they were passive and accepting as more blows followed, until they lay, doubled in pain on the shore by the causeway.

Michel's men rowed eastwards, rounded a point and made for the cog they had seen in the afternoon. There was a single light, there to guide the smugglers to the rope ladder at the boat's stern that was their way on board.

There was no reason for the lone watchman to suspect danger. He was awaiting a rowing boat, lit by a single lantern and with two men in it, and that was what he saw approaching. The routine nature of the arrangement, repeated so often, created in him a state of careless boredom, and he had his back to the ladder when the Englishman appeared on deck.

The watchman was despatched efficiently, silently, the Englishman's hand covering the man's mouth as a dagger pierced flesh and bone.

The tattooed Frenchman climbed the ladder. Together, the two men did a reconnaissance of the deck. Three smugglers slept there.

The Englishman checked the hold. It was full of barrels of wine. At a rate of one barrel each night, the smuggling must have been going on for several weeks.

There were no other men there. The boat had only a skeleton crew. Most probably, the cog was used as a transit boat, taking the wine out to a larger one offshore for the Channel crossing.

Michel's men had come with no plan, intending to improvise depending on what they found. But they had one instruction from Michel. The boat must be wrecked. Saving the wine was not as important to him as ending the smugglers' ability to carry on their enterprise, here or elsewhere.

They saw a barrel of pitch, and an idea formed. They rolled it quietly so that it was near where the sleeping men lay. Then they dropped the lantern into the barrel.

At first, the pitch just smoked, but within minutes it was ablaze and spewing out noxious fumes. The smugglers started to wake up, sleepily becoming aware there was a fire then realising they were trapped between the inferno and the boat's bow. There was no way for them to reach the rope ladder. The only option available was diving headlong into the sea. Two did so, but the third, a non-swimmer, chose to run the flames. It was a fatal choice. His screams of agony caused even the hardened Englishman and tattooed Frenchman to grimace and turn away.

Michel's men had time to take a barrel each from the hold, then make their way to the stern and the rope ladder. They rowed back towards St Malo, leaving the two surviving smugglers to their fate. They did not care whether the men lived or drowned.

Once they had enough distance from the boat, they stopped and watched the flames rise as the wooden vessel burned brightly, the reds and oranges providing a beautiful spectacle against the blackness of the night sky for anyone who did not know the horrors they contained.

Meanwhile, Michel had followed Jack to his house, which was not far from the causeway. He waited until Jack reached the door, then made his presence known. He stepped out from the shadows and leaned against a post; arms crossed. "Nice night for a boat trip," he said.

Jack was surprised and puzzled. He did not immediately connect Michel's words with his own activities. He was not yet aware he had been found out. He looked up at the night sky. "Warm enough, and a bit of starlight," he replied. Then he saw the glow in the direction of the islands.

"Indeed it is, especially with a glass of wine in hand. Or maybe a barrelful."

Now Jack understood. "Ah," he said. "Is my game done?"

"That it is."

"So?"

"Well, by now your boat will be a wreck and your stolen cargo gone. I expect you are not the mastermind for the scheme. You will have to answer for the loss."

"To the authorities?"

"That is a point on which you can have some choice. I can turn you in and you will hang, or…"

"Or what?"

"Or you cede your half of the business to me, at the very generous price of a groat. By chance, I have the document here, prepared for you. All you need to do is sign and seal it. I even brought the wax."

"You would ruin me."

"I would. And enjoy doing it. But, as I say, you could choose the alternative."

It was no real choice. Jack would undoubtedly hang if he was handed in. If he signed Michel's document he would live, albeit in poverty, and still with the risk of punishment from the chief smuggler. He might even die at the smuggler's hands. But that fate was not certain, while the alternative would certainly lead to the hangman's noose. And he was already thinking how to avoid it. He would flee.

He took the document and signed it, then pressed his ring into the wax and added his seal. Without another word, he went inside his house.

As Michel began to walk away, he heard a scream of despair from within. And frowned. He had liked Jack, larger-than-life and good company. But in the world of commerce, trust was everything, and Jack had betrayed him.

When he got home, Michel found Ishraq, Edwina and the two men who had torched the cog. They opened one of the barrels that had been retrieved and talked and drank through the night. There was no atmosphere of triumph. Michel forbade it. Instead, there was reflection on a job well done and on the stupidity of Jack, who had now lost everything he had worked for. And for what? A relatively small, though regular extra income. The man had been wealthy beyond the dreams of many men, but greed had been his downfall.

It was almost dawn when Ishraq left. "Don't give up on your dream," Edwina said to him.

"Go to Marseille," said Michel. "It is the best place to find passage east on the southern sea."

"I might do that," replied Ishraq. "But maybe Florence is now my goal. What of you, Lady Edwina?"

Edwina sighed. "You still call me lady." She thought for a moment. "I have done all I can here. But, as I told you, I have one more thing to do before I return to England."

He said an awkward goodbye. "I wish you luck, and safe journey."

She hugged him as she would a brother.

Ishraq returned to the Santa Lucia. Preparations were already under way to set sail, and his late arrival earned scolding looks from his overworked shipmates. So he immediately set to his jobs, and it was not until the carrack had sailed that he was able to check how James was.

He found his friend awake, but immobile. There was a stink of excrement, so he cleaned James and the area around James' hammock. As he did so, he could see how weak his friend had become. James had lost weight so quickly because he was neither eating nor drinking but was haemorrhaging fluids from his bowels. Ishraq tried to give his friend water, but James was disinterested, as if he had given up.

There was no specialist surgeon on the ship. Instead, the captain dictated how sick or injured men should be treated, and by whom. In this case, Ishraq volunteered to nurse James and the captain agreed.

Ishraq did what he could, trying to make James comfortable, clean, fed and watered. In truth, it was little more than a concerned, watching brief.

By evening, James had passed away. His dying act was to whisper in Ishraq's ear. "Sing merrily, cuckoo."

When James passed, Ishraq said a prayer. He had been raised in the Christian religion and as a child he was taught the words of a prayer to be used for the dead and dying. It was the 23rd psalm. When he finished, he cried.

Later that day, James was buried at sea. The captain made no ceremony of the burial. It was done with no emotion.

Ishraq stared in the direction of England. He wondered whether James' family, wherever they were, still hoped that one day they would see their son again. And he wondered whether his path would again cross that of Lady Edwina.

Chapter Fifteen

Avignon, June 1378

It was not long before the new pope's representative made an approach to the man whose fame was spreading ever wider in southern France.

Matty was washing his undergarments in the Rhone. His monk's habit had gathered dust and grime on the hot roads from La Rochelle. The old monk it had belonged to had not taken great care over its cleanliness, and Matty was struggling to get it clean. He had washed it several times but still it was grubby. So he wanted at least to have clean clothes underneath.

A woman appeared at his side, gently eased him to one side and took over, using a homemade soap to scrub the linen garments.

It was a feature of his life now that everyone seemed to want to do things for him. Part of him appreciated it, but there were times when he just wanted to be left alone, to succeed or fail like everyone else.

A voice came from behind him, addressing the woman. "You need not do that. I will arrange for his clothing to be properly cleaned at the palace."

Matty turned and there stood a tall, angular man with silver-grey hair in a tonsure. That marked him as a cleric, but his clothes said more. He wore a short, hooded cloak, a Manteletta covering his shoulders, the clothing of a bishop. He was with Frere Jean.

"On second thoughts, perhaps new clothing would be more appropriate" added the bishop as he watched the woman struggling to make a difference even with her soap.

Matty shrugged. "I have worn these for a while now and feel quite attached to them. They have become part of me, I think."

"They look as though they have a life of their own." The bishop made a face in disgust. "But as you wish. Now, let me introduce myself. My name is Angelo. I am the Bishop of Florence." Matty wondered whether he should drop to his knees or bow but did neither. The bishop did not seem to care. "So, you are Brother Stephen, the English black monk who seems to inspire devotion from so many."

"It was not my intention to do so," replied Matty.

"Which is even more impressive, I think. There are many who contrive to achieve notoriety. Most fail miserably."

"I don't understand why anyone would want such a thing. And surely the church is against idolatry."

"Indeed. The second commandment. But there have always been prophets and their followers. If your followers find inspiration from you that is acceptable to the church. Only when they start to revere you as a god is there a sin committed."

"Either way, it is not right."

"Perhaps you need to share your views with the man who is, above all others the spokesman for our Lord on earth, the man chosen by his peers to be the rightful head of our church. Pope Urban asked me to come here and find out more about you. Ideally, he wishes to meet you in person."

Matty was taken aback. "For what purpose?"

The bishop shrugged. "He simply wants to know about you. He has heard of your healing and sent me to invite you to Rome. Frere Jean has been most helpful in telling me of your story."

Matty was growing angry. He scoffed. "No doubt you have heard how I saved a man's sight then cured another who the day before was dead. I'm told there's a story going round that my eyes contain a million stars. People have vivid imaginations."

"I understand what you say and praise your honesty. Maybe some people have exaggerated what you have done, but our Lord works in mysterious ways, and already I find you interesting, different. Many men would cut off a hand to have your abilities and, I think, wisdom."

Matty felt a shiver down his spine. The bishop's words had triggered another memory.

It was not like the previous ones. He had no vision of a place, an incident or people he had known. It was just hearing the words the bishop said. *Cut off a hand.* Somehow, the words had meaning for him.

He stared into space, trying to recapture whatever memory was there waiting to be found. The bishop turned to Frere Jean. "Is he seeing a vision?" he asked excitedly.

"In a way," answered the priest. "I told you he cannot recall parts of his life, but he sees things from his past that are sometimes not clear at first. He strives to interpret them."

"Visions, eh? Intriguing."

Matty had come out from previous episodes of recall very quickly. This time was different. He stayed transfixed, oblivious to those around him. Something told him this memory was his most important yet. He wanted it to continue. And more came.

He saw his parents and his dead brothers. They were smiling. Why were they smiling?

His mother stepped forward and hugged him, then stepped aside. Behind her was a group of new people. Immediately, he knew who they were.

There was a woman holding a baby. The woman was Alice, and the baby her child. His child. His daughter, Edwina. Another woman stood beside them. Charlotte. His wife. Beside her stood their three children. Gylda, Maude and Edward.

Matty's mother spoke. She was still smiling. "You lost us, but look at what you still have," she said. "So much love."

Then the memory jumped forward in time. The baby was now a little girl. She was crying out as a vicious hound mauled her. And he knew why he had shivered at the bishop's words. He felt Edwina's pain as the surgeon removed her bloodied hand from her arm.

The memory stopped as suddenly as it had come to him, his mind shutting it down as it became too painful.

He was breathing heavily. "I have a family," he announced to no-one.

"You look tired," said Frere Jean. "Come. You should rest."

The bishop's eyes widened. "You *have* had a vision, Benedictine," he declared, almost to himself, his voice full of hope and expectation. "Frere Jean says you see the past, but what if you can also see the future? I can see why the Archbishop of Cambrai is so interested in you, and Pope Urban will also be. The people are right. You truly have a gift."

So, there it was. The reason the pope in Rome wanted to know about Matty. It was because of the archbishop's interest in him. He felt like a pawn in a game. Then his attention was suddenly drawn to a man of middle age standing nearby, trying to look innocent but failing to achieve it. "It seems we are being watched," he said.

The bishop laughed. "Of course we are. I represent Rome, so I am the enemy here. My every move is noted and reported."

"So they watch you, not me."

"Of course. I am an important man. Ignore it. There is no danger, so long as we are careful not to offend the people of Avignon."

Another sight now caught Matty's eye. There were some dogs scavenging amongst rubbish that had been thrown into the river and had washed up on the banks. Nearby, a child played in the mud. His memories of his daughter being mauled were still fresh in his mind and he ran to chase the dogs away from the child.

The bishop walked to his side, his interest growing by the minute.

"How can I know what I remember is real?" said Matty. "I think it is, but how can I be sure? I feel like a child, born that day when I awoke in a French bed only months ago, then reborn today. Sometimes I think I have never existed at all. Yet I believe I have a family somewhere, wondering where I am, thinking I have abandoned them. And that is the hardest thing."

"You have many questions about yourself," said the bishop. "I know only one man who can answer them for you. Come with me to Rome and speak with him."

"I have already met one man of importance and he lied to the people about me."

The bishop nodded. "He is false. I represent the one who is true."

Matty looked round for the man who had been watching them. He was no longer there, gone no doubt to report to Archbishop Robert.

He wanted to vomit.

Chapter Sixteen

The Papal Palace, Avignon, June 1378

The bishop had been allocated rooms in the papal palace. He was the representative of the new, official pope and as such was given a grand suite, though not the papal chamber itself. The Archbishop of Cambrai was notably absent, avoiding the indignity of having to welcome Pope Urban's representative when he believed he, not Urban, should be the new pope. It would have meant having to make polite, respectful conversation through gritted teeth.

The bishop insisted that Matty spend the night in the palace, and Matty was allocated a grand room, befitting the level of importance he had attained.

There were many bedrooms in the palace. Matty's room had a high ceiling and was decorated with scenes depicting Moses leading his people out of Egypt. A tall glass window caught the moonlight and for an instant the light illuminated Moses' eyes, as though sending a message to Matty that he was being watched.

There were heavy curtains that Matty considered closing, but he left them open. Most places where he had slept were dark at night and his best nights' sleep had always been when he slept out in the open air. This was the next best thing.

At first, he lay awake, watching shadows on the whitewashed walls. He thought about the memories that had come to him of a quite different place, the one in which a single room served as living space, kitchen and bedroom for a whole family. His family's home. But where was it? He still did not know.

He settled down and slept well, the best he had known since La Rochelle. He was woken by a servant bringing him a magnificent breakfast of bread, two fish courses and some fresh eggs. There was high quality wine to wash it down. *Wine for breakfast*, he thought to himself. Frere Jean had told him that the Avignon popes were known to be connoisseurs of fine wines. They had even planted their own vineyards all along the Rhone, creating new communities around humble villages such as Chateauneuf-du-papes, a place that was now famous for its red wines.

It was a breakfast fit for a king.

After breakfast he wandered the buildings of the palace. The previous day he was exhausted and hardly noticed the scale of the place. Even when he met the archbishop, he saw only one or two rooms, but now he was able to explore.

There were people busy everywhere. The palace was more than just a huge church. It was the centre of a vast undertaking, administering the business of the Christian church across Europe. The tax collection task alone involved an army of administrators.

He passed offices with clerks and scribes hard at work. There were dozens of cleaners and attendants in the corridors. And clerics of all levels of importance were there. In total there must have been hundreds, if not thousands of people inside the palace and its grounds.

He went outside and walked round the perimeter, then into the commercial area of the city. It gave him a greater insight into the wealth there, so much of which was generated by the presence of the holy city. Although its geographical location made it a centre for trade, Avignon owed much to the presence of the popes, but for how much longer?

He walked round a market, still thriving despite the slow exodus he had seen previously. A host of traders were selling wood carvings, alabaster statues, jewellery, clothing. There was a thriving industry for souvenirs to pilgrims; surely one area of trade that would suffer greatly from the move to Rome. In the meantime, Louis and Francesca had chosen a lucrative business for themselves.

He stopped to look at a stall selling small brass figurines. He picked one up, admiring the detail and intricacy of the workmanship. It was shaped as a woman with hair twisted and knotted. The trader saw his interest and spoke to him. "Africain. You like?"

Matty nodded, then turned out his pockets to show he had no money. The trader understood and indicated some bead necklaces he was also selling. "Maybe these?" he offered. This time, Matty pointed to his chain of shells. "All I need," he replied.

Moving on, he saw there was activity down a side street and went to explore. The street housed banks and moneylenders, as well as strategically placed pawn shops doing brisk business. It was not only the poorest who took their valuables there. He saw several noblemen doing the same. It was not unusual to pawn items as a means to finance an investment or wager.

He watched for a while as a series of farmers' carts delivered high quality produce to the palace gates and wondered what would become of those farmers in the future.

His tour gave him a better understanding of the scale of impact the return to Rome would have on Avignon.

He looked amongst the sea of faces. There was the usual good humour that was a feature of all markets, the traders working hard to entertain their prospective customers, hoping that would earn them favour and a sale. But there was also noticeable unrest. Tempers flared for the slightest of reasons. People were worried. Their livelihoods were at risk. Families that had lived comfortably would know hardship. Not everyone would suffer, because Avignon's position on the Rhone would continue to be a point in its favour, but the city would be significantly diminished from its current level of importance, no longer the centre of the Christian world, no longer the place kings and queens visited.

He wondered what would happen to the moneylenders, most of whom were Jews. He remembered that a downturn in economic fortunes often ended with the moneylenders taking the blame.

There was a great deal at stake.

He wanted some peace and quiet and drifted further from the palace. He knew he was being followed, something he now took for granted. It had been happening for days. This time it was a younger man than before, a man of about twenty years. And whereas the previous watcher had been unarmed this one wore a sword. Matty had none.

He decided to test how far his stalker would go. He started walking and crossed the river into the countryside south of Villeneuve.

After a while, the young man raced to catch him up and stood in the road, barring his progress. "Where are you going?" the man asked in heavily accented, but good English.

"What business is it of yours?"

"You cannot leave the town."

Matty held the man's gaze and stayed stock still, while the young man twitched nervously, uncertain and unsure of himself. That in turn made Matty nervous. Such men were unpredictable. Nevertheless, he was determined to stand his ground. "Is that a threat?" he asked, keeping his voice level, not wanting to escalate the situation.

"I have orders and will carry them out. You must return." The man's manner was aggressive, but not confident. It was clear this was an unfamiliar role he was playing. "Please," he said, tilting his head and almost pleading now.

"Very well," replied Matty. "But first I wish to know whose orders you are under."

The young man hesitated, trying to decide whether to give out the information. Matty started to walk on and the young man moved again to bar his passage. "I said…"

"What is your name?" asked Matty.

"Domenico."

"Well, Domenico, I know what you said, but you have not answered my question so I will continue on my walk."

"If you do, you will be killed. Look over my shoulder. Try not to be obvious."

Matty did what he was bid. "Now tell me what you see," said Domenico.

"Two men, trying to look casual, just going about their business."

"But you see they are not what they seem."

133

Matty shrugged. "They are hired thugs. I have seen the type, many times before They are with you?"

"No. I am here to protect you from them." Matty had to resist the inclination to laugh out loud. The young man was clearly no bodyguard.

"So tell me who sent you. I will not turn back until I know," said Matty. Still there was hesitation. "It is up to you," he added. "Tell me or draw that sword, because that is the choice you have."

Matty was taking a risk but thought it a small one. Domenico did not have the same look as the two other men. He lacked the sense of menace. He was a messenger. It meant his master wanted Matty unharmed, or he would have sent someone more capable of doing it.

Suddenly there was movement from the two other men. They started to run towards Matty and Domenico.

Domenico turned, realising what was happening. He drew his sword and faced the two men. Matty cursed himself for being unarmed and he lacked faith in Domenico to protect him. He had made a mistake walking away from the town. Out here, away from the heart of the city he was vulnerable. "We must go," he said.

Domenico nervously watched the two men getting nearer. "Follow me," he said.

Matty had no knowledge of the area. He had no option but to trust Domenico.

They ran a short distance to where a huge man stood holding three horses. This man was unlike Domenico. Many men wore swords for effect. Domenico was one. But this one also wore a brigandine, a coat made of leather with rivets for added strength and straps for adjustment. Armour. He also wore a hard look, a look of hatred, perhaps hatred towards Matty but more likely towards the world in general.

The second man started to draw his sword, then saw that Matty was unarmed and left it sheathed. He gestured for Matty to mount one of the horses, a grey mare.

There was no point protesting. If Matty had been armed, that would be different. He obeyed, sure now that this was no act of rescue. He looked at Domenico, who wore a slightly apologetic look and stayed quiet.

The three men rode for more than an hour, hugging the river north from Villeneuve, passing miles of vineyard from which the wine Matty had with his breakfast had most probably come. Every few minutes they stopped and the armoured man checked to see if they were being pursued. Each time they did, Matty looked for opportunities to kick his horse into a gallop and try to escape, but he judged it would be suicidal. His horse had been chosen well. It would never outrun the armoured man's stallion.

Matty tried to engage the man in conversation, hoping for information, clues, any sign of a weakness. But the man refused to respond and simply employed a stare that cut through him like a knife. This was not someone to be underestimated. He was clearly an experienced guard or soldier. After a couple of attempts, Matty gave up the idea.

They turned into a valley, a tributary of the Rhone. Trees and dense vegetation replaced the manicured vineyards, lining the valley sides. To all intents and purposes, it was an area of wilderness.

A rusty gate came into view, evidence of perhaps a run-down shack or farmhouse. In such a remote place, that was what Matty expected to see. As they passed through the gate, more overgrown bushes seemed to confirm that first impression.

But then a house appeared. Not a farmhouse, but a grand house set in grounds. The stonework was not elaborate but chunky, solid, and was expertly dressed. There were glazed windows. The building seemed out of place here, too elaborate. And it was very well hidden.

The horses were taken into small stables while Matty was led into the house and then to an enclosed courtyard. The day was warm but the courtyard was sheltered and cool. A fountain stood in the centre, spraying refreshing water into the air.

A man lounged beside the fountain. He stood up at Matty's approach. He was a big man, both in height and girth, with a mass of thick black hair on his head and chin and a sharp, pointed nose. He wore a ring in his ear. But the most striking feature was a deep scar running from his left ear to his eye, or where his eye and ear had once been. All that was in his eye socket was the eyelid pulled over and stitched permanently in place, while the ear had been severed. It looked like a single sword swipe had done the damage. "Welcome to my humble home, monsieur," he said. There was only a trace of accent, and not a French accent, more guttural.

Matty was looking round, trying to avoid staring at the man's disfigurement. In the yard were statues, an olive tree and a palm, plus some bowls filled with herbs. Dogs lounged in the shade.

"I see you admire my home," said the man. "Beautiful, is it not? She was once a Roman villa. I found her purely by chance, a neglected ruin in a sorry state. I brought her back to life and gave her a new name. The Villa Libera. It's the name of an ancient Roman goddess, the goddess of wine. Also the goddess of fertility." He laughed. "Both of which are fitting for the house of Erich, I think! But my story can wait. Please sit and let me refresh you after your long ride in this heat."

Two drinks were brought for Matty, a fruit drink of some kind and a cup of wine, with a bunch of grapes, bread and olives to accompany them.

The heat had indeed been fierce, so he drank his fill.

"You will be wondering who I am and why you are here."

"I assume you are hired by the Archbishop of Cambrai, or maybe the Bishop of Florence," replied Matty.

The man laughed again, this time raucously. "Ha! A good guess. But sadly, you are wrong. I will explain in good time, but first I will show you my humble abode."

Matty was given a tour of the house and its outbuildings. Domenico stayed in the courtyard but the second man Matty had arrived with followed everywhere they went, his eyes always on Matty.

The general layout was square around the courtyard. There were three bedrooms, a kitchen and dining/living room (the former triclinium of the Roman villa). Each room was extravagantly furnished but without any thought to how one thing related to another. Random pieces were simply placed wherever the owner decided.

As they toured the buildings Matty noticed servants. They were without exception young, female and with dark skin. He thought of Erich's joke about his own fertility. No doubt the servants were chosen with that in mind.

The triclinium was most elaborate, with a huge oak table in the centre, a fireplace made of marble, a beautiful Persian rug and another life-sized statue, this one a genuine Roman relic. "The goddess Venus," declared the host proudly. "Is she not beautiful? See the detail in her hair and her cloak."

On the table was fine silverware and a pair of carved wooden candlesticks. But the most striking things were dotted around the room. They were stuffed birds, some placed on shelves and others standing like statues. Matty had a vague memory of having seen such things before, but never in such numbers.

The host was eager to talk about his collection. "See this one, a kite, and here a beautiful owl." But his pride and joy was a huge golden eagle. He caressed the lifeless plumage lovingly as he would a child. "What do you think?" he asked Matty.

Matty could see residual beauty from when the creatures lived, but the overall effect was disturbing, claustrophobic, a vision of death, made worse by the almost maniacal way the one-eyed host stroked each piece in turn. He felt as though he was in a bizarre nightmare and had to fight to stay calm. "Fascinating," he answered truthfully.

Erich beamed. "Glad you like them," he said, misunderstanding Matty's response. He patted Matty firmly on the back.

Finally, Matty was shown the rooms that had once formed the Roman bathhouse. The area was now a huge basement, almost as big as the rest of the house, in places extending beyond the house footprint.

"The villa had two storeys," explained Erich. "Many people lived here, the family with their slaves. When I found it, the upstairs was in poor condition so I consolidated the buildings into one storey." Erich was trying to impress Matty, but Matty's mind was on the people, because he suspected slavery was still present in the villa.

Erich explained how the bathhouse had worked. "Each room had a different purpose," he said. "Bathers started in the hot room and worked their way through to the coldest, then to a dressing room and exercise room. The Romans lived the good life. I envy them. I have plans to renovate it all and use it myself one day. But come now, it's time to eat."

"We've only just eaten," quipped Matty.

Again there was Erich's laugh. "In Erich's home, it is always time to eat, drink and enjoy the company of friends."

"Am I your friend?"

"Erich the Dane is friends with everybody." Another laugh and pat on the back.

"Dane, you say. I thought you were not French, though you sound more English than Danish."

"I will tell you my story while we eat."

They returned to the courtyard. More food had already been laid out in preparation. Clearly, those who attended Erich knew not to keep him waiting for his food and drink.

The man in the armour stood in a corner, silently keeping guard. Domenico was in a chair. One other adult was also there, a woman in

138

her mid-twenties. She was beautiful, tall and elegant with skin as pale as alabaster. Her hair was long, dark and simply braided.

Beside the woman were two children, boys, one of about eight years and the other maybe five. They sat still as Erich went to them in turn. He lifted the woman's chin and gave her a full kiss on the lips, turning to Matty as if to make him envious. If the kiss could speak it would say: *'look at the gorgeous creature Erich the Dane shares his bed with every night'*. Then he patted the heads of the boys. There was pride in his eyes, but the boys' reaction was regimented rather than warm, dutiful rather than loving.

A maid attended to their needs, one of the dark-skinned beauties. She was filling Erich's wine cup before it was drained. Erich gave her a lecherous look and touched her arm a little too intimately. Her hair was like that of the brass figurine in the market. The style had the effect of allowing her face to be fully on show, accentuating how smooth her skin was and how beautiful her face, a face that showed no joy.

But the maid did not wear African clothing, because all the women in Erich's household wore long white robes, like the togas worn in ancient Rome. The boys wore simple white tunics, again in the Roman style. It was clear what effect Erich was trying to cultivate. Matty imagined him lounging on a couch, posed as an emperor while being fed grapes by his female slaves.

Erich settled back into his chair and began to hold court. "Have you heard of Sequin de Badefol?" he asked Matty.

Matty shook his head. "My memory is not good, so I cannot say."

"Ah, of course. I was told you had a problem with that. A strange thing, to lose your memory. It's not a problem I have ever had. I remember every man I have sent to the grave, or at least every important one. You know, the nobles and suchlike. Anyway, I digress. Sequin was my old commander. We fought together at Poitiers. Then there was a break in the war against England and we all needed money, so Sequin led us as mercenaries, soldiers of fortune. We were

139

the scourge of France and then Italy. At one point we held so many castles it was like Sequin was the king of the Saone and Rhone. We laid siege to Avignon and the pope paid Sequin to leave the area." Erich laughed at the memory. "So we went to loot and spend our money elsewhere for a while. But all good things come to an end and, sadly Sequin died."

Erich laughed again, even more raucously than before. "He had survived so many battles, but do you know what killed him? He ate some bad fruit?" More laughter.

When the fit of laughter subsided, he took some more wine from the servant girl and continued. "But he had accumulated great riches, and when death takes away, it also gives. So, Erich the Dane gathered his share of Sequin's wealth. Of course, I had to use a little friendly persuasion here and there to get it." Another laugh. "Then I decided it was time to retire and came back to Avignon, where we had such good times before. I found this place and have stayed ever since."

"Are you in hiding?" asked Matty.

"No need. I am a pillar of the community here. My money sees to that. I am a successful entrepreneur. I own quite a lot of land, including several vineyards and olive groves, an orchard, a mill, some houses, oh and several bishops." That brought another raucous laugh. "I could afford to live in the city and some think I am strange for living out here but I like the privacy it gives me. Security also."

"You don't seem well guarded for such a rich man."

"All round this part of France are castles, built to defend against the English Angevin empire. But that is in the past. There are still local rivalries, but I stay out of them, keeping a low profile and going unnoticed. I also have respect. No-one dares do me harm. And they know that if they did, I have plenty of mercenaries in my pay I can call upon when needed." He laughed yet again. It seemed he thought himself hilariously funny.

"And your accent? You said you would tell me more. Are you Danish?"

"Partly. I was born in England, but my mother is Danish and named me after a Danish king. As a child I spoke both languages. I considered myself English and went to war to serve King Edward in France. The English soldiers gave me my nickname. But I changed sides when I thought the French would win at Poitiers. It seemed the right thing to do. Big mistake." This time there was no laugh, only a sigh. "You can see the wounds I got in the battle. But it was eventually a fortunate mistake. Joining Sequin made me rich beyond my dreams."

"So what does a successful *entrepreneur* want with a simple monk?"

"All in good time. First, I should introduce you to my friends here. Domenico you know. He is my vineyard manager and wine salesman. He was here when I bought the vineyards and I kept him on to work for me. After all, what did I know of growing grapes and making wine?"

"I thought he was no soldier."

"Yes, but the other man you came with is just that. I fought with him under Sequin." He pointed to the fierce, armoured man in the corner. "This is Jaro. He is Germanic. As you will know, he is a man of few words. But he is the most loyal man I have ever met. His only problem is that he looks as dangerous as he is. When I wanted to bring you here, I decided Domenico would be less likely to frighten you away."

"You were right. Were the two men we saw yours as well?"

"Oh, no. They were genuine thugs. Domenico and Jaro probably saved your life." Erich laughed his raucous laugh again. Each time he did, Matty thought him more maniacal.

Erich went to the woman. This time he gently kissed her hand. "And this is the lovely Lella. She is Italian. Her name means *'dark'* but she is the light that shines on me and makes my darkness brighter. She has given me two beautiful sons." He went to the two boys. "This is Jacques and the youngest is Henri. One day they will inherit all the riches I have collected." He returned to his seat, beaming with satisfaction. "We are a collection of oddments from all over Europe.

141

And now we have you, a famous monk and an Englishman to add to the collection."

"You are also English."

Erich shook his head. "No longer. Neither am I Danish, nor French. I am a man of the world, and this is my home now."

"What will you do with me?"

"I wondered when you would ask. Most would have asked as soon as they walked through the door. Which makes me realise you are not the simple monk you described yourself as. But the answer is I am not sure. All I can say is that you will be my guest for a while. You can have the run of the house while Jaro is there to watch you. At night you will sleep in the bathhouse and you will go there when I have visitors. The thick walls make it soundproof. No-one will hear you. As a matter of fact, there are people coming tonight for a meal. So I'm afraid you will be having an early night."

"I can't believe you have taken me prisoner without any plan," said Matty.

Erich spread his arms in a gesture of comradeship. "My friend, you are no prisoner. You are my guest. As for a plan, who needs one? My life is unplanned, yet I thrive. Don't worry, I will think of something. You are important, and I collect important things. They always prove their worth, given time."

Erich paced the room, then spoke again. "When I came here, I was happy to retire from a life of drama. But it can be tedious. So when I heard about you, I was intrigued. I needed to know if you really were a miracle worker, and Domenico told me how you seem to have become important to the politics of the church. I sensed a chance for sport. I don't need more money, though I haven't ruled out making some by selling you to the highest bidder. Who has the most money, do you think, Rome or Avignon?" Again, the Erich laugh. "So, how will my sport play out? I don't know. But tonight is the first move. I have invited a bishop to dine with me. It will be an interesting meal."

Matty opened his mouth to speak. He wanted to know if it was the Bishop of Florence. But Erich held his hand up. "Enough talking now," he said, then barked an order to Jaro. "Take him to the bathhouse."

"To my prison you mean," said Matty

"As you wish. Call it what you will. But that is where you will go."

Chapter Seventeen

Off the coast of Brittany, June 1378

Ishraq lay in his hammock, too weak to care that it was stinking and sodden from his sweat. Beside him was a bucket, full of a yellow-brown liquid. The contents of his stomach, emitted from both ends.

Whatever it was he had eaten, it had bitten back and taken all his energy. Plying a coastal route had its advantages, because the ship could pick up fresh food along the way. So scurvy was never an issue, but rancid meat and overripe fruit was. Ishraq was not the only crew member who was suffering.

In addition, he was grieving. Until James' death he had not realised how much his friend meant to him. Now he knew. He had shed tears each night.

A sailor came to remove the bucket in order to toss the spew and shit overboard. His name was Carlos. He gave Ishraq a look that Ishraq understood. Carlos was generally on good terms with Ishraq and knew the stench was not Ishraq's fault, but nevertheless *somebody* had to be made to feel guilty for causing him such an odious chore, and Ishraq was the obvious candidate.

Ishraq rolled over, trying to ignore the look. And vomited again, this time missing the bucket. That earned him more than just a look. Carlos tipped the bucket over him.

He felt desperate and so physically weak but had to get out from the mess. He swung his leg out of the hammock and urged his body to follow, then grabbed the bucket out of Carlos' hand and summoned his reserves of strength to go on deck with it. There he flung the remaining contents overboard and went to where another bucket was tied to a rope. He threw that one over the side then hauled it up, full of sea water. It was heavy and the effort was draining. He used the water to douse himself, then threw the bucket over again and hauled once more. This time he transferred the water into his own bucket and took it down to sluice his hammock and the floor around it.

The hammock was now even wetter than before, but no matter, he fell into it and almost immediately was asleep.

It was as if he was too tired to fend off a flood of thoughts joining as one and creating a dream. He saw people he knew. The faces were blurred but he sensed who they were.

There was the man he had known as his father, who had bought him in a Florentine slave market. Edwina was also there. And so too was James.

The three people who had been the most important in his life were talking together but not looking in his direction. They were talking about him and not with him.

His father was berating Edwina, waving a finger at her. *"The lad is my property,"* he was saying. *"I have every right to do what I want with him and I will not have you interfere."*

Edwina replied. *"You are an evil man. You should never have taken him from his home. You even took his name from him."*

"Home, you say! Home! He has but one home and that's with me."

James was crying. *"I will never see my home now,"* he said. *"The cuckoo no longer sings."*

Ishraq wanted to comfort James, but discovered he was unable. It was his dream but he was not in it. Yet Edwina suddenly looked in his direction. *"Don't give up on your dream,"* she whispered, her parting words when last he saw her. Then her form melted away and all that was left was a corpse, James' lifeless body.

He woke with a start, sweating profusely. And knew what he had to do.

****

By the time the Santa Lucia reached La Rochelle, Ishraq was feeling better, though not well enough to resume his duties. His days of rest and recovery had given him time to think, time to consider the next chapter in his life.

Edwina's words stayed with him. But it was the death of his close friend that gave him the push he needed to resurrect the dream he had put on hold, the dream of finding his homeland.

When the ship docked once more in port, the captain asked if he was up to his usual task. He said he was.

He found a flower seller quite easily. This one had sold him flowers before and when she saw the Santa Lucia's arrival, she knew she would have a sale. "A good trip?" she asked in broken English. He shrugged and nodded. Why tell her the truth? What would be the point, because she was just asking idly, with no real interest either way? She only wanted his money.

He made his way to the captain's cabin.

The captain took the bunch of flowers but was more interested in something laid out on his desk. Ishraq leaned over to peek. The captain looked sideways at him, because Ishraq had never shown such interest in what he did. He was intrigued. Why now?

"Charts," said the captain. Ishraq kept looking, and the captain realised there must be a reason. "See here is where we are now, in La Rochelle. All down here and along here is the west coast of France."

"What are these?" asked Ishraq, pointing to spots in the sea.

"They are the reason I study the charts. They are rocks and islands we must avoid. The charts help us steer clear of those dangers in the sea. I look at them now and then to remind myself. It is important not to become complacent even after fifty or a hundred trips."

Ishraq nodded slowly. "Is Baghdad on the charts?" he asked.

The captain gave a little laugh but could see how intensely Ishraq scoured the charts. "No," he replied. Then he rolled the charts up and brought out another piece of parchment. He rolled it out. "This is a map," he said. "You will see there are no little spots like in the charts. Instead, you have the whole of the Mediterranean Sea, with all the major ports. See here is Cadiz, and here is Venice, and here Athens, my home city."

146

"And Baghdad?"

"First, tell me why you want to know."

Ishraq decided to tell the truth. "I think I was born there."

The captain frowned, not sure where this was leading, but pointed to an area at the end of the map. "See here is Jerusalem. Baghdad is further east still. The map doesn't go that far."

"So, it's a long way."

"Yes. A very long way. Why, are you thinking of going?"

Ishraq looked troubled. "I don't know."

The captain understood. "You miss James, I think."

"Yes, I do."

"Well, I would hate to lose my flower buyer, but if you ever decide to go, the best way from here is by land to the southern coast then by sea to Jerusalem." He drew the route with his finger across the map. "It will not be easy though."

"Somebody has told me to start at Marseilles."

"Yes." He pointed to Marseilles on the map. "My life has been at sea and I have sailed the Mediterranean many times. It is beautiful. If you never got to Baghdad, you would not regret seeing the southern sea."

Ishraq nodded. "Thank you," he said. "I know now what I must do."

The captain reached into a drawer in his desk and pulled something out. "This will give you luck," he said. It was a small box. Inside was a four leafed clover, dried and carefully preserved. "One of these was taken by Eve from the Garden of Eden," he said. "A souvenir from Paradise."

"Do you not need it yourself?"

The captain pointed to his cat tattoo. "I have plenty to keep me safe. But if you sail the southern sea, you will need this more than I."

Part Four

Coucy

Chapter Eighteen

Amiens, June 1378

There was still much danger in the French countryside. Michel had tried to persuade Edwina not to go. "Just write to her," he suggested. But she felt it was the only way. She had to be certain the request got through and wanted to hear the answer directly.

So Michel went with her. He took one of his men, the Englishman. Michel had decided it would be better to have him along than the tattooed Frenchman, simply because Edwina could converse with him. Not for conversation, but because, in times of danger, good communication was needed.

Michel had told Edwina the Englishman's story. The man was known only by a nickname, one he had since he was a boy. His father, a sheep farmer, was cruel, beating him, his mother and siblings regularly and mercilessly over many years. Then one day, when he was aged eight, an elderly ewe passed away during the night. The boy's father wanted to go gambling and drinking but wanted the fleece of the dead sheep to be removed from its body. He told the boy to do it, then left him.

It was a task the boy had not done before, though he had watched his father do it. He made a poor job of it, ruining the fleece. When the father returned, drunk and angry at having lost money from a card game, he beat the boy for the crime of costing him money.

The father then settled down in a barn to sleep off his ale. The boy found him and stood over him, recoiling at the rank smell that rose from the sleeping man. Years of stored hatred surfaced until the boy could take no more and snapped. Calmly, and without emotion, he grabbed the sheep shearing scissors. They had a sprung handle. He opened them only partially, so creating a twin bladed weapon, which he plunged into the unprotected stomach of his sleeping father.

The boy's mother heard her husband's cries. By the time she found him he was bleeding profusely and dying. The boy was kneeling over him, already cutting the skin from a man not yet dead, shearing him just as he had sheared the ewe. He was laughing at the blood oozing from the wounds. It was a bloody mess.

In that moment the boy was half mad. His mother tore him away but could not save her husband. She asked him why he had done it. "I wanted to see what was under his skin," was the reply. She was angry and gave the boy yet another beating. But she understood and was somewhat relieved to be free from the torture that was her marriage, as well as the pain and worry of watching her children suffer. So she hid the deed from the authorities, claiming her husband's death was an accident, that he had fallen on the shears. She was sure they never believed her, but farming accidents were common. If they did suspect the truth, they chose to ignore it, knowing what the man had been like. There were few mourners at his funeral.

Despite the death being officially accidental, everyone around seemed to know what the boy had done. Months later the people round and about still talked about the boy who had tried to skin his father. And they started using only one name for him. They called him Fleece. And that was what he came to be called ever afterwards.

Michel said that Fleece still had a kind of madness about him, but also possessed gentleness and loyalty and led a life that was simple, with no emotional ties. He had left his family without notice. He just got up one morning, mounted his horse and disappeared. He was thirteen at the time. He took work here and there until seeing a poster advert for hired hands. It was Michel's poster. He had worked for Michel ever since.

Fleece was not to be feared, Michel told Edwina. But woe betide any man he met whose cruelty to those weaker than himself reminded Fleece of his cruel father.

They were halfway to their destination and Michel thought they should rest a day or two. Edwina reluctantly agreed. She would have preferred to push on but had to admit to tiredness.

When they found a place to stay, Michel decided to go and pray at the great cathedral for a safe journey. He asked Edwina to join him, but she declined. "You go, she said. "Pray for us both. I need some time to myself."

Alone in her room, Edwina gave some thought to her relationship with Michel. He had accompanied her on a dangerous journey in the past, and now here he was again her protector and travelling companion, asking nothing of her, loyal and faithful. He had a woman waiting for him in Winchelsea but seemed to have forgotten that fact.

She took out her precious amulet for the first time in a while, closing her eyes and touching it lovingly. She imagined the presence of her mother and her friend Mary and knew they would tell her she was mad not to encourage the relationship to blossom. But there was always another voice holding her back.

She dozed. She could not have slept long. It was still daylight when she woke. She rubbed the sleep from her eyes, then completed a daily routine. She carried a balm with her that soothed the stump where her hand had once been. She rubbed the balm over the hard area of skin.

Inexplicably, she began to sob. It came as a surprise to her. She must be tired. There could be no other explanation.

A knock came at her door and woke her.

She answered the door, opening it just enough to see who was there. It was Michel. He was smiling and holding something out to her. "A gift," he said. "To help you in your quest."

It was a metal badge. In the centre was a face. "John the Baptist," said Michel. "The cathedral sells them as souvenirs. I bought it for you."

"You shouldn't have," said Edwina. But she was glad he had. He was a kind man and truly cared for her. She heard her mother's voice once again inside her head. *'Marry him or die a maid.'* It was not so simple, but why?

Michel bowed lightly then was turning away, but Edwina grabbed his hand and held it. He turned back to face her, then dared to kiss her.

Edwina felt guilty, thinking of his woman, Wenna. She drew back, but Michel saw a rare opportunity and seized the moment. He kissed

151

her again, and this time Edwina lost herself in the sea of emotions she was feeling. Before she knew it, they were lovers.

The next morning they set off again. Edwina was quiet. Michel had hoped that the passion of the night before marked a turning point in their relationship. He hoped she would be in high spirits, full of the joys of life, but she was not. He had seen her like this before, withdrawn into a shell. At the time it made him realise she did not love him. And it was happening again.

She wore the badge he had given her. The figure of John the Baptist stared out at him, proudly fastened to her cloak. The badge mattered to her. *He* mattered to her. But she did not love him.

Michel let Edwina ride ahead with Fleece, allowing him to be alone with his thoughts. He thought about Wenna. If Edwina had not come back into his life, he would surely have married Wenna and settled down, had children, grown old with her. He was wealthy, so their lives together would have been good. Not exciting. Edwina was exciting. There was always adventure with her. It was one of the things that made her so attractive. But Wenna was lovely. He was such a fool.

He sighed. He was bewitched. Not supernaturally. Just the kind of bewitching that some women had the ability to do to some men. He had to snap out of the spell and think again of Wenna, because she was where his future lay.

They stopped to rest. Michel sat apart from Edwina and Fleece while they busied themselves tending the horses. He watched Fleece for a while. As far as he knew, Fleece had no personal ties, carried no personal baggage. How good it must be to live such an uncomplicated life, living day to day without regard for anything but your own immediate needs. Fleece never lacked casual female company, with no strings attached. His own mistake was to want more intimacy, a companion, someone to share his life with. He was beginning to believe it was a costly error.

Edwina came across and sat next to him. "Are you alright?" she asked, her voice unsteady but heavy with genuine concern for him.

"Why wouldn't I be?"

She looked to the ground. "Last night was lovely," she said, almost in a whisper, unsure of the reaction she would get.

"But today you regret it." His tone was sharp, not accusatory but frustrated, angry with himself.

She grimaced. "No. Never. It's just…."

He sighed. "I know. There's no need to say it." His tone was now more even, with a hint of self-pity.

"I'm sorry."

"Time to move on." He looked away, then stood up and went to his horse. No more was said.

As they rode on, Fleece slowed to ride alongside Michel. "You are hurting," he said.

Michel looked sideways at him. Fleece had never spoken to him like that. He had doubted Fleece had enough sensitivity to notice the moods of others, let alone speak words of sympathy.

"We have all been through the same," added Fleece, his voice level, his words caring yet with no emotion in his voice.

"I thought you were a rolling stone, gathering nothing lasting along your way."

"There have been women, as you know. But each time I get close I start to see rivals and think my woman unfaithful. And I remember my name and how I earned it. Then I walk away before I pick up another set of shears, or an axe, or anything else, and end the life of the woman I care for."

Michel nodded, understanding. "You hide your burden well. I would never have guessed it," he said. "As for me, I am ready to go home. The person Edwina wants to see probably won't be there or won't agree to see her. So we're wasting precious weeks of our short time on this earth. I should never have come."

"You are a good man. You would never have left her to make the journey on her own. It's too dangerous."

"But what of my Wenna? Who is looking after her while I am away?"

"Wenna is used to you going off on your business trips to England."

"You are right. But this feels different, a betrayal. Right now I just want to go home to her."

"If you want to go, I will stay with Edwina."

"No. It's right what you said, that I need to see her safely to her destination. Let's finish what we started."

Chapter Nineteen

Coucy-le-Chateau, Picardy, June 1378

It was a beautiful early-summer morning. Edwina, Michel and Fleece approached the fortifications of the town, beyond which was a hill. They could see the castle and its enormous circular keep, the largest anywhere in France, and its equally imposing corner towers.

A company of knights appeared, riding out. They wore shields emblazoned with a common coat of arms, quartered with red and white horizontal stripes and depictions of castle towers. Symbols of strength. The overall effect was of a uniform, giving the appearance of an army.

At the head was a man in full battle armour but no helmet. Edwina stared at him, sensing his importance. His beard was close trimmed and his hair short, while his eyes were sharp. His head was back, with a prominent nose pointing to the sky. He held himself confidently, a man who knew his own status, his own place in the world.

As the knights passed by, two stopped. They were outriders, doing their job, ensuring the strangers posed no danger to the column. Michel spoke with them and they went on their way, re-assured.

Further on, the sheer size of the castle became evident. It was defended by huge outer walls and a moat. At the castle gates they were able to see how thick the walls were, twenty feet or more. This was a place built to withstand attack. The location required it. Coucy was in the heart of Picardy, an area much fought over for centuries.

Michel spoke with one of the castle guards, a huge man dressed in full armour. They spoke in French.

He introduced Edwina by her formal title, the Lady Edwina de Lucan, then explained the purpose of their visit and requested an audience. He added some words of praise for the castle lord for good measure, reaming off the lord's list of titles. The idea was to earn favour and show that this was no idle visit. The list of titles was extensive. Lord of Coucy, Lord of Marle, Lord of La Fere, Lord of Crecy-sur-Serre,

Lord of Oisy, Count of Soissons, Earl of Bedford and grandson of the Archduke of Austria.

It earned him a round of applause from the guards. "No-one has ever managed that before," said one. "But I'm afraid you are unlucky, monsieur. Our lord is not in residence."

"I know. We just passed him. But it is his lady we have come to see," replied Michel in his most assertive tone. "The Countess Isabella. The Lady Edwina is a friend of hers."

The guards looked at one another, unsure. "From England," added Michel, moderating his tone. "She has come a long way."

"Follow me," said the guard who had previously spoken. They started to do so. "Not you," said the guard, pointing to Fleece. "And not you," pointing to Michel. "Only the woman."

Michel made to protest but Edwina held up a hand. "It's all right," she said. "I will be fine."

Another of the guards beckoned the two men. "Jouer aux des?" suggested one.

"He's inviting us to a dice game," said Michel to Fleece. "There's nothing else to do. Shall we?"

"Why not?"

Edwina passed through the gates and saw the chateau in the far corner of the fortified area. It had three circular towers, the centre tower being the biggest. That was where she was taken.

****

Isabella, Countess of Bedford, was approaching her forty-sixth birthday. Edwina thought it showed. Isabella did not look how she did last time Edwina saw her. The beauty had faded and she did not look to be in the best of health.

It had been a year since the royal wedding. The countess, who had for years resisted marriages arranged by her father, had inexplicably married off her young daughter Phillipa.

After the wedding, Phillipa would go to live in the home of her new husband, at Hedingham in Essex. And the countess felt anxious, guilty about sending her daughter away. Because Phillipa was aged eight years. Isabella wanted someone to be close by, watching out for her, and charged Edwina with the task.

Edwina went, as instructed to Hedingham as Phillipa's lady's maid. Her role was to be as a surrogate elder sister, and the countess slept a little better at night knowing she was there. But things did not go as planned.

"You let me down," said Isabella. "You left your post and failed in your duty, leaving my precious child alone in a strange place, at the mercy of a man she hardly knew."

Edwina protested. "It was you that made her marry so young. You cannot blame me for that. And anyway, I was forcibly taken from her. I was held prisoner. It was not my fault. You forget that I suffered greatly. If you wanted a proper guard for her, you should have chosen a soldier."

Isabella wanted to smile. She admired Edwina's pluck in standing up to her. She hid it, staying in role as the stern mother who had been let down. "You *suffered!* You **suffered**!" she shouted, her eyes widening to cut through Edwina like a knife. "Wait until you have a daughter of your own. Wait until you, too must let her go. Then will you know real suffering."

"Your daughter was not as helpless as you thought she was. She is strong, for her age."

"She needed to be, because you were not there for her."

Edwina sighed. She had come to ask Isabella's help but had ended up arguing with her. She needed to find a way forward. She lowered her tone. "I have regretted not being there for Phillipa," she said. "If I could have my time again, I would do things differently. But I can't change things. Please, can we just talk about the reason I am here?"

Isabella scowled. "I know why you are here. There's always a problem in your family that you need me to solve. No doubt you have got yourself into some sort of trouble again."

Edwina protested once more. "My father saved your life!"

"He came to my rescue once. Looking back, I'm not so sure I needed it. I had men-at-arms with me."

"You were surrounded. My father drove them off with his arrows."

The countess was a little chastened, but not fully. "Even so, I have repaid the debt many times over. I intervened when your father was on trial in Lincoln. I helped him get into Oxford. I persuaded my father to let him have the lodge in Windsor Forest. And do you think you would have been invited to a royal wedding but for me?"

"You are right. We owe you much. Though the wedding was not a good experience for me."

Now it was the countess' turn to sigh. "I have much to do. My maids will make you comfortable in one of the chateau's best rooms. We will talk again tomorrow." With that, she marched out, leaving Edwina stunned at the suddenness of her departure.

An hour later, still smarting from her encounter with the countess, Edwina left the chateau and went to the village, seeking out Michel and Fleece. She found them in an inn where they had rented a room, and where the dice game was in progress.

If she had wanted a sympathetic ear or a shoulder to cry on, she was not going to get it. From the stacks of coins on the table she could tell that Fleece was doing poorly in the game, and that Michel was faring even worse. Their expressions were grim. Their company would not be enjoyable. All they were interested in was the game and trying to win back their losses. She suspected that for them it would be a long evening, most probably into the night.

There were no other women in the room where the gambling was taking place. The room itself was dark, the atmosphere oppressive.

So she walked away. Michel did not even know she had been there.

When she returned to the chateau, she decided to spend some time exploring before settling down for the night.

The rooms were sumptuous. There was much wealth here. Everywhere there were symbols of prowess in battle, with paintings of the lords of Coucy going back generations. Mostly, they were painted astride their battle horse There were also paintings of members of Isabella's own family, the royal family of England, King Edward, the Black Prince, John of Gaunt.

She visited the library then went to sit in the chapel, alone with her thoughts, until a man appeared at the door. His features were familiar, the same features Edwina had seen on some of the paintings. And she recognised him as the leader of the band of knights she had seen earlier in the day. It was Enguerrand, Lord of Coucy, husband to Countess Isabella.

"So you are the girl with one hand," he said, causing Edwina immediately to cover her hand with her sleeve. "I have just come from my wife. She told me you had arrived at our home." The fluency of his English struck Edwina, until she remembered he had been captive in England for years, held by Isabella's father, King Edward as ransom. That was how Isabella had met and fallen for him. "I have heard much about you and your family," he added.

He had taken off most of his armour but still wore his half-greaves, his leg armour. They were splattered with blood. He saw how that distracted Edwina, so took them off. "I own a lot of land and sometimes I have to remind my people of their place on it," he explained. "It can get bloody."

Edwina knew how things were done. She was not naive. Many landlords used violence to keep their tenants in check. The kind ones were the exception rather than the rule. It sickened her. "My father served in the English army for a while," she said. "I've heard many stories from him, about the senseless slaughter of defenceless peasants and their families. It sickens me. And, so often, it is justified because a lord decided to remind them of *their place*."

Enguerrand took a deep breath. He was tired. "You speak to me without fear, but also without respect," he said, a mixture of admonition and admiration in his tone.

She shrugged. "I speak my mind, things I see as true. If you want me to fear you, I'm afraid I will have to disappoint."

He stifled a laugh. "That was never my intention. You are our guest and as I said I have heard so much about you that I look forward to some proper conversation. Just one thing, though." He leaned forward to within a few inches of her. His tone hardened. "Don't ever speak to me like that in front of anyone else. If you do, you will regret it. I will not be responsible for the consequences."

She held his gaze but softened her approach. "I should not have said what I did. I'm sorry. Though it is what I think. I've come a long way to ask your wife for help and she won't hear my request. I don't know what to do. I'm still a little angry with her."

He nodded. "You cannot know it but she has problems of her own, believe me. But give her time. She will hear what you have to say. In the meantime please enjoy our hospitality." He looked at the bloody armour. "While I get somebody to clean that for me."

Just then a young lad appeared at the door and coughed gently to attract his lord's attention. Enguerrand went to him and spoke with the lad in whispers, then returned to Edwina. "It seems you have things of your own to attend to here," he said. "The two men you came with have been arrested. They killed a man in the village, on their first day here. That is something of a record. My squire will take you to them."

Edwina was stunned. This was the last thing she needed. She followed the squire out of the library. He took her to a room in one of the corner towers. Two guards stood outside. They let Edwina and the squire pass into the room.

It was not a prison, not a dark, damp basement room. Light came in through a window and candles were lit where the room was in shadow. The furnishings were simpler than in the main tower, but still

160

comfortable. The overall effect was that the men were not yet being held for punishment but awaiting a decision what to do with them.

Edwina went to Michel. His face was covered in bruises and one arm was held limp by his side. He tried to smile in re-assurance but the attempt made him spasm. She held him by the shoulders until the spasm ended. She was still angry with him, but also sorry to see him in such a pathetic state.

She looked over to where Fleece sat. He was in an even worse state. He was naked from the waist upwards and sported a newly stitched gash in his side. As ever, he showed no emotion.

"What happened?" she asked Michel.

"We were playing dice," he replied.

"I know," she said, her voice tetchy at his elusive answer. "I saw how much you were losing. No doubt you lost a lot."

"I did. Then there was a wrestling match, so I decided to bet on that and recover some of my losses."

"But instead you lost more."

"No. I bet well that time. I won quite a bit of my money back."

"But that got you into a fight."

He shook his head and pointed to Fleece. "*He* got me into fight."

"How?"

"There was a group of men at the wrestling. They were drunk and had lost money. A woman was there with a child, a son of maybe six or seven years. The boy had a harelip and when he talked it was hard for anyone to understand him apart from his mother.

"One of the men started shouting at the boy's mother, saying she must be evil to have given birth to such a child. The boy was brave and went to try to protect his mother. The man turned on him and started beating him.

"Fleece saw what was happening, a man beating a child for no good reason. Like I told you, abuse of a child is the only thing that stirs his

161

emotions. He loses his mind. He lost control and attacked the man, beating him half to death. No more than the man deserved, if you ask me. But the man was not alone. He had gone to the wrestling with two brothers and they had friends there. They all set upon Fleece. It took them all to get Fleece off the vile man. As for me, I had no choice but help him and you can see the result. As you know, I am no great fighter."

"I'm told a man died."

"Yes. One of the brothers. Fleece hit him, a single punch, and the man never got up. When Fleece saw what he had done he stopped fighting."

"Too late."

"Yes."

"You are lucky to be alive, but now you will both hang."

"Undoubtedly."

"What happened to the boy?"

"He will live, thanks to Fleece. I saw him being comforted by his mother. So at least some good came from it all."

Fleece now spoke, his voice weak. "The boy was doing no harm. The man who was beating him had lost money gambling and was the sort that needs to take it out on somebody, usually a child or woman. He was a coward picking on the weakest victim he could find."

Edwina shook her head in disbelief. "Why are people so cruel?" she said. "But you killed a man. I can't see a way out from this, for either of you."

"And we have destroyed your chance to get help looking for your father."

"There never was a chance of that. We should not have come here. It has cost your lives. I'm sorry."

Chapter Twenty

Coucy-le-Chateau, June1378

For three days Edwina was in limbo. There was no sign of the countess making further contact with her, and no decision had been made on the fate of Michel and Fleece.

She made no more visits to her travelling companions. She had such mixed emotions, conflicting feelings. Despite her own apology to them, she was angry with them. Their actions had jeopardised her quest, and more importantly, put their own lives at risk. And yet, what Fleece did was right, admirable.

She was at a writing desk, composing some letters. She had been in this situation before. She knew she should contact home and let her mother know she was safe and well, but beyond that was unsure what to say. She was not even sure she was, in fact, *safe and well*. She could well suffer the same consequences as her companions, guilty by association and sent to the hangman. She most definitely could not say when she would be going home, and she had no news of her father.

She also needed to let her father's wife Charlotte know she was still searching for him. But the deadline for Charlotte and the children to be evicted from their home was getting nearer and Edwina had nothing to report, no progress made in her search.

It was a fine day outside. She decided the letters could wait. Perhaps the fresh air would inspire her to find the right words to say.

She walked aimlessly for a while, until reaching one of the village wells. A group of women had gathered, meeting there to collect water and enjoy the local gossip.

As she watched, she forgot to keep her sleeve down over her stump. As she got older, she had become less embarrassed about the disability than she once was and was less careful to cover it up. She could never predict what response she would get if someone saw it. Sometimes there was kindness and sympathy, but mostly derision, even fear at the sight of something they did not understand.

One of the women at the well saw the stump. Edwina wore a leather glove that had been specially made for it. But the missing hand was obvious.

The woman became excited and started shouting and gesticulating.

Edwina's French had improved during her time in France, but this woman was almost screeching and her words came so fast that Edwina could not keep up with what was being said. The woman gestured for Edwina to stay where she was and Edwina understood that much.

A short while later, the woman returned. She had a child with her, a boy of maybe six years. He wore an expression of uncertainty. His mother encouraged him not to be afraid, and they moved closer to Edwina.

Now the woman spoke more slowly, calmly and clearly. Edwina could make out enough to know that she was being thanked and that it was to do with the boy. Edwina quickly made the connection to what Michel and Fleece had done. The woman had been told that the men who defended her boy were travelling with a woman with a missing hand. Edwina had worried about being judged by association, but this woman was doing just that, and Edwina was judged a hero.

Edwina felt awkward. Only an hour or less earlier she had been cursing what the two men had done because it affected her chances of influencing the countess. Now she was being lauded for their act of kindness and bravery, and when she looked at the helplessness of the boy, she felt ashamed of herself.

When finally the woman left, Edwina made straight for the room where her friends were being kept. But as she approached the tower, she saw Count Enguerrand in the courtyard. It was an opportunity to ask about the men's fate.

The count was once again in full armour, preparing for another outing to ensure his tenants *knew their place* in the scheme of things. He looked weary but accepted Edwina's approach graciously. He knew what she wanted.

164

"You wish to know what will happen to your friends," he said flatly. "Well, I can tell you that oaths have been sworn by the dead man's family and associates. They have all stated that the man known as Fleece started a fight for no reason and that the one he killed was unarmed, defenceless and innocent."

"You do not believe them, surely?"

"They swore on oath."

"But Fleece only went to help a poor child who was being set upon."

"That is what he claims."

"It's the truth."

"Maybe it is, but he was given the opportunity to speak to the court and chose not to."

"What? Why? But also, ask the child's mother. She will tell you what happened."

"The process is done. The court has considered all sides and has ruled on the evidence. A man has died and the killer must be punished according to our laws."

"What about Michel?"

"A lesser punishment has been decreed. The Englishman will die slowly, confined in a cage. Your merchant friend will merely be flogged."

Edwina stood with her mouth open. Words would not come. She watched. transfixed as the count mounted his horse and rode on, unsympathetic, to terrorise another village.

She looked at the towers. She could not face Michel without trying to secure a better outcome for him and for Fleece. Her gaze turned to the central tower. She had to try to see Isabella again.

She told the guards what she wanted. One went to tell the countess and to Edwina's surprise came back with the news that Isabella had agreed to see her.

When Edwina entered the room, she was struck by Isabella's demeanour.

The countess was sitting by the fire, her face drawn, looking sad and melancholic. She spoke but without looking in Edwina's direction. "You come again! Seeking my help, of course."

"Yes, if it pleases you, I am."

"*If it pleases* me. Ha! What in this life pleases me now?"

Edwina stepped nearer. "Are you unwell, my lady?"

Isabella turned her head, now looking sideways at Edwina. "My husband is a good man, you know. Gracious and principled."

"I don't doubt it. But I see no justice in a man sentenced to death for going to the aid of a defenceless child."

"The courts are there for a purpose. You cannot argue against a system that has worked for hundreds of years. And besides, Enguerrand must uphold the law, not undermine it."

Isabella stood up and poked the fire, then went to the window. "Let me tell you about the man I married, a man I married for love, remember. He was a rich lord when my father took him as prisoner at the battle of Poitiers. Marrying me made him even more important, a Knight of the Garter in the country he had fought against. But he remains French and swears allegiance to the French crown. For years he achieved the impossible, staying true to both countries, a friend to each, avoiding having to fight on one side or the other. But when my father died, things changed. Enguerrand had to renounce his English titles and I, his dutiful wife, gladly did the same. I became penniless while my brother ruled England as regent and my father's mistress made merry at Windsor."

She paused and Edwina waited, knowing more was to come. "Did you know that King Charles wanted Enguerrand to be Marshal of France? Enguerrand turned him down. Or that he is the son of an Austrian princess but is denied his inheritance? So be careful what you say about my dear husband. He is a good man who could have had wealth beyond his dreams if he had wanted it."

Isabella sighed. "I'm tired, Edwina. Don't ask me to help your friends. I lack the energy. And don't ask me to look for your father."

"So, you know why I came."

"Of course I do. I have taken an interest in your family for years. Do you think I would not know he is missing. After the skirmish at Rottingdean I made enquiries, but alas to no avail."

"Then help Charlotte."

"His wife? Why, what happened to her?"

"She is to be evicted if he doesn't return by the end of the year. That's why I came here, to ask you to help her."

"I see. But I have just told you, I no longer have influence at court in England. There's nothing I can do."

"You could at least try."

"No. My days of rescuing your family are gone. You must sort your own affairs out. Our conversation is ended."

Edwina knew she was beaten. She turned to go, then hesitated. "Last year, when I was missing, my father sacrificed everything trying to find me. I will not give up on him."

"I would expect nothing less. Now go and leave me be."

167

Chapter Twenty-One

Coucy-le-Chateau, June 1378

Edwina did not attend Michel's public flogging. Part of her thought she should, to show him her support. She knew he would be taunted by the elements in the crowd who hated the English and those who just enjoyed such public spectacles of human suffering. She could not bring herself to witness it. She prayed he would understand.

She did go to see Fleece in his cage.

Fleece had also been flogged, then beaten and placed in the cage, the cage then hung from a wooden frame. His last days on earth were pitiful as he slowly starved, on view for all to see, a deterrent to others.

The mother of the boy he had defended was there every day, saying her prayers and making offerings of any small possession she could afford to give. Edwina saw tears well in the woman's eyes as the gifts were carefully placed where he could see them. And she saw his weak smile in acknowledgement of her kindness.

Edwina spoke to Fleece, hoping her words would offer him some small comfort. "To me, you are a hero," she told him. At that stage, he was too weak to reply. She hoped he heard her.

Michel was released and came to stand gingerly next to Edwina, watching Fleece's life ebb away.

"I'm sorry I didn't come," said Edwina.

"I'm glad you didn't."

She touched him gently, not wanting to add to his pain. "Let me tend your wounds," she offered.

"I will, but later. I am not going to die. We have time. For now, let's pray one last time for a brave man."

He started to say the 23rd psalm. She joined him.

Fleece's body moved as his last breath came and went, and he passed into another life. A man in the crowd spat at his lifeless form.

"What will happen to his body?" asked Edwina.

"He is judged a criminal, a murderer," replied Michel. "There will be no marked grave. But he is with God now, so none of that matters."

She sighed. "Tomorrow we will go home. Where will you stay tonight?"

He shrugged. "None of the inns will have me. I'll find somewhere, don't worry."

"Come to my room."

He looked at her quizzically. "I seek no sympathy, nor new complications in my life," he said.

"And you will get none. You will sleep on the floor. But it will give me the chance to tend your back. It's the least I can do."

"We will be seen. You will be labelled a harlot or worse for taking a convicted man to your bedroom."

"Well, I do need more excitement in my life," she replied with heavy irony in her voice.

They walked to the tower, Michel unsteadily but accepting no physical support from Edwina. As Michel had predicted, they drew hateful looks and catcalls from people they passed, mostly addressed to Edwina.

Once in the room, Edwina carefully removed Michel's shirt. Try as she might she could not avoid gasping at what she saw. Michel's back was crossed with deep cuts. She was able to tell that there had been more than one episode of flogging, with signs of healing from the first then new lashes delivered over the healing wounds. The pain must have been excruciating, but she thought Michel would not welcome any sympathetic comment about it. Instead, she concentrated on what must be done.

"The main thing is to prevent infection of the areas around the wounds," she said. She did not know where to start, because *'the area around the wounds'* really meant the whole of his back. "I will make up some balms. Are you in pain inside?" She gently pressed her fingers where she knew his vital internal organs were located.

169

He understood. "I ache all over my body, but only on the outside."

"Good. Then you will heal in time." The words sounded callous, but he did not want mawkish sympathy from her, and she had personal experience of scars healing, though hers had never quite healed as well as she had hoped they would.

There was an apothecary in the village. The shelves were well stocked and the owner had a small area of garden for growing herbs he sold. Edwina told him she was helping a man with severe cuts but stopped short of saying her friend had been flogged. The apothecary was very helpful and quite knowledgeable, but Edwina was unsure about some of his advice. When he produced a jar of honey and some camomile she nodded her thanks, but she was not so enthusiastic when he offered her the blood of a badger to add to her balms. She decided to stick with what she knew would work.

She bought her ingredients plus bowls, a mortar and pestle and a storage jar. Then she saw some spiced wine on one of the shelves and added that to her purchase, thinking how Michel needed internal as well as external rejuvenation.

When she got back to the room, Michel was sleeping in a chair. She left him while making up her balms. When he awoke, she administered the balms, and gave him some of the wine. Then he slept again, this time for the full night and into the next morning.

So it was into the afternoon before they set off. Edwina applied more balm to Michel's wounds. Michel decided to pay for a cart and driver for the first few miles of their journey back to St Malo, allowing himself to curl up and rest in the back.

Edwina rode alongside. She thought of home and family. It seemed such a long time since she spent her days idly sitting by her Moses tree, reading fantasy stories from *The Golden Legend* and thinking about the heroes and beautiful maidens depicted in the book. Her days then were easy but her life was empty, devoid of adventure. Perhaps she should have stayed there instead of going to a wedding, one that changed her life forever.

She thought of her mother and her friend Mary, still where they had been for years, safe and certain about their tomorrows. But she did not envy them. She thought of her half-brother Daniel, who was steward for an important family, living in a castle no less. Like her, he had enriched his life by leaving home.

She wondered about her friend Martia, an outgoing young woman who had surprised her by opting to live on an island on The Medway with an old woman, Dolly. She hoped Martia was content ploughing through Dolly's extensive library, clothes collection and wine store.

Then there was Ishraq, the slave boy who had found freedom and a life for himself on the high seas but had not got to Baghdad.

All these lives that had touched hers seemed so far away now. Only Michel was near, like a pet dog, faithful and reliable, but now bruised and battered simply because of his decision to accompany her to Coucy, her last throw of the dice on behalf of her father's wife and children.

They reached their first overnight stop, an inn they had stayed at on the way to Coucy. It was in Noyon and was within a short walking distance of the cathedral. They ate at the inn, then Edwina left Michel to rest again while she went to light candles, one for her father and one for Fleece.

There were only a few people in the cathedral, so it was quiet and peaceful. A young nun approached her. The nun seemed to sense that she was English. "Welcome to our wonderful place of worship," she said. "Are you a traveller?"

Edwina never liked to talk with strangers who came up to her. She always suspected they had some ulterior motive for doing so. This time, though she needed to talk to someone. She felt melancholic and needed some friendly company.

"You look lost, my child," said the nun. Edwina thought the nun was too young to be calling her *my child* but still warmed to her and thought she was right. She did feel lost.

171

The tears came without warning. They flowed easily, expelling the emotions that had built within her through the horrors of Coucy. She allowed the nun to put an arm round her and gave herself to the warmth of the physical contact.

"Do you want to tell me?" asked the nun. And Edwina found herself nodding. "Come, there's a place I go to."

It was a side chapel. They were alone. The nun settled down on a cushion in a corner. "It's always peaceful here," she said. Edwina sat beside her and shared the burdens she carried, laying out her feelings of guilt about Michel and Fleece and her sense of anguish that she had made no progress finding her father.

The nun offered no words of wisdom. Her experience of the world was limited. Instead, she told Edwina a little about herself. She said she had felt the call to enter a life of prayer at a very early age and knew little of the outside world. But it did not matter that she lacked inspirational words. Her presence was enough. Her kindness and care made a difference. Edwina felt her burdens become lighter, lifted from her.

They prayed together then sat for a while in silent contemplation.

It was Edwina who broke the silence. "Thank you," she said. "I feel much better. You have a gift. My father is a healer, a physician, but I think you are a healer also. Your kindness heals my spirit."

The nun shook her head modestly. "I am at peace inside. That is what I try to share. I see people come here who are not so fortunate as I, and I want to help them experience what I have."

The nun paused, then went on. "I have heard tales of a man I wish to meet. He is an Englishman, a black monk and is the talk of all my sisters in the convent. We are told he truly has a gift, as a healer like your father but also a healer of souls. I plan to make a pilgrimage to see him. He is at Avignon. I am told he is known only as the Benedictine."

"I hope you find him and that he lives up to your expectations."

172

The nun suddenly became excited. "Perhaps he can help you. Perhaps he has second sight. Why not come with me?"

Edwina frowned. "No, I can't. I'm tired and must go home to England. Anyway, I don't believe in magic."

The nun noticed that Edwina wore a token around her neck. It looked like a homemade cross threaded with a strip of leather. It was crude yet beautiful. "You wear an amulet."

Instinctively, Edwina's hand went to her cross. "Yes. My brother gave it to me."

"Does it serve to protect you?"

"It's a long story."

"Perhaps there is a part of you that does believe in magic, just a little. I think you have stories to tell that I would like to hear, and the journey to Avignon is a long one." Edwina did not answer.

"Will there be answers for you at home?" added the nun.

"No."

"Then what have you to lose? Look, just give the idea some thought. I will be leaving after the Feast of The Assumption."

"The middle of August."

"Yes."

"I will think on it. But if I do return, how will I find you?"

"Easy. Until I set off for Avignon, I'll always be here. If you need to ask for me though, my name is Briony."

"Thank you. I'm Edwina. Perhaps we will meet again."

"I think so. I sense our paths might cross again."

Edwina touched her amulet again. She wondered whether Briony was right.

The walk to the inn was short but by the time she was there she had made her decision. She set down two candles on a desk in her room and composed two identical letters for Michel to take across the

Channel, one for her mother and one for Charlotte. She could not go home just yet. Briony had been right about that. Partly, she was afraid to go back now, with so little achieved. So why not take a leap of faith and go with the young nun?

She kept the wording brief:

'Dear Mother (Dear Charlotte), I trust you are well. I am still in France with Michel. My spirits have been lifted by new information and I will shortly be travelling south to follow it up. I will write again when I have more news. Your loving daughter (Your friend) Edwina.'

She had chosen her words carefully. There were no untruths. She was indeed planning to head south. The *new information* was the Benedictine. It was a deceit, leaving the recipients of the letters thinking she had a new lead to her father's whereabouts. But she felt no guilt. The deceit would be a good thing, she reasoned, keeping their hopes alive. It was the right thing to do. Why add to their worry? Maybe something would turn up, a change of fortune. She must continue to hope and pray.

Before she retired, Edwina looked in the room where Michel was sleeping, opening the door just enough to see him. He was tossing and turning, not at peace.

A tear came to her eye. They had crossed a line and shared one night of intimacy. She had built his hopes up. She did not love him. She felt sorry for him. She was about to confirm her rejection of him yet again. He did not deserve her rejection, nor her pity, but it was the right thing to do. For him. For Wenna. For herself.

She went to her room and collapsed, face down on her bed. She sobbed. She felt dirty and, in that moment, she hated herself.

Part Five

Lella

Chapter Twenty-Two

Avignon, July 1378

Erich was right. Sitting in his bathhouse prison Matty could hear no sounds from the rest of the house that once had been a Roman villa. So he had time on his hands. Time to think.

It seemed pointless planning an escape. The walls were so thick, the floor was made of concrete and the iron bars that formed the entrance were formidable.

Instead, he spent time reliving his memories. He jumped from one memory to another. He was with Edmund and Meg, then with Marianne, Alice, Edwina, or his friend Tom.

It all seemed so long ago.

He got sharply to his feet and paced up and down the bathhouse. Memories were fine, but he had to get home, to those he loved who were not mere memories but were alive in the here and now. He wanted desperately to see them all.

The following day Erich was as good as his word and Matty was free to roam the house. Free, that is, if he could forget the presence of his shadow, the imposing figure of Jaro.

Around midday Erich found him. "You missed a good evening's entertainment and gossip, Monsieur Le Benedictine," he said. "It was very…informative."

Matty had questions prepared, but Erich held up a hand to stop him. "Now I will sleep," said the Dane. "Because tonight we do it again with a different bishop and a few cardinals. It's tiring work, you know, eating and drinking all night. You should feel sorry for me, resting comfortably as you do in the bathhouse." He laughed and disappeared to his chamber.

Matty tried in vain to engage in conversation with Jaro. There was a language barrier but even without it there would still have been difficulty. Jaro would have no interest in talking with him. The man was as impenetrable as the villa's walls.

He ventured outside and found Lella in a wicker chair, reading. He turned away, thinking she would not want his company, but she beckoned him back. He was surprised when she spoke in English. "You look in need of company," she said. "So am I." She patted the seat next to her. "Come and sit for a while. Jaro will be my chaperone."

Matty hesitated, then did as she suggested. "What are you reading?" he asked.

"The Decameron," she said.

His expression was blank. He had not heard of it.

"It's a selection of stories about people during the Great Plague."

"Sounds depressing."

"In a way, it is. But it's written by an Italian and I never find Italians depressing. There's always some, how shall I say, moments of passion. But also, the book is helpful. Did you know there is plague still in Europe? In fact, I have heard it is back in England, at a place called York. Perhaps you know it."

"You know that my memory has been poor of late and I'm not sure of many things. The name rings a bell. I think I have been there, but maybe I'm imagining it."

"Anyway, the book says that to avoid the plague you must leave the towns and cities, find an out-of-the-way place to hide and tell one another uplifting stories."

"Leaving towns sounds a good idea. I think that's what I did once. Plague seems to like the towns and cities. But I'm not sure how telling stories would help anyone."

"Neither am I. I haven't finished the book yet. Maybe I'll find out."

"It seems to me you have a comfortable life here, but you see no-one other than Erich and his henchmen."

"I have my sons. And there are parties like the one last night."

"How exciting for you, meeting stuffy old bishops. I bet you danced the night away with them."

She frowned. "I know what you're trying to do. But it won't work. And you're wrong about the bishops. Some of them are young and full of life. More than once I've had unwanted stares from one. But you have annoyed me now. I think I will go back to my reading, if you would kindly leave me to it."

"Of course."

Lella gave an instruction to Jaro, and Matty's time out from the prison of the bathhouse was ending prematurely. But he had sewn a seed. He wondered whether it would germinate. He needed an ally and his hope was that behind her veneer of happiness Lella felt as much a prisoner here as he was.

Before he was back at the bathhouse, he saw the young black maid who had attended to Erich the day before. He tried to catch her eye, but she looked down and away as Jaro ushered him to his prison.

****

Over the next three days a pattern became established. Matty would find Lella sitting in the same place and they would talk, each day a little longer. They talked again about the book, which led Matty to tell Lella about the loss of his family to plague. She told him she also had lost family members, during The Great Plague of 1348. It was before she was born but all her grandparents died and when plague returned a few years later her younger sister was taken.

Matty was glad of the opportunity to talk with someone about his family and sensed the same was true for Lella. She seemed to enjoy his company, though she was cautious always to stay in control, saying nothing out of turn about Erich or her relationship with him.

On the third day she confided more to him about herself. He already knew from Erich that she was Italian. It turned out she was from a small village near Turin.

"I was eleven years old," she told him. "Mercenaries were raiding in Italy and came to our village. They were not Sequin's men but some had been with him before that. One decided to abduct me from my family. He brought me to Avignon. I was with him for three years."

Matty could see how hard it was for her to tell him this. There was loathing in her eyes as she mentioned her captor. It was all she said, offering no details of how she was treated, but it was clear the memories were painful. He suspected she had suffered greatly.

She continued with her story. "Then Erich and his mercenaries came and for a few days the two bands spent their evenings together, drinking and singing their songs. I saw how Erich looked at me and there was something about him, a spark of life. He was a rough diamond but had more tenderness than the man I was with. So I dared to look back at him the same way."

"A risky thing to do," said Matty.

"Yes, but I didn't care. If my owner killed me for it, I would have seen it as a mercy."

"Your *owner*?"

"I have no other word to describe him."

"What happened?"

"Erich offered to buy me. It was not accepted. But Erich always gets what he wants. He set up a card game with me as the prize. He won, but my owner was not going to part with me. There was a fight and much bloodshed. Erich and his men won, and I was his."

"A different man, but another owner."

"Yes, but as I said, Erich can be tender when he wants to be."

"And brutal when he doesn't?"

She ignored the suggestion. "I am better off with him," she said.

"How long has he owned you?"

"Careful. You are on dangerous ground. We have *been together* ten years."

179

"And you have two sons. They seem quiet, not as boisterous as most their age."

"Erich is strict. They know not to make mischief when we have guests."

"I should think he would be a father not to be crossed."

"He adores them," she replied. Her responses now were sharp.

Matty decided not to say any more about Lella's husband or sons. He was already pushing her a little too far. He changed the subject. "I see you aren't the only beauty here. The maid who served us was striking."

Lella frowned and drew her lip in. Matty thought that was telling. He had touched another nerve. He was trying to achieve a balance and was at the edges of how far he could go, but this time she did not send him to the bathhouse.

He was feeling she had warmed to him and looked forward to seeing him. He decided to test his progress, arriving a little later the next day. Sure enough, she had put her book down and was straining to see if he was coming. He smiled inwardly, encouraged.

That same day Domenico spoke to him, only to ask if he was comfortable in the bathhouse and to assure him that he would not be there much longer. Domenico said that Erich sent his apologies for having had no time to be with him, because he was busy *'finalising the arrangements'*. That alerted Matty. Something was going to happen to him soon.

The next day Matty decided to push Lella harder. It was risky. She might pull back and end their meetings. But he felt he had no choice.

He delayed going to her just a little longer than before. But this time, when he got to their meeting spot she was not there. He wondered whether she felt she was telling him too much about herself, letting him get too far inside her world.

He waited a while but she did not come. Eventually he gave up and wandered round the house as before. And came across the maid.

She was alone in the main reception room, polishing the marble fireplace. For once, Matty's shadow, Jaro had given longer him longer rein and stayed in a nearby corridor. It gave Matty an opportunity to speak with the maid. "Hello," he said.

Her response was to cower, whether suspicious of him or afraid she might be seen talking to him. He tried again, using his most non-threatening voice. "My name is Matty."

She looked in his direction but not at his face. She was looking at his monk's robes. He saw it and wondered whether the robes made some bad connection for her. "Don't be afraid," he said. He could not be sure she understood his English. All he could do was convey meaning through his tone and by keeping his distance, allowing her some safe space.

It was all he had time to say. He heard Jaro approaching and hurried from the room. Jaro turned a corner and saw him descending some stairs, giving no hint he had been in the room with the maid.

Back inside the bathhouse, he pounded a wall in frustration. He needed an ally but had spoiled his chances with Lella and made no progress with the maid. Then he noticed something. There was a piece of cloth underneath his wash bowl. It was not there before.

He took it out. There was a crude drawing on it. He turned it this way and that, until it made sense. It was a map of the bathhouse. He held his candle close and positioned the cloth to be sure it was orientated from where he stood. Then he saw a mark, a small cross in one corner, above the area that had been the caldarium, the heated plunge bath.

He made his way to the spot that was marked.

Like the rest of the bathhouse, the caldarium had a concrete floor. He found the area marked on the cloth. It was very dark and it was hard to see anything. He ran his hand in the dirt and there, placed underneath an overflow pipe, was a metal lever with an upturned end. A crowbar.

Why was it there, in that place? Did it explain Lella's absence? Had she put it there for him and left the map so he would find it?

181

He took hold of the pipe and twisted it in his hand. It moved. The mortar around it was loose. He twisted again and more mortar came away. Another twist and a yank pulled out a piece of the pipe. It was rusty and had cracked along part of its length.

Removing the pipe did not create an escape route, but it made a small hole above a course of stonework in the internal wall. Using the crowbar he was able to lever one of the stones out, then another.

Lella must have known about the weakness. He stepped back and took a closer look in the light of the candle. The reason the mortar was soft was because of years of exposure to water from the outside through the broken pipe. He touched the mortar and sure enough it was damp. Evidence of the water seepage would be clear in the external wall, while hidden from view inside. He could not have noticed it, but anyone familiar with the house would know about it. Lella wandered the grounds. Erich did not. He was probably unaware of the dampness.

Matty continued prising away mortar and then stones until he had access to the cavity below. When the hole was big enough, he squeezed down into the area of the hypocaust, the channels that originally allowed hot gases to pass under the caldarium and heat the rooms above.

There was still no way to get outside, but Matty now had access to crawl through the space under the floor. It was tight, claustrophobic. He wriggled through, not sure where it would take him, hyperventilating with the fear of becoming stuck. Finally he reached the domed space where fires were once lit from outside the building, heating the air that was then circulated under the bathhouse. It was bigger than the space under the floor. He crawled through, then hurriedly scrambled amongst thick brambles and nettles that had grown around the abandoned dome and its surroundings, earning himself a few stings from the barbs where his skin was exposed. Then the growth thinned and he was out and in the open air.

He rolled away from the brambles and lay for a moment on his back, relieved to be drinking in the fresh air. Then he realised he had dropped the crowbar scrambling through the bushes. He could not

182

leave it. It was his only potential weapon, but more importantly he knew it would implicate his helper when found.

As he found the crowbar, a sound caused him to turn and he saw a figure in the trees, a woman. It had to be Lella. She walked away a few paces then stopped and turned to look back. She wanted him to follow her.

When he got to where she had been, there was a short sword there. Lella had put it there for him, but was keeping her distance, expecting him to collect the weapon and run. But he could not. He knew what she had done would put her in danger.

He picked up the sword and followed her. She tried to run but he easily caught her, gently pulling her down to be out of sight of anyone passing. It caused him to drop the sword.

Lella was looking away. Matty turned her face to him and saw why. She had a black eye and swollen lip. More evidence of the danger she was in.

There were some rocks ahead. "Behind there," he said. She shook her head. "Go!" he repeated, and this time she did. He picked up the sword and joined her at the rocks. "Tell me!" he said. It was not an order but a plea, his voice gentle and caring. "Did Erich do this to you?"

She nodded. "Jaro told him about our meetings. Erich can be a very jealous man."

"I'm old enough to be your father."

"So is Erich."

"But you still risked helping me. Why?"

"Once Erich knew you had been meeting me, I worried what he might do to you. Besides, the house does not need another prisoner. There are plenty here already. Also, there have been two bishops come here, one from Avignon and the other from Rome. They both said you are an important man, a holy man. I am devout. My faith told me I must try to help you."

She looked sharply into his eyes. "Living in this isolated place I never have the chance to do anything worthwhile. By helping you I can feel better about myself, and maybe God will reward me somehow."

"Domenico told me Erich had a plan for me. It has to be something to do with the archbishop."

"You are right. The French have not given in. They will try to overturn the decision of the College of Cardinals to appoint an Italian pope. To do that they need to plead a case and they think they can use you. If you are with them it will count for much when the votes are cast. But the Italians know that and want to prevent it. So Erich plays a game. He plays one side against the other. He has told both sides he would be willing to use his contacts to find you but that it would cost him a great deal in bribes. He will sell you to whoever bids highest, though he is in no hurry. He enjoys the game more than he needs the money."

"Erich will know you helped me escape. He will hurt you more than that black eye. He likely will kill you."

She shook her head. "Erich lacks imagination. Jaro will mostly be blamed. He was supposed to be guarding you. Then Erich will see the loose masonry. It's been neglected for years. He will curse himself for not having it repaired. He won't suspect anyone would dare help you, especially me. He thinks I have no spirit left to do anything brave. I didn't believe it myself until today."

"We can be miles from here before they even miss us."

"You don't understand, do you? I have been somebody's property for more than half my life. What would I do if I was free again? The idea frightens me. At least here I am fed and kept warm. And I cannot leave my children."

"I understand that, but no human being should be owned by another."

"Many thousands are. It is just how it is. You can say prayers for me if you wish, but I won't change my mind. Just go, I beg of you."

It was clear Lella's mind was made up, and Matty knew she had to stay because of her boys. He took her hand in his and squeezed gently, a gesture of thanks for the risk she had taken.

"There's one more thing," he said. "The African maid. You choose to stay here. It's your choice to make. But the girl has nothing by comparison to you. I want to help her."

Lella sighed. "You cannot save the world."

He shrugged. "I am the Benedictine. Perhaps I can."

Lella pulled at her hair. "Why, oh why did you have to come here and make my life too complicated?" She thought for a moment. "Leave the girl to me. I will find a way."

"You promise?"

"Yes, I promise. Now go. In God's name, go!"

Matty went out into the low sunshine of the evening, feeling free, but also guilty for leaving behind two vulnerable women. He reached a rise in the landscape and looked back. "God be with them," he whispered under his breath.

Chapter Twenty-Three

Avignon, July 1378

Lella was right. Erich's anger was directed not at her but at Jaro. Matty's escape was discovered next morning and when Erich was told he immediately assumed that Jaro had metaphorically, and perhaps even physically fallen asleep on the job, allowing his charge to somehow get hold of a tool while he was not looking. It was a surprise that their prisoner had discovered the weak area in the bathhouse wall, but Erich never suspected a conspiracy. Instead, he was impressed by the resourcefulness of the man known as the Benedictine. It meant he would have to match such skill and cunning.

Jaro accepted his responsibility. How could he not? He stood motionless while Erich berated him for his negligence. He took the verbal assault fully and without protest. Fortunately, he had built enough credit over his years of loyal service for Erich that he knew his mistake would earn him nothing more severe. But he felt embarrassed. He had cost Erich a lot of money. He was determined to make amends.

On one thing Lella's instinct was wrong. Erich's intention for the Englishman had never been to sell him to the highest bidder. Instead, the plan was to make money from the Roman *and* French bishops. He would take payment from both for the invented costs of hiring men to search for the black monk.

That plan would give him two sources of income rather than one, as well as the satisfaction that came from the game he was playing. Neither bishop would know he was working for the other. It would be deliciously clever.

Erich knew there would come a time when the Benedictine was no longer on everyone's agenda, no longer a cash cow. Events would move on. Other things would rise to prominence. Until then he would milk the situation, and when the monk was no longer of value, he would dispose of him in some suitably gruesome manner.

In fact, it had occurred to him that he did not need to keep his captive alive at all. He could pretend to organise searches even if the monk was dead, never to be found. But he reasoned that it made sense not to kill the man just yet. That way he kept his options open. Circumstances could change. Perhaps there would be new opportunities to cash in.

The escape changed everything, and Erich was angry. He gathered a group of his most trusted mercenaries. Jaro was to be the main man in terms of muscle but it would be Domenico who was the cerebral leader. The meeting was brief. Erich made no speeches. He said just one thing. "Find the Englishman and bring him back. Dead or alive." All aspects of detail were left to Domenico.

Domenico explored the area round the house looking for evidence of where the Englishman might have gone. But the trail grew quickly cold, evidence that the quarry knew how to cover his tracks.

The city was an unlikely destination for the escaped man. The Benedictine was a recognised figure. He would be spotted and his whereabouts reported.

It was even more unlikely that the Englishman would have crossed the Rhone. The only crossing points were in the city, bringing the same risk of being spotted. Trying to swim across would be suicidal. The river was too wide and deep, with vicious currents.

Two options remained. The Englishman might follow the west bank of the river, going north; or he might head further west along the river's tributaries. So Domenico split his force into two.

Of the two possibilities, Domenico's instinct was that the Englishman would follow the tributaries. All along the Rhone were mills, forges, fishermen and those who made their living from boats transporting goods. It was the area's major highway. The monk would run almost as big a risk of being seen as if he went to the city. Leaving the great river meant fewer people and therefore less chance of being reported and captured. The monk might try a cross country route but was more likely to stay near the water courses. Domenico sent Jaro, his main man, that way.

Jaro had four men with him. He also had Erich's best tracking hounds.

The hounds were normally used to following animal rather than human scents. They were excellent hunters of foxes and deer, but not men. So Jaro tore a piece of the cover that had been on Matty's bed in the bathhouse and took it with him. Every now and then he gave it to the hounds to sniff, introducing them to the scent of their new quarry.

*****

The following day was fiercely hot. Matty was travelling light but making only slow progress in the intense heat. He knew to stay away from main tracks. There were few anyway in this part of the countryside.

He rested for a moment to drink in a small pool that had been filled during a previous storm. When he started walking again, he stumbled into an area of bracken and a new memory came to him.

He was fleeing, being chased, just as he was now. He could hear horses pass by. They failed to see him. In the distance was a church spire. His village. He was running away from home and everything familiar, including the people he knew and loved. Plague had taken his family and the people of the village feared him, believing he was a carrier of plague. He felt cowardly. He had left his dying family behind. He had no choice, he knew it, but still it felt wrong.

A sound brought him out from his daydream. It sounded like a woodpecker. He had been hearing other sounds since he left Erich's house. An owl. A vixen. Too many distinctive sounds in a short period of time. They were the calls of men, one to another.

He climbed a mound and scoured the area ahead. And there they were. Three men on another area of raised ground, watching the direction he had come from. A coincidence? Or were they waiting for him? His escape had been remarkably easy until now. Perhaps Lella had betrayed him.

Suddenly all three men raised crossbows, cocked and loaded.

He turned to see where they were aiming. There was a group of men with hounds ploughing their way through the growth, about three hundred feet from the archers. Well within range and in full sight. He recognised the leading man in the threatened group. It was Jaro.

The archers waited, choosing the right time to strike, then stepped out from the trees and released their arrows. Two hit home. The screams of the men who were hit filled the air.

Jaro's men were surprised. They panicked, shouting at one another in confused response, unsure yet where the attack came from. Jaro calmed his men and ordered them to take cover, then checked the damage. He saw that one man was fatally wounded. The other would live but no longer able to fight. It left Jaro with only two fit fighting men.

Matty watched the archers reload. They had no mechanical loading aids, and the manual process was slow.

Jaro could not be sure how many he was up against. The sensible thing would be to regroup and move carefully forward, keeping low and hidden under the growth. Instead, he rushed out, sword in the air, charging. His two uninjured men needed no instruction. They trusted him, or maybe feared him. They followed suit. And with them went the hounds.

Crossbows were never easy to reload in a skirmish. On the practice fields archers honed their skills to reduce how long they took, and they could be very efficient firing from ramparts. But in the heat of a skirmish nerves played their part. In the crucial first minute the three archers fumbled. They heard the hounds and saw the huge figure of Jaro charging them. They had loaded their arrows but were not set ready to fire. They panicked, releasing their arrows without properly aiming, and sent them high and wide of the advancing group. They were now sitting ducks.

Jaro was now upon one of the archers, despatching him with his sword. Without breaking stride he was on the next man, while his men

189

took out the third. Matty closed his eyes as the hounds tore flesh from the dying men.

Matty crouched down and watched Jaro search the dead men, possibly to identify them but more likely to steal anything of value. Then Jaro and his two fit men moved on, leaving the bodies where they were. Jaro's wounded man was left to fend for himself.

What was it Matty had witnessed? It was certainly an ambush but meant for who? Were the archers waiting for him or Erich's men? He had no way to know.

Either way, he was in the middle of something, and he thought it must have something to do with himself.

When Jaro had gone, Matty went to the bodies of the archers. There was nothing to tell him who they were. They wore none of the insignia that would identify their allegiance to either the pope in Rome or the archbishop in Avignon. He could be sure only of one thing. An ambush required knowledge. The archers had known to expect their targets to come here, in this remote location.

He picked up one of the crossbows. Jaro had decided not to take any of them, preferring a sword, a weapon that was easier to carry, more mobile. The crossbow was more suited to a battlefield encounter.

But Matty needed another weapon. He remembered practising with a longbow in his youth. He had no memories of using a crossbow, but still he slung the weapon over his shoulder, along with a quiver and three arrows.

Jaro and his men were now ahead of him, still heading east. So Matty turned away, heading north towards the Rhone.

Chapter Twenty-Four

Avignon, August 1378

Ishraq looked up at the Palais des Papes. It had taken him two months to get here, walking from La Rochelle. His ultimate destination was Marseille, which his captain had told him was the gateway to the Mediterranean and where he hoped to find passage east, to Baghdad. And the best route to Marseille was via Avignon then down the Rhone through Nimes.

Going to Avignon also gave Ishraq an opportunity to discover more about the man whose name seemed to be on everybody's lips. Who was the Benedictine? Was he really a saint, a messenger from God, a great healer? Or just a man? And could he be Edwina's lost father? That idea was absurd. Impossible. Too unlikely to waste time thinking about. Yet Ishraq was drawn to this city where the answer lay.

He already knew that the Benedictine had gone missing. As he neared Avignon there was talk of nothing else in the taverns, and a plethora of theories abounded.

One theory was that the black monk had been so appalled by the behaviour of the people in the city, the prostitution, gambling, drunkenness, avarice, that he had decided to move on, to share his gifts with a more deserving place, more deserving people. The problem with that theory was that there were no reported sightings of him elsewhere.

Another theory was that the monk had retired to a monastery, to a life of prayer, and had chosen anonymity, which was why his whereabouts were unknown.

One woman claimed to have seen him, standing on a hillside looking upwards to the sky, arms outstretched. She said she watched as a shaft of light hit him and pulled him to his place in Heaven. It was just like the story of Elijah, she said, but without the chariots of fire.

Ishraq thought these ideas fanciful. He suspected there was an earthlier explanation for the monk's disappearance.

He walked for a while. There were people dancing in one of the city squares. Their heads lolled and they had their eyes closed. The watched the puzzling sight until he heard a commotion on the other side of the river and went to the old bridge to see what was happening.

People were heading away from the river, so he followed. Before long he saw what was attracting everyone. There was a long stretch of field. Ishraq judged it at about five hundred feet in length and a hundred in width. At each end were two men holding flags, and at one end five men were mounted on palfreys, all facing down the length of the field. Some of the riders wore brightly coloured clothes. They were knights and the colours were from their coats of arms. The different patterns and colours were a useful means for distinguishing each of the riders and their horses.

In between the riders and flag wavers the grassy track was lined with people from all walks of life, and nearby was a lively market. This was a spectacle, a day out for families and friends. A regular event not to be missed. With a horse race as its main attraction.

Ishraq had been to races before but they were just local affairs, usually between two men who had made and accepted a challenge in an English tavern. *'My horse can beat yours'.* This was much more of an organised event. As well as the market traders there were various kinds of entertainers, all making money from the hundreds of spectators. Several moneylenders were busy, and in the distance was a livestock market.

At every race he had been to there was betting involved but here things were different. It was not just the riders and their immediate friends wagering a day's pay. This was big business. Several men stood halfway along the racetrack receiving bets from rich and poor alike. Ishraq watched and listened. The bets being placed were mostly small coins but sometimes much larger amounts.

He discovered that most of the bets seemed to be placed on one horse and rider, a black stallion whose rider wore a crimson shirt of pure silk adorned with its owner's crest. Ishraq could understand why the horse was so favoured. It looked magnificent in comparison with the

192

other four. He heard the odds being shouted. A winning bet on the stallion would earn less than a winning bet on any of the other horses, but better to win a little than lose.

He ambled towards where the five riders were gathered, each busy keeping their mounts calm in the last moments before the race. Up closer, he saw that the black stallion was indeed a beautiful horse. But he also saw it had weaknesses.

In England Ishraq had worked at Hedingham Castle. There was a marshal there, a man called Tuder ap Win. Tuder was responsible for the stables. He was an evil man, but an expert when it came to horses. Ishraq learned a great deal from him about what to look for when buying for the castle stables. Some horses were best for the plough, others for pulling carriages. Palfreys were riding horses, good for racing.

The black stallion was strong and sturdy with thick bones and good muscle. But it was proving difficult for its rider to control. It was nervous, headstrong.

And there was one horse that Ishraq thought could match the stallion for speed. It was a grey mare. Its rider was the only rider who was clearly not a knight. He wore a simple, undyed linen shirt without a crest, but his bearing spoke of assured confidence. Ishraq wondered whether he was a merchant or a farmer, then thought again. Perhaps he was a professional rider, a former cavalryman maybe. And his horse was calmer than the stallion. It was well balanced and its muscle was in the hind quarters, the most important area for speed.

He compared the riders. The one in crimson also oozed confidence, but in a different way from the rider of the mare. He had too much confidence. Ishraq saw it as arrogance. Whereas the rider in the plain shirt gave only the impression of a man doing his job, something he had done many times before, going about his business with certainty built upon experience. He was undoubtedly a professional rider.

Ishraq needed money. He had used almost all his savings travelling from La Rochelle. His plan was to stow aboard a boat at Avignon, then again at Marseille, but if he could make a little money on this race, he could pay for passage instead. It would make for a more comfortable journey and one with less risk. He checked in the pouch he carried on his belt. He had four deniers, about fourpence in English money. It was enough to buy a decent meal but nowhere near enough for passage.

He decided to take a risk. He approached one of the men taking bets. The man wore a straw hat and a sour look. "What are the odds for the grey?" asked Ishraq.

"One denier wins three. It's all written on the slate there," was the reply.

Ishraq examined the slate by the man's side, on which was written the odds for all five horses. He decided to ignore it. "Make it ten for three," he offered.

The sour man gave a suitably sour response. "I set the odds," he said. "Not you. Anyway, is that all the money you have?"

"Yes."

"Well keep it. Buy some ale with it. The stallion will win."

"Ten for three," repeated Ishraq.

The sour man shrugged. "As you wish. But don't say I didn't warn you." He took the coins and moved on to the next customer.

Ishraq retired just a few paces. He never trusted men who took his money on a promise. He would keep his eyes on this one.

Suddenly there was a roar from the crowd. Ishraq turned to see a flag held high where the riders were. The flag waver waited until the five horses were roughly in line, then swung the flag downwards to his toes. It was the signal for the race to start.

The stallion reared up, over excited, and the grey had made ten yards before the crimson rider regained control.

By contrast, the grey mare moved gracefully, powering forward. But the stallion showed its strength and started to make up ground. The other three horses were heavy footed and slow, and by the halfway

194

point it was a two-horse race. The grey was still ahead but not by much, and with another 150 feet to cover the crowd sensed a victory for the stallion. Ishraq looked round and saw that very few cheered for the grey. Everyone had money on the black.

The horses were now nearing the finish line and the stallion edged ahead, but Ishraq remained confident. He saw a contrast between the two riders. The rider of the mare remained calm, keeping his horse's gallop even and smooth, while the rider of the stallion was putting his horse under pressure, whipping it, his body moving about in the saddle and causing the horse to veer from side to side.

With sixty feet to go the grey edged ahead. The stallion's energy was spent, unable to respond, and it veered further from a straight course. Ishraq smiled. He had won some money.

He went to claim his reward, noting how few others were doing the same.

"You've had a bit of luck there boy," said the sour man as he counted out ten deniers. "You'll be able to spend it all and get drunk tonight."

"Are there to be any other races?" asked Ishraq.

"It's a five-day festival. There's another race this evening and two each day after that. But don't be tempted to try again. You've been lucky. Don't count on more of the same. You'll lose what you've won."

"Thank you for the advice," replied Ishraq.

He took out his pouch and put eight deniers into it. The other two would be his meal and drink for the day.

That afternoon he repeated the exercise, betting his eight deniers and getting thirty back. He could afford a night in a bed at one of the city's inns. And after two more races the following day he had more than a franc, the equivalent of an English pound. It was more money than he had ever held in one go.

At each race the pattern was the same. There was a favourite but that was not the best racer in the field. Ishraq marvelled at how easily the betters were drawn to bet on an inferior horse just because of its looks and because others had.

On the third day he avoided the sour man and went to a different one to place his bets. He reasoned that would be safer than taking a lot of money from a single source.

He now had enough for his passage to Marseille but decided to have one more day at the races. He thought another day might earn him enough for passage even beyond Marseille. So on the morning of the fourth day he went to the track as before and followed the same routine, weighing up the horses and riders before going to place his bet. His chosen horse's rider wore a blue shirt, its crest a griffin.

He decided to bet with the sour man again, but as he waited in a queue it seemed the sour man was deliberately ignoring him, serving others before him. Only when the queue had gone did he receive any attention. He soon discovered why.

"You again," said the sour man, avoiding eye contact.

"Yes. I've come to take a few more deniers from you." It was meant in jest but was not taken that way. "I'll wager a franc on the blue rider to win."

The man lowered his voice. "Now listen here. You have been noticed. I waited for the queue to die down so I could warn you. Winning again today would not be good for your health."

Ishraq scoffed. "I've won a mere fraction of what you earn. An insignificant amount. How can that be worth troubling yourself about?"

"Not me, you fool. There's a man organises the races and takes the lion's share of what I and the others make. And he's a proud man. Doesn't like being bested by a young man of low birth. The amounts don't matter. His pride does."

"So don't tell him."

The sour man lost patience. "Do as you please," he said, snatching the coins from Ishraq's hand. "A full franc at odds of five to one. Your bet is accepted." Another customer was approaching and the sour man turned his back on Ishraq, ending their exchange.

Ishraq retired to watch the race, but his attention was now elsewhere. He was looking for signs of trouble. There were so many faces. More than once he thought he saw someone staring at him, only to find they were returning his own stare.

He settled down to watch the race. He was sure he had bet on the right horse and at first there was no reason to believe otherwise. Then things changed. His chosen horse came under pressure from its rider and was struggling to make ground. It was inexplicable. He knew he had bet correctly.

The favourite moved up and the sense of expectation in the crowd was palpable. The favourite was now alongside Ishraq's horse, then overtook it, winning by a horse's length.

Ishraq was stunned. In one race he had lost almost all the money he had won over the previous two days.

He picked out a figure in the crowd. This man was not just returning Ishraq's stare. He was grinning at Ishraq, mocking him.

And Ishraq knew he had been outfoxed.

Chapter Twenty-Five

Avignon, August 1378

Domenico was still grinning at Ishraq, as if inviting him, daring him to approach. And Ishraq did not disappoint.

"You set that up just to put me in my place," said Ishraq.

"You have an eye for a good horse," replied Domenico. "But you made one bet too many. Come. I will buy you ale as consolation."

Ishraq was intrigued. And thirsty. So he agreed.

As they drank, Domenico told Ishraq his name. "You are the race fixer," said Ishraq.

"No, but I work for the man who is."

"And you decided to teach me a lesson."

Domenico laughed. "You are less important than you think. The favourite was always destined to win that race. Think about it. If favourites never won nobody would bet on them. And my master doesn't bribe all the riders, just the ones he thinks have a chance to win. Occasionally he gets it wrong and another wins, which is good. It adds to the credibility. It's all part of the game. You were just unfortunate, or maybe you should have stopped while you were winning. But tell me about yourself. How do you know about horses?"

"I learned in England. My teacher was good, with horses at least. He was not so good with people."

"Many men are better with animals. But let us talk about you. Now you have no money to finish your journey to Marseille."

"You know about that."

"Of course. Information is everything in my business. So what will you do?"

"Find free passage. That was my plan before and will have to be again."

"Or you could earn some money working with me for a while, to pay for passage in luxury. Unless you are in a hurry, of course."

"Working with you?"

"Yes. You saw the livestock sales. You would be my buyer and seller."

Ishraq nodded, understanding. "Picking out the best."

"Not always. The favourites must be carefully chosen also. They have to look better than they are."

"You would have me deceive honest people out of the money they need for food on the table."

"Gamblers deceive themselves. They need no help from us."

"I'm not sure. It feels wrong."

Domenico stood up. "Come with me, Meet the man you would be working for. He is buying a horse as we speak. Maybe he will persuade you."

Ishraq agreed. He had nothing to lose. So they walked together to the sales ring. Some sales were happening by auction and others by private sale. A man was negotiating a purchase. Domenico made the introductions. "This is Erich," he said. "And this is the man I told you about, Erich. The one who has been doing so well at the races. This is Ishraq."

"Greetings, Ishraq. What do you think of this fine mare I'm buying? I'd welcome your thoughts."

Ishraq felt he was on trial, but went to gently pat her, soothing and calming her. He gave her some hay before checking all round, paying most attention to its back, neck, belly and legs. "A fine horse," he said. "But for one thing."

Erich was taken aback. "What? What have you seen?"

"She chews only on one side of her mouth, and her breath is bad. She has a problem, maybe a broken tooth. If I'm right, she will be irritable and unmanageable. I would have it checked before buying."

Erich looked at Domenico, then at the man who was selling the mare. Domenico stepped forward, taking hold of the horse's mouth, intending to part the lips to see inside. As he did so, the horse reared. Domenico was lucky not to get hurt. But it was clear that Ishraq had been right. The horse was in pain.

"I'll let you have her for half the price," said the seller hurriedly.

Erich grabbed the man by the collar. "You knew!" she hissed, then kicked the man in the stomach as punishment.

"I've ridden horses all my life," said Erich to Ishraq. "I know more than most do and would have spotted that before too long. What impresses me is how quickly you saw it. You saved me money. I think you can be valuable to me, and I pay well."

"I need only enough to get me to Marseille."

"Then it's agreed. You will work with me until you have the money for Marseille." Erich gave Ishraq a firm pat on the back.

Whether Ishraq liked it or not, he was now Erich's employee. "I will take no part in your fixed races," he said. "I will advise on your stock and no more."

"As you like."

Ishraq still felt uncomfortable, but at least he had placed a limit on his complicity. It eased his conscience just enough. He had a new job, and his prospects for Marseille had improved immeasurably.

Chapter Twenty-Six

The Villa Libera, Avignon, August 1378

Lella was surprised to meet the new addition to Erich's kingdom. Ishraq was unlike most of Erich's men.

The first task Erich gave Ishraq was an audit of the stock in the stables at the Villa Libera. Lella watched the process.

Ishraq was slow, purposeful, thorough in his approach. He picked out several issues with the horses, mostly minor but in one case more serious. One of Erich's favourite horses had a fetlock weakness, caused by wear and tear or possibly an underlying fracture. Ishraq was able to point out that the condition might worsen over time if the horse was overused.

Lella was impressed. She was also at a loose end since Matty left, and the opportunity to spend a little time with Ishraq, to get to know him more, appealed to her.

So they talked, and Ishraq shared with Lella his dream of finding his home, the place from which he had been taken and enslaved. And as she listened, Lella felt a sudden emptiness.

The following day Ishraq had little to do. The stable hands were competent and there were no new horses to examine. Domenico told him there was a big fair they would be going to within the week, but until then his duties would be light. It seemed he was being paid well for little work. He did not mind. It was a means to an end, but he was already feeling bored.

Lella found him a short distance from the house, sitting by a tree. She sat beside him. When she spoke, her words were slurred. She had been drinking despite the early hour.

She launched into a monologue. "I envy you. We're very alike, you and I, except that you have a plan to escape. I will be here for as long as Erich wants me. Though maybe that won't be for long. He comes to our bed now only occasionally. Why? Because he hires younger girls as servants and uses them when he wants to. I'm old now in his eyes."

Ishraq thought she was telling him very personal things considering they had just met. He was unsure why, and he felt uncomfortable. "You are young and beautiful," he told her, almost in a whisper.

"How old are you, Ishraq? Sixteen? Seventeen? Not yet twenty, that's for sure. You will have eyes now for girls your own age, but as you get older you will still look for the same girls, young ones, just as Erich does. I know. Ever since my flowering I have had to endure old men, ugly and stinking of sweat and ale, panting as they take their fill of me. And that is why I am now afraid. If Erich tires of me completely, I will have to go back to that. It will be how I will survive."

She sobbed. He put his arm round her to comfort her. She drew away. "If Erich sees you do that you will not survive the day."

"I'm sorry. I thought…"

"No. It's I should be sorry. I said too much."

They sat for a while with no more said, until Ishraq broke the silence. "I told you the dream I have. What is yours?"

"I'm glad you dream of better things, but for me, and for the others here, it is dangerous to dream. Forgive me. I seem to be pouring my heart out these days to anyone who comes here. I did the same with the English black monk."

Ishraq's eyes widened. "The Benedictine? He was here?"

Lella was flustered. "No, no. Forget what I said. Nobody comes here."

Ishraq knew she lied. The man known as the Benedictine had been here. He wanted to know more.

Before he could ask, Lella's mood changed. She looked vacant, her eyes high in her head, oblivious to Ishraq's presence. It was as though she was possessed. He knew she had been drinking but he had never seen such effects from alcohol, and if wine was the cause why had she seemed more alert minutes earlier?

202

She started to dance, turning in circular motions round and round, head bent backwards and eyes closed. Her arms were held out wide.

Then Ishraq witnessed another sudden change. Lella wore a terrified look, staring open-mouthed into space, focused on a single point. She screamed. "Va via!" she shouted. She fought the air, as if fighting an invisible foe, telling it to go away, then convulsed and fell at Ishraq's feet.

Ishraq did not know what to do, but fortunately Lella's episode did not last long. He heard her moan and she began to come back into the world she had temporarily left. He helped her to sit up and the colour returned to her face.

"What happened?" he asked.

"I don't know. It was like a nightmare. There was a beast. I shouted for it to go away." She fought the air again as she remembered her encounter with some demon. Ishraq held her hands until she stopped fighting the imagined creature.

"Has it happened before?"

She hesitated. "Yes," she said.

"How much wine did you have?"

"No more than usual. And I've had the dreams when I haven't been drinking. They are never quite the same. The beasts are horrible but always different. This time it was a wild boar, taller than the tallest man. It had big teeth, and human hands." She shuddered.

"Have you told anyone?"

"No. If I tell Erich he will think the same as you, that I drink too much. And if I tell a priest or physician, he will say I have a demon, or must have done something evil to be punished so."

"You were dancing."

"Was I? When it comes on, I feel hot, like I'm on fire. I didn't know about the dancing."

203

A memory came to Ishraq. "There were people dancing when I arrived in the city. I thought nothing of it then, but now I think of it they danced just as you just did."

"Coincidence?"

"Maybe. But the thing I did notice was that the dancers seemed to be in a world of their own. You were the same."

"I'm feeling tired," said Lella. "I think I will retire to my room."

She stood to go. "Just one thing," said Ishraq. "Do you go to the races?"

"No. Never. Erich wouldn't let me."

"Try to persuade him. You would enjoy it. There's much to see and the races are colourful and exciting. I will be there at the next ones, because it's my job here."

"I will ask him. Maybe he will let you be my chaperone."

****

The following morning was again quiet for Ishraq, until Erich saw him. "You are going to earn your pay tomorrow," said Erich. "I want you to go to a small country house near Villeneuve. Domenico will take you."

"Am I buying a horse?"

"No. You will be pretending to be interested in one the owner has for sale. The owner knows you will be coming. But I have no wish to buy anything. I have no need for another horse."

"What then?"

"The owner has entered one of his horses in a race this weekend and I want you to find out about it. Is it a winner or a loser?"

"You have no influence over this man?"

"No. That is why I need to know how good it is."

Ishraq decided to be bold on behalf of Lella. "I spoke with your lady yesterday. She says she doesn't get to the races. Forgive my forwardness, but I think she would enjoy them."

Erich frowned and gave Ishraq an angry look. "You are more than forward. You are insolent." But then he considered the suggestion. "It might be a good idea, though. I will think on it," he added.

Chapter Twenty-Seven

Villeneuve, Avignon, August 1378

It was a short journey. Ishraq and Domenico arrived at their destination by noon.

The chateau was typically French, built on a hilltop plateau overlooking the valley. It's position had been chosen for defence and it had a dry sunken area around it where a moat had once added another layer of protection. Conical towers and a bridged entrance drew the eye on arrival.

They were taken into the cool of the chateau's hall. Ishraq was glad to be out of the midday heat. The cold fruit drinks the host provided for him and Domenico were welcome refreshment.

There was no rush to get down to business. A plate of fish followed the fruit drinks and then there was ale, pork and bread, all served on silver tableware.

The host's name was Oudin. Ishraq did not know if he was titled, a former mercenary like Erich or simply a merchant made good. He did not care to ask. Instead he just enjoyed the food and ale while Domenico did the small talk. It was clear that Domenico and Oudin knew one another well. They discussed a range of things of little interest to Ishraq, such as the likely quality of the year's grape harvest.

When the conversation turned to politics, Ishraq listened only half-heartedly. But he did hear what was said about the word from Rome. It seemed that the decision to appoint an Italian pope rather than a Frenchman was being reconsidered.

According to Oudin, the man who had been made pope was already proving a disappointment to the cardinals. He was joyless, they said. Oudin was gleeful, because it meant Avignon was not yet done, and he still had hope for his businesses, whatever they might be.

Finally, they ran out of things to talk about and moved on to the purpose of the visit. Oudin did a hard sell, extolling the virtues of the horse he had for a sale. It was a foal, a filly. According to Oudin, it was the product of a match made in Heaven between a wonderful stallion and a superb mare.

Domenico had explained Ishraq's presence. Oudin took them to see the foal and Ishraq's job began. He examined, poked and prodded, nodding or shaking his head as he did so. All for show. "A fine beast," he declared.

Domenico scratched his forehead. "I agree. A bit young, though," he said. "We're after something more mature. Perhaps next year. I wouldn't mind another ale, though. It's thirsty work in this heat."

"Of course," replied Oudin, only a touch of disappointment in his voice. He enjoyed being the host. "Let's retire to the hall for the afternoon."

Domenico gave Ishraq a look, a signal. "Is it all right if I have a wander," Ishraq said. "I've had enough ale for one day." In truth, he would happily have downed several more tankards.

Domenico looked to Oudin for approval. "Feel free," said Oudin. "But don't be tempted by my silver. You'll be searched when you leave."

Ishraq laughed, sharing the joke, if that was what it was. Then he strolled around the chateau grounds, acting as casually as he could but heading back to the stables.

He visited the stalls, which were open and accessible. Several boys were busy grooming the horses. They were good horses, but not racehorses. They were all workhorses for the chateau's farm. So he explored further. And found a fenced compound. If Oudin possessed more valuable horses, this would be where they were kept.

He saw the rider of the first horse he had bet on, the skilled rider who had worn the undyed linen shirt. The man was walking towards the enclosure's gate. Ishraq followed him and tried the gate, but the rider had barred it from the other side. Whatever was inside was not for public viewing.

He wandered some more until Domenico and Oudin found him. "Are you ready to go?" Domenico asked him.

"Yes," he replied. Then he made an aside to Oudin. "The silver is loaded on my horse."

Oudin laughed and patted him on the back, while Domenico thanked Oudin for his hospitality. "Shame about the foal," he said. "Maybe in a year's time if it is still for sale."

"Come back any time, just to eat, drink and talk."

On the journey home, Domenico asked Ishraq if he had discovered anything of value. "Oudin has at least one horse he keeps from prying eyes, and a good rider to go with it," he replied. "If I am allowed to bet on the race, I will bet on Oudin's horse."

"Did you see it?"

"No. I didn't need to."

It was late when they got back to Erich's. They parted and Ishraq made for his dormitory room. But he was intercepted before he reached it. Lella had been awaiting his arrival.

"A successful day?" she asked.

"I suppose so. Tiring though." It was an attempt to get her to leave him alone. It was too late for this.

But Lella did not take the hint. "I owe you a debt," she said. "Erich says I can go to the races this week."

"I didn't think he would listen to me."

"He asked me whether I wanted to go and I have ways to get him to say yes. By the time we had finished he was the happiest man in Avignon."

Ishraq did not want to hear the details. "Good," he said. "But now I must sleep."

"Of course. See you tomorrow."

That night, Ishraq slept fitfully. There was a great deal on his mind. About his new job. Had he sold his soul to the Devil? About the Benedictine monk. Where had he gone to? But mostly about Lella. She wanted to spend time with him. It was just friendship, totally

208

innocent. But would Erich see it that way? Lella seemed unafraid but Ishraq thought she was playing a dangerous game, one that also meant danger for himself. Both their lives were at stake.

****

On the day of the races, Erich's entourage set off for the city. As well as Domenico, Ishraq and Lella, there was one of Erich's mercenaries there as protection in the absence of Jaro, who was still out searching for the Benedictine. The group was completed by a lad to see to the horses and two young maids.

One of the maids was there to see to Lella's needs and the other, a young African girl, was for Erich. After what Lella had told him, Ishraq could not help but wonder what that girl's duties entailed.

Erich's personal maid was very young, maybe thirteen or fourteen years old. Ishraq watched her as they rode, trying to glean something about her mood. But she kept her eyes down all the while, silently hiding her feelings, her emotions.

As they neared the race field, Ishraq saw another group of people dancing, eyes closed as before. He watched them for a while. He saw again the similarities to Lella's dancing. It could not be a coincidence.

Erich was busy, talking with other men who had come for their day at the races. So Ishraq took the opportunity to go to the dancers and try to find out more. There was a priest there, helping a young man. Ishraq asked what was happening.

"Holy Fire," said the priest. "That's what's happening."

"Holy Fire?"

"You don't know of it? It's a plague, of sorts. No buboes. But like the plague it won't go away. It's an evil thing, the work of the Devil."

"It makes them dance."

"Sufferers tell of visions. Some call it St Anthony's Fire because he had similar visions when he was tempted by the Devil."

Ishraq thought about what Lella had told him she saw. "Do they see strange beings, part man and part beast?"

"Yes, and other things. Bright lights."

"Do they feel on fire?"

"Yes. You know someone with those symptoms?"

"Maybe. What becomes of them?"

The priest rolled up the breeches of the young man he was examining. "Look," he said. "And smell." The young man's skin was black and rotten. "His leg will rot away. And look here." This time he revealed the young man's arm. It also was black and rotten. "Holy Fire will kill him, in time."

"Is there a cure?"

"Prayer to cast out the demons. There's something the Benedictine monks make that some say works, though I've never seen it used. All I know is that many die, though the poor always seem worst affected."

Ishraq wanted to ask more but heard Erich's voice calling him to join the entourage. They were about to go to the race field.

He re-joined the group and watched Lella for signs she had noticed the dancers. If anything, she seemed deliberately to look away from them. And it came to him. She knew. She saw them and with that knew her own future. It was why she wanted Erich not to know. If he did, her time with him would surely be brought to an end.

With that in mind it was good for him to see Lella's joy as the day unfolded. Erich advised her which horses to bet on and without exception she chose a winner, joyfully unaware the races were fixed.

One of the horses she bet on was Oudin's. Ishraq could not help but notice how Lella looked at the handsome, confident rider in his pale shirt. He hoped Erich had not noticed. And the race went as predicted. There was a favourite, just like before, but it was no match for Oudin's horse.

Ishraq had earned his pay. Erich gave him a smile of approval. He stood to win a great deal, both by betting on the winner but also because he controlled the betting. His men had taken large amounts from all those who bet on the favourite. Erich celebrated by taking wine and the young African maid to an empty hospitality tent. There were no smiles for Lella.

The day was declared a success, and the entourage visited a tavern before setting off back to the villa. When they did, Ishraq excused himself. He told Erich he wanted some time to himself, to pray at a nearby church.

Erich was surprised. "You're Christian? I thought you'd be Muslim."

"I was brought up in the Christian faith, yes."

"You're full of surprises. Well, don't run away. My spies will find you."

"I have passage to Marseille to pay for, remember. I'm staying until then." In truth, a few days earlier he would indeed have made his escape despite the risks. He did not like the situation he had got himself into. But now he felt a responsibility. Lella's story haunted him and he wanted to help her, and maybe the African girl as well.

The church was near to where the priest had been helping the victims of Holy Fire. He hoped it meant it was the priest's church. And he was in luck. As he entered, he saw the same priest laying out the vessels for the evening Sacrament.

"If I may," he said. "We spoke this morning and you told me something. I would like to know more. You said the Benedictines have a cure for Holy Fire."

"There's an abbey that has the relics of St Anthony. Wine is made there, blessed with the relics. It is said to be a cure."

"Where is this abbey?"

"Far away. More than a hundred miles. Almost to the Alps. But there's another Benedictine abbey not far from here, the abbey Saint Andre in Villeneuve. It's an important place, a royal abbey, charged by the king to oversee many of the priories in this part of France. Cardinals from all around come to it for their vacations. Perhaps a place of such status will have some of the wine."

"Have you tried the remedy?"

211

The priest looked contrite. "To my great shame, I long since gave up hope for the poor unfortunates. I believe their fate is preordained. You must have somebody you care about to go to this trouble, and I wish you well. Perhaps you will find the cure. If so, I would ask you to tell me what you find."

As Ishraq re-joined the entourage, a man approached Erich and started hurling abuse. His clothes were ragged and his appearance dishevelled. It was clear he had lost heavily at the races and he looked like a man who could not afford the loss. He was accusing Erich of fixing the races.

The man's rage subsided and he asked Erich for help, saying he would have no means to feed his family for the rest of the week.

Erich's response was calm and reasonable. He told the man that he would help him, then turned to his bodyguard and told him to go with the man *'to assist him fully'*. When the bodyguard returned there was blood on his tunic.

Ishraq knew what *'assistance'* the man had been given. He felt sick and even more angry with himself for accepting work with such a man as Erich.

On the journey home, Lella's mood was euphoric. She fawned over Erich, whose response was muted politeness. Ishraq worried that she might slip into another episode of Holy Fire. Thankfully she did not.

Ishraq rode with Domenico. "Oudin's horse was impressive," he said. "Perhaps Erich should buy it." He was planting a seed, because he wanted to return to Oudin's, from where he could slip away and visit the abbey where there might be a cure for Lella's disease.

Part Six

The Cave

Chapter Twenty-Eight

The River Rhone, August 1378

Matty was hungry. He had foraged a few berries and had spring water to drink but it was not enough. At home he was able to discern the plants that were edible, but the plants here were things he was unfamiliar with. Were the mushrooms poisonous? Were the roots and leaves of other plants safe? He had no way of knowing. So he decided he had to find a human route to food, a farm or village.

Instead, he came upon a boat moored by the river. He watched from a distance and saw it was a large river cog carrying salt and heading towards Avignon, the place he wished to avoid. But he needed food. He could see two men on deck and one in the aft cabin. He decided to take a risk.

He had no money and nothing to trade. He would have to plead to the men's mercy and kindness. He slung the crossbow over his shoulder. Carrying it in his hands would have looked more threatening. He hailed the men in French. The response was in English.

"Your accent is terrible, monsieur. But come anyway," said one of the boatmen.

Matty boarded the cog. "Are you after a free ride?" asked the boatman.

"I offer a couple of hours' labour in return for a little food and drink," replied Matty. "But I must be put ashore on the far bank of the river before we reach the city."

The man looked at him with suspicion. "I don't like cities," added Matty.

The boatman decided to ask no questions. It was none of his business. But one thing bothered him. "There's always work to do on my boat," he said. "But you would have to give me the crossbow. I don't allow such weapons on board." Matty nodded and handed over the crossbow and arrows. The boatman was satisfied. "I have loose salt that needs to be put into bags," he added. "Can you do that?"

"Gladly."

The boatman showed Matty what needed doing and he set to work. As he did, another memory came to him. His last one had been of running away from his home village, pursued as a possible carrier of plague. Now he remembered what happened next.

He had been hungry, just as he was now. A family of canal boat people had helped him. Martha and her family. He remembered their kindness, and Martha's wonderful cooking.

After Matty had toiled for more than an hour, the boatman came to him. "You need a rest," he said. "Sit. And have this." It was a piece of fish with a jug of ale to wash it down. Matty ate and drank greedily.

"You've not eaten for a while then." It was a comment, not a question. "Are you heading for the abbey?"

Matty was puzzled by the question, then realised he still wore his monk's clothing. He nodded. It seemed a good way to avoid other questions about his origin or destination. "How far is it?" he asked.

"We'll drop you on a bend north of the abbey. It's as near as we can get without you being seen." He gave Matty a knowing look. "It's a short walk from the river. Just head south. And you can relax until we're there. You've done enough to earn your food and ale for one day, old man." Matty was grateful. He baulked a little to be referred to as an old man, but he was relieved there was no more work to do. In truth, he was no longer able to do a full day of manual work without suffering for it afterwards.

Alone now as the boat slowly made its way along the Rhone, Matty reflected again on his latest memories, hoping to trigger more. But nothing new came to him. He wept inside as he revisited the frustration of knowing he had a wife and children who were out there, alive, somewhere beyond his reach, somewhere in England.

His childhood and young adulthood were the most complete pieces he now had of the puzzle. He had names. Meg. Edmund. He had pictures of his family in his head. There were sights, sounds and smells he could associate with his past. But the pieces that were still missing were crucial. Things in his most recent years of life. In a real sense he felt no further forward. He wondered how long it would take for them to come back to him.

The boat started to pull into the shore. The boatman pointed out a rough track. "Just follow that," he said. "You can't go wrong. The abbey is protected by a fort. Once you see that you will find the abbey."

The boatman gave Matty the crossbow back and Matty said his thanks. He looked back across the river and saw that he was opposite the tip of a river island. "That's Barthelasse," said the boatman. A man was there, weeding in a field. The man put down his hoe and stared at him, a moment of recognition.

Matty cursed his monk's habit. It was too easily recognisable. By the end of the day Erich would surely know where he was.

He looked to the sky. There was not much light left in the day. He was desperate for more food and a good night's sleep. He decided he would be safe enough at the abbey just for one night, so followed the track towards Villeneuve.

The wind was getting up, gusting and making progress difficult, and he had to climb a steep hill, but he arrived at the fort just before dusk. Its stone walls looked recently built.

A guard at the fort entrance was about to close the gate for the night but saw Matty approach. The monk's robes Matty wore earned him a respectful welcome.

"Juste à temps," said the guard. *Just in time*. He made a motion with his hand indicating the strength of the wind. "Mistral," he said.

The guard asked no questions. It would be for the monks at the abbey to decide whether to let the visiting monk have a bed for the night. The guard knew it would be a formality. They rarely turned anyone away. He led Matty to the abbey door, knocked and immediately left Matty alone, waiting to be admitted.

The duty monk opened the door and took Matty straight to the kitchens. Pilgrims at this time of night were invariably hungry after a full day's walking. "Do you speak English?" asked Matty.

"Oui. Yes. I do," was the reply. "Do you wish to stay long with us?"

"One night only, thank you. I will leave at dawn."

"As you wish. I will take the weapons you carry. You will get them back when you leave. Will you join us for prayers at midnight?" It was an assumption based on Matty's apparel. Matty was tired but nodded. It was easier than trying to give reason why he would not.

So it was that after little more than an hour's sleep Matty awoke to the sound of a hand bell calling the monks to Mass. He was in one of the guest houses for visiting monks. He had expected a dormitory but the abbey was so large he had a room to himself. There were guest houses for the poor and larger ones for visiting dignitaries. Drowsily, he followed a group of several monks They walked to the quire near the high altar. Lay brothers sat separately in a quire by the nave.

He tried to follow the service but struggled. It was all he could do to stay awake, and to avoid giving away his lack of familiarity with the proceedings. Somehow, he managed by miming the chants and prayers.

When the service finished, he expected to return to the guest house. Instead, one of the monks approached him and wordlessly beckoned him to follow.

They passed through the cloisters and came to the abbot's accommodation. The entrance hall had a high ceiling and there was a grand staircase leading to an upper floor.

Matty was taken into a study. There sat the abbot, reading by candlelight. The room was cold even though a lively fire was burning. The abbot's mitre and staff were on a table nearby.

The abbot put down his book and half turned towards Matty, beckoning him to sit, then looked him up and down. "I know who you are," he said.

"I am nobody," replied Matty.

"No. You are somebody. Because all southern France seems to seek you. I have been visited by a priest, Frere Jean and representatives both from Rome and the Archbishop of Cambrai, all wanting to know if you have been here. Also, I am well informed of the movements of local, how shall I say, entrepreneurs. One of them is looking for you with utmost diligence. So I told my people here to let me know if you turned up at our humble abbey."

"Humble?"

"Maybe not in size, but in spirit, I can assure you. Our calling is to work tirelessly and be self-sufficient. But of course you know that being a Benedictine yourself."

"I mean no trouble. I will move on at dawn."

The abbot now fully turned to face Matty. "I do not think that would be wise. I fear for your safety."

"I was seen this evening as I arrived in Villeneuve."

The abbot nodded. "We can offer sanctuary."

"This is a big place. You have a bakery, a mill, stables and daily visitors from the town. It only takes one to realise there'd be a reward if he reported me to whoever pays most."

"It might still be your safest option until they lose interest in you."

"I don't know."

"Think on it. But also, I have a request to make. I'm told you are a healer."

"Of sorts."

"A young man arrived yesterday. He seeks help for a friend. We have a fine infirmary, one of the best in France but could not help him. Your reputation intrigues me. Perhaps you can succeed where we failed. Would you see him before you leave tomorrow?"

"I need to leave early, but yes I will see him if he rises early enough."

"Good. I will see that he is brought to you. Now, get some sleep. You will need it. And I will pray for you, my son. God be with you." He made the sign of the cross.

Matty was given a lantern and returned to the guest house. It was pitch black and completely silent. It felt a little eerie. He opened the door and put a foot inside. Then he realised there was something wrong. He had left a window open, but in the moonlight, he could see it was closed. Cautiously, he entered the room.

He held his lantern high. It cast a shadow on the whitewashed wall behind him, the figure of a man with his hand raised, holding a dagger. Matty rolled away just in time before the hand came down. He extinguished the lantern and moved to a position in a corner opposite the window, away from the light. And waited.

There was a rustling as his assailant tried to find his way in the dark. Matty remained still until he saw what he had hoped for, a silhouette cast against the glow of the window. He jumped up and grabbed the arm that was holding the dagger, then put his forearm around the man's neck.

The assailant still had one hand free and he was strong. He took hold of the arm Matty had round his neck and started to pull it away. Then, just as suddenly he let go and used his elbow to deliver a blow to Matty's ribs.

Matty was winded. He tried to hold on to the man's dagger hand, but a second blow to the ribs doubled him over. He was now at the mercy of his attacker. Without the strength to stand and fight back he stayed low and rolled away into the shadows of the room.

The attacker needed light so he could see where Matty was and finish him off. He found the lantern and took out a flint to light it. It was a mistake. The flash gave away his position.

Matty pulled at the attacker's foot and used his body to unbalance him. He went for the hand with the dagger for a second time. This time, he managed to twist the attacker's wrist and take the dagger from him, but that sapped his remaining strength and he rolled away again, finding another corner. He was panting from the effort he had expended.

Matty's assailant could hear him. He lit the lantern and now could see him. But Matty had the advantage of the dagger. For a moment there was a standoff. Matty's opponent was uncertain. Matty awaited his next move.

Voices came from the corridor. People were running. The alarm had been raised. It forced the attacker to consider his position, and he chose to flee, running out and pushing past two monks who had responded to the commotion in Matty's room.

Matty did not give chase. He was simply glad still to be alive.

The two monks came into the room. There was much confusion, much chatter, questions being asked. Until the arrival of the abbot calmed everyone down.

The abbot looked concerned. Matty re-assured him that he was unharmed. "Now you see why I cannot stay," he said.

"I think this is not the reason you wish to leave. We can protect you. I will post men at your door. But you are troubled, my son. I feel it. You do not think you belong here, but you do not know just where you do belong. Stay. We can help you."

"You are right to say I am troubled. But the answer is not here. The answer lies in England, where I belong."

For the rest of the night, Matty stayed awake, keeping alert against another attack. As dawn approached, he made his way to the infirmary as promised.

The young man the abbot had spoken about was there, waiting for him. A warm herbal drink was provided while they talked.

Ishraq's visit to Oudin had been brief. He asked if Oudin's prize horse was for sale. Oudin said 'no' and Ishraq left for the abbey, only to learn they had none of the wine that might cure Lella. Then he was told of the arrival of a man who might be able to help him. So he stayed the night.

He introduced himself, then got straight to the point. "You are the Benedictine, the healer," said Ishraq. "There's a woman who needs your help. She has the Holy Fire."

Matty knew of the disease. Holy Fire, or St Anthony's Fire. He had seen it in England and northern France. Often it was mistaken for plague. There was no known treatment.

"I was in a battle in England," he told Ishraq. "I was wounded and lost my memory. For a while I thought my name was Stephen and that I was a monk. Now I remember who I am. I am not a Benedictine. My name is Matty. Stephen was my friend, and he was a great physician. I have tried to be like him, but those who think I am special have it wrong. I am not who they say."

"So you will not help me."

"I cannot help you. There is no cure for Holy Fire."

Ishraq pleaded. "You are my last hope."

Matty thought for a moment. "When Stephen was faced with a new problem, he always asked questions that other physicians did not. They relied on old explanations or signs in the stars. He used the information he took from the sick themselves."

"Then ask me some questions."

Matty nodded. "What are her symptoms?"

"She talks of burning inside. She is hallucinating and has a rash on her skin. But so far her skin has not blackened like the others in the city."

"All things that are evidence of Holy Fire. Where does she live?"

"In a grand house in the countryside."

"Are there other sufferers there?"

"No. I don't think so. But there are in the city."

Matty thought some more. "When plague came it was worst in the towns and cities, where people congregated together. I took my daughter away to keep her safe. But you say your friend is already living apart from other sufferers. That is interesting. You must talk to her. Look for clues. Find something she has in common with the sufferers but not those she lives with. Use your wisdom. Search for connections. That is the way you may be able to help her."

"Is that all you can do? Can't you call upon some higher power to protect her? Pray for her even?"

"You are her best hope, not me. As for prayer, I have my doubts that it works. I do pray, because I see no reason not to."

Ishraq shook his head. "I hoped for more."

"Most people do. I must go now."

There was one more thing for Ishraq to do. He had to be sure, for Edwina's sake. "You were wounded," he said. "I too have been in a battle. In England. The battle at Rottingdean."

There was no moment of recognition. The name meant nothing to Matty. "Were you hurt?" asked Matty.

"No. But many were."

Matty shook his head. "Why do men have to wage war?"

"I don't know. It's a mystery to me."

They parted. Ishraq was satisfied. The man known as the Benedictine had no memory of Rottingdean, so could not be Edwina's father. He set off to return to Avignon, to the Villa Libera.

The monks gave Matty some food, two candles and a flint to light them with. He reclaimed his weapons, the sword, crossbow and arrows. Then he headed north, because England was to the north. He would follow the North Star. Somewhere in England was his home. *Get to England*, he told himself. *Then find your family*.

Chapter Twenty-Nine

The Villa Libera, Avignon, September 1378

When Ishraq got back to the villa, Domenico was quick to scoff at the unsuccessful trip to Oudin's stables. "I knew he would never sell," he bragged. "Now get back to doing what you are paid for."

There was no sign of Lella. It was frustrating. Ishraq wanted to talk to her in the way the monk had advised. He had no optimism about the outcome, but it was all he had to give him hope for her. He felt a bond with her. They both knew what it was to be a slave.

In the daytime he busied himself around the stables. He observed the men and women around the Villa Libera. He was looking for signs of anyone who seemed disaffected, unhappy working for Erich, or who simply had too loose a tongue. He also hoped to see the African girl.

One man stood out. He was an older man. He was known as Brasero, meaning fire pit, the name given to him when he was the blacksmith in Erich's old mercenary company. Now he was just a general dogsbody. His demeanour was sour and he drank more than was good for his health. Ishraq decided to cultivate him for information.

There was no tavern near the villa. There was no need for one. Plenty of ale and wine was to be had from Erich's personal store. Each evening the main villa staff would meet up in the grounds and share jokes, play music, sing songs and slake their thirst.

One evening, Ishraq saw an opportunity. When everyone else had retired for the night, he was left alone with Brasero.

Brasero had already drank too much, but Ishraq plied him with more. And before long it began to pay dividends.

"They tell me you were an important man," said Ishraq. "Good with metal. No-one finer, they say."

Brasero's speech was slurred but his mind was clear. "I was that. Without me, Erich's men would have lost many battles and skirmishes. Blunt swords are a death wish."

"You and he must go back a long way."

"Yes, though you'd never know it. All I do here is fetch and carry. *Brasero get me this! Brasero get me that!* And its humiliating. Today my job was to collect a whore from the city and bring her here. Tomorrow, I take her back. What sort of job is that?"

"Your loyalty is commendable."

Brasero was being listened to for once and opened further. "And something else. Erich plays a dangerous game with the church. He courts the bishop sent by Pope Urban while keeping counsel with Archbishop Robert." He leaned in conspiratorially. "Did you know there are rumours of a meeting. Some cardinals want Robert to be pope. And he loves it. There will be a war and Erich will find himself having to choose sides. No good will come of it, mark my words."

Ishraq was not interested in the politics of the church, or in Erich's scheming. But Erich's whoring was of interest. "You say you brought a woman to him and he is with her now. What of his mistress, Lella?"

"Ha! He keeps her in her own apartments, out of the way. When he wants her, he takes her to his bed, but when his eyes land on a maid or a woman from the city, Lella is forgotten."

Brasero was now feeling the effects of the alcohol. He felt sick. He was also realising he was saying too much. He leaned in again. "You will not tell anybody what I have told you, will you?"

"Of course not. I am to be trusted for my discretion."

Brasero nodded, but now he was losing his senses, drifting into a drunken stupor. Ishraq got up and left him slouched in his chair, hands holding on to the edge of the table.

The information from Brasero created an opportunity. Erich was occupied with his whore. Lella would be in her own rooms. Ishraq could go to her without risk of disturbance from Erich.

He had never been to the part of the villa that was Erich and Lella's private domain, but he knew which stairs led there. He climbed them. There were two corridors, one to the right and one to the left. He had no idea which led to Lella and which to Erich.

224

He went to the right, passing some storerooms and what looked like a small reception room. Lella's personal maid was there. She heard him and stared at him. "What are you doing here? This area is forbidden. If the master finds out you are here…"

"I need to speak with your lady. It's urgent. I have information for her ears only. She will want to see me. Please, tell her I am here."

The maid hesitated. "Stay here," she said. "If you move one step further, I will scream and you will be dead before the scream fades."

He held up his hands in a gesture of acquiescence, and she went into the room. When she came out, she wore a stern look. "You will get us all killed," she said. "My lady says you can go in. But be brief. I will keep watch for anyone coming. But remember what I said. One wrong word, one step too many and I will call the guards."

"Understood."

He went in. Lella was sitting in the dark. A solitary candle provided the weakest possible light, just enough for him to avoid bumping into furniture, but not enough to illuminate her face. She did not look directly at him, but he thought she had been crying.

"You are brave to come here," she said. "Or foolish,"

"I'm assured Erich is busy for the night."

She laughed. "Of course. But if you were seen, it will be reported."

"A chance I take."

"So, what do you want with me?"

"Your sickness. Is it worse?"

"No. Neither better. I look at my arms and legs every few minutes. Waiting for the blackness to appear."

"I spoke with a great healer. The one they call the Benedictine. I told him about you."

Now she turned her face towards him. "What did he say?"

He decided to be honest with her. "He said he knows no cure for Holy Fire but told me what to do. I need to ask you some questions. I have been thinking what to ask."

She frowned and sighed. "No cure. My last hope gone."

"Please, answer my questions. It might help. Is anyone else at the villa afflicted with Holy Fire?" She shook her head. "Do you go to the city, to the poorest districts where others have the sickness?"

Again she shook her head. "Why would I?"

He paused for thought. "The monk said I must search for connections between you and the other sufferers. If you never go to the city, I cannot think what else to ask."

"My maid goes to the city. She has family there."

"Are they poor?"

"Very."

"Does she carry the sickness?"

"No. She is well."

He stepped forward, daring to enter Lella's personal space. "There must be something. He told me to look for clues, to find something you have in common with the sufferers but not those you live with."

She thought for a moment. "My maid brings me bread. Her mother works where they bake it. It's awful but I eat it because it pleases my maid to bring me a gift. She has no money to buy me anything. The bread is all she has to give."

"Do you have some here?"

"Yes. There's a piece on the table. Light another candle to see it."

Ishraq lit a candle and saw the bread. It was dark in colour, not unusual for bread made with cheap rye flour, the food of the poor. He examined it but was struggling still to make a connection. He remembered Matty's advice. "So no-one else here has the sickness and the only connection between you and those in the city is this bread. Is that right?"

"I suppose so."

"Then stop eating the bread."

The extra candle improved the light, and Ishraq could see Lella's expression. She was cross. "Tell me, please. How will that help me? You have doubt in your voice. You don't really believe the bread is the cause."

He frowned. "All I know is that I trust the monk, but I don't want to give you false hope."

"Hope? Is there such a thing?"

"It's there for those who choose to take it. And what have you to lose? At worst, you'll be eating nicer bread than this muck."

"I will offend my maid."

"Don't tell her. Pretend to eat, then throw the bread away."

There was a polite knock at the door, then a whispered voice. It was the maid. "You take too long. You will be found out. You must leave."

Ishraq understood. His mission was done. But he had one more thing to say to Lella. "You never leave your room. I need to know how you are. Could your maid carry messages to me?"

"Why do you care?"

"I don't know. Maybe because I have my freedom. And you do not."

****

Next morning, Ishraq was in the courtyard. He saw Jaro for the first time in a while. Jaro was talking with Erich. He ducked behind some barrels and listened to the conversation.

Jaro was telling Erich that the search for the Englishman had not yet been successful but that new information had come to light. A sighting had been made. The Englishman was seen getting off a boat near Villeneuve. Jaro had been to Villeneuve and made enquiries, speaking with some men there who were in Erich's pay. One was a monk from the abbey. The sighting was confirmed. The Englishman had been there only days previously. They saw him head north.

227

Erich was angry. He said Jaro was not doing enough. The search must be intensified, concentrating on the west of the river. Those who were on the east should be redeployed to Villeneuve, to help scour the countryside beyond. The Englishman must be found.

When Jaro left, Ishraq walked back into the open courtyard. He pretended he had not seen Erich but walked close enough to make his presence known. He wanted Erich to speak to him. Information was all. Anything he could discover, about Lella or about Erich's plans for him, could be valuable.

Erich saw him and, as Ishraq had hoped, hailed him. "Ishraq, my boy. Come here," he said.

Ishraq dutifully went to Erich, but Erich was in no mood for a chat. He gave him a task. "You are too idle by half. I'm paying you to do nothing. I have a job for you. Come."

They walked to the stables. Ishraq anticipated there was an issue with one of the horses. Instead, there was a horse and covered cart readied for a trip out.

"Get in," ordered Erich. "There's a woman in there," he said. "Take her to her home in the city. Normally, I have a man whose job it is, Brasero, but he is missing, lying in a hedgerow probably after a night on the ale. She will tell you where to go, then come straight back. Hear?"

Ishraq nodded his understanding, and his acceptance, then urged the horse forward following the trail towards Avignon.

For the first mile, he resisted the temptation to turn and look at his passenger, and she did not speak to him. Then the sky darkened and the Mistral brought a fierce lashing of driving rain with it. Within minutes, he was struggling to keep the horse on track and the rain was defeating his clothing, drenching him through to the skin. It was then that the woman spoke. "We must stop," she said. "Come inside until it passes. It looks like it will. The sky is blue further west."

The voice was soft and alluring, with a hint of foreign accent. And she was right. Ishraq needed to get under cover. So he eased the horse to a stop and joined her in the covered part of the cart.

Ishraq had seen many pretty women in St Malo and La Rochelle. But he had never seen such beauty as now faced him. The alluring voice belonged to a woman, little more than a girl really, of similar age to himself. She was small, delicate. Her skin was a tone darker than his own. Her hair was black as the night. Her eyes were bigger than any he had ever seen. Her perfume of musk was intoxicating in the enclosed space of the cart.

She wore a brightly coloured silk garment that covered her from her neck to her toes. On her head was a scarf in the same material. On her feet she wore simple sandals.

Ishraq knew who she was, or at least why she had been at Erich's. She was the one he had been told about the night before. A lady of the night, a prostitute, a whore. Call her what you would, it took nothing away from her beauty. He was transfixed, speechless. And the way he looked at her, she could not have failed to notice. "My name is Lakshmi," she told him.

Ishraq had always been shy around women, but with Lakshmi he could not even get words past his lips. It made her smile to herself to see his awkwardness, but she hid it well.

They sat in silence until the rain stopped, then Ishraq resumed his place on the box seat and they continued to the city. He expected to be directed to one of the poorer areas, but instead he was taken to an area of wealth, a quarter where bankers and lawyers lived. They stopped in front of a house with two storeys, both built in dressed stone. He helped her down from the cart and watched as she went to the door. Then she was gone.

He was in no hurry to return to the Villa Libera, so wandered the streets. He soon found himself in a poorer quarter of the city, an area he had been to before, but this time he paid attention to the people there. The signs of abject poverty were unmistakeable. Some of the faces wore smiles but he was at a loss to understand why. Their clothes were dirty and ragged. Street urchins watched him, weighing up the chance to steal something of value. But the thing that shocked him most was the number of amputees begging for alms. He had seen men with missing limbs before. It was an occupational hazard for seafaring men. But here he knew it was largely caused by a disease. Holy Fire. And his mind painted a picture of another face amongst the beggars. Lella's face. Was that her fate to come?

As he walked back to the cart he was struck by a thought. There had only been one woman he had cared for in his life. He had felt a bond with Edwina. Now there were two more. Lella was a friend, but Lakshmi, a girl he had only met that day, was his new goal.

When he got back to the villa, he immediately sought out Lella's maid. "How is she?" he asked.

The maid rounded on him. "My lady is tired," she said. "And no thanks to you. Keep away from her. Take your lust elsewhere."

"You don't understand."

"Don't I? You're a man and she is a beautiful woman. What is there to understand?"

"Have you not seen how ill she is? I'm trying to help her for God's sake."

"You will get her killed. My lord Erich is a jealous man."

Ishraq opened his mouth to protest, but as he did Erich came into sight and the maid hurriedly left.

"I have another job for you," said Erich. "We found Brasero in a ditch as expected. What I didn't anticipate was that he would be dead. Choked on his own vomit. Which means there's a hole to fill in my staff here, and you will fill it while I find someone else. Tomorrow you will fetch the girl back for me."

"The same one?"

Erich smiled. "Yes. I have developed a taste for the exotic."

"Is there no horse work?"

230

Erich shook his head. "Race days happen at short notice, usually after a challenge. When the challenge is made it takes time to organise things. There's food to provide, entertainment to be arranged and moneylenders to be informed. You know the kind of thing. What I'm saying is that it doesn't all happen overnight. So, be patient. I will let you know when I have word of the next event."

"Until then, I am to be a fetcher and carrier."

"You will be making money for your trip to Marseille. That's all you should be thinking about."

It was true. Ishraq had almost forgotten why he was there. What did it matter how he earned the money?

It was all right. More importantly, he would get to see Lakshmi again.

Chapter Thirty

Woodlands west of the Rhone, September 1378

Matty had made little progress. He knew not to follow the Rhone, because it would take him north-east rather than due north. But the nights had been cloudy and the North Star was obscured. And everywhere he turned there were men searching for him. So he had to stay away from the main thoroughfares.

He was tired. He felt trapped. He needed to rest and think.

It was early evening and the sun was starting to go down. Through the trees he saw a ridge. High ground would give him a vantage point, a chance to assess the numbers that were against him and how close they all were.

He made his way through the woods towards the ridge. The rocky hillside was easy to climb. There were goats in the rocks and there was a rough track of sorts. It looked like an old shepherds' track. Before long he was near the top.

He decided this could be somewhere to stay for the night. He could have just settled down amongst the rocks, but that would not be safe enough. He had to explore further and find somewhere less obvious.

The sun was now on the horizon. It would soon be dark. He dropped down from the ridge on its far side. And he got lucky. There was a cave. He had not seen it from above. To find it, anyone would either have to know it was there or be just as lucky as he had been. It was the safest place for miles around.

He went inside. There was still enough twilight to enable him to see that the cave was not very deep. It was no more than a space within the rocks. But it would do.

He gathered some branches, broken from their trees by the Mistral but still with their leaves on. He placed them at the cave entrance in a way that would give the impression they were bushes. A passer-by would not see the cave.

He took out his candle and placed it as far back in the cave as he could, then lit it with the flint. He went outside to see whether the light would give away his hideout. "It will do," he said to himself.

He climbed the rocks again. At the top, he looked back towards Avignon, and saw groups of men, maybe two or three miles away, threshing through the undergrowth, searching for him. He could even hear commands being shouted.

There was some distance between the two groups. Were they together, or were they competitors? It did not matter. Either way, his situation was precarious. But the daylight was fading and they would have to stop the search before they reached him. He felt safe enough for the night.

He returned to the cave and sat for a while, listening to the rooks in nearby trees. He thought about Lella and the African girl. Then he thought of Ishraq, and suddenly found significance in something Ishraq had said. Ishraq told him he was at a battle, at a place called Rottingdean. And Matty now remembered that name.

He was there, in the same battle. He could see the sky raining with arrows that he and the other English archers showered at the advancing enemy forces. An order was given, and he joined the infantrymen in the town square, fighting hand to hand, with no room to manoeuvre, no room to breathe. He felt his own claustrophobia and feelings of panic.

Out of the corner of his eye he saw a wooden shaft, then the outline of a pike head. Then his head spun. He was still conscious, though barely so. He was in a dream, detached from his body, confused. In between life and death. Then there was blackness.

He remembered it all.

It changed things. He was heading for England with no idea where to go, if or when he got there. While in Avignon there was a young man who had been at Rottingdean and shared his experience of the battle.

233

He sighed. Ishraq was his best chance to discover more, and maybe give him the clues to reconnect him with the pieces of his life puzzle that were still missing.

Avignon meant danger, but he had no choice. He must go back. His memory of running away from his village haunted him. He would not run away again. He would face whatever awaited him in Avignon, good or bad.

He slept fitfully. His deepest sleep came just before dawn.

****

He awoke sharply, hearing a sound. A new sound. The yapping of hounds.

He jumped up and went outside, scrambling up the rocks as before. The searchers had started out early. He could see them within a mile of the ridge. There was a houndsman, dangling something in front of the hounds, offering them the scent they needed to hunt their quarry. He was the quarry.

The leader of the party wore armour. It was Jaro.

The scent was working. The search party was heading straight for the ridge. He scoured the horizon for the other group he had seen the night before, but they were not there.

He tried to count the number of men. There were at least eight plus the dogs. Too many. His crossbow could account for one, two, possibly three. Not eight.

During his restless night he had done much thinking, and he had a plan.

He made his way along the ridge, in the opposite direction to Avignon, making sure to leave tell-tale signs of his presence. He tore some cloth from his shirt and pressed it on to the thorns of a hawthorn bush. Manna for the hounds. Further on, he dropped the remnants of his candle and left the flint with it.

He reached the ridge's edge. The shepherds' track ended there, with no single route onwards. He doubled back and found a spot suited to

234

his plan. Then he wedged the crossbow between two rocks, making it level enough for his purpose. And waited.

As the search party neared, he forced himself to be patient. The distance had to be right. When he judged that it was, he fired his arrows in quick succession. He aimed high. He had no wish to kill.

His pursuers took cover.

He ran back along the ridge, adding more of his scent, then jumped down to the cave, hoping the false trail would be stronger than the real one.

When no more arrows flew, Jaro and his men started the search again. They let the hounds do their work. Matty listened to what was happening above him. He was afraid his rouse might not have worked and fully expected men to appear at the cave entrance. He held his sword tightly, ready to defend himself. But the noise passed over. The false trail had been taken.

Matty knew that the trail would go cold when Jaro reached the ridge's edge. But that could be explained because of the many ways Matty could have gone from there. It would take Jaro time to explore all the different options, even with the hounds. And Jaro would not think that Matty would turn back towards Avignon. Why would he?

By the time Jaro had worked things out, Matty would be well on his way back to the city. He set off, keeping to the woodlands. He had been able to see Jaro's men the day before, visible from the ridge. He had to stay hidden beneath the trees, away from the open plain.

He made better progress than before, partly because he was retracing his steps and had no need to navigate by the stars, but also because he had lost the searchers.

The afternoon temperatures rose to an uncomfortable level. He needed water. He saw signs of a gorge and made for it. There he found something unexpected. There were several bodies, men and horses together. A lone live horse was drinking in the stream, beside floating bodies. Other bodies were in the growth along the stream's bank.

There had been a skirmish. He had seen two groups yesterday. This must have been the other one.

He lifted a body in the hope of getting clues about what had happened. The man wore the blue and yellow checks that were the coat of arms of the Archbishop of Cambrai. His throat had been cut.

He examined more bodies. All had their throats cut. If this was a skirmish, there would be sword wounds in other parts of the bodies. It was no skirmish, but a mass execution following a capture or maybe a betrayal. Jaro had eliminated a rival force, for reasons Matty could only guess at.

A sound caused him to turn, grasping his sword. There was a man, badly hurt but alive, crawling towards him. He sheathed his sword and went to the man's aid.

The man's face was blistering from lying in the open under the hot sunshine, lips dry and cracked. Matty went back to the stream and gathered some water in his hands, then returned and put a tiny amount to the man's lips and face. The man was suddenly lively, demanding more, but Matty refused. "Not yet," he said.

The man seemed to understand and calmed down. Matty examined his injuries. For some reason, his throat had not been cut like the others. He had bruising to his forehead and, more worryingly, a wound in his chest that was oozing blood. Matty's priority was to stem the flow.

He sat the man up and pulled the clothing away from his chest. He investigated the wound looking for signs that the tip of the sword might be lodged inside. It was not. Re-assured, he placed his hands over the man's chest and pressed firmly down. Then he tore a strip from the shirt of one of the corpses, dipped the cloth in the stream, then placed it over the wound, tying it over the man's shoulder.

It was as much as he could do. He now had a choice to make. The man was not well enough to travel. Matty could stay with him, at the risk of being discovered by Jaro. Or could simply leave the man to his fate.

It was no choice. He could not leave the man to die. He had to hope Jaro would spend a full day following the false trail. Because helping the injured man meant Matty could not move on.

There was one piece of good news. Some of the possessions of the victims were there. Presumably, Jaro had enough provisions of his own and decided he did not need them. So there was food and the means to start a fire.

A fire would be another risk. Smoke could be seen. But again Matty had no choice about. The injured man needed warmth. Matty cursed as he lit a fire and made use of it to cook a piece of pork. It had been pre-cooked but Matty knew that if he cooked the meat again it was less likely to poison him and his patient. A hard biscuit finished the meal.

He rummaged some more among the discarded belongings and found a leather flask with its stopper intact. He pulled the stopper out and discovered the flask was full of wine. If Jaro did find him here, at least he would die well fed and with wine at his lips.

He gave the wounded man a little diluted wine and a tiny piece of the cooked pork. Then he settled by the fire to await whatever the rest of the day would bring.

He did not have long to wait.

Jaro had seen the smoke. He still thought Matty was heading north, away from the city. He thought the fire must belong to a shepherd. Nevertheless, he sent two men to check out the fire, just in case. One was an experienced soldier. The other was a young recruit. It was almost night by the time they reached the fire. There was a crescent moon shining.

There was no way for the men to enter the small gorge without scrambling down a hill. Silence was impossible. When they reached the stream, they found one man, asleep by the diminishing warmth of the fire. They knew him. They had left him for dead. He had put up a fight, costing him the sword wound and persuading his comrades to surrender, expecting mercy which never came. Jaro's men were so certain the wound was fatal they did not bother to apply the coup de grace. But now he was easy meat. They would finish the job and return to tell Jaro what a good job they had done.

They did not need stealth. Their prey was in no state to resist. So they walked up to him. They were laughing, relaxed, unafraid. They spoke together in French, playing a game of words to decide which of them would do the deed. Finally, one was chosen. He moved towards the helpless figure; sword raised.

Matty was behind some rocks. He moaned, a ghostly sound, then stepped out and threw his cloak wide. He had remembered what the little boy said months earlier, that his monk's robes made him look like a big bird. In the half-light of the crescent moon and the weak light from the dying fire, the effect was ghostly.

He held his sword up so that it was caught by the moon, keeping his hand inside his cloak sleeve. To the two men it looked as though the sword was held in the air by magic.

The two men looked at one another, eyes wide in astonishment. Within a heartbeat they forgot about the injured man. The young recruit panicked and started to run. The older man was braver and shouted for him to come back. When he did not, the older one felt suddenly alone and vulnerable. He was not going to stay to face the spectre. He ran after his companion.

When they thought they had gone far enough away they stopped running. They were panting, exhausted. The younger man spoke. "What do you think it was?" he asked.

The older man groaned. "I think we have been tricked," he replied.

The younger found his courage at last. "Then we should go back."

But the older was not sure of his own judgement. "Best not," he said.

"So how do we account for the campfire?"

"We'll say we found the dying man and finished him off. Jaro will be none the wiser." The younger agreed and was relieved.

****

238

The following day, before dawn, Matty was on his way to Avignon. The wounded man was barely fit to travel, but they could not stay in the gorge. It was too dangerous. He thought about giving the dead men a decent burial, but there was no time. Ever mindful that his own family did not know where he was, he promised the dead men he would let people know what had happened to them. Then he put the man on the stray horse and walked alongside.

He was going back to find Ishraq, the young man who had been at Rottingdean. He would go first to the Palais des Papes, to deposit the injured man, a soldier of the archbishop. Then he would search for Ishraq, the key to completing his life puzzle.

Meanwhile, the two men from the gorge had reached Jaro, who was still in the area around the rocks. He had been going round in circles, cursing the hounds as useless for failing to find the trail.

The young recruit stayed silent, while the older, more experienced man took the responsibility of telling Jaro the story they had agreed. He kept it simple, with no mention of the spectre in the dark. They had found an injured man and finished him off.

Jaro thought the story plausible. But he knew his men. He turned to the younger one and addressed him directly. "Now *you* tell me what happened," he said.

The man was flustered. He had not expected this. He was not prepared for it. "The same," he said. "I say the same as him." His voice was uneven. Jaro thought he was hiding something.

"Tell me in your own words," said Jaro.

The young man was breathing heavily now and unable to get his words out. Jaro knew there was more to this. "Spit it out, man!" said Jaro. "We don't have all day."

The young man was unable to think straight. He gabbled. It was a mistake. "He was wounded," he said. "We had to finish him. The ghost..."

Jaro was now in the young man's face. "Ghost? What ghost?"

239

The older man sighed to himself. He felt he had to intervene. "He's been at the ale since we got back. Ignore him."

Jaro rounded on the older man. "I smell no ale on him. There is more to this, I know it. I will have the truth or else you will both suffer the consequences."

"I tell it true," said the younger man. He spread his hands, emotions overcoming him. "The ghost was there. It had no hands yet it held a sword. I feared for my life."

Jaro lost patience and struck the man. It was a savage blow. He turned to the older man. "No more lies," he said.

Within the hour, Jaro and his men were on their way back to the gorge. Jaro had worked things out. The lack of a scent at the end of the ridge and the appearance of a *ghostly figure* with a sword in the gorge told him all he needed to know. The Benedictine had turned back. It was puzzling. Why had he done that? But it was the only explanation. And Jaro vowed to find him.

Part Seven

Briony

Chapter Thirty-One

The River Saone, September 1378

The countryside was beautiful, but Edwina was tiring of it, and regretting her decision to go with Briony.

They were about halfway to their destination, but at least they had the hardest part of the journey behind them. They had left the rough roads. The Saone and then the Rhone would take them on more quickly and comfortably to the city of Avignon.

Travelling by river was safer than going through the countryside, especially for two young women. Edwina still had vivid flashbacks to an incident almost exactly two years before. She was on her way to Windsor, to the royal wedding. She and her escort, Tom met a group of players. During the night, two of the players tried to rape her. They were caught before the act, but still the trauma remained with her and resurfaced every time she ventured out on the dangerous roads of England and France. She felt safer now they were on a boat.

Edwina discovered that Briony had led quite a sheltered existence. She told Edwina she was brought up on a lakeside. It was remote, with few visitors, and few dangers other than the odd wild boar. So she was more relaxed than Edwina, less expectant of bad things happening to her. Edwina had insisted they buy some protection on such a long journey, and Briony had agreed reluctantly, feeling it unnecessary.

Michel had been, as ever, supportive. Despite his disappointment that Edwina chose not to accompany him back to St Malo, he readily found the money needed to hire an armed guard. He even helped vet the applicants for the role, though leaving Edwina the final choice.

Some of the applicants came with descriptive names. Edwina rejected Frederic the Accursed, for obvious reasons. Equally though, she turned away Paulus the Good, thinking he sounded too nice, too soft to be any good in a fight, even though he assured her he was an experienced soldier.

She chose a young man named Philippe. There were several reasons for her choice. Firstly, she liked the name. It sounded noble somehow, and she had been reading about Philip the Evangelist, whose daughters had the gift of prophecy. Some said Edwina had the same gift. Edwina liked the associations, however obscure.

Another reason was that Philippe was quite handsome. He was not like Michel, who was tall and thin. In fact, the contrast was obvious. Philippe was stocky, muscular, earthy. His arms were tattooed with depictions of snakes and his long hair was tied in a knot on top of his head. His appearance made Michel feel uncomfortable about hiring him. Michel would have preferred somebody more conventional

Michel put Phillipe through a series of tests, which he completed calmly and with skill. Even Michel had to acknowledge how well the young man completed them. And Edwina saw a kindness in Philippe's eyes and general manner. When Edwina decided on Phillipe, Michel lacked strong reasons to object.

On the journey so far, Philippe had already proved his worth. There had been two incidents on the roads, both involving men who had drunk too much ale and who approached the two women, thinking them vulnerable. The men made typically suggestive remarks and got too physically close, making the women feel uncomfortable. On neither occasion did Philippe need to draw his sword. He avoided escalation, putting himself between the men and women assertively, protectively, and without fuss or violence was able to defuse each situation, easing the men away.

One other incident occurred. It was more serious. Briony had been able to secure letters of introduction from her prioress that meant that she, Edwina and Philippe would receive welcome at any of the hundreds of monasteries, convents and other Christian houses lining the route. It was common practice, on a *quid pro quo* basis. Briony's priory provided accommodation to travellers in the same way. A small fee was charged, but the main benefit was removal of the need to take rooms in some seedy inn.

So the three were able to stay mostly in safe places. But there was one occasion when poor weather delayed their arrival at the planned resting place and they had to take what was on offer locally. It was not even an inn, just the house of a couple they met who heard of their plight and kindly offered them a place to rest for the night, a room for the women and a barn for Philippe.

Acts of kindness are not always what they seem.

It was two days later, twenty miles down the road, that Edwina discovered one of her possessions was missing. She had checked her bag when she left, but not thoroughly enough.

Looking back, she realised she had allowed herself to be taken in. And it was the woman who had given her re-assurance, both in her kind manner but also in her attention to matters of safety. The woman said she understood that Edwina and Briony might feel unsafe in the house with Philippe in the barn. So she showed them a latch they could fasten on the inside of their bedroom door, to keep them safe and secure from intruders or unwanted attention.

But somehow the latch had not prevented the theft. Edwina could not work out how or when it happened. Most likely it was when she and Briony left the room door open and went to eat at the kitchen table.

Edwina had enjoyed a comfortable life as the daughter of a lady of the manor and had accumulated several personal possessions of some worth. But the thieves took only her most valuable piece of jewellery, an item that had been given to her by Michel when a romantic relationship was developing between them. It was a brooch, made of gold with an enamelled scene added. It was of the highest quality.

The scene on the brooch was of a lifeless tree, above which flew swallows against a blue sky. Michel had it made specially, depicting a moment in Edwina's life, one she had told him about, a moment of inspiration she had sitting under her favourite tree, her Moses Tree. She saw swallows flying south and took it as a sign. The sight of the birds made up her mind to go to the wedding at Windsor. Edwina told Michel there were times when she regretted the decision, but to Michel it was a beautiful decision because it led her to him. The brooch symbolised his thanks for that.

The thieves knew what they were doing taking the brooch. At first, she thought it strange that was all they took but Philippe explained it. With just one small item taken, she was less likely to notice the theft and raise the alarm. The bag looked as normal and she did what most would do, neglecting to examine it and missing the fact the brooch was not there.

Briony also had some things stolen. One was a purse. It contained a small amount of money, which she had saved for the trip through working extra-long hours at the convent school. But the loss of money was nothing compared with what else the thieves took of hers. She had a silver cross attached to prayer beads. It was something Briony's parents gave her when she decided to become a nun. The value to a thief would not be huge but the sentimental value to Briony was great. Like Edwina, Briony had not noticed her things were missing.

When the thefts were discovered, Philippe said they should turn back and confront the couple, but neither Edwina nor Briony wanted to. Edwina was frustrated by the length of time it was taking to complete their journey and wanted to carry on. She also reasoned that going back would be pointless. The stolen goods would already be sold and they had no proof that it was the couple who had taken them.

Edwina was affected by her loss. It left her feeling even more guilty about Michel. How would she tell him she had failed to keep safe something he had bought her, something that was such a special thing to him? He would, of course be understanding about it, as he always was, and that would make her feel even more guilty than she already did about him. Because she found herself looking at Philippe just a little longer than she should.

It was absurd. After all, Michel knew she did not want a relationship with him beyond simple friendship. Still, it felt like a betrayal when she stared longingly at Philippe as he went about his duties.

Briony said nothing about her loss, displaying no shock and showing no emotion. Edwina thought it a strange reaction but understood. The girl was the most content person she had ever encountered. Nothing bothered her. She lived in a state of constant trust in her god, accepting in full whatever life put before her.

Edwina could never be like that. She was restless, desperate to end this chapter in her life. She hoped Avignon would mark a change for the better. The day was ending and she was sulking.

Briony suddenly appeared. "Come with me," she said. "I've set up a small chapel on the boat."

Edwina sighed deeply. It was the last thing she needed. But Briony tugged at her arm, insistent. And Edwina thought, *'why not?'*

As expected, Edwina was bored in the makeshift chapel. Briony had fashioned a cross from pieces of wood she found on deck, then decorated the scene with stones. It was very simple, yet Edwina saw beauty in it. Afterwards, she said what was on her mind. "You must be devastated having your cross and beads stolen."

"Everything is part of God's plan," replied Briony.

"Everything?"

"I believe so. He told me to find the Benedictine. The theft must have a purpose within my journey."

Now Edwina was irritated. "How can that be possible?" she barked.

It had no effect. Briony just shrugged. "Only He knows."

Edwina suddenly realised something. Briony's faith was everything to her, yet she had never once asked about Edwina's faith, or lack of it. And Edwina felt compelled to say something all the same.

"My mother went to church every Sunday and Holy Day," she said. "I was made to go with her, but I knew she only went because it was expected of her as the Lady of the Manor."

Briony listened intensely.

Edwina continued. "My father isn't religious. He saw terrible things in the war."

Briony nodded. "And you?" she finally asked.

"I used to sit by an old tree. I felt a connection to something. It was where my grandparents had died. I never knew them, but I felt safe there, as though they watched over me. It was silly. For years I stayed at home because I was afraid of the outside world. Now I find myself so far from home it scares me."

"You are homesick and lonely. It's natural."

"I witnessed a battle once. Men were killing other men for no obvious reason. Afterwards, my brother went off to get married and my friend went to live on an island with an old woman. They were both sure what they wanted. I see the same certainty in you. Don't you ever doubt yourself?"

"Always. But I never doubt God."

Briony took Edwina's hand. "I felt called to ask you to come with me on this journey. I don't know why, but I feel it was right. You will find your place, I'm sure of it. There's a purpose that we don't yet understand."

"I wish I could believe you, but if you could say a magic word to take me home in an instant, I would be happy in that."

Briony squeezed Edwina's hand. "You are not alone," she said. "Have no fear for what might be to come."

"I will try."

Chapter Thirty-Two

South of Lyon, France, September 1378

Progress was now good. Since they left the Saone and found passage on the Rhone, they had been eating up the miles. But still there were a hundred miles to go to Avignon.

At Lyon there had been a wide choice of boats to take. The town was a hub for trade and Avignon was its gateway to Marseille, the Mediterranean and beyond.

But the loss of Briony's purse had an impact. Edwina still had money, but it was ever dwindling. Overland they had been able to sleep in religious houses at no cost, but river passage over such a long distance did not come cheaply. And the more comfortable the ride, the greater was the fare.

So the boat they chose was modest, affordable. It was a small cog taking silks for export to Italy. Its name was *Le Julienne*.

The silk industry in Lyon was thriving. French produce was cheaper than Italian produce, and therefore saleable. The scale of production, however, was much smaller, and not enough to warrant larger boats. The Julienne only had berths for its crew and they had been given up for the three travellers. For the impoverished crew the extra money was worth the inconvenience of sleeping on the deck for a few nights.

Midstream was a safer place than dry land, so the cog made as few stops as necessary, only to take on fresh food and water. Edwina got to know the crew quite well. They were all from a single extended family. The captain and mate were brothers and the rest of the crew (four in total) were either cousins or relatives through marriage. The captain told Edwina it was a sensible arrangement. He trusted blood relations more than hired labour. In fact, the whole enterprise was conducted within the family. Back in Lyon, the men's wives and sisters worked the silk. The family would never get rich but earned enough while enjoying the closeness of a purely family enterprise.

As the boat continued its relentless way, Edwina learned more about Briony and Philippe.

Briony's story was straightforward. Her family was devoutly religious and she had always wanted to take her vows. It had never occurred to her to do anything else. Her life was totally void of complication. Edwina did not know whether to envy or pity her. She took to thinking of her as Eve before The Fall, pure and innocent. On one occasion, she called Briony *'Eve'* by mistake, to Phillipe's amusement.

By contrast, Philippe's life had been full of highs and lows. His was a story she had heard before, born the second son in a landowning family. The first son inherited the lands while Philippe was destined for a military life. In a time of war with England, there was no shortage of action or opportunity. He was barely in his teens when serving with the Duke of Burgundy's men. It was 1373. The duke was playing a game of cat and mouse with John of Gaunt's forces, drawing them out but avoiding pitched battles, the strategy being to drain the English army of its resources. It worked. The Treaty of Bruges was signed in 1375 and a lengthy period of truce followed. By the time Edwina was seeking a bodyguard, Philippe was bored of the idleness of being a soldier in peacetime and was drawn to apply.

One afternoon, the captain announced they were within a day of Avignon. Edwina had something to ask Philippe. It was the question non-combatants tended to ask of fighting men. "Have you ever killed anyone, Philippe?"

"I don't know," he replied flatly. "I've cut some in battle but never stayed to find out if they lived. I was otherwise occupied by then. Maybe they died. Maybe they didn't. It was a case of kill or be killed."

Edwina was shocked by his lack of emotion. It was as if he was talking about cutting barley or branches from a tree rather than human flesh. It bothered her and dampened the feelings for him that had been building. He was handsome, but not as thoughtful or as sophisticated as Michel. It made her appreciate what she had given up. But that bird had flown for good. There was no way back.

She was still only twenty years old, but she was despairing of ever finding love, even though she was no longer self-conscious about her missing hand and the scars still visible on her neck. Michel was not

249

the only man who had looked on her with desire. Even on the boat, more than one crewman gave her a look or a wink. So she knew she was pretty enough, and her friend Mary found love at a similar age. But that was unusual. Most women were wedded mothers by twenty.

Her thoughts were broken by a shout from one of the crew. "Chaines!"

She looked where he was pointing. The river was at one of its narrowest points and she could just make out a chain draped across the surface, stretching from one bank to the other. She looked at Philippe. He was putting on his sword. "River pirates," he said.

Philippe went to the bows, but the crew knew where the attack would come from and waited at the stern. Then Edwina saw why. Two boats approached from behind. They were smaller and faster than the Julienne and were using the current to catch it up.

The Julienne reached the chains and was held there, unable to go further downriver. Philippe realised what was happening and ushered Edwina and Briony as far forward as they could go, then positioned himself to defend them.

There were six pirates in each boat. Twice the number of the crew. They boarded. The Julienne's crew fought well and for a while Edwina thought they would repel the raid. Philippe knew differently. The crew were tiring with the effort of fighting one against two. He turned to the women. "Jump!" he said. "It's your only chance."

Edwina looked down into the water. She knew how to swim, but at this narrow part of the river the flow was fast, with dangerous eddies all around. She looked along the boat to where the fighting was taking place. Philippe was right. The pirates were gaining the upper hand. She took Briony by the arm. "Come," she said.

But Briony stood firm, shaking her head. "It's too dangerous," she whispered.

"We have no choice," Edwina told her.

Briony shook her head. "God will save me," she declared.

Edwina was exasperated. "You must jump. It's the only way. I choose to live. You must do the same."

"No." And with that Briony sat down on the deck, immovable.

"Leave her," said Philippe. "Go now!"

Edwina hesitated, then bent down to Briony. She took off her wooden cross, the amulet she had been given by her brother.

Briony had worn no cross since hers had been stolen. Edwina knew how important it had been to her. She placed the amulet in Briony's hand. "God be with you," she said, and kissed Briony on the cheek.

Briony clutched the amulet. She managed a weak smile. "And with you," she said, her voice weak with fear.

Edwina turned, took one step then jumped into the water. She sank deeper than she had expected to. She was struggling, unable to climb back to the surface. The current took her in a circle hit her head on the chain the pirates had put across the river. She was dazed but reached out and grabbed it, pulling herself up, her head now out of the water.

She gasped as she took in breaths of lifegiving air. Then she looked to the riverbanks, thinking she could use the chain, hand-over-hand to reach them. But that way lay more danger. There were pirates at each end of the chain, ready and waiting.

She looked up at the Julienne. The pirates had reached Philippe. The crew must be dead.

Philippe was agile, shifting from side to side, cutting and thrusting. The pirates goaded him. First one prodded, then the next, keeping just out of his reach, making him respond to each thrust, tiring him as they had done the crew. And Edwina saw the fatal blow, a sword through the heart. Philippe collapsed to his knees.

Briony was now at the mercy of the pirates. Edwina saw one pirate grinning and she knew what Briony's fate was to be. The pirate had a full beard and wore a distinctive, gaudy hat with peacock feathers. For a moment, Edwina was distracted by him. Briony looked back in her direction, smiling and holding up the amulet, then at last summoned the courage to dive headfirst into the river.

The young nun hit an eddy and disappeared. Edwina moved along the chain, hand over hand, to get near where Briony had entered the water so she could help her friend. Briony did not surface, so Edwina dived down. It was brave, because she was not a strong enough swimmer against the currents. She found no sign of Briony and re-surfaced, then waited as long as she dared, but still there was no Briony.

The pirates on the riverbank were now removing the chain, pulling it to one side. Edwina had to let go. She tried to swim with the flow of the river but it was impossible. The river was in control, not her. She was swept along. Several times she was dragged down, but mercifully the river coughed her back up again each time. Until finally the river widened and calmed. And Edwina was able to clutch an overhanging branch, using it to swing on to a mudbank and the safety of land.

Exhausted, she lay on the grass, her breathing deep and uneven. Then she saw the Julienne go by, crewed by the pirates. They would sell everything, the cargo but also the boat. For them this was a good day. Edwina shouted a curse at them, then sobbed for Briony and Phillipe.

When she regained her composure, Edwina realised she was lost and alone. She knew she could follow the Rhone and would end up in Avignon. But for what purpose now without Briony?

The answer came immediately. She had to fulfil Briony's pilgrimage. It had never been her own. She had just been along for the ride. But it was a reason to continue. If Heaven existed, Briony was there now watching, and would take great pleasure if Edwina completed the journey and found the Benedictine. She only hoped the monk she now so wanted to meet was worth the lives of two young people. If not, she would not be responsible for the consequences.

But first she had to get to the city, with no boat, no horse, no food and no water. She sighed then took the first step of many thousand.

She followed an old mule track. It was dry and dusty. She saw no people, only sheep and wild goats littering the hillsides. She also saw a creature she had never seen before. It was small, the size of a small rat, and appeared quite still, standing on a rock, basking in the sunshine. It's skin was scaley and it had large feet. Suddenly, it scurried, and Edwina flinched. Then it was gone.

Edwina shuddered. She would be glad to get off this track.

As nightfall approached, she ploughed on. Tiny insects swarmed around biting her. Her mouth was dry and her tongue parched. She was relieved when she came across a corn mill. She had to take the chance of making contact. There was a boy fishing at the riverside. She approached him. He turned and shouted, not to her but to someone or something behind her. She heard a sound that had haunted her for years. The panting and slavering of a hound at her back.

She braced herself for the attack. This time would be different. She would not suffer for a second time.

Chapter Thirty-Three

Avignon, September 1378

Ishraq's mood was sour. His new duties were harder than he had anticipated. Each time he deposited Lakshmi at Erich's door he felt sick in his stomach. His fondness for the little dark-skinned girl had grown to near obsession. She was all he thought about, day and night. He told himself it was her eyes, like bottomless pools drawing him in. She was unlike any other girl he had met.

He had no idea what she thought of him. She rarely spoke or looked in his direction.

And as his love for her grew, so his hatred of Erich matched it. It was a mixture of helpless jealousy and a feeling of impotence because he could not protect Lakshmi from Erich's grimy hands.

He started to imagine ways to rescue her. On one occasion when he collected her from her home, he came close to saying what was in his mind. *'Let me take you away. Let's go to Baghdad'*. But he lacked the courage, fearing that she would reject him and laugh at his stupidity.

He had seen nothing of the other woman in his life. He had received no further news from Lella. Her maid had not contacted him. He did not know whether the advice he had given her had worked. He imagined it had not, and that her limbs were now black and putrid, her mind turned to mush.

So now, as he pulled up outside where Lakshmi lived, he felt only despair.

She came out as normal, but Ishraq saw there was something different. She had never been enthusiastic about going to Erich's, but now he saw she was more anxious, fearful.

He said nothing and helped her up into the cart as normal. As always, she wore a dress that covered her, neck to toe. Other women covered their form, but Lakshmi's silk sari hugged her figure, accentuating rather than hiding the shape of her body.

He noticed that she was holding one arm limply by her side. And he thought she was in pain.

She saw him looking at her arm and withdrew it behind her back. That made her wince. He dared to reach for it, tenderly bringing it back to her side. It was done in such a caring way that she let him do it.

He pressed gently on her wrist and she winced again. He looked her in the eyes for the first time since they had met. "It's broken," he said."

"I want no fuss," she said meekly. "It was an accident. I fell." It was said in an unusually hurried way.

"You must get it wrapped, to ease the pain and let it heal."

"I have to go to the villa."

"Erich would understand."

Lakshmi turned her head away. She was crying but trying to conceal the tears. And Ishraq understood. "Erich did this," he said.

"We must go. He will be waiting."

Ishraq gently took a sleeve of Lakshmi's dress and began to lift it to reveal the skin beneath. At first, Lakshmi resisted, then she let him.

Her arm was covered in bruises. Ishraq closed his eyes in shocked realisation. He was sure that if he examined other parts of Lakshmi's body he would find more, but he had no wish to embarrass her just to confirm what he already knew.

"You can't go back there, to the villa," he said urgently.

She stared at him blankly. Her tone hardened. "Who are you to tell me what I can and can't do? You know nothing about me."

"I know this much. He will kill you before long."

She laughed. "And you will stop him?"

"I care about you."

She was angry now. "No you don't. You see me in the same way as Erich does. Where I live there are women you would never look twice upon. If I looked the same, you would not be doing this. You don't

255

care about me, you only lust after me. Anyway, I'm safer with Erich than I would otherwise be. I'm kept just for him, while the other girls never know from day to day who will turn up to use and abuse them. Half the men who come don't think of us as people. They buy us as they would a coat or a dog. Some despise us and yet still they come. Others despise themselves for doing so. We have armed men to protect us but still women have died there. No, I'm safer as things are."

"I have plans," said Ishraq, his eyes widening as he started to tell her of his dreams. He thought she would be excited. "When I've earned enough money, I'm going to Baghdad. You can come with me."

She scoffed. "You work for Erich. He won't let you leave. You are as much a slave to him as I am."

"No. You're wrong. We have an agreement."

Lakshmi's patience was being stretched. She spat in the dirt. "That's what any agreement with Erich the Dane is worth."

Just then two people came from the house to see why they had not yet left. One was a middle-aged woman with a stern face and the other was a brute of a guard. Ishraq guessed the woman to be the madame of the brothel. "We must go now," urged Lakshmi. "They are not a pair to be crossed." She sat back in the cart, and Ishraq did the sensible thing, urging the horse forward away from the inquisitive pair.

On the journey to the villa, Ishraq considered what Lakshmi said. She was right. He was a fool. Any agreement with Erich was worthless.

He took out his purse and counted the money he had saved. It was a pitiful amount. What little he earned had been easily spent just on ale and gambling. At this rate he would never have enough for Baghdad.

When they reached the villa, Ishraq's heart was full of hate but he could do nothing. Lakshmi went to Erich while he found a quiet corner and sobbed. Until Lella appeared.

"She is very pretty," said Lella.

"Is she?"

"Maybe you haven't noticed. But I think you have. She is too pretty by half. I can see what is happening. It won't be long before she replaces me here."

The thought was too much for Ishraq. Lakshmi permanently at Erich's beck and call. He rounded on Lella and had to hold back from hitting her. "Leave me alone," he said. "My life is bad enough."

"I'm not trying to hurt you, but it's what happens and will affect me more than you. A young girl comes along and the old one is discarded with the rubbish. I will end up back doing the work she now does; work I did in the past. In ten years' time Lakshmi will be replaced in the same way."

"I will kill him before I let him have her."

Lella grunted. "Men! You're all the same. The Benedictine monk wanted to save me just as you want to save her. He didn't understand."

"The Benedictine was here?"

"Yes. You know him?"

"It was he who told me how to help you with the sickness."

"And it worked," she said. She showed him her arms and legs. "I stopped eating the bread and now my sickness is gone. I can go out now in public." She beamed a smile Ishraq had rarely seen from her.

He was amazed. "You are cured?" he gasped. Then his tone changed. "Cured to live as a slave. If I was you, I'd rather die."

"But you are not me."

"If it is the bread that causes the sickness, we can help the people in the city. I promised a priest I would tell him."

She sighed. "Then they die starving instead of by Holy Fire."

He nodded, understanding. "Because the dark bread is all they can afford. But I will tell the priest anyway. But what about Lakshmi? What can we do?"

"It seems we both want the same thing, to get her away from Erich. It is time for us to join forces."

257

Chapter Thirty-Four

The Palais des Papes, Avignon, September 1378

Matty was still dressed in his robes. They were a uniform, announcing to the world he was a monk, a man of God.

He had thought about discarding them and finding common clothing, but he realised that for a little while longer he had to be the Benedictine.

He was returning to the city to find a young man. The only thing he knew about the man was his name, Ishraq. With such little information, it would be much easier to let Ishraq find him. And that meant Matty must stay in his uniform.

He approached the building and handed over the injured man. He reported the skirmish outside the city and said other men lay dead there, needing burial. He asked that their families be informed.

The ne waited. Before long, the inevitable crowd formed. But this time it was what he wanted. Ishraq was not amongst the crowd, but no matter. Matty had a small army of disciples. He put the word out that he needed to see the young man he had met at the abbey. He said it was a matter of great spiritual importance. He allowed himself this one small deceit. He felt he had earned it in a way.

It was not long before a guard arrived, to usher Matty into the palace. It was what he had expected. After all, hadn't the archbishop been looking for him?

He was shown into an anteroom. He sat alone, waiting. An hour passed, then another. This was not what he had expected. He thought he was important. Clearly, he was not.

By the time someone came he was growing anxious, puzzled by the slowness of the reception.

He was taken into another, larger room with a long table. It was a room Matty had not been in before, a formal meeting room. He wondered to himself just how many rooms there were there in the palace. He could spend a year here and still not see them all.

There were three men in the room. The archbishop was not there. There was not even a cardinal. Instead, there was Frere Jean, Jaro, and another of Erich's henchmen. It did not feel right.

Jaro grinned. "You took your time," he said. "I got back yesterday."

Matty shrugged. He was not interested in preliminaries. He knew this was going to be an unpleasant encounter. He decided to let Jaro make the next move.

But it was the priest who spoke next. "We thought you had decided to escape Avignon," he said.

"I realised I have done nothing wrong," replied Matty. "I have no fear of this place. Why should I wish to escape from it?"

"Well said," laughed Jaro. "And it's true, there's nothing to fear here."

"So why did you hunt for me?"

Jaro looked at the ceiling and stroked his beard, as if thinking. "I think we both know the reason," he said. Then he gave an almost imperceptible nod, and without warning the other henchman seized Matty, pulling his arms behind his back.

Jaro put his sword to Matty's chin. "For which you will hang," he added with glee.

Shocked, Matty looked toward Frere Jean. The priest had his eyes closed and was saying a prayer. "God have mercy on the soul of this wretched man."

Jaro barked out an order and two more men came into the room. He punched Matty in the stomach. The punch winded Matty and he doubled up in pain. He was then dragged away and taken deep into the bowels of the palace, to a dark dungeon.

The guards left, and slowly Matty regained his strength. He tried to think what reason Jaro could use to justify a hanging. Erich had to be behind it, but to what purpose?

There was no bed in the dungeon, just a stone floor. He curled into a ball to conserve body heat. Still he shivered in the cold and damp.

He tried to sleep, but the cold kept him awake. His situation triggered a memory of similar circumstances. He was in Lincoln castle prison, awaiting trial, falsely accused of murder. He was taken up to the castle court to face a jury, and he saw familiar faces on the jury bench. Faces of men who hated him. His chances were slim but there were people on his side, people who cared about him, and they gave evidence that his main accuser, his childhood friend, Edmund was a liar.

He wondered whether he would again face trial by jury. If so, this time would be different. He was in a foreign land, far away from anyone who cared one way or another about him, whether he lived or died.

He had felt lonely before, but never so helpless.

He thought about his decision to return to Avignon. It was a mistake. He had come back into danger. He had hoped to find Ishraq, to learn about the battle at Rottingdean and maybe discover a way to find his family. He thought he would be safe enough, given the esteem in which he was held. He was wrong.

He started to drift off. Then, finally, the last, and most important piece of his life puzzle came back to him.

There was an old building, set in the heart of a forest. He knew where it was. It was in the great forest of Windsor.

He was standing ankle deep in a stream. Nearby were three children playing in the water. He had seen them before and knew who they were. Gylda, Maude and Edward. His children. They were laughing and splashing him. It was a picture of joy. And he was happy.

A woman stood on rocks midstream, watching, her face beaming with pride and love for all four of them. It was Charlotte, his wife. In her eyes was pure pride.

He let his mind dwell on the scene, watching his eldest daughter, Gylda. She was growing up and wise beyond her years. He could see how she looked out for her brother and sister, just in case they slipped on the stones and fell. The water was not deep, but she still thought it her duty to watch.

He smiled to himself as he remembered a conversation he had with Charlotte about their firstborn. Charlotte was insistent they name the child Gylda after Matty's mother. She understood how important that would be to him. He was fortunate to have such a wife.

The memories faded. In the dark, he lost track of time. When the dungeon door finally opened, he thought maybe a full day had passed. Or was it just an hour? There was a figure holding a lantern. It was Frere Jean. Behind him was a woman carrying a tray with some food and drink. She set it down then left.

Matty was not hungry. He ignored the tray. Jean sat on the floor beside him, hands clasped as if in prayer.

"Did you sleep?" asked Jean.

"I dreamed. I finally know myself. I have had a good life. If there is a god, he has let me see it once more before I am hanged."

"I know you have doubts about God. I pray you find faith in time."

"What exactly am I accused of?"

"There were dead men on the road north of the city. Jaro says he saw you kill them. He and his men have given identical accounts. They say you used a crossbow, and yesterday you fetched up at this place carrying just such a weapon. We have it now, as evidence."

"I brought back a wounded man. Why, if I had killed the others?"

"The wounded man was one of the archbishop's men. The dead also. They were following you. Perhaps you had reason to murder them."

"No. I didn't know them. I didn't kill them. Jaro did. He is a thug. And a liar."

"Jaro works for Erich, who is a respected member of the community here. Erich vouches for Jaro as an honest man."

Matty laughed. He repeated the words. "Erich vouches for him. And you believe Erich. I was falsely accused before, in England. I faced trial by jury. Witnesses saved me. There must be those who can testify to what Erich and Jaro are. Is it to be a jury trial again?"

261

"No. Pope Clement has decided otherwise."

Matty looked surprised. "Pope Clement? I thought Urban was pope."

"A lot has happened since you left. We now have two popes. Robert of Geneva, the Archbishop of Cambrai has been elected by the same council who elected Urban. It's all a bit of a mess, if you ask me. But Robert's appointment directly affects you. He no longer has need for the support of the Benedictine. He has achieved his goal without you."

Matty struggled to take in what he had just been told. "Robert of Geneva, a mass murderer, is now the pope, the head of the Christian church. How could the cardinals do such a thing?"

Jean looked round anxiously. He knew they were alone, but even the thickest walls had ears. "Hold your tongue," he whispered. "You will get us both killed."

Matty shrugged. "That fate already awaits me. Whatever I say can't harm me more. So how will they decide to execute me if not through trial by jury?"

"The new pope favours God's judgement rather than the judgements of men. You are to have a trial by ordeal."

"What does that mean?" asked Matty.

"I'm not surprised you are unfamiliar with it. It's an ancient method, and unusual now. The pope used to be a lawyer. He believes trial by ordeal is fitting in your case. The question to be asked is whether you are sent by God or the Devil. That is not something for men to judge. Only God can do so. The trial will allow God to answer. If you are innocent, you have nothing to fear."

"Now that I have my memory almost restored, I know that wherever an Erich or a Jaro has taken a dislike to me I have *much* to fear."

"Your memory is fully back?"

"Almost. And with it came knowledge that I have a precious family in England. If you had told me a week ago that I was to be hanged for a murder I did not commit, I might have thought it a blessing. I was in despair. Now I have reason to live."

"If you are innocent, you will live to see them."

"So, what exactly will happen at this trial?

"It is yet to be decided. There are a number of options."

"Any pleasant ones? Trial by feasting, perhaps?"

Jean's face hardened. "Do not be so cynical in the face of your god's judgement. It is not a matter to joke about."

"Of course, you are right. I must face this trial that will determine whether I live or die with cheer and enjoy the suffering I am going to endure before my death. In fact, I will be like a flagellant, relishing the pain, enjoying the lashings or drownings or whatever else is deemed to be suitable justice for me."

"You are truly damned. I will pray for your soul."

The priest called the guard and marched out of the dungeon.

Matty was left with his thoughts. He closed his eyes and watched his children playing once more, reliving happier times. Times he may never experience again.

But what he said to Jean was right. He now had so much to lose by death that he was determined he would not go there without a fight.

Chapter Thirty-Five

A corn mill north of Avignon, September 1378

Edwina was lucky. The miller could have killed her for what she had done.

At the sound of the approaching hound she had panicked. She had lost a hand to a vicious hound and was not going to let this one take more of her. So she waited until she knew the hound was close, then spun round and kicked it with all her might.

The sound of her foot on the animal's head was sickening, as was the sight of one of the smallest dogs she had ever seen lying still in the grass, its neck broken. Her imagination had got the better of her when she heard the hound approaching, magnifying the panting and slavering to the level of a huge beast.

The boy fishing by the river was distraught, his pet's life ended by a chance encounter. Edwina was mortified by what she had done, but too late to make amends.

The miller was calm, gentle, kind, understanding. He consoled his son and took the dog's body for dignified disposal. His son was less forgiving. Edwina said sorry as many times as she could. Her apologies sounded hollow.

The miller's wife was as kind as her husband. She saw the state Edwina was in, contrite and with clothes still wet from having been in the river, her face covered in insect bites and hands caked in mud from her scramble out on to the bank. She boiled water for Edwina to wash and loaned her a linen dress while she scrubbed her clothing then dried it in the late evening sunshine.

After washing, Edwina sat by the mill pond. She was tired from the effort of fighting the river. The miller's wife watched her for a while, wondering why there was such sadness in her face, not knowing about the deaths of Briony and Philippe.

When Edwina's clothes were dry enough to put on, she hurried to get ready. She did not want to overstay her welcome. The miller's wife gave her some food and fresh spring water. To Edwina, such kindness felt like a punishment. She felt she deserved scorn. The dog was so tiny and was loved so much by the boy. But more importantly, she felt guilty to be alive when Briony was not.

The miller's wife gave her directions to Avignon, along an easier path than the mule track had been but still away from the more dangerous main highway.

Edwina thanked the woman for her kindness but could not face saying goodbye to the little boy. Before long, she found herself on a rise in the landscape. She looked back towards the mill, thinking there were good people as well as bad in the world. Then she looked up at the sky. To the west she saw no clouds, just the oranges and reds of a sunset. But elsewhere it was grey and black. A storm approached. She walked faster, but within minutes the clouds reached her and the wind was on her.

It was like no wind she had ever known. The moorland winds near her home in England were fierce and cut through her bones without mercy, but this was even stronger, more powerful. She was pushed backwards and could not stay on her feet. It felt like some devil was expending its fearsome breath just on her.

She made for the comparative shelter of nearby woods and crouched behind the largest oak she could find, praying for the wind to cease.

She expected such a force of nature to last long into the night and beyond, but amazingly it stopped abruptly after only a short burst. And she thought her prayers must have been heard.

She shook her hair to get rid of some of the dust the wind had created. Then she saw that she was beside an old oak tree. The tree had been struck by lightning some years before. Shoots of recovery told of the tree's fight for survival. It was so like the tree she had grown up with, the one she knew as her Moses Tree.

God spoke to Moses through a lightning tree, so the name was given to any tree similarly struck. But it was not a lightning bolt that struck

Edwina's tree. Men had burned down her grandparents' home with them and their children still inside. The tree burned with the house.

Seeing this oak tree gave her mixed emotions. She was already feeling homesick. As a reminder, it gave her some comfort, but it also reminded her just how far from home she was.

Nevertheless, she felt a calmness as she sat for a while under the tree. She closed her eyes and thought of her family and friends, remembering good times playing with her brother Daniel; helping her mother pick herbs in the manor garden; and playing hide and seek with her father round the grounds of the hunting lodge.

She instinctively felt for her amulet, but she had given it to Briony. She felt naked without it.

Thoughts of her father reminded Edwina why she was there. And thoughts of Briony reminded her how the young nun had given her new hope in her quest to find her father. She wondered whether she would ever get to meet the Benedictine monk Briony had so wanted her to. Perhaps he would give her some guidance, some avenue to follow in her search. She had to believe it, because otherwise she was drifting, without purpose, ever further from home.

There was only a little daylight left, but she set off again, this time with a spring in her step. She had a new determination. She would not let negative emotions overwhelm her.

By morning she reached the outskirts of the city. Her food had run out but her spirits remained high as she passed a series of waterside industries, each one dependent in some way or other on the river.

She passed another mill. This time it was a fulling mill. A water wheel drove fulling stocks, hammers pounding loosely woven wool to produce a tighter weave. Pounded wool was drying on frames.

Further along there was a flour mill, then a cottage outside which a woodturner was busy fashioning handles for farming implements.

Girls and boys were going back and forth to the river, yokes on their backs and buckets at either end. And there was smoke from blacksmiths' fires.

The heart of the city was not yet visible and she was unsure which way to go. She saw a young woman with baskets loaded on a donkey heading in a direction where the river seemed to widen. She thought it must be the way to the city centre. She approached the woman and asked in French if she was right. The woman replied politely, but in a local dialect. Edwina could not make out what was being said. She decided to trust her instincts and follow the woman anyway.

She passed more light industry then the environment changed as dwellings replaced workshops. The scene was like any of the cities Edwina knew in England. The houses were roughly built, timber framed, some with wattle and daub infill, others fully timbered. A few had an upper storey but most did not. A large proportion verged on being derelict.

The streets were muddy and the mud contained all kinds of detritus, including animal excrement. At least, she thought it was animal excrement. She hoped that was all it was.

Pools of standing water were everywhere. And the people looked just like the needy she had seen in the poorer areas of Lincoln or London. And just like in England, there were those who lived life with a smile on their face, full of joy. They had few possessions but found joy in the simple humour and companionship of family and friends.

It was the afternoon. The woman with the donkey turned into a street at right angles to the river. It felt wrong. Edwina was sure the city was further on. She was anxious about continuing, not knowing how far she still had to go and not wanting to be alone in a strange city at night. And she was tired, having walked far and missed a night's sleep.

She saw a small stone building. There was a roughly made wooden cross at the entrance. It was a place of worship, a chapel.

The door was open and she ventured inside with caution.

The chapel was tiny, only big enough for individual, private worship. There was a locked case set into the stone wall. In it was a silver cross, visible but safe from theft. There was an inscription above the case, written in Latin. Edwina's Latin was patchy but the quotation was one she knew. *Come to Me, all you who labour and are heavy laden, and I will give you rest.* Flowers, votive offerings, a candle and some grapes had been lovingly placed underneath the cross. Otherwise there was nothing in the chapel but a single bench and stone floor.

She went outside. There was nobody about. Everyone had retired for the night. She decided to stay in the chapel. It would be safer than wandering the streets. She went back inside. She was starving and the grapes were tempting, but she resisted. They were an offering, lovingly left by some devout worshipper. They were not hers to take. She curled up on the bench. It was cold, but she was so tired it didn't matter. She soon fell asleep.

Her night was peaceful, undisturbed, and she was still sleeping when dawn broke and an old woman carrying fresh flowers came into the chapel. Edwina was not the first person the woman had found using the place for shelter, but a new discovery was always a shock. The woman coughed deliberately, to wake the sleeping Edwina.

The old woman cocked her head to acknowledge Edwina but said nothing, waiting for Edwina to decide between fight or flight. She sighed with relief when Edwina started to apologise for being there.

Communication was again difficult. It was more than just a difference in dialect. The local language was Occitan, which was quite unlike French. But the woman understood and held up a hand. No apology was needed. She pointed to the quotation. The chapel was there to serve everyone who needed to pray or was lost, or simply tired. She finished her daily task, changing the flowers.

Edwina thanked the woman for her kindness, keeping to the simplest of French and using gestures. "Merci pour votre gentilesse," she said. The woman cocked her head again and smiled.

Edwina went out into the day. The new resolve she had found was still with her and she was determined to stay positive. She told herself so. She remembered her friend Mary's words to her. *'Go with strength of purpose'*.

It transpired that she was nearer the city centre than she had imagined. Within a few streets walk she was staring at the ramparts of the main city. But what to do next? She knew no-one. Her resolve faltered slightly as she struggled to formulate a plan. She was here to find the Benedictine, but there were practical matters to resolve first, the basics of food and a roof over her head.

She spent the day wandering aimlessly. It gave her a sense of the layout of the city and the vibrancy of its people, but she needed to do more than take in her new surroundings. She kept returning to the same place, going round in circles. She had neither food nor money to buy it. She drank water from a well. It was a risk. Her father had always told her to avoid well water, especially in large towns or cities. But she had no choice.

Before she knew it the day was ending and she had achieved nothing. Worse still, she had nowhere to bed down for the night. There was only one thing she could do.

She returned to the chapel. The door was open just as it had been the night before. She went inside and curled up once again on the bench. But this time she sobbed and struggled to sleep. She had felt lonely before in her life. She had felt homesick before. But never like this. Despair washed over her like the water when she was fighting for her life in the river.

The next morning she was awake when the old woman arrived with another bunch of fresh flowers. This time the woman saw the tear lines on Edwina's cheeks, and understood, offering her hand, making a physical connection. "Viens," said the woman.

Edwina was led to a long building. It looked like a typical farm outbuilding, a byre perhaps. As they got nearer a sound grew. Not animal sounds but human activity, despite the early hour.

269

Inside, women were working. It was an unusual sight. In Edwina's experience, industry on such a scale was done by men. The work women did was invariably smaller scale and done at home.

The old woman led Edwina along to the end of the workshop. They passed women beavering at their work stations. The work was all textile related but the tasks varied. A group of women worked on blankets. Others unpicked used clothing, which then transferred to other stations to be remade as something new. There were women applying buttons, and in one corner were ropemakers.

They reached the end, where a man sat reading a ledger. He was clearly a foreman of sorts. The old woman said something to him in the local dialect. He turned to Edwina. "Can you sew?" he asked in good English.

Edwina nodded but drew back the sleeve of her dress to reveal the stump where her hand should be. The foreman stared angrily at the old woman, then pointed to the door. "No use to me," he said.

Edwina hated needlework. As a child she avoided lessons by pretending that her missing hand made her useless at it, but she had also seen it as a challenge and in private developed some skills, using various parts of her body to compensate for her missing hand. She enjoyed being the only one who knew her ability. It was a game, something to amuse herself with as she was growing up.

But now she needed money for food and accommodation, and that meant she would have to work, at least until she could decide her next steps in life.

She walked over to one of the women, who was cutting cloth. The woman used one hand to cut and the other to hold the cloth still. Edwina ushered the woman to stand and took her place, then finished the cutting, using her knee to serve as the steadying hand.

The other women in the room were now watching with interest.

At another station a woman was using a lucet, a small wooden tool shaped like a catapult, to make cord and braids. This time Edwina sat down and took hold of a lucet, placing it under her armpit, then threaded the end of a length of wool through the hole in its centre and took the thread in her teeth. Her good hand could now wrap the wool as expertly as the other woman had been doing.

Her eyes were bright as she enjoyed the minor triumph of showing how she had mastered her disability. But she had to make an admission. "There are tasks here that are beyond me, or I would be slow to complete. But I can do most of the jobs."

The foreman laughed then nodded to the old woman. Edwina had made her case successfully. She had work. "I need a place to stay," she said to the foreman. "And money today."

He looked at her, weighing her up. "You can stay at one of our houses and you can eat there, but you will get no money until you have earned it." Three of his words stood out for her. *You can eat.* He turned away, ending the conversation. For Edwina it was enough. She would have a roof over her head and food in her belly.

The old woman placed Edwina at a station. The women there were fashioning mid-quality garments. It was a test. If she could match their quality of finish she would be kept at that station. Otherwise, she would be put on to simpler tasks, earning less money.

At the end of the day the old woman examined Edwina's work. It was good, but the old woman gave no congratulation, only a criticism. "Trop lent," she said. *Too slow.*

Having missed a night's sleep and worked hard for the day, Edwina was tired. She was taken to a house where she was given a bed in a dormitory. She recognised some other women from her place of work but there were others who worked at other sites.

She washed then joined the women at a long table in a dining room. She made no connections with them, because of the problem she had with the local language. She ate greedily, finally nourishing herself, then retired early and was asleep within minutes.

The next day, she was roused at dawn and taken back to her new place of work. The day passed slowly. Still there were no connections, no new friendships. She tried to work more quickly. The work was hard, with little reward other than the food that was supplied.

The station she had been put on earned some small extra privileges. There was more variety of food on offer and even a cup of weak wine at the end of the day. But working quickly was taking its toll. She had cramps in her leg and her stump throbbed. She made mistakes that needed correction, reducing her overall output. The woman had been right. She was too slow. "Tomorrow, there," said the woman, pointing to a less demanding station. So she would lose the extra benefits.

The repetitive nature of the work reminded her so much of her life as a ten-year-old. In a way, her life had come full circle. She was again a singleton spending her days with the women doing *'women's things'*. But at home she had at least been able to converse to pass the time.

The pattern continued for several days. At evening meals she remained an isolated figure. The other women seemed kind and tried to communicate with her but she was feeling sad, trapped. She had no time to do anything but work, eat and sleep. She almost forgot why she had come to Avignon. She decided things must change.

An opportunity arose for her to speak with the foreman. She now knew his name to be Garnier. He came to her station to examine her work, interested to see what someone could achieve with only one hand. She stopped working and spoke to him. Some of the other women gasped. It was something they would not dare do.

"Monsieur Garnier, might I speak to you?" she said.

He shrugged, as if to say, *'if you must'*.

"I do appreciate having this job," she said. "But I need to know where it is leading me."

He frowned. "Go on," he said, expectantly. This could be entertaining, he thought.

"I am getting fed and have somewhere to sleep, and I thank you for that, but have received no payment beyond that, and have no free time to myself."

He raised his eyebrows. Then he looked round in mock survey of the surroundings. "Are the doors locked here?" he said. "Are you free to walk out whenever you have had enough?" His eyes bore into her.

Then he leaned forward, his nose almost touching hers. He whispered; his voice laced with sarcasm. "Perhaps I could organise a tour of the city for you on a fine sunny day. Would you like that?" She avoided his gaze and did not answer. "But of course you would not eat that day. How could you, after doing no work? But you are not a prisoner here. You are free to leave." He pointed to the door. She did not move. He straightened. His voice sharpened. "You will be paid when your work deserves it," he said, and walked away, smiling to himself.

Edwina was angry and tired. She sat for a moment trying to regain some composure but it was hard. She had a strong sense of justice. This was not right. Her mood built until, for the first time in a long while she fell into a fit, one of her seizures.

The other women watched in horror. Such things were to be feared as signs of possession. They moved back as far as they could in the cramped workshop.

But one woman stepped forward, knowing what to do. She supported Edwina in the way Michel had done a few weeks earlier, making her comfortable and safe from harming herself.

It was brief. Within minutes Edwina was alert again, though disorientated. She realised what had happened and felt a mixture of fear and shame. Fear at what the reaction might be from those around her. Shame because although she knew the seizures were not her fault, she never liked being the centre of attention and when all eyes were on her she always felt she was on display, as if naked.

The foreman showed some uncharacteristic humanity. "Take some air," he told her.

She went outside. It was a sunny day with a bright blue sky. She sat alone, thinking about what had just happened. She remembered her father's views about her fits. He once said she was more likely to have a seizure when under acute stress. It seemed to accord with her current circumstances.

She had been grateful for the work here. It had served a purpose she desperately needed. But it was not far from being a form of slavery. At home, tenant farmers toiled long days only to owe their landlords more at the end of the day than at its beginning, but at least they worked in the open air and usually were accompanied by their families. Here, women hardly saw the light of day, and how often did they see their children?

She went back inside and approached one of the other women. "Combien de temps êtes-vous ici?" she asked.

"Six ans," was the flat reply. Six years.

Edwina asked another woman, who answered four, and another said eight. It made up her mind. She courteously thanked the foreman and the old woman for the bed and food she had earned, then walked back out into the sunshine. She had no plan. She was taking a huge risk. But she knew it was the right thing to do.

She made her way to the ramparts, for no reason other than to be in the heart of the city. A feeling came upon her. It was something she had felt before, when she was held prisoner in a cottage on the English coast. She had dismissed it then but later discovered its truth. So now when she felt it, she accepted it as genuine. She sensed his presence. Her father was nearby.

Briony's words came back to her. The young nun said there must be a reason why they had met. Now she knew. It had brought her here, to where her father was.

She wandered the streets and lanes just hoping to see him round a corner. In some side streets she saw people preparing to settle down to a night sleeping rough. They looked purposeful, as if this was a regular routine. It scared her, not because she feared they would do her harm, but because she was gaining insight into what she might become if she lived like they did. She saw one woman rocking

274

backwards and forwards as if possessed by some demon, and a young man cried softly to himself.

She thought about going back to the chapel but dismissed the idea. That would take her full circle back to a place she had only escaped by entering the clutches of the textile workshop. She needed to move on, even if that was a dangerous thing to do.

She went to the old bridge, thinking she could shelter underneath. It would give her protection from the wind and be a good place to sleep. There she found whole families and she knew this was their regular spot. One or two looks told her not to invade their precious space.

She sat down by the river and said a prayer, seeking guidance. Her eyes were closed. She felt a hand on her shoulder and jumped up, turning to face whatever new threat was there. She recognised the person. It was one of the women from the workshop, the one who said she had been there four years, the same one who helped her during her seizure.

The woman held up a hand in apology for startling Edwina. "Viens," she said, and Edwina followed her.

The woman's home was a long way from the city centre. They seemed to walk forever. As they did, the woman collected twigs, until her arms were full. Edwina decided to do the same, hoping it would be of benefit to the woman. She thought how, as well as doing a full day's work, the woman made this lengthy journey twice each day.

The house was not even in a residential area of the city. There were more workshops, heavier industries than the ones she had seen before. There was an ironworks, around which the air was filled with noise and soot, with flakes of ash flying and floating in the air.

In side streets were some lighter industries. Here a pottery, there an enamelling workshop.

Finally, they were at a building where leather bellows were made, specifically for the ironworks. Edwina was taken up stone steps at the side. The woman and her family lived above the workshop; their air polluted by the stench and ash flakes.

275

The woman was greeted by her children, two girls and a boy all aged under five. There was no sign of a husband. An older woman was there, boiling stew on a fire, sleeves rolled up showing tanned, muscular arms. She did not acknowledge Edwina, who thought the woman was most probably the grandmother of the family.

There was a chimney, the only benefit of living above the workshop, with its own fire below. In winter the room would be warmer, and of course the fire was good to cook on. But on this late summer evening the heat outside was intensified by the heat from the fireplace, making the room almost unbearable. There was one window, shutters opened, but no cooling breeze passing through it.

The fireplace provided a focal point for the family's activities. As well as the pot with the stew, there were smaller pots hanging from nails at the fireside as well as a basket holding the twigs collected on the walk home. They provided the fuel for the fire. Edwina added her twigs to the basket, earning a smile from the woman.

The woman finally introduced herself with a single word. Her name. "Lorraine," she said, offering her hand to Edwina.

"Edwina," was the simple reply.

The old woman dished out the stew, including a bowl for Edwina. She did not ask her daughter why she brought a guest home. She simply filled the extra bowl. It was generous hospitality, a kindness from one person to another, needing no explanations.

Everything was understood. Lorraine had taken pity on Edwina, knowing how hard it would be for Edwina to survive without work, and the whole family joined with that sacrifice. It was a potentially lifesaving gesture, and all Edwina could do was to show her thanks through expressions and the occasional 'merci'.

After the meal, one of the children saw Edwina's arm where her hand should be. It was innocent inquisitiveness. Edwina let the child touch her leather glove and felt a sisterly kind of joy in the moment.

Before they all settled for the night the woman told a story to settle the children down. Edwina sensed it was one they all knew, because

276

there were looks of anticipation in the children's eyes at what was to come. She made out some of the words, enough to know the story was about a knight and a shepherdess. There was something of interest for the boy in the knight's daring, and something for the girls as the knight's love for the shepherdess grew.

Edwina was given a blanket and a place to sleep on the floor. It was hard and unforgiving, but safe and warm. She lay awake, Lorraine's family's kindness triggering thoughts of another kindness she had experienced on this journey.

She had often wondered to herself why she agreed to accompany Briony to this city. She now knew. It was the nun's warmth and naive sense of purpose. How could anyone not find comfort with such a person.

A tear formed in remembrance of a friend lost.

But as she settled down under her blanket, watching the fire burn and listening to the sounds of the sleeping children, she had a sudden cosy feeling. After the hardships of the past few days she now felt uplifted. She thanked God for Lorraine and her family. They had welcomed her into their home and it felt good. She was smiled to herself and thought that tomorrow might quite possibly turn out to be a wonderful day.

Chapter Thirty-Six

The Villa Libera, September 1378

Ishraq was working with the horses, preparing them for a race meeting to be held the following week.

Erich came to the stables to tell him where the race meeting was to be held. "It's not far from Oudin's place in Villeneuve. It's at the home of a cardinal," he said.

Ishraq showed surprise. "Cardinals racing horses?" he said.

"Indeed," replied Erich. "You sound surprised, but many of the cardinals owe their appointments not to their strong faith but to the nepotism of the popes, past and present. Rome or Avignon, it's all the same. Brothers, cousins, brothers-in-law…relatives, friends and dubious associates of all types have been appointed over the years. Pope John appointed three of his nephews as cardinals. Inevitably, some are more interested in the world of men than the realms of angels. And horse racing is one way to pass time profitably when you have few other duties to perform. Now, I will leave you to do some work for a change."

Ishraq had delivered Lakshmi to the Dane the previous day, and his mood was low. His handling of the horses was a little rough as he struggled to contain his emotions. A stable boy decided to intervene and took over handling the horse. Ishraq shook his head, angry with himself for losing control and taking things out on the poor beast.

Jaro came into the stables. "Erich has a job for you," he said. "Go to his chambers immediately."

Erich's chambers were bigger than Lella's. There were two large rooms and one small. The large rooms were used as the main bedroom and its anteroom. The small room was more of a private dressing area that also served as a storage place. Erich allowed few people into the rooms. There were two maids who came in to clean, serve food and drinks and, if required, carry out *other duties.*

Ishraq waited in the anteroom. It was the worst kind of torture as his mind whirled with thoughts of what had been taking place in the next room. When the bedroom door opened, he wanted to catch a glimpse of Lakshmi, but Erich closed the door behind him.

Erich was in an impatient mood. Ishraq thought it was because the Dane wanted to return to his fun with Lakshmi. The thought made Ishraq want to scream.

"I want you to go back to Villeneuve tomorrow," said Erich. "When you went to Oudin's before you did well, but I need to find out more about his horses before the races next week. Information is everything."

"Won't Oudin suspect that's why I'm there?"

"Of course he will. But it's part of the game we play. Oudin will try to outfox you. You will need your wits about you."

"Am I taking the girl back today?"

"No. She's staying longer this time."

It was another blow. Ishraq would not see Lakshmi before going to Villeneuve and would be constantly worrying about her in Erich's clutches. If he had a weapon, he might well have sacrificed all then and there in a reckless, suicidal attack on Erich. Even with no weapon, he was tempted to try, until Jaro came in, saying he needed a word with Erich. Ishraq was ushered out and the moment was lost.

As he returned to the stables, he saw Lella leaning on a fence, looking in his direction, smiling. It was a false smile. He saw through it. She curled her finger to beckon him. They had not spoken since Lella gave him food for thought by suggesting they had a common interest in getting Lakshmi away from Erich.

"It's happening," she said, the smile now gone.

"What's happening?"

"There's a race meeting coming up."

"I know. I have orders to go and spy at Villeneuve."

"He's taking *her*, the whore who stirs your loins. He's taking her to a public place. Showing off his trophy. You know what that means. My days with him are numbered. If we don't act now, it will be me working at the brothel instead of that bitch."

"Don't call her that, please."

"I'm sorry, but she is a rival. For that I hate her."

"I need to see her."

"Why?"

"I don't know. I just do. I can't think straight. Maybe it will help."

Lella scowled. "Your brains are in your balls. That's why you can't think straight. But if you really think it might help, I will arrange it this afternoon. Erich is going to the city. Find out what she knows about his plans. But don't just waste time mooning over her. And don't turn to jelly. Get me some information."

"I will."

****

Ishraq waited nervously. Lella had bribed the guard whose job it was to loosely watch over Lakshmi. In the remoteness of the villa, there was never a risk of her attempting to run away, but Erich thought she might try to escape in another way. He knew she loathed him. He thought she might take her own life, which would be inconvenient.

"It's a sign of how confident he is in her happiness," joked Lella. "I have bribed the guard. I told him I'd like a few minutes alone with the girl, to talk about *women's things*. I gave him enough so he will not tell Erich about it. So I've bought some precious minutes for you. But don't dare take advantage. If you so much as touch her and Erich finds out, neither of us will see this day out. Understood?"

Ishraq nodded. There was never any danger of him making a physical approach to Lakshmi, nor of him telling her how he felt about her. He worshipped her, but only from afar, a lovesick puppy.

Lella opened the door partially, then whispered, "You have a visitor, my dear." She opened the door the rest of the way and Ishraq stepped inside, head bowed, nervous, heavy with humility.

"I will leave you for a little while, but I will be nearby, listening for any sound that concerns me," said Lella pointedly.

She left and closed the door. Lakshmi was brushing her long hair. She was seated at a small desk on which were two wooden figures. They were carvings of beautiful women dressed in exotic dresses like the ones Lakshmi wore. She saw Ishraq staring at them.

"They are goddesses," she told him. She picked one up. "This is Ganga, who cleansed the world by bringing a great river into it." She put it down gently and picked up the other one. It was of a woman with four arms instead of two. "And this is Lakshmi."

His eyes lit up in surprise. "You?"

"No. Not me. But I was named after her. She is the goddess of wealth."

"It's a beautiful name," he said, then felt awkward having said it.

"They are my constant companions. They keep me safe. What about you? Do you have gods to protect you?"

"I was brought up by a Christian man, but he taught me nothing about the faith really. It was just there, like an old coat. He never prayed."

"Your skin colour is like mine."

"I think I was born to the east and sold at a market."

"Perhaps the same one where I was sold."

Ishraq's emotions were running high in her presence. "You were sold?" he gabbled. "How could anyone wish to sell you?"

"I was one of many children. My parents could not afford to feed us all. I was chosen to be sold because I would bring the best price. I was glad to be of worth to my family, to help them survive."

"That was a selfless act. You were brave."

She felt embarrassed. Nobody had ever given her praise in that way before. "Why are you here?" she asked.

281

"I have seen you many times but we have spoken little. I wanted to know you more."

"For what purpose?"

"I don't know," he lied. "I think, maybe you are like me."

The door opened and Lella appeared, far too soon for Ishraq. "Time is up," she said.

Ishraq wanted to object but words would not come. Lella had warned him to use the time well and he had failed. What they were doing was dangerous. He was angry with himself. He had wasted his short time with Lakshmi. He stammered some words. "I, I, I am glad to have, to have talked with you," he managed before Lella ushered him out.

Lella called the guard to return, then found Ishraq sulking in the courtyard. "Well?" she asked. "What have you learned from that?"

He was lost for words. He had learned nothing of value. Then something came to him. "I have learned an important lesson," he said. "I now know what true love is."

"Gods above! You think now of love? Like I said, your brains are in your balls."

"That's not what I meant, though maybe I do love her, and not just for how she looks. No, what I meant was that true love is sacrifice."

"So would you sacrifice yourself for her?"

"Yes, I would."

Part Eight

The white stallion

Chapter Thirty-Seven

The Palais des Papes, October 1378

Matty had a visitor. Jaro had decided to have some sport with him.

"We are all waiting," said Jaro. "Waiting for the famous monk who works miracles. We are wondering why he is still here when he could magic his way out." He gave a flourish, depicting a flight, an escape.

Matty did not bite. He stayed calm and silent. What was the point in responding to Jaro's taunts? He knew what would follow either way. Jaro would resort to violence. And he was right.

Matty was sure he had suffered worse beatings but he could not remember when. By the time Jaro finished he was bent double, holding his stomach, and covered in bruises to body and face. Jaro just kept yelling the same two words. *'Say something!'*. It seemed Matty's refusal to speak was fuelling the big man's anger.

Soon after Jaro left, Jean arrived. He was shocked, but not surprised to find Matty in such a state. He made to offer some comfort but Matty waved him away. "Don't worry, I will live," Matty told him stoically.

"Are you well enough to receive some news?" asked Jean. Matty nodded. "The arrangements for your trial have been made."

Matty's greatest fear was confinement. He had long suffered from claustrophobia. "Am I to be buried alive?" he asked weakly.

"No. As I told you, the church has long since banned such trials."

"Forgive me if I have little trust in your church."

"I told you Pope Clement wanted your trial to fit the crimes for which you are accused. He has decided. You will be given the Eucharist."

Matty looked puzzled. "The bread and wine? Is that it?" He laughed, which made his ribcage hurt.

"Do not think it a weak test. It is quite the opposite. It has been used before and in your case his holiness believes it apt. He was struck by your refusal to take the bread and wine when he presented you to the cathedral congregation. He believes there was a reason for your refusal. The Devil's disciples cower at the altar of Christ. If you are a man of God, the angels will rejoice when you take the Eucharist and survive, but if, as he suspects, you are an imposter, a devil in disguise, God will surely strike you dead at the sacrament table."

Matty laughed. "You are telling me I just take the bread and wine then either die or walk away."

"You sound sceptical, as though you don't believe in God's will."

"What I find hard to believe is that I am that important to Him."

"We are all important in the eyes of God."

"I have never claimed to be what they say I am. If God knows that, how will I be judged?"

"I cannot answer that."

"I thought priests were his representatives on earth."

Jean scowled. "You try my patience."

"I'm sorry," said Matty. "But this is all too much for me. Tell me, will I be allowed to speak at the trial, to explain all that has led to this?"

"No. You will simply take the bread and wine. You will say nothing. And the date is set. One week from today."

"It will feel like a year."

Jean turned to go, then paused at the door. "There's a crowd outside. They are here for you. Some are calm and peaceful but others are shouting and throwing things at the doors. As far as they are concerned you are one of them, sent to be among them, just like our lord. There is already concern what would happen if you were convicted. The crowd might turn ugly. But the new pope is standing firm. The trial will go ahead regardless."

"What do *you* believe of me?"

"I have seen you do good things. But we all know how cunning the Devil is. Perhaps your good deeds are a veil, hiding your true self."

Matty shook his head. Sometimes he could not understand the world he lived in. "So any man who is good must be judged, in case he is

285

false. It does not encourage goodness. No wonder the world is as it is."

Jean scowled as he was leaving. "You would test the patience of the saints."

"I might just do that, after I have tested the patience of God."

Chapter Thirty-Eight

Villeneuve, October 1378

Oudin cut an impressive figure strutting round the grounds of his home, supreme in his environment, confident, positive, decisive.

He was not surprised to hear Ishraq was back. He went to the stables and greeted Erich's spy with a smile and a forthright welcome. "Get straight to the point," he said. "What does Erich want to know this time?"

Ishraq saw no point in lying. "The strength of your horses," he replied.

"Of course. Then come and see for yourself."

As they walked to the stables, Oudin asked an unexpected question. "How is Lella?"

Ishraq looked at Oudin with curiosity. "You know she has been unwell?"

"Yes. Erich has his spies, including yourself, but I also have mine. I know all that goes on at his stables. I know his horses and your ability with them, but my spies also tell me other things happening at the villa. Lella has been staying in her room. I'm told she has a sickness."

Ishraq did not want to betray a trust. "I cannot tell you things she would keep secret, but I can tell you she hopes to come to the races."

"Good. She has never been before. And she must be feeling better."

They reached the stables and Oudin introduced Ishraq to his horses, at least the ones he wanted Ishraq to see.

"What about the others?" said Ishraq, pointing in the direction of the hidden compound he had discovered before.

Oudin laughed, but duly led Ishraq to the compound. And there was indeed a new horse, a white stallion, not pure white but still a handsome beast. "He's a good horse, nothing special, but people will bet on him just because of how he looks," said Oudin. "Gamblers can be a fickle lot."

"So he could be the favourite."

"He probably will be. But he won't win. For one thing, I know Erich has acquired a young chestnut mare that will have the better of my stallion. It is usually the way, is it not, that a good woman can get the upper hand even against a good man." He laughed. "And there will be other good horses in the races. The cardinal who hosts the event has some excellent mounts."

Ishraq remembered what Erich had said. *Oudin will try to outfox you.* Perhaps he was doing just that. He tried a different approach. "Can I ask you to tell me a bit about yourself?" he said. "You don't have the local dialect."

"As you wish. I am just turned thirty years. I was born a Corsican nobleman but had to flee in 1372 when the Aragonese took control of the island. I managed to bring enough of my family wealth with me to be able to set myself up well enough here in Avignon, but I soon discovered that Erich the Dane was the main man here. He rules the city just as surely as the church does. So I try to get the better of him now and again."

"In the races."

"Yes, and with trade deals and so forth."

Ishraq suspected Oudin must have reason to be so open with him. Oudin asked for directness, so he gave it. "Why are you so helpful, showing me your prize stallion when you know I spy for Erich?"

"Erich and I are wealthy men, perhaps the richest round here, apart from the popes of course. But sometimes, making money gets boring. So we play our games with one another to pass the time. Erich expects me to tell you nothing about my new horse, so I do the opposite. It will make him think, just as you are doing, *what is that cunning Oudin up to?* He will probably think I have deceived you and that the horse is a winner, though I think you know enough about horses to form your own judgement about that. Either way, I enjoy knowing he is trying to work it out. He would do the same given the opportunity."

"*Are* you deceiving me?"

Oudin's eyes narrowed and he touched his nose mischievously. "That would be telling." He laughed.

Ishraq could see differences between Erich and Oudin. The Corsican possessed charm, a sign of his noble birth. Erich was anything but noble and thrived not through personality but the muscle of men like Jaro. Oudin was a persuader, and a successful one.

Ishraq took a longer look at the stallion. Oudin had been honest with him. The stallion was beautiful but lacked the strength to win races. Erich's mare would certainly beat it.

"By the way," said Oudin. "I believe you are acquainted with the monk they call the Benedictine."

Ishraq shrugged. "I have met him," he said, wondering briefly how Oudin knew, then remembering what Oudin had told him. The Corsican had his spies.

"You might be interested to know he has been arrested and is in a dungeon at the palais."

That caught Ishraq's attention. "For what crime?"

"For being himself, of course." Oudin laughed and walked away.

The news was upsetting. The monk had helped Ishraq to help Lella, and Ishraq hoped he would be soon released. But he had more immediate concerns of his own. Lakshmi.

There was no more for him to do at Oudin's. He crossed the old bridge into the city, then found himself heading towards the brothel where Lakshmi lived. He knew she was not there and he had no reason to go, but still, it was where he went.

He stood at the gate looking up at the building. He had been here many times before but never noticed its condition. The façade had a faded grandeur. It must have been a place of some importance in the past. It was near enough to the palais to perhaps have been the home of one of the bishops. But now, stones needed replacing and the windows were too dirty to see through. Ishraq thought that might be deliberate, a good way to keep out prying eyes. Nevertheless, the overall sense was of somewhere that had former glory but was now neglected.

He had no plan. He just wanted to be near where she lived.

A cart drew up and a well-dressed man got out. Most carts were simple things, but this one had springs for a more comfortable ride on the rough roads, plus steps at each side, with carved rails to assist passengers climbing in or out. There was even an awning to give a degree of protection from the wind and rain.

The man was tall, muscular and wore distinctive clothing, including a gaudy hat with peacock feathers. He strode past Ishraq and went through the gate. The door of the house was kept permanently locked but before the man reached it, it opened for him. Ishraq saw a figure behind the door, a young woman. She saw him but quickly closed the door behind the man in the peacock hat and was gone. Ishraq heard a bolt being drawn across. There was no way in for him.

He sat for a while. Then, to his surprise, the girl he had seen came out and approached him. "You are Ishraq the coachman," she said.

"My name is Ishraq, but I am a sailor, not a coachman," he replied.

"As you wish. Lakshmi speaks of you."

The words took him aback. He had thought he was invisible to Lakshmi, yet she spoke to this girl about him.

"She sees how you look at her," added the girl with a giggle.

Ishraq was flustered. "I mean her no harm," he gabbled.

The girl smiled. "She knows that. She thinks you are kind. She likes you."

That hit him even harder, like a thunderbolt. She *likes* me, he thought. It was all he could do to stay calm. But his face betrayed his thoughts. "I see that pleases you," said the girl. "But you must be realistic. Madame de Bruler will not allow Lakshmi to become close to you."

"But would Lakshmi like to become close with me?"

The girl's face was suddenly stern. "You have not heard what I said. It would not be allowed. So you must stop dreaming. Find another pretty girl. Avignon is full of them. Now, I must go back in. I will be missed. There are customers waiting."

"One with feathers in his hat."

The girl looked back at the house. She did not like Ishraq's questions and the man with the hat frightened her. "I must go," she said.

She went inside. Her aim had been to warn him off, but instead she had given him hope. *Lakshmi likes me*, he thought again. And the thought grew in volume. **Lakshmi likes me**. But she had also given him new reason to fear for Lakshmi's safety. Because the girl feared for hers.

Back at the villa, he once again gazed hopelessly at a building. This time it was the window of Erich's bedroom. He seethed, but now possessed a determination he previously lacked. There was a glimmer of hope. Lakshmi might just want to go with him, away from this life of slavery. But he needed to act quickly. Lella was right about that.

He went to his room and took out the pouch he kept his money in. Maybe he could buy Lakshmi's freedom.

He counted the coins. It was a pitiful amount. Ever since he discovered that Lella's illness might be the result of the cheap bread she was eating he had been telling people not to eat it. It meant giving them money to buy better bread. It was a futile effort. Those few who did buy better bread with his money still bought the cheap bread with their own. Most just spent his money on ale. And Ishraq's meagre funds had dwindled to almost nothing.

The chances of buying Lakshmi out from prostitution had always been extremely low. The madame must be earning a great deal from Erich. But with so little money, the idea was ludicrous.

He would have to find another way. He had to speak with her again, this time with a clearer idea what he wanted to say.

Chapter Thirty-Nine

Avignon, October 1378

Edwina wanted to earn her room and food. She offered to help Lorraine's mother in the kitchen but it was the old woman's domain and the offer was refused. The same applied to cleaning the home or washing clothes. The only way Edwina could make herself useful was by playing with the children, keeping them amused while teaching them a few basic words of English. She did that in the mornings, then used her free time in the afternoons, during the children's rest periods to wander the city looking for signs of her father.

Each time she saw a monk she approached him. Surely monks knew where to find the Benedictine, one of their own. But the language barrier always proved too difficult. She could never quite convey what she wanted. When she mentioned the Benedictine they recognised the name, and she constructed various non-verbal ways to ask if they knew where he might be, but none worked.

One afternoon she came across a monk on the steps of a small church. He was giving alms in the form of fruit and cheese to some ragged children. Despite her previous failures, she tried again with this monk.

As she struggled, a voice came from behind her. "Can I help you, mademoiselle?"

It was a priest who spoke English. She felt elated. Her luck had changed.

"I hope you can," she replied. "I am trying to find the man they call the Benedictine. Do you know where he is please?"

The priest nodded. "I do indeed. But why do you seek him?"

She hesitated. If she told the priest she thought the monk might be her father he would think her mad and walk away. "I believe I have met him before and would like to see him again," she said. "He made a big impression on me."

"Well, I too have met him and can understand you being drawn to him. He has unique qualities. I don't think I've met another who is so easy to warm to. My name is Frere Jean, by the way."

"And I am Edwina de Lucan, from Nottingham in England."

"England. You are a long way from home, mademoiselle."

"I am. But please, can you answer me a question and tell me how old he is? I want to be sure he is the same man I met before."

Jean gave a brief description of the Benedictine.

"He is the right age," said Edwina. "It might be him. Can you tell me where he is so I can go and see?"

The priest pointed at the imposing structure of the palais. "I am sorry to tell you, but he is in a dungeon in there, awaiting trial."

Edwina gasped. Her face drained, and Frere Jean bid her sit down on a nearby bench. "Whatever they think he has done, he is innocent," she said.

Jean frowned. "Opinions are divided about his guilt or innocence."

"What is the charge against him?"

"It's a question of who he is. Men who perform miracles attract interest, because some aren't what they seem to be."

"I'd very much like to see him."

Jean shook his head. "Impossible, unless of course you are rich enough to pay substantial bribes." He paused. Edwina said nothing in reply. "I thought not," he added.

Edwina's attention was taken again by the nearby monk's activities. "They do good work," she said.

"They do God's work," said Jean. "I have not been in the city long but this is somewhere I like to come to and help the monks when I can. I have been doing some fund-raising for them."

She was suddenly angry. "It's good that you do that, but the man awaiting trial in there also does God's work. I don't know about miracles, but I do know he helps the sick. He does not deserve a prison

293

cell. There must be something you can do to help me at least get to see him. I beg you, please."

He sighed. "You seem very upset about a man you say you met only once," he said.

She was getting nowhere, so decided to take a chance and trust the priest. He seemed kind. "I have not told you the full truth. I believe the Benedictine is my father," she blurted.

The priest sighed, and her fears proved right. He thought her mad. "Go back to England. There's nothing here for you," he snapped.

Edwina had a mixture of emotions. She now knew where her father was but his situation was not good. She left Frere Jean and wandered around the city until it was time to meet Lorraine. Each day they had been meeting on the old bridge at the end of Lorraine's day's work, then together they had walked on to Lorraine's home.

For the first time, Lorraine was late. Edwina waited until the point where she began to be worried. She walked in the direction of the workshop. Within sight of it, she stopped as she heard a quiet voice sobbing behind an old, abandoned cart. She knew it was Lorraine.

She found Lorraine doubled in pain, clutching her stomach and holding a piece of moss under her skirts. "What's wrong?" asked.

"I have my flowering," answered Lorraine. She had learned to speak slowly to give Edwina a better chance of understanding her. "I've been in pain all day and my work has been slow." She looked up.

Edwina saw bruises around Lorraine's eyes. Slow work had earned Lorraine a beating from the foreman. She helped her friend to her feet and supported her. They made slow progress home but managed to complete the journey. Lorraine's mother immediately came to assist and, for the first-time acknowledged Edwina's contribution, offering her warm eye contact by way of thanks.

The old woman disposed of the blood-covered moss, then gave her daughter something to ease the stomach pains and applied ointment to the bruises. As Edwina watched, she realised this was a routine they had developed. It was not the first incident of its kind.

She was angry and became animated, trying to convey that something should be done to punish the foreman and protect Lorraine from future harm. But the old woman calmly shook her head and Lorraine added some simple words, said firmly, leaving no room for challenge. "Merci, mais non," she said.

Edwina took a deep breath. She knew they were right. Justice was rarely available to the poor. If Lorraine complained it would likely result in losing her job, and how would that leave the family? She felt sickened. The old woman could see it and put an arm around her. "C'est la maison aussi," she said. French words she understood. They would lose their home as well, unable to pay the rent.

Edwina had watched helplessly as Briony lost her life. Now she was faced with two more situations about which she was powerless. The Benedictine monk lay helpless in prison on charges she did not understand, and her new friend Lorraine was being mistreated just for being a woman. It was too much. She went outside and let out a howl in frustration. Life was too cruel.

When Lorraine's mother served the day's stew there was silence. The children would normally chatter and bicker, full of energy. But they were quiet, subdued. They sensed their mother's discomfort. And the adults were lost in their own thoughts.

It was Lorraine, stoic and determined to alter the mood, who broke the spell. She remembered to speak slowly for Edwina. "Demain, courses des chevaux. Nous y allons. Vous aussi?"

Edwina had no interest in going to horse races, but refusal would seem ungrateful. This family had gone out of their way to help her when they had problems of their own. "Oui," she replied. "Moi aussi." She would go with them to the horse races.

Chapter Forty

The Palais des Papes, October 1378

Matty was thinking. There was nothing else to do.

His memories now were clear, his mind fully recovered. He was thinking about Stephen, his friend and mentor. It was Stephen's name that came to him when he regained consciousness in a ship off the coast of Brittany those months earlier. It was a sign of the monk's importance to him.

If anyone asked Matty to define *'saintly'* he would have given them a description of Stephen. Matty met Stephen at a time of personal crisis. Stephen took him in, gave him food and shelter, then showed him the importance of caring for the unfortunates in society, the *truly* unfortunates, including lepers. He taught Matty so much.

In all things, Stephen paid no regard for his own welfare. Eventually, it cost him his life. His tireless efforts to help the poor was never matched by any thought for his own welfare.

It was ironic. People lauded Matty as a healer, while Stephen, a true believer and skilled physician, lay forgotten in the graveyard of a minor monastery.

Matty wondered what Stephen would say to him now. What words of wisdom would come? And he found himself praying to Stephen, asking for his help, his intervention. He was tired and just wanted to be home with his wife and children. He missed them beyond words. He found himself begging Stephen's spirit for help, for an intervention with the angels to let him go free so he could return to England and be with them.

He smiled to himself. Did he believe in angels or spirits? Most people did. But did he? Did he believe he was communicating with his dead friend? Possibly not. But while he made his plea to Stephen, this room, this prison, seemed to melt away and he felt close to something that was hard to describe, something untouchable, intangible. He felt less alone and less suffocated by claustrophobia and foreboding.

It made him think of the monks at Villeneuve. They spent most of their time alone in rooms like this. Even when they were gathered, they were still alone, forbidden to talk or acknowledge the presence of others. He understood for the first time. He was alone here, isolated, but felt peaceful.

He thought about his daughter, Edwina. She was once kept captive like this, facing the uncertainty of what her captor might do to her. But she never gave up hope. He would try to do the same. He wondered where she was. He hoped she was safe and well in England, married perhaps and with a child of her own. The child would be his grandchild. He would like to be a grandfather. It seemed unlikely, because Edwina preferred adventure to homeliness. He could not imagine her as a dutiful wife nursing her infant by a fireside.

He lay down. There might not be many days of life left for him and using any of that time in sleep seemed a waste. But it was necessary. He was about to close his eyes, then saw that he had a visitor to his prison cell. A tiny mouse had found a way in. He wondered how. The walls and floors were so thick. He noticed the smallest of gaps under the solid oak door. It must have come in that way.

Watching the little mouse took his mind off his worries. It sniffed in search of food and found a few crumbs of bread that had flaked from his latest meal. He thought about cornering and capturing it, just for the company it would provide, but decided that one prisoner here was sufficient, so chased it under the door and out. "Stay free," he told it.

The distraction helped him settle and he was soon asleep.

He dreamed of being at the hunting lodge that was his home in England. He dreamed of a simple picnic by the nearby stream, his wife Charlotte beside him and their children playing in the water.

It was a night of restful peace, until he woke with a start. Because in his final dream of the night he saw them leaving the lodge, their most precious personal possessions loaded on to a cart. Charlotte looked back towards the place that had been her home for many years. There was a tear in her eye.

He sat up, wondering what it meant. And it came to him. He had not considered the reality of his family's situation. Now he did. If he was missing, presumed dead they would lose their home.

He clenched his fists in silent rage. And resolved even more that he must survive the ordeal and go home before it was too late for Charlotte and the children.

Chapter Forty-One

The grounds of a chateau, east of Avignon, October 1378

Ishraq rode behind Erich, Lakshmi, Jaro, and two of Erich's henchmen. Beside him was Lella. Behind them were two stablemen leading Erich's racehorses.

It had been two hours' ride from the villa. Lella was in a chatty mood, talking to Ishraq about a wide range of things he thought trivial. The weather. The prospects for Erich's new mare in the main race. Whether the cardinal's food and wine would be any good.

It made Ishraq uncomfortable. Only a matter of weeks earlier, Erich would have had him killed on the spot for talking with his woman. The difference now was plain to see. Ishraq and Lella could talk as much as they wished. Erich had moved on to a new relationship.

Ishraq could not take his eyes off Lakshmi. She rode a filly. Her silk sari was draped around her and over the horse's rear. His gaze was only broken when the sun caught the circlet she wore in her hair, dazzling him.

Lella leaned over to him. "Don't be too obvious. There are many eyes here," she warned him.

The chateau came into view. It had a moat, around which was a clearing, originally created to provide an unobstructed view from the chateau of any approaching raiders. A defensive arrangement. It seemed the cardinal thought stone walls and a moat were not enough.

The cleared area of grass had been scythed the night before and was covered in shining pearls of dew that were rapidly disappearing as the day warmed. It was readied as a racecourse.

Lella told Ishraq the chateau's owner had chosen not to attend his own race meeting. He considered himself above the likes of Erich and Oudin, so although he would make a lot of money from the event, he chose to stay away, avoiding having to commune with them.

At the previous races Ishraq had attended, Erich made money because he owned the men who took bets. He also took a slice from the profits of the many and various vendors and stall holders. Here it was different. It was the cardinal who would benefit. It meant the races themselves were more important to Erich. He could only make money here with a winning horse or by placing astute bets.

Other horse owners had already arrived and were gathering by tents near the chateau drawbridge. Ishraq saw Oudin and his entourage, including Oudin's professional rider, the one in the plain shirt. There was an area of light woodland where the work horses were looked after, and a special area set aside for the racehorses.

Erich barked out orders for Ishraq and the other stablemen to take his horses to the gathering area and make sure they were in the best condition after the journey from the villa. "You know what to do," he said to Ishraq, then made for the tents.

Ishraq nodded his assent. "Where will you be?" he asked Lella.

"I will be at the hospitality tents, but not in Erich's company. I have someone else I want to see today. I probably won't see you again until after the races. Don't let Erich down. It would not be good for you."

In the woodland, Ishraq supervised as Erich's horses were fed and groomed. There were to be five races during the day. The first two were for locals, mostly farmers racing their best farm horses. Then came the more serious races with specialist horses trained for the purpose. Erich had brought three, one for each of the lucrative races.

When he was satisfied that Erich's horses were being well prepared, Ishraq wandered the woodland gathering information about the other contenders. He saw Oudin's mounts, the white stallion taking pride of place. But then he was drawn to another horse, another stallion. Its coat was black but it glowed with an orange sheen that changed shape as the horse moved about, like the flickering flames of firelight.

A small, middle-aged man was grooming it. The man had dark skin, a similar tone to Ishraq's own. "He is beautiful," said Ishraq.

"Arabian. From the finest stock."

Ishraq drew closer and examined the stallion. "Who owns him?" he asked.

"My master is a prince. His horses are his pride and joy."

"I can see why."

Ishraq moved on but found no other horses that might threaten Erich's. The cardinal's horses were no match for Erich's, Oudin's or the Arabian stallion. He made his way to the tents to make his report.

Erich was lounging with Lakshmi on cushioned chairs, sipping wine and enjoying sweetmeats provided by the host. Ishraq told him about the Arabian horse. "It will take some beating," he said.

"Arabian, you say?" Erich stood up and paced the tent. "A prince, you say?" He was deep in thought, distracted enough for Ishraq to steal a glance towards Lakshmi, but she discreetly kept her head down.

"This changes things," said Erich.

The plan had been clear. Ishraq had advised Erich to bet modestly on the first four races, each of which were one circuit of the track round the chateau. The outcome for such short races was uncertain, with too many unknown factors. They were, therefore, hardest to fix.

Erich would bet bigger money on his own mare for the final race, a race of three circuits. He would get favourable odds because Oudin's stallion would be the clear favourite. But the new threat from the Arabian stallion worried him. "What must I do?" he asked.

"Bet on the Arabian horse," advised Ishraq

Erich thought for a moment. "I don't like it," he said. "What if it is all show and no substance?"

"It will win, trust me."

Erich shook his head, not in disagreement but in concern. He had a difficult decision to make. He did not like risking his money. He needed certainty. "Very well," he said. "I will heed your advice. But fetch Jaro for me."

301

Ishraq turned to go but could not resist another glance towards Lakshmi. She had not said a word in the time he was there. This time, Erich saw it and rounded on him, grabbing him by the neck. "Never do that again. Do you hear me?" Ishraq stayed calm and did not reply. "*Do you hear me*?" bellowed Erich. And this time, Ishraq nodded.

Erich let go and Ishraq went to find Jaro. He cursed himself. He should have been more careful. Or maybe he should have been braver and stood up to the Dane. He dismissed the thought. Erich was much stronger than he was and had his henchmen with him. There would surely come a time, a better opportunity, one chance that he would have to dare to take, regardless of the consequences for himself.

He found Jaro and told him Erich wanted to see him, then went to find Lella. She was the closest thing he had to a friend here. He went to the hospitality tents, looking for her.

He heard her before he saw her. She was in high spirits. The cardinal had organised a fair and she had spent some time and money at it. She had bought some Chateauneuf wine and the effects showed. She was shouting at, rather than talking to a well-dressed youth half her age. The youth looked embarrassed and Ishraq's arrival gave him the excuse he needed to make an exit, looking relieved.

Lella put her arms round Ishraq's neck. She was drunk. But her arms slipped away as her body control evaded her and her legs gave way, leaving her kneeling on the grass. Ishraq helped her up and eased her out into the fresh air. There was an empty chair. He put her into it.

In the background, he heard the pounding of hooves. The first race had begun. Lella also heard and tried to stand up. "We're missing the race," she said, her words slurred. This time she collapsed completely, falling into the mud where numerous feet had softened the earth round the tents. He helped her up again and looked for somewhere they could go away from prying eyes. He saw a small hut that was empty. A fire burned inside, with the remnants of cooked chestnuts. It seemed the vendor had abandoned his enterprise when the race started and his customers disappeared to watch it.

Ishraq sat Lella down then went to fetch water. When he returned, Jaro was there, staring intensely at the state Lella was in.

"She has done no harm," said Ishraq hurriedly. He was worried there would be repercussions for Lella's poor public behaviour.

Jaro's response surprised him. "I know." There was uncharacteristic kindness in his voice, affection even. Ishraq had never seen Jaro show concern for anyone or anything. He clearly had a soft spot for Lella.

"Erich wants you," said Jaro. "Don't worry. I will see to Lella."

Lella smiled. "It's all right," she said to Ishraq. "Jaro will look after me. He always does."

In the weeks since he was hired by Erich, Ishraq had never suspected any kind of relationship between the two. Of course not, because they would have been hiding it from Erich.

He left them and went to find Erich. In the background, the horses and riders were being readied for the second race.

Erich was surprised to see him. Jaro had not been sent to fetch him and had lied to have time alone with Lella. But Erich did have business for Ishraq and took him to one side, away from the crowds.

Erich spoke quietly. "The Arabian horse has been dealt with," he said. It will go lame before the first circuit is ridden. Jaro has seen to it. But we must deal with Oudin's horse. I know you think my mare has the beating of it, but I don't trust him. If he bought me a beer, I'd smell it before drinking to make sure he hadn't pissed in it."

"I told you my opinion," said Ishraq, a little too firmly, as if a rebuke.

"You're sailing close to the wind, lad. First you look at my woman and now you cheek me. This is your last warning. Understood?"

"Yes."

"The point is that we must tilt the odds in our favour. It won't be as easy as the Arabian. Oudin would be suspicious if Jaro was around his horse. You will have to do it."

****

303

Edwina never expected such a long walk to get to the races. They had walked for three hours, starting at dawn. She now knew why Lorraine's mother chose not to come.

It was two days to the trial of the Benedictine. She had not wanted to leave the city, but she could think of no way to help him. So she came, hoping the distraction might help clear her mind.

The children walked without complaint. Towards the end of the walk Lorraine carried the youngest, her three-year-old. Edwina thought about the return journey at the end of the day. By then Lorraine would be exhausted.

But for now, as the chateau came into view there was only excitement, anticipation. The first thing the children noticed was a line of banners stuck in the ground beside the numerous tents. Then they saw the magnificent horses and the rich colours of the riders that identified the horses' owners. Edwina was struck by the grandeur of the chateau, while Lorraine was almost as excited as her children at the spectacle.

On the journey, Edwina had learned a few things about Lorraine. This was an outing Lorraine had known as a child and she carried on the family tradition when she became a mother. Edwina learned that the children's father was alive somewhere, or at least Lorraine thought so. She had not seen him for two years. He simply left one day, leaving her as sole breadwinner, mother and father. But she seemed happy with her lot. Her husband was not missed. She liked her independence.

They sat on the grass and ate the food and drink they had brought with them, mainly pieces of fish Lorraine's mother scrounged at Avignon's quayside then cooked and salted to preserve them. The children ate quickly, eager to see all that was going on. Edwina noticed how little of the food Lorraine ate, giving her portions to her children.

They toured the fair. There was a falconer showing off his prize hawks. He sent one gliding to a tree then called it to return, then let the children stroke the bird.

A woman had a small brown bear on a leash and was charging people to come forward and touch it. And there were events for the older children, including running races and an archery contest.

All was not calm at the fair. A group of men had been drinking. Each had a hound on a long leash. The hounds snarled as they pulled and strained, frightening passers-by, to the amusement of their owners. Edwina ushered the children away, remembering her own mauling.

They found a group of players performing. Edwina did not understand the words, but she could understand the overall meaning. The play mocked the monk who was about to face trial by ordeal, an actor portraying him as a minor devil, with the head of a goat. The watching crowd laughed. Edwina urged Lorraine to move on.

They spent the early afternoon watching the races. Lorraine took the opportunity to doze, a rare time of rest for her with Edwina there to watch over the children.

The fourth race was starting, then it would be the grand finale, the big race, the one that drew the most enthusiasm from all present. It was due to start in an hour. Edwina was tiring but led the children to a better vantage point. On the other side of the track was a figure. Someone she knew.

It was Ishraq. What a small world it was to see him here in Avignon. Then she remembered. He had told her, all those months ago in St Malo that he planned to travel to Marseille, then on to Baghdad. So he had made it this far, at least.

She raised a hand to wave in his direction but could not catch his attention. And there was something wrong. He seemed anxious, furtive, looking around, wary of being seen. She saw him go where the horses were being prepared for the final race.

Lorraine woke up. "I have something to do," Edwina told her, then went to follow Ishraq.

****

Edwina was right. Ishraq was nervous. His instructions from Erich were clear, to administer a potion, a sedative made mainly from chamomile and valerian. It was for Oudin's horse. He was instructed to give the horse the potion plus half a bucket of water. "It will not harm the horse," Erich told him. "But it will slow him down."

Ishraq had argued it was not necessary. Erich's horse would win anyway. But Erich was adamant, taking no chances, and Ishraq had little choice.

He easily convinced Oudin's stable lad that the white horse needed help. "The heat is affecting the poor thing," he told the lad. "He needs more water. Go fetch some." The lad went for the water, giving Ishraq an undisturbed opportunity to do what he had come to do.

But he hesitated. Erich had said it would not harm the horse. But Ishraq did not trust Erich. He sniffed at the potion to discern exactly what was in it. And his concerns increased.

A familiar voice came from behind him. "Ishraq." He turned and saw Edwina. His feelings were mixed. He was glad to see her, but not at this moment. If he failed to carry out Erich's orders, he would suffer the consequences, but he could not do it with Edwina there.

So his response was off hand. "Edwina. It's nice to see you! Perhaps we can meet up after the races and talk about old times."

It was dismissive. The cold welcome was unlike him. Edwina knew there was something wrong. "Are you alright?" she asked.

"Yes, of course. Busy that's all. I have things to do for the big race. But please leave. I will have time to talk with you later."

Her eyes narrowed. "Something tells me you are up to no good."

"Me? Never. You know me better than that."

The stable lad returned with the extra water for the horse. Ishraq drew a heavy breath. He had missed his chance. He had hesitated, then Edwina's appearance taken away his opportunity.

"Shall I give him the water?" asked the stable lad.

Ishraq had been unsure about what he was doing. Maybe this change in circumstances was for the best. "No," he said. "He has cooled."

"Come on," he said to Edwina. "Let's watch the race together."

"Not so fast. " It was Oudin. With him were two of his men. "Search him," he ordered.

The search did not take long. Ishraq had the sedative mixture in his bag. Oudin beamed. "Caught in the act," he said.

"I gave none to the horse," said Ishraq.

"Because we got to you first."

"No. I had the chance. I couldn't do it."

Oudin spread his arms. "Either way, it's what Erich sent you to do."

It was true. Denial was pointless. "What now?" asked Ishraq.

"You will both enjoy my company for the rest of the day."

"This woman had nothing to do with it. I have never seen her before."

That was a mistake. It drew Oudin's attention to Edwina and he looked on her with greater interest. "She comes with us," he said.

"Can we watch the race?" asked Edwina.

"Why not? But don't try to escape. My men would stop you."

They walked towards the tents, passing Erich's entourage. Erich was there with Lakshmi, Lella, Jaro and his other henchmen. Oudin shouted to him. "I've invited Ishraq to join me for ale," he said. Erich's eyes narrowed with suspicion but he had no reason to object. He just hoped Ishraq had done the deed and given the stallion the sedative.

Ishraq saw Jaro standing beside Lella. The way he stood looked protective. They surely were more than just friends.

When they reached Oudin's tent, Oudin spoke to Ishraq. "What are you doing with such a pretty girl," he asked.

"I don't know her. We met today by chance," replied Ishraq.

"I don't believe you. But I hope she will stay a while." Oudin gave Edwina a lecherous look. She looked away to avoid his gaze.

307

"I am nobody," she said, pointing in the direction where Lorraine was. "I'm just here with friends for the races. I went to look at the horses, that's all. I have nothing to do with this man. I should go back to them." She made to move, but one of Oudin's men blocked her path.

"I will not hear of it," said Oudin. "You must stay and help me celebrate. It is a day for stallions." Edwina understood. Oudin was not talking about his horses. He planned to seduce her. She decided to call his bluff. He would surely not harm her in such a public place.

"You bore me," she declared, and pushed past Oudin's man. As she had hoped, she met no resistance.

When she got to Lorraine the normality of the scene there hit her, a woman and her children enjoying a family outing. It stood in stark contrast to the sense of menace around Oudin's group. Whatever Ishraq had got himself into, it involved danger. But she could not help him. Her priority was her father. Ishraq would have to look after himself. She hoped he knew what he was doing.

Chapter Forty-Two

The racetrack at the cardinal's chateau, October 1378

Seven horses and their riders lined up; the riders' eyes fixed on the man with the flag that would signal the race to start.

Edwina surveyed the scene. There were people everywhere. Some were even on the chateau roof, getting the best view possible. At one point she saw some colours moving above the crowd. At first, they reminded her of the peacock feathers worn by the pirate on the *Julienne*. She did a double take but there was no-one there. She chided herself for having too much imagination.

Most of the riders wore strong colours. The rider of the Arabian horse wore a blood red shirt. Erich's rider wore sky blue. There was one exception. Oudin's rider wore his familiar plain linen shirt.

The crowd was noisy, expectations high. There was nervous excitement. Men had wagered a lot of money on the outcome of the most lucrative race of the day. While some could afford to lose what they had bet, others could not. What they all had in common was belief they would be going home richer than when they arrived. A group of chateau guards watched from a distance, prepared to intervene if any who lost too much turned nasty.

By the tents, Lella had sobered a little. She spoke to Ishraq. "The Arabian stallion is magnificent. I have put most of my money on him."

Ishraq shook his head. "Then you will lose your money."

She looked at him. He had said it with such certainty. He knew something. It dawned on her. "Erich!" she exclaimed.

"Yes, with Jaro's help." He wondered whether Jaro had been more successful than himself in following Erich's orders.

The flag was raised, the noise grew, and then they were off.

One of the riders decided to set a fast pace. It gave him his moment of glory as he headed round the first bend two lengths ahead of the field. By bend two the lead was down to one length. He was caught by bend three.

The other riders knew better than to go too early, so there was general caution and little between them. The three favourites stayed close to one another, each rider keeping an eye on the other two, just in case one made a break.

As they approached the end of the first lap, the three had edged ahead of the rest. They were back in sight of the main body of the crowd. Cheers of encouragement rang out louder still.

Suddenly, the Arabian stallion reared up. Its rider regained control and urged the horse forward, but the horse was in pain and started limping. The rider ignored the beast's distress, spurring it on again, only to cause more pain and damage to the injured leg, until the rider had to accept the inevitable and pulled the horse up.

There were gasps from the crowd. Edwina looked across to the prince's entourage. They showed no emotion. It was a piece of misfortune. It happened in races. There would be others.

A group of men who had bet on the horse were animated, distraught. The chateau guards kept an eye on them as the race went on.

Ishraq saw a look exchange between the two riders who were now out on their own. There was mutual respect mixed with determination, saying. They kicked their mounts into a faster gallop.

Oudin's white stallion and Erich's chestnut mare showed no signs of slowing as they reached the halfway point. Erich was surprised. He thought the stallion would be tiring by now. He looked towards Oudin's tent, but Ishraq avoided his gaze.

The horses entered the final lap. Erich's and Oudin's were in front but there was one other left. Ishraq recognised the blue and yellow checks he had seen before, the colours of the archbishop, the new pope. It trailed by several lengths. The rider applied his whip and the horse responded, making up some ground but still well adrift.

Ishraq thought Oudin's rider was the best in the field. The young man in the linen shirt exuded total calm each time Ishraq saw him ride. But the emotion of the contest was affecting him and he was losing his calm assuredness. He started making mistakes.

Ishraq could see how the race was going to end. He smiled to himself.

Edwina was also smiling as she watched Lorraine enthusiastically shouting encouragement to no particular horse. The children jumped up and down. For a moment, Edwina forgot her troubles, enjoying their simple joy.

She heard groans from the crowd and she saw the horses come into view along the final straight. The two in front were fighting tiredness, both riders whipping with frenzy but with little effect. Their horses were slowing, energy spent.

Then it was over. It was an unexpected result. The tortoise had beaten the two hares. Tonight Pope Clement would be even richer.

There was some trouble in the crowd as men counted their losses but it was quickly dealt with by the chateau guards.

Oudin was laughing. He found it all amusing. He went to congratulate the pope's rider.

Ishraq looked for Erich but could not see him. He expected repercussions. If he had sedated the white stallion there would have been no energy-sapping duel and the pope's horse, a horse of lesser ability, would never have won. So he would be blamed.

He was about to set off to the Villa Libera with Lella when Oudin approached him. The Corsican was still in a good mood. "Stay with me a day or two," said Oudin. "Both of you. It will be safer."

"Erich will certainly be angry," replied Lella. "He has taken a blow to his pride and his pocket."

"There are things you don't yet know," said Oudin. "But you'll find out soon enough. In the meantime, don't go back."

"If we don't, it will be bad for us," Ishraq said to Lella. "And we all know why Oudin wants you here."

Oudin smirked. "Maybe I do want the company of a beautiful woman," he said. " But I have only Lella's interests at heart."

Lella was torn. Oudin was offering her an escape. It would be dangerous to go back to Erich just now. But she wanted to be with

311

Jaro. Then she saw something that made her gasp. "Look!" she said, pointing to Erich walking back towards the race track. With him was the maid, the young African girl. "See what she wears," added Lella.

They saw it. The girl wore a gold necklace that was a series of rings inset with jewels. "It seems I was wrong," said Lella, almost in a whisper. "It isn't Lakshmi who is my greatest rival. That's Erich's most valuable possession. It's from Africa, just like the girl. He showed it to me once but has never let me wear it. That tells me how he feels about her."

Ishraq felt elated. Perhaps Erich had most his interest in Lakshmi.

There was renewed cheering coming from the track. They went to see what was happening. Two horses and their riders were at the starting point. It looked like an impromptu challenge between locals, nothing to do with the planned race programme. A bit of fun.

The race began and they watched, just for some light relief from the more serious events of the day. But as the horses approached where they stood, a figure ran out into their path. Lella gasped once more then looked away, knowing what was happening, and the cheers of the crowd hushed as the young African girl stood erect and proud in the path of the horses. The riders saw her too late. They tried to evade her but could not. The crowd went silent as first one horse then the other trampled her under their hooves.

Ishraq saw Erich. The Dane was in shock, open-mouthed.

Edwina rushed out from the crowd and went to the stricken girl. There was nothing she could do. The girl's ribs were crushed and she had taken blows to her head. Yet she had a strangely contented look on her face. She spoke one word as she drifted out of consciousness and faded away in Edwina's arms. "Libéré". Edwina understood the meaning. Released. Freed.

****

On the way back, Erich rode ahead with Jaro and Lakshmi. Ishraq was with Lella. Little was said, until finally Ishraq voiced some thoughts.

312

"There's something I can't understand," he said. "Erich is in a bad mood, but so should Oudin be. He knows Erich asked me to sabotage his horse, and then his horse lost because his rider failed to stay calm. *Things you don't yet know*, he said. What can he mean?"

Lella shook her head. "Who knows?" she said. "But my mind is churning as I think what this all means for me with Erich. I never saw the maid as a threat. I was too concerned about the other one, the one you lust for. But Oudin is no answer to my problems."

"Because you prefer Jaro."

She laughed. "You've noticed. You know, there's more to him than meets the eye. He can be cold, a killer of men, just like Erich and so many others I've known, but with me he is kind and gentle. I don't think he would ever hurt me. And he would be a very good protector."

They were a mile or so from the villa. There was a glow in the sky above their destination. "Something's wrong," said Ishraq, spurring his horse on. Lella did the same.

Flames licked the air. The villa roof blazed. Timbers cracked and gave way. People ran backwards and forwards with buckets of water, to little avail. The whole house was burning.

"*Things you don't yet know*," said Ishraq under his breath.

"You think Oudin did this?" asked Lella.

"Without doubt. And he has started a war."

They rode on and joined a group watching helplessly as more of the villa collapsed. A woman ran out. Ishraq recognised her as one of the senior maids. She was shouting and pointing, desperate for some help.

It was Jaro who responded. Without hesitation or thought for his own life, he ran into the stricken building. People held their breath as they awaited his return.

Someone screamed. Jaro had come out with a young maid in his arms. She had been overcome by smoke. He laid her on the grass and the woman who had raised the alarm tended to her.

313

Lella rushed to Jaro, who was on his knees, coughing his lungs out as his body tried to get rid of the acrid smoke he had inhaled. One side of his face was burned, the skin blackened. The burns looked deep, permanent. Some of his hair was burned away at the temple. He was in a state of shock and unaware of the injuries. She held his hand.

Erich appeared. He was barking orders to his men. He kept saying Oudin's name. He clearly suspected Oudin had done this, torched the villa while Erich was at the races. Ishraq thought he was right. *'Things you don't yet know'*. It fit.

Ishraq could not see Lakshmi anywhere. He went as near the burning villa as he dared. She could be in there. He was almost in the fire, feeling its heat against his face, then stopped as he saw her on the edge of woodland. She was away from everyone else, sitting on a mound of grass and hidden from general view by a huge oak tree. He went to her. "I thought I'd lost you," he said.

She was in shock and looked sad but was otherwise unhurt. "It should have been me running in front of the horses," she said.

Erich was still preoccupied, vaguely and haphazardly ordering his men to take retribution against Oudin.

On impulse, Ishraq grabbed Lakshmi by the hand and pulled her into the trees. He thought she would resist, but she went easily with him.

They continued deeper into the woods. Then he stopped, took one of her shoes and tore a piece from her dress. She looked aghast, wondering what he was about to do. "Trust me," he said. "Wait here."

He ran back to the tree where they had been, checking no-one was watching him, then scorched the shoe and silk cloth on cinders that had been carried by the wind. He placed them as near as he could to the villa in a spot where they would be unlikely to be further burned but would be found. Then he ran back into the woods.

When he got back to Lakshmi, he explained. "You are dead, Lakshmi. You died in the fire. Now we make our escape."

"I am afraid," she replied. "They will find us."

314

"You are right to be afraid. What we are doing is dangerous. So I will not force you to come with me. But if you go back, you will be Erich's property for years to come. You must decide."

She sighed, then nodded enthusiastically. "You are right. I am already dead. I have nothing to lose. Let's go."

Part Nine

Trial by Ordeal

Chapter Forty-Three

Avignon, October 1378

Edwina was distraught. She had waited for hours where she first met Frere Jean, hoping to see him. She had thought long and hard how to gain access to the man she was sure was her father. All she had was the priest. Even though he had dismissed her claim to be the Benedictine's daughter, he was her best hope. But he was nowhere to be found.

Lorraine arrived from work and they met at the old bridge as was their routine.

As they walked to Lorraine's home, Edwina saw a group of people gathered in a small square down a side street. A woman stood in the middle of a circle of people, telling a story. Lorraine stopped to listen, so Edwina did. She only understood a small percentage of the words, still finding the local Occitan difficult, but one word was repeated several times. *Benedictine.*

When the woman finished, there was applause. Edwina looked at Lorraine for some hint of what was going on. In her frustration, she spoke in English. "What is she saying? Why are they clapping?" Lorraine shook her head. The language barrier was there again.

Nearby, an older woman heard Edwina speak and saw her frustration. "She tells of meeting the Benedictine monk," she told Edwina in accented English. "Her house was destroyed in a flood. She and her family would have died, but the monk had a vision and saw the flood coming. He warned her and saved their lives. When she heard he had been put on trial, she wanted to come and tell her story."

Another woman made her way to the centre of the group of people and began telling her own story. The older woman once again interpreted what was said. "The monk was passing through her village. Her husband had lost all feeling down one side of his body and lost the use of an arm and leg. The local priest said the man had a demon in him. The woman asked the monk if he would visit her husband, and he did. He said her husband was suffering an affliction

317

that had been known about since the Greeks and Romans. He said it was nothing to do with demons, but there was no known cure. He told her that with rest, care and simple exercises her husband could regain some or all his feeling. She followed his advice and her husband improved. Like the first woman, this one wanted her story to be known to those who have put the monk on trial."

Edwina was now certain that the Benedictine was her father The stories were not of miracles, but knowledge and wisdom, typical of things he would do. She had to find a way into the palais. But how?

The gathered group stirred. "What's happening," asked Edwina.

"They march on the palais," replied the older woman. "They demand an audience with the new pope."

Perhaps this would be Edwina's opportunity. She joined the march. The numbers were not great, about thirty people, mostly women.

The woman who Matty had saved from the flood was at the forefront of the delegation. At the gates of the palais she pleaded passionately with the guards for an audience. At first, the guards stood impassively. Then one lost his patience, striking the brave woman across the face and using his halberd to keep the others at bay.

Edwina tried to push through to help the woman who had been struck, but the delegation was tightly massed, trying to force their way through into the palais. The guards grouped together, forming an impassable wall behind their weapons. There was no way past.

She saw two women fall to the ground, and the rest retreated. There was a panic, and more women fell in the chaos and crush of people.

There was a voice. "Cesser!" It made no difference, until raised louder. "*Cesser! Je vous commande!*"

The guards stepped back. That allowed Edwina to reach the woman who had been struck first. She was bruised and bloodied but otherwise she was dazed and shocked more than physically hurt.

The voice was that of a member of the Curia, one of the four hundred or so administrators who worked at the palais. To Edwina, he looked like any other priest, but his importance was attested by the obedience he had so easily commanded from the guards.

He introduced himself as Frere Paul, then helped the injured woman to her feet. Edwina looked round for signs of others who had been injured. Thankfully, she saw no dead bodies, only minor injuries as the fallen were led away from the palais gates by their friends.

Frere Paul helped the woman up. She was still dazed. He led her and Edwina inside the building. He assumed Edwina and the woman were together, friends or associates, and dealt with them as a pair.

They were taken to a huge internal courtyard with beautiful gardens. It was quite dark, the high gothic buildings keeping out the sunshine across much of the space. Edwina wondered how much darker and how dank her father's prison cell must be.

Two nuns arrived with water and bandages, and Frere Paul went to work on the woman's wounds while Edwina was offered water, which she took gratefully. "Thank you," she said to them.

Frere Paul turned round, "You are English?"

"Yes."

"And you come here because of the man we have here awaiting trial?"

She saw an opening. "He means much to many in England," she said. She thought news of the Benedictine was unlikely to have reached England's shores, but a small lie seemed justified in the situation.

"Your friend seems not too badly hurt."

Edwina bristled. "She was struck for no good reason with a lethal weapon. I've seen such things before. The shock comes later. She will need care and attention for at least a day and has no money to pay for it." She gave him a withering look.

He sighed. "Very well. We will take her into the infirmary for the night and watch over her."

"Good. I will stay with her."

He shook his head. "That is not possible."

319

"And if she dies, will you answer when I tell the world of her murder?"

He held up his hands. "You are being needlessly dramatic."

"Am I? Tell that to her."

He looked at the injured woman, who was still dazed. "Very well," he said. "Stay with her. But if she does die, I have done all in my power to help her, would you agree?"

"Yes. You have been kind."

Frere Paul gave some more orders, and the two women were escorted to the infirmary. Edwina smiled to herself. She was inside the building where her father was being kept. It was one step nearer getting to see him, to at least offer him some comfort and let him know she knew he was there and he was not alone.

The injured woman was regaining her senses. A nun explained to her why she was there. She was puzzled by Edwina's presence, but glad of the company in this alien place. Before long she was dozing.

When she awoke, Edwina was gone.

Chapter Forty-Four

The towpath of the Rhone, October 1378

Lakshmi asked Ishraq what his plan was. He had no answer, because he had no plan. He felt guilty. He had been reckless and now there was no going back. But ever since Rottingdean he had been a man who seized the day, taking opportunities as they presented themselves. And so far, it had worked in his favour.

They followed the river back into the city. The Mistral was blowing, making navigation of the river difficult. Ishraq watched several boats struggling to make progress upriver as the wind pushed them over to the east bank. The boats travelling downriver were faring better.

In the main mooring area, he was drawn to one of the largest vessels there. It was a Moorish cog like ones he had seen in La Rochelle, plying trade routes along the Atlantic coast from southern Spain. But this one had a cross on its mainsail, a Christian emblem.

The crew had skin tones like Ishraq's. Some dressed in clothes that could be from any part of western Europe, but others wore kufiya headscarves and full-length, flowing robes. Clothing from the east.

Whatever the origins of the boat and its crew, the vessel stood out because of its sheer size. There could be only one explanation. It belonged to the eastern prince who had been at the races, the owner of the Arabian stallion that Jaro had ensured did not last a single circuit of the track.

Seize the day, thought Ishraq. He led Lakshmi to the boat. There was a makeshift boardwalk. It was uneven, with some of the planks worn. He offered her his hand, to help her across. When she took it, her touch sent tremors up and down his body. He tried his best not to squeeze too tightly, or to look quite as ecstatic as he was feeling.

Preparations were being made for sailing. He looked up at the sky. The weather dictated there would be no sailing today. But the prince clearly intended to leave at the earliest opportunity. Ishraq hoped so.

He was an accomplished sailor, and sailors were always in short supply. And his skin tone would work in his favour. He was sure the captain would take him on. This could be what he had come to Avignon for. Passage downriver towards Marseille, then Baghdad.

The complication was Lakshmi. How could he secure passage for her? They had no money. He would have to use his wits.

A crewman was giving orders to the rest. The first mate. Ishraq shouted in Spanish from the quayside. "Where are you bound?"

The first mate stopped what he was doing. "Byzantium," he replied.

"Is that east?"

"About as far east as you can get."

"Do you need an experienced and cheap deck hand?"

"Always." The mate saw that Ishraq was not alone. "But we can't take a woman. We don't carry passengers."

"I can do the work of two men."

"Sorry, but we have no spare cabins."

One of the other sailors went to the mate and whispered in his ear. The mate laughed, then shouted down to Ishraq. "Perhaps we can help you. Come aboard. But you will not like what we have to offer."

Ishraq and Lakshmi followed the mate down some steps into the bowels of the boat. They arrived at a small, enclosed space. It was humid and smelled foul. There was hay on the floor. Much of the stench was from the hay. There was evidence of excrement. "There was a horse in here," said Ishraq.

"Yes."

"But no longer?"

"It got lame in a race. A shame, because it was a fine racehorse. My master didn't want it to suffer the return journey so he sold it. The lucky horse has a new job servicing a dozen mares to produce future race winners. Now that's what I call retirement."

322

"We'll take it," said Ishraq, trying to ignore the look of disgust on Lakshmi's face. In truth, he felt ashamed. Here he was, dumping the woman he loved in an airless hole full of horse shit. "How long will it take to get to Byzantium?" he asked.

"It depends on my master. He likes to visit places. The journey here took us a year."

"You kept a prize horse in here for a year?"

The mate laughed. "No. The master bought him in Naples."

A year. And then more to get from Byzantium to Baghdad. Ishraq could not subject Lakshmi to a year in this room. But they must leave Avignon before Erich found them. At least she would be safe here. They could leave the boat at the next port.

The boat was called the *Hero* after a famous Byzantine scholar. The mate told Ishraq about the learned man who knew about geometry, but whose biggest achievements were in the art of siege warfare

"Now you work," said the mate. "I hope you are as good as your word, because I will keep you to it. You have the work of two men to do."

"Go," said Lakshmi. "I will be fine here."

Ishraq went on deck and started work. He worked hard but kept an eye on the steps down to Lakshmi's makeshift cabin. He was worried for her on this ship of men. It was an anxiety he would have for as long as they were on board. He resolved to protect her.

Lakshmi cried when he left her. She was unsure whether her tears were tears of unhappiness for being in this place or relief for having escaped the brothel and Erich the Dane. Tears were tears. How could anyone tell the difference? She could not. All she knew was she would be much happier when Ishraq came back from working.

Hours later, Ishraq's work was done. He was anxious to get back to her, but the mate halted him. "You're a good worker," he said. "Here, you deserve a drink at the end of your day."

The mate gave Ishraq a cup of something strong he had never tasted before. It tasted strange and Ishraq was not sure he liked it. "Greek," said the mate. "Ouzo. Very strong."

As Ishraq drank, he watched some of the crew having a little fun to wind the day down. One of the prince's guards threw a barrel over the side. It was empty and attached to a length of rope. When it reached as far as the rope would go, he took out a bow and arrow. "Target practice," said the mate. "To keep sharp. Some of the men wrestle, he does this. We must be ready for the next fight."

Ishraq watched for a while. The archer's first three arrows hit the target and stuck. The fourth fell short and was lost in the water. The archer shouted a curse. "That will cost him a tenth of his wages," said the mate. "Arrows are costly. It's a good incentive. He rarely misses."

The archer grabbed the rope and started to draw the barrel back in, cursing all the while. And finally, Ishraq was left to go down into the bowels of the boat, to where Lakshmi waited.

The relief on her face spoke volumes and he wondered once again whether he had done the right thing bringing her here. Until she hugged him and kissed him lightly on the cheek. "Thank you," she said. Lakshmi did not share his doubts. She knew he had made the right decision, whatever the outcome might be. They lay down holding each other and settled down for the night, not yet as lovers but as a couple contented because they were going to face the future together.

Ishraq smiled and felt happy beyond his wildest dreams.

Chapter Forty-Five

The Palais des Papes, October 1378

Frere Paul had more important things to attend to, and the nuns had been told only to see to the woman with injuries. So when Edwina slipped away, she was not missed and there was no alarm raised.

She was concerned she would stand out and draw questions. In the corridors and quadrangles she kept her head bowed whenever anyone passed by. She imagined that everyone here must know everyone else, and that she would be identified as an intruder.

But as well as the many priests and nuns there were dozens of lay people, all wearing ordinary clothing just like her own. In addition, there were many casual visitors, some on pilgrimage. The place was full of strangers and she wandered unchallenged, invisible.

She searched aimlessly, not knowing where to go. Did she expect her father's prison cell to just appear before her? How could she ask where he was when she lacked the language skills? And what would she ask? *Please take me to the prison cells. S*he would be laughed at.

It was hopeless and she was about to give up. It was getting late. Then she turned a corner and saw a familiar face. It was Frere Jean. She was uplifted. She had found him at last. He would be able to help her.

She stopped in her tracks. He was at a side entrance to the palais, his back to her, talking with another man, one she recognised, someone she had first seen on a boat, the man who caused Briony to dive into the waters of the Rhone. He wore the same gaudy hat he had worn then, with its peacock feathers. So she *had* seen him at the races.

What was Frere Jean doing talking with a murderous pirate?

She hid behind a pillar and watched. Frere Jean's whole manner was different from before. It was furtive, and he was in a hurry to conclude the conversation. He clearly did not wish to be seen with this man.

She saw the priest give something to the pirate. It was a bag. From the pirate's reaction, she thought it must contain something of value, money or gold perhaps. That raised her suspicions even higher.

The pirate left and Frere Jean walked in Edwina's direction. She had to act. The priest was still her best chance to find her father.

She stepped out from behind the pillar, striding as if she had simply been walking along the corridor. Then she feigned surprise to see the priest. She greeted him. "Frere Jean, we meet again."

Jean was nonplussed. His heart was racing with the anxiety his meeting with the pirate had caused. He just wanted to get to his rooms. He wanted to tell Edwina to go away. Instead, he managed a weak response and smile. "Good day," he said.

The priest's composure quickly returned as he realised that she should not be there. "How did you get in here?" he asked.

She decided the truth would suffice. "I was with a woman who was hurt. Frere Paul helped us. I couldn't resist exploring. It's such a wonderful place, all the high ceilings, the frescoes…"

He was only partly convinced. "Where is the injured woman now?"

"That's the problem. I'm lost. Perhaps you can help me find my way back to her."

"Of course."

She gave him a description of the room she had been in and he led the way. "The Benedictine *is* my father, you know," she said, in a matter-of-fact voice. "I have proof now."

"I'm sorry," he said. "I'm very busy. Go along this corridor. Now I must go."

"His hat is very distinctive."

"What? Who?"

"The pirate with the peacock hat. The one you just bought a boat full of silks from. The one who murdered my friend to get them."

"What?" he repeated. "You don't know what you are talking about."

"It will be easy to prove. A boat full of silk is hard to hide." She was making a leap. She knew the pirate had the boat and silks but had no proof that was what Jean paid the pirate for. But Jean made no denial.

326

He shifted uneasily. "What do you want?"

"To see my father before his trial. That is all."

"Out of the question."

"Then I will go to Frere Paul, He will be interested in your activities."

Jean reddened with anger. He relented. "Half an hour. No more."

"Thank you. It's all I want."

He led her through corridors and down steps to the cells. Edwina saw Jean slip the guard a coin and the cell door was opened.

She took a deep breath, then went in. The prisoner was asleep, his back turned to her. A single candle illuminated his face, enough for her to see it was her father. She felt elated to have found him, but it also confirmed the danger he faced, awaiting trial.

She nudged him awake. At first, he did not acknowledge her, thinking he was dreaming. Then she spoke. "Hello, father," she said softly.

He rubbed his eyes in disbelief, then took her in a loving hug. And they both wept.

"How did you find me?" he asked her.

"I heard of a man who was well-loved, an Englishman who helped people. I thought, *that sounds like someone I know*. I almost didn't recognise you though. You've lost weight. Have you given up pheasant."

He laughed. "It's good to see you," he said. And they wept more.

They had only a few minutes together before the guard ushered Edwina back out. It was enough time to share the bones of their stories. Edwina left out the part where her life was endangered by the pirates and did not mention having seen one of them in the city. She was not going to burden her father with any more worries. He was much more interested in her visit to Charlotte.

"I think they will have to leave the lodge," he said.

"Don't worry. I went to see Princess Isabella and she will help them." It was the second lie she had told that day, but it gave him comfort.

When she emerged into the warm air of the Avignon evening, she felt satisfied. She could not affect her father's fate, but her visit had lifted his spirits and it helped him to know that she would be able to tell his family what happened to him. She left him smiling.

As she drank in the air, she glimpsed peacock feathers above the crowd that always gathered at this time of day.

She gently pushed through, and there he was, the pirate responsible for poor Briony's demise. She followed him, keeping her distance. He met and joined a small group of men. The other pirates? Possibly, but amongst them were two she recognised. They were Oudin's men.

Another unexpected connection. The pirate, Jean and Oudin.

The group of men made their way towards the river. On the way, they collected something. Edwina could not tell what it was. But as they reached the river, the men stopped and formed a circle. When they emerged, they each held a lit torch.

She looked round. There were a few people, all looking away, walking away, knowing something bad was about to take place. She stayed and watched from the corner of a building as the group of men set kindling by a warehouse door and lit it.

It took only a few minutes for the blaze to fully catch. The warehouse was stone built but with tinder dry wood in the doors, windows and roof. The men laughed and joked as they watched the flames rise. She heard a name. They were ridiculing Erich the Dane. It was his warehouse that burned, along with everything in it.

She looked for signs of a response from the city authorities to battle the fire. One or two official-looking men came to see what was happening, then abruptly left, not wanting to get involved.

She was tired and her stump throbbed. It had been a hard day and her emotions were high. She cared nothing for Erich or his possessions but wanted justice for Briony, which meant following the man with the peacock hat.

Chapter Forty-Six

The Hero, Avignon, October 1378

The night sky was red. Ishraq joined a group of sailors watching the flames shoot towards the stars. Although the fire was some distance away along the quayside, the Mistral was still strong. There was danger that it would spread to other warehouses, and that would put the wooden boats at risk. Captains and first mates watched anxiously.

So Ishraq was sent with another sailor to report on the progress of the fire. When he got to the warehouse, he could see that the fire presented little risk to the *Hero*. The location of the warehouse was far enough away and the wind direction was favourable.

He wondered whether the blaze was accidental or deliberate. Fires happened regularly. The wooden buildings were vulnerable. But there had been no lightning strikes and it had rained heavily, so everything was soddened, rather than tinder dry.

He looked round, surprised that no crowd had gathered. But there was a group of men. He looked for possible suspects among them. Arsonists often stayed to see their handiwork unfold. He saw Oudin's men within the group, as well as a distinctive man he had never seen before; one who wore a hat with peacock feathers.

He heard loud shouting from over the river and turned, to see Jaro leading a group of Erich's men in a charge towards the group.

Oudin's men ran away, lacking enough numbers for a fight. Jaro and his men chased them as they scattered. Ishraq managed to catch the attention of one of the chasers. "What's going on?" he asked.

The man was breathless, and eager to pursue the chase, but recognised Ishraq and quickly replied. "It's war between Erich and Oudin."

"Is Lella safe?" shouted Ishraq, but the man was gone.

Ishraq returned to the *Hero*.

Edwina saw him go, but he did not see her.

There was a man on deck, striking in a full robe of pure white and with a white kufiya headscarf. Ishraq had seen the prince at the races but only from distance. This was his first sight on board the boat, because the prince tended to stay in his cabin. The prince stood proud and regal, watching the glow in the sky. He was a handsome man of about thirty years, with a close-cut beard and a sharp nose.

The prince looked down and recognised Ishraq. Ishraq knew he was in trouble. Orders were shouted and men rushed down to seize him.

They took Ishraq to the prince's cabin. Two men held him, hands now tied and a curved sword blade pressed to his cheek. The room was opulent, decorated in red velvet and gold, a stark contrast from the dirty cabin Lakshmi was in. He thought of her and hoped she was safe.

The prince sat in a sumptuous chair, his feet resting on a magnificent Persian rug. There was polished silverware, including a wine goblet the prince drank from.

"So, Erich's horseman is now one of my sailors," said the prince. "I wonder what mischief you have planned for me."

"I only want passage to the sea," replied Ishraq.

The prince frowned. "I know Erich was responsible for my stallion going lame. And you, as his horseman, are my prime suspect."

Ishraq shook his head. "Not me, your highness," he said, not sure whether that was the correct address for the prince.

The prince thought for a moment. "Oudin has declared war on Erich," he said, hoping for a reaction. There was none. He tried again. "He is making a play for Erich's empire. He wants to be the unofficial king of Avignon. The Villa Libera is gone, and now Erich's biggest warehouse has been razed to the ground, with many things of value inside it. Oudin has struck at Erich's wealth."

This time there was a reaction, but an unexpected one. "Is Lella safe?" asked Ishraq, his tone filled with concern.

The prince's eyes narrowed. "Erich's woman. What is she to you?"

"A friend. We have things in common. We both know what it is to be owned by a cruel man."

The prince nodded. "I'm told you came aboard with another beauty. Why are two such women so close to a simple sailor? What's your secret?" Again, Ishraq did not reply. The prince clapped his hands and barked another order. "Let's find out," he said.

Minutes later, Lakshmi was brought into the room. Ishraq struggled and strained but was held fast. "Don't harm her," he pleaded.

The prince was clearly surprised to see Lakshmi. He recognised her from the races, where Erich had shown her off, boasting how he owned her. The prince whistled. "You must not value your life very much," he said to Ishraq. "You dabble with Lella *and* Lakshmi, *both* of Erich's women, and this one is the most dangerous for you, I think. Erich is no longer so bothered about the other."

"I will free Lakshmi. I won't let her die like the African slave girl."

The prince stood up. "That was a sad thing to see." He ran his finger along the back of the curved sword that had moved to Ishraq's throat. "You will free Lakshmi? You cannot even free yourself." he mocked.

"I have never known a freer man." It was Lakshmi, wanting to help Ishraq and emboldened by the helplessness of their situation.

The prince smirked. "It seems beautiful women are indeed drawn to you. Maybe it's because you promise them things like freedom that are not yours to give." He thought a moment. "But what to do with you?" Then he barked an order in Arabic and the pair were taken to the stinking cabin, with a guard posted to watch them.

Edwina saw them being manhandled along the deck before descending into the boat's depths. "What have you got yourself into this time, my friend?" she whispered to herself.

Chapter Forty-Seven

The Cathédrale Notre-Dame des Doms d'Avignon, October 1378

A large crowd had gathered. Normally, legal matters of importance to the papacy were heard in the palais, in one of the great halls designed for the purpose.

But this was to be a public event. It was a Sunday. Every Sunday began with a grand parade, involving hundreds of the religious personnel of the city. This day was no exception.

After the parade was a blessing of the assembled crowd and an open-air Mass, conducted by Pope Clement himself. After that, he distributed special gifts to those priests, nuns and bishops who had served him well in some way he wished to reward.

For Edwina, it all meant the building of tension. There was a pain in the pit of her stomach. She felt like running away. She longed for the main event, her father's trial, to be over.

And then it was happening. A fanfare drew attention to the palais entrance, and she saw her father being escorted towards the cathedral.

She pushed her way through, shouting words of encouragement to him. He did not look in her direction. She was too far away and her words floated away on the breeze.

There was no sign of Pope Clement. He had decided to distance himself from this. He had wanted to be associated with the Benedictine when it would help his cause, but now took a neutral position, a wise thing to do. He was keeping his options open. If the monk survived, he could re-claim him. If not, he could denounce him.

But there was someone Edwina recognised. Frere Jean was one of the clerics walking in front of her father. She was surprised to see a lowly priest there, in such exalted company, with bishops and cardinals. Even the Bishop of Florence was there, Pope Urban's man. Perhaps Urban had insisted on a representative at the proceedings, or maybe the two popes had set aside their differences when it came to the matter of the Benedictine.

They reached the cathedral and stepped inside. The parade of dignitaries had already entered and were seated. A choir sang chants. Smoke rose from censers, the aroma of incense filling the air.

Once the church personnel were inside, it was the turn of the common people to be allowed in. There were hundreds, squeezing through the door then finding standing room wherever they could.

Edwina got through but was at the back. She needed to get nearer the altar. A bishop was delivering a sermon. She edged forward, but the crowd was suffocating and she was still a long way from her goal.

She pushed harder and wriggled through to a gap at the side of the cathedral, earning protests from those she kicked and elbowed to get there. She was now close enough to see her father sitting near to the altar. There were guards at either side of him.

She heard a scream and looked in its direction. It was the woman her father had saved from the flood, the woman who she had seen before, crying out in anguish at the unfolding spectacle.

Looking back to the altar, Edwina was struck again at the prominent role Frere Jean was playing. It was he who was cleaning the cup and preparing the bread and wine. She thought it odd.

The bishop finished his sermon. Everyone had their attention on him, quietly listening as he spoke in Latin. Edwina recognised some words. "Per deum unum sumus" - *through God, we are one.* Her father was calm, bravely accepting his fate, dignified in the face of supreme judgement.

Frere Jean passed the bread to the bishop, who gave it to Matty, saying the words of the Eucharist in English for Matty's benefit. "I am the bread of life…" Matty ate the bread without mishap.

Then Jean passed the cup of wine to the bishop, and he gave that to Matty. "The blood of Christ…"

Matty held the cup and slowly lifted it to his lips, sipped the wine but then spat it out. There were gasps from the congregation and the bishop looked annoyed, berating Matty for lacking courage. "You must drain the cup," he ordered.

But Matty knew there was something wrong. The wine tasted foul, and he knew why. As a skilled physician he understood herbs and plants. And he recognised the musty, bitter aroma of the hemlock plant. He refused to drink the wine.

The bishop was incandescent. He called for a guard and instructed him to hold Matty down, then he forcibly put the cup to Matty's lips.

Edwina desperately pushed further forward. She saw Frere Jean shifting uneasily. He had something secreted in his hand. No-one else was watching the priest, but Edwina was sure he was not what he seemed. She had seen his furtive meeting with the pirate and now he was in this special place at the altar. He must have reason.

She could not see what Jean was holding, but she trusted her father's instincts. He refused to drink. It would not be through lack of courage.

Matty held up a hand, agreeing to take the wine. He had no choice. The congregation was silent as everyone waited for him to drink.

Suddenly, Edwina worked out why her father was resisting, and who was responsible. She pointed at Jean and shouted out. In the absolute silence she could be heard throughout the cathedral. Her voice echoed from the walls. "Il a du poison! The priest has poisoned the wine!"

For a moment, no-one stirred. There was shock, disbelief. Until the woman from the flood also shouted, joining with Edwina, repeating the accusation. "Poisoner! Poisoner!"

More voices joined in. The bishop looked round, trying to work out what was happening He took the cup and smelled the aroma of the wine, then recoiled. It was indeed foul. He hesitated. Had God made the wine foul? Surely that was the whole point of the trial by ordeal.

The bishop wanted to speak with Frere Jean, but the priest had slipped away. It raised the bishop's suspicions. If Jean had stayed, perhaps the bishop would have continued to administer the wine. But Jean had fled. Perhaps the accusations were right.

A scramble developed as the commoners in the church fought to get to the altar to protect the monk they revered. Guards formed to stop the forward movement of the crowd, then panicked and fell back as they realised the numbers were too great.

The bishop told the guards to release Matty, thinking to save himself from the crowd's fury. He hurriedly made an exit away from them.

Matty saw an empty vial behind the altar. He picked it up and held it to his nose. It smelled of hemlock.

Edwina fought her way to her father's side. He was astonished to see her, but there was no time for greetings. She beckoned him to follow her and took him through the side exit she had seen Frere Jean use.

Outside the cathedral, they looked for Frere Jean but he was nowhere in sight. His actions puzzled them. "Why did he do it?" Edwina asked. Matty shook his head. He did not know. She thought of Jean's association with the pirate. It did not explain the priest's actions.

The crowd inside the cathedral was still noisy, but there was another commotion outside. It was coming from the direction of the bridge. Across the river, thirty or forty men were approaching, fully armed and armoured. And facing them, on the near side of the bridge, was an even larger group. Battle cries filled the air.

Some people on the bridge were caught in the middle and tried to get away. Some were successful, but for others it was too late. When the men came together in the centre of the bridge there was no thought given to the safety of any innocent non-combatants. Swords clashed. There were screams of agony. And the bodies began to pile up.

Edwina had no wish to watch the carnage. The sounds though were impossible to avoid.

Matty took her hand and led her away. They needed to find Frere Jean.

On the bridge, the fighting continued. Neither side had the upper hand, until the pirate with the peacock-feathered hat and his men arrived. They joined with Oudin, and it changed the balance. Erich's men were gradually pushed back into defensive positions, then were slaughtered, their bodies dumped unceremoniously into the river.

Erich had stayed back. He paid for fighting men, but now was forced to join the fray. His right-hand man, Jaro. was alongside him. They fought like wild men, demons. Both were skilled and experienced in close combat. Between them, they were worth five men, maybe ten. But it was not enough. There were simply too many against them.

Oudin had waited years for the chance to topple Erich's empire. It was the arrival of the pirates in the city that made the difference. Oudin struck a deal with them; help him to defeat Erich and a share of Erich's wealth would be theirs.

At the far side of the bridge, Lella watched helplessly. She saw Erich with Jaro. Oudin and the pirate made straight for them, Oudin facing Erich and the pirate squaring up to Jaro.

Years of overindulgence weighed against Erich. He was slow, cumbersome, while Oudin was younger and fitter. It was no contest. Erich parried the first strikes but lacked the energy to sustain his defence and was cut down.

The pirate's fight with Jaro was closer, lasting longer. But the pirate had more cunning than Jaro, drawing him forward then chopping at his legs, the only area where Jaro had no armour. With Jaro on his knees, the pirate delivered the fatal blow, a slash to Jaro's throat.

Lella saw Jaro fall and ran to his aid, reaching him as he breathed his last breath. She lay across his body and sobbed.

****

Matty and Edwina were on one of the moat bridges. They had looked everywhere for the priest. Then Edwina saw the pirate with the peacock hat. The fight on the bridge was over, but he was striding with purpose. He had his men with him, and his adrenaline was pumping. He wanted loot, and knew a great prize was moored nearby.

"Follow him," she told her father. "He is in league with the priest."

"I need a weapon," said Matty. There were plenty to be had. He found a body, one of Erich's men, and took the dead man's sword.

Matty and Edwina followed the pirates to a boat. She recognised it as the one she had seen Ishraq on. "I think my friend is on that boat," she said. "And I have a score to settle with those pirates."

The pirates boarded the *Hero*.

****

Ishraq and Lakshmi were still confined to the stinking cabin that had once housed an Arabian stallion.

They heard activity on the deck above them. The guard who watched them was restless, itching to join the fight but unsure whether to leave his post. Ishraq asked him what was happening. "We are being raided," replied the guard.

Ishraq recalled the raiders at Rottingdean. He would not go easily this time. "Go, and fight!" he told his guard. "And I can fight with you."

The guard hesitated. He had his orders, to stay with the prisoners, but Ishraq was right, he was of no use below deck. He should be helping his comrades. He raced up the steps, leaving the prisoners unguarded.

Ishraq followed him, poking his head through the gap enough to be able to see along the deck. He surveyed the scene.

There was fighting at either end of the boat. Nearest to him the prince, majestic in his flowing white robes, fought alongside the mate. The prince flashed a curved sword with great skill, fending off two pirates. The mate made a thrust and one of the pirates fell. But Ishraq could see the numbers were in favour of the pirates.

"Stay here," he said to Lakshmi, then leaped out on to the deck. He was unarmed, but his sudden appearance distracted the pirates and the prince cut another one down.

There was a break in the fighting as the pirates regrouped. The prince took a moment to speak to the mate. He was smiling. "We could have sailed this morning," he said. "But I chose to stay because things were getting interesting. I wanted to see whether Erich or Oudin triumphed.

337

It was a mistake. I should have been wiser and left when I had the chance. My decision has cost you your life."

"If I die here with you, it will be an honour," replied the mate. "But I'd rather not. Let's kill the bastards." They both laughed.

One of the pirates raised his sword, aimed at the prince. The mate rolled into him, knocking him off his feet. The prince smiled again, then turned his attention to yet another of the boarders.

Matty and Edwina reached the boat. Edwina saw Ishraq on deck, unarmed. The fighting was fierce. "That's my friend," she said. "He is trapped."

"I know him," said Matty. "He is the reason I came back to Avignon. He fought at Rottingdean. I was there. I thought he could help me remember things."

Matty had the sword he had scavenged. Edwina was unarmed. "Stay here," he told her, then ran on to the boat.

Edwina was a spectator at Rottingdean and then again as the pirates killed Briony and Phillipe. She could not, would not stand by this time, armed or not. So she followed her father into the danger area.

One of the crew was trying to fight his way to the stern but was outnumbered. Matty went to his aid. The sailor was glad but also puzzled that a stranger, a black monk was making this his fight. He pointed to some barrels. "I have to get to them," he told Matty.

Edwina was near enough to hear. The pirates had seen her come on board but ignored her. In their world, an unarmed woman was no threat.

But she was resourceful. She slipped past and got to the barrels. And she saw why they were so important to the sailor.

She summoned all her strength to wheel one, then another barrel out, creating a defensive barrier across the deck. Her father saw what she was doing and gestured to the sailor to follow him. Using their swords to keep the pirates at bay, they worked their way to the cover and protection of the barrels.

"Over there," shouted Edwina, pointing to what she had found. Matty looked and saw the bow and quiver of arrows sailor was trying to reach. He had left them there after his target practice.

Edwina risked a glance to where Ishraq was. The prince and mate were holding out, but against overwhelming odds. It was only a matter of time before they were defeated, and Ishraq was helpless, still unarmed, behind them.

Matty turned to the sailor he was fighting alongside. "Can you hold them for just a minute?" he asked. The sailor nodded. Matty gave him his sword, and the sailor fought two-handed from behind the barrels. One of the pirates approached from the side, and Edwina threw a tin cup she found, distracting him enough for the sailor to shift position.

Matty knew the sailor could not hold out for long. He picked up the bow and quickly nocked and loosed his first arrow. At almost point-blank range he hardly needed to aim. The arrow pierced the chest of a pirate who was no more than a few feet away.

The arrow had barely left his bow before he was loading another. One of the pirates fighting the sailor turned his attention to him, but Matty fired his second arrow and pierced the pirate's heart.

The other pirates at that end of the boat stopped in their tracks. Matty already had a third arrow loaded. It was instinctive, learned at the butts of Lincolnshire then the killing fields of France. The speed of his work was astonishing.

The pirates stepped back. Beyond them, their leader, the man in the peacock hat, was weighing his options. He still had ten or more pirates on the boat, half fighting the prince and mate and the rest facing the archer monk, one sailor and a woman. He liked the odds, but the monk was fast and his bow posed greatest threat. The monk had to be dealt with. He called two men away from the prince and mate, then ordered the rest, all seven of them to charge the archer monk.

Seven men would overwhelm Matty, Edwina and the sailor, but at a price. Some would die. And they knew that. They froze, none wishing to be first in line against the ageing monk who had arrived out of nowhere to wreck carnage on their numbers.

The pirate leader became angry and waved his sword at his own men. If they did not charge, they would face his blade. Some responded and moved forward, but too slowly. Matty's third arrow cut the first one down, another shot to the heart. And now, the pirate leader had a mutiny on his hands. Half his men made for the boarding plank to escape from the hell that was the *Hero*.

The sight heartened the prince and mate, who redoubled their efforts. The mate cut down one of the three they faced. It was now two against two at that end of the boat. The pirate leader was suddenly indecisive and Ishraq saw an opportunity to rush him, knocking him to the ground. The pirates were in disarray.

Matty drew a fourth arrow, and another pirate ran for his life.

The prince and mate drove back the two who remained, and they also fled. Only the pirate leader remained. But he was not finished. He grabbed hold of Ishraq and held him as a shield, a hostage, and edged his way to the boarding plank and safety.

Lakshmi was at the hatch. She saw Ishraq with a sword held to his neck and she screamed.

The prince and mate were exhausted, but joined Matty, Edwina and the one other sailor who had survived. Matty had his bow raised. "I can't shoot," he said. "I might hit the wrong man." Nevertheless, he kept his arrow trained on the escaping pirate leader.

Edwina went to the boat rail. The pirate leader was almost on land. He had one arm round Ishraq's neck and held his sword a matter of inches from Ishraq's face, keeping his eyes on Matty as he backed away. Then he missed his step on the uneven boards. His grip on Ishraq loosened and Ishraq reacted quickly, slipping from his grasp and ducking down. Matty's reaction was instant. His arrow flew. The pirate leader took the arrow in the chest and fell into the river, disbelief on his face. For a few moments he fought, splashing and trying to keep his head above the water. Then he disappeared and did not resurface. All that was visible was a red patch on the water and a peacock-feather hat floating on it.

Edwina thought of how Briony drowned. It seemed fitting that the pirate leader should die in the same way. But there was no time to celebrate. Frere Jean was still at large.

Lakshmi ran to Ishraq and hugged him. Edwina smiled at the sight.

Matty hugged Edwina even harder. There were tears in his eyes. It was infectious. She felt her own tears flow.

The prince examined the bodies of his crew, one by one. There was guilt written on his face. "I should have left when I had the chance," he said, his voice uneven with emotion. "I must inform their families."

"You were not to know of the pirates," said the mate.

"We must find the priest," said Edwina.

"But where?" asked Matty.

"I have an idea."

Edwina led her father to the small church where she first met Frere Jean. Ishraq went with them as an interpreter. Lakshmi stayed behind on the *Hero*. At the church, the same monk was there as before, distributing alms. Ishraq asked if he had seen the priest who had been there. The monk shook his head. Edwina was disappointed, but not surprised. "It was worth a try," she said.

They made to leave, but the monk said something. Ishraq explained. "The monk says the priest sometimes goes to a boat. It's moored about a mile downriver."

"The *Julienne*," said Edwina. "I was right about the silks. It's the connection between Jean and the pirates."

"The monk also says the priest is a very good man," added Ishraq. "Because he brings money to pay for the alms the monk gives out."

"He is a complex man," said Matty.

They returned to the *Hero*. They were all hungry. No-one had eaten for hours. The sailor who had fought alongside Matty cooked some fish and they ate together. Ishraq pulled a face. "Fish again," he joked.

The light was fading, so they decided to wait until morning to look for the *Julienne*. They considered talking to the city authorities but rejected the idea. This was something they must do themselves.

The prince would have to find a new crew. He offered Ishraq a post as second mate. Ishraq discussed it with Lakshmi, then took the job. "But can Lakshmi have a better cabin this time?" he asked.

"Agreed," replied the prince. "You have earned it."

"It's a step nearer Baghdad," said Edwina, then saw that her father looked glum. "What's troubling you?" she asked.

"I'm thinking about Charlotte and the children," he replied. "I must get home before they are evicted from the lodge. I can't spend too much time here, regardless of Frere Jean."

"Of course. Let's find him tomorrow, then go home."

"Yes. Now, tell me about this boat we'll be looking for."

"I came here on it. It has a cargo of silk. The pirates took it. That's when I first saw the pirate leader. Then I saw him here in Avignon. I recognised the hat. He was with Frere Jean."

"We didn't kill all the pirates. We can expect a warm welcome tomorrow. Let's get some sleep."

On the old bridge, Oudin stood over Lella, who was draped over Jaro's body. "You have no choice but to live with me now," he said.

She spat at his feet. "I would rather die," she said. She knew he might take her at her word. She hoped he would and end her misery. But he just walked away.

She got up and strode, head held high, to the only place she knew where she could now survive. Madame de Bruler was at the door as she got there, almost as if she had been expected. Without a word, she went inside, back to the world of slavery and abuse she thought was in her past.

Chapter Forty-Eight

The Rhone, south of Avignon, October 1378

They found the *Julienne*. It was discreetly moored round a bend in the river. Two pirates who guarded it recognised Matty as the archer monk, and he had his bow.

Matty drew the bow. Ishraq lit an arrow and gave it to him, then lit two more and held them ready to load. Matty hailed the pirates. "Send out your leader," he demanded.

"We have no leader," replied one of the guards. "You killed him."

"There's always a leader. Send him out. Or the arrows fly."

The guards conferred, then one went below deck. And the new pirate leader emerged. He was a youth, no more than seventeen or eighteen. He looked nervous.

Matty shouted to him. "Now send out the real leader." There was no response, so he sent his first arrow flying, aiming for a clear area of the deck. The pirates quickly put out the fire.

The rest of the deck was a mess. The pirates had neglected it. The sails were down but just left lying, while cloths, pieces of timber and two barrels of pitch were also on deck. Matty took aim at the barrels. "My next arrow will light up the boat," he shouted. "Now, send him out."

The young pirate froze. Behind him, a figure appeared. Frere Jean. He was no longer wearing his priest garments.

"How did you know?" Edwina asked Matty.

"It takes a certain kind of man to want to be a leader. A man who thinks himself above others. A man like Jean." He shouted up again. "No longer a man of God, then?"

"I am always that, but the church is no longer my home. It has let me down. I will do God's work without it."

Ishraq spoke up. "We spoke to a monk who says you are a good man. So why did you try to poison the Benedictine?"

343

"I travelled across France with that man," said Jean, hissing the last two words. "I saw the adulation he got but had to suffer his blasphemous words. Then he rejected the Eucharist when the archbishop offered it. He is ungodly. Pope Clement should have dealt with him as such, instead of ordering a mockery of a trial."

"You didn't trust God. You had to use poison," asked Matty.

"The Devil has cunning beyond any understanding of men. He would have conjured your freedom. I had to act to ensure justice prevailed."

"Justice? You don't know what that is," said Matty.

"I do what I must do. And now, I have been given a second chance to rid the world of your evil. I have enough men here to deal with you, your one-armed daughter and the young infidel." He turned to the pirate crew. "Kill them all," he ordered.

One of the pirates responded, running to the boarding plank and charging across it. He never reached dry land. Matty still had a flaming arrow at his bow and sent it into the pirate's body. The pirate screamed in anguish and dived into the river.

The other pirates stopped. They had seen the archer take down their comrades the previous day and now one more was dead.

"Cowards," shouted Jean, waving his sword at his own men. He chose the weakest, the youth who had said he was the leader, and attacked him. But the others mutinied, defended the youth, falling on Jean, disarming him then holding him down. One looked towards Matty. "What now?" he asked.

"I want no more bloodshed. You will leave the boat. We will take it back to the people you stole it from. Tie Frere Jean up, then you can go peacefully."

The pirates agreed.

Edwina was shocked. She wanted *all* the pirates to be punished for Briony's death. But she understood. No more bloodshed. No more waste of young lives. And the boat with its cargo of silks would go back where it belonged.

The pirates left. They considered offering themselves to work for Oudin, but they were tired of life on the river and wanted to go back to sea. So they made for a tavern where mates went looking for new crew. The mate from the *Hero* was there, doing just that. He recognised them but ignored them. They were not the sort he wanted.

Matty marched Frere Jean to the palais. Edwina accompanied him. Ishraq said he had other business to attend.

They asked to see Frere Paul. When he came, they told him what had happened and asked him to have Frere Jean arrested. But Frere Paul shook his head. "Do you have proof for what you claim?" he said.

Edwina began. "I saw Jean talking with the pirate leader," she said.

"Talking is no crime," said Paul.

"He tried to poison my father at the altar," she added.

"What did you see, exactly?" asked Paul.

She considered. "He poured the wine. My father took a taste and it was bitter."

"It had the odour of hemlock," added Matty. "And I found a vial."

Paul shrugged. "Wine can be bitter. Did you see Jean put hemlock into the cup?"

"No, but it had to be him that did it."

Jean laughed. "They have no proof, just speculation, idle guesswork."

"I'm afraid he is right," said Paul. He gave Jean a knowing look. "I know what you did. The bishop believes the same as these people. But without proof I cannot act. Release him," he ordered the guards.

The guards let Jean go and he walked away, grinning.

"I wish I could do more," said Paul. "But I am a lawyer by trade and your accusations would not stand any legal test. I'm sorry."

"This is outrageous. And what about Oudin?" said Edwina. "Will he also escape punishment for what he has done?"

"There are many Oudins and Erichs in Avignon. If we arrested them all the cells would be overflowing. But Oudin has shown his true colours. He will be *persona non grata* to the pope. If he hoped to get rich by killing Erich, he will find he has made a mistake. Pope Clement has the power in this city. Oudin will find he is unable to trade in the way Erich did. And although he has men-at-arms, the pope has more. Oudin's future is not as bright as he will believe."

"It is not enough," said Edwina.

"No. But it is how things work here," replied Paul.

Matty and Edwina returned to the *Hero*. They ate with the prince. They were despondent. Jean and Oudin had escaped real punishment.

****

Ishraq was at the house of Madame de Bruler. He was sure that's where Lella would be. He asked to see her. "It will cost you the normal rate," said the madame.

He pleaded just to have a few minutes with Lella, just to speak with her, but without success. He did not have much but had to use what he had to buy an hour with Lella.

She was not glad to see him. "I have customers waiting," she said. "So go away."

"I have paid to be with you. You can't refuse me."

She shrugged and started to disrobe. "No," he said gently.

She sighed and calmed. They talked for a while. He told her his plans for himself and Lakshmi. "Come with us," he said.

"Are you building a harem?" she responded.

"Of course not. But the prince needs able workers, women included."

"I can't do anything. I can't cook, sew, clean..."

"Lakshmi can. She will teach you."

"No thank you. I cannot come with you. This place is my life now."

He was annoyed at her stubbornness. "So stay a slave," he said. "but what of your sons?"

Her eyes closed and tears formed. "They are with Oudin. They will be trained as squires. I have abandoned them. I had to. It's my biggest regret; that and my failure to keep a promise to help a young maid. She, too is Oudin's now."

"Then let us hope he treats her better than Erich did. You won't change your mind?"

"No. I cannot. Please, just leave me in peace."

****

Matty had finished his meal. "We have nobody on the *Julienne*," he said. "I will check that all is secured for the night."

Edwina offered to go with him. "It's not necessary," he said. "You are tired. Rest." She was falling asleep where she sat, so she agreed.

When Matty got to the boat, all seemed well. He made some checks and worked to secure the decks against the weather, then went down into the hold. The cargo of silks was still there. It would be good to return them to their rightful owners.

He heard a noise on deck, and a face appeared at the top of the steps.

"Thought you were rid of me, didn't you?" said Frere Jean. "I guessed you would come here. Didn't expect you to be alone, though."

"And I thought you would have fled like the coward you are."

"Why? I am an innocent man, free to do as I please in the city."

Matty saw that Jean held a taper. A barrel of pitch had been rolled to the top of the steps. It was clear what he intended.

Matty had a sword, useful against men but useless against a wildfire. He edged towards the steps, the only way out, but was cornered. Frere Jean laughed as he jammed the barrel in the hatch, stepped back and dropped the taper into it.

The highly flammable pitch caught immediately and the flames blocked Matty's exit. He was trapped. He tried in vain to get near the barrel to dislodge it, but it was impossible. The heat was already intense, and the flames were like a wall. He felt his face burning.

Once the cargo of silks caught, the whole area below deck would be an inferno. He moved the sacks away from the fire. It bought him a little time but he prepared himself to die a horrible death.

Jean was still laughing as he made his way towards the boarding plank. When he got there, someone was waiting.

Edwina had felt guilty leaving her father to do the work on the Julienne, so doused herself with water to wake up, then followed him. Now she stood between Jean and an easy escape. "Not so fast," she told him." He laughed maniacally.

She knew why. Her only weapons were words. "I can't understand it," she said. "You are a man of God. You help the poor. There's goodness in you. So why join a gang of pirates?" .

It was the right tactic. Jean wanted to explain. It halted his escape. "You are right," he said. "I've fallen low since I arrived in this city of greed. I was so enthusiastic, expecting something holy, different from the cesspits such as Paris. Never have I been so shocked. In the end I decided that if that was the way of things here, I may as well take my share and steal from men who did not deserve their wealth. Then God spoke to me and I knew I had to do one more thing for my salvation. He told me the Devil had sent a demon here in the form of a monk, the Benedictine. I tried to kill him but failed. This time I will not."

"It was not God but the Devil who spoke to you. You were tricked."

He shook his head. "No. It was God. I know it."

"The pirates you fell in league with were evil. I saw them take this boat. They killed innocent god-fearing people, poor people. I watched a young nun take her own life rather than suffer rape." She let the words sink in and saw they made him think. She went on. "You let the Devil in. His cunning invaded your soul, telling you to do an evil deed, persuading you to kill a good man, my father. You are a fool."

348

Jean was taken aback. "I, I, I did what I thought was right," he said. There was little conviction there. Edwina thought Jean had harboured doubts about what he was doing all along but persuaded himself that what he was doing was right, because it suited him to do so.

"And now you must right the wrongs you have done."

Jean's face contorted as he wrestled with his thoughts and emotions. He looked up to the sky, hands spread wide. "Tell me what to do," he shouted. "I don't know what to do."

"You do know," said Edwina, her voice low and even. "You know what evil looks like. My father is good. Choose good over evil."

Jean kept his hands wide but his head turned and his eyes landed on the fire that was now engulfing the hatch and steps down to the hold. He screamed and ran to the hatch, then wrapped his arms round the blazing barrel, ignoring his own safety. With enormous effort, he hauled the barrel out and on to the deck. His clothing was ablaze, his skin red and his hair melting like wax with the heat.

The steps to the hold had burned away. Matty was weak because the fire had sucked the air from the hold. Until Jean removed the barrel, he had been close to losing consciousness.

With the steps gone, there was a gap in the flames. He summoned what strength he had left and threw himself at the hatch, grabbing hold of the deck and hanging there for dear life. If he fell, he would die.

Edwina saw him and dragged the edge of a sail to within his reach. He grabbed it, hauling himself up. She took his arm and helped him out. Much of the deck was ablaze. She helped him to his feet and they ran to the smouldering boarding plank and rushed across.

They looked back at Frere Jean. He lay across the burning barrel, still alive but screaming in pain. They saw him look once again to the heavens and heard him ask for forgiveness, then succumb to the fire.

Matty was coughing out some of the smoke he had inhaled, while Edwina retched at the sight of the priest's blackened body. When she

349

recovered, she looked again at the charred remains of the priest. "Will he be in Heaven or Hell tonight?" she asked.

"When I was waiting to take the Eucharist, I wondered how I would be judged," he replied. "The priest is not the only man to have done terrible things. I still remember my part in the English army, bringing death and destruction to the villages of Normandy."

"How can good and evil deeds be weighed?" said Edwina.

They watched the boat burn to ashes. There would be nothing left of it or its cargo to return to the rightful owners.

Chapter Forty-Nine

Avignon, November 1378

The meeting was informal. Pope Clement was in the papal gardens. There was, of course, an entourage, but only a small one.

Edwina and Ishraq were not invited. There was only Matty, accompanied by Frere Paul. Matty no longer wore his Benedictine robes. He had finally cast them off. He wore a simple short tunic. "No longer a monk, I see," said the pope.

"I never was," replied Matty.

There were no preliminaries. A table was set, the polished silverware filled with local fruit. But Matty was offered no refreshment. Pope Clement did not like to dwell on matters of business and wanted this matter to end. He got straight to the point. "I have given your situation a lot of thought," he said. "Many hours in deliberation and prayer. You will be wondering what I have concluded."

Matty stayed silent. He did not think he was expected to speak.

"Frere Paul told me what Frere Jean did." Matty assumed the pope was referring to the attempted poisoning and Jean's dealings with the pirates. He was not. "It was a wonderful, selfless act, giving his life to save you. It was the act of a pious man who knew right from wrong. He saved your life on that boat. That was your trial by ordeal and God chose Frere Jean as His instrument to save you. You are free to go."

Matty thought to object. He carried very different memories of Jean. How could a man who attempted to murder him be God's instrument for anything?

"I will, of course make sure Frere Jean is remembered in some way," added the pope. "Not a statue, I think, but something worthy. A plaque, perhaps."

Matty could not believe what he was hearing. "Are you aware what you are saying?" he said, earning him a sideways look from Paul.

"Of course I am," said the pope. "But there is a Bible quote, fittingly from the book of John. *Greater love hath no man than this, that a man lay down his life for his friends.* And that is what he did."

"Friends? He was mine once, or so I thought. I have known better."

The pope had made his decision and had a busy schedule. "Think what you will," he said. "Now, I have things to do."

Matty was ushered out. At the palais entrance, Paul asked him how he felt. "The pope sees things differently from me, but I no longer care," he said. "All I want is to go home and see my family."

Paul nodded. "England. A troublesome place. Your young king, or rather his uncle, John of Gaunt, raided Brittany this summer. His army was sent back to England with a flea in its ear. Will England and France never end their interminable war?"

"I want no part in that. I simply wish to be home, if I still have one."

"Well, God speed, but don't ever forget that God has pardoned you today in this holy city. Find a way to serve Him. Maybe one day you might even become a real monk."

"I think not."

****

Back at the *Hero*, Edwina was getting things ready for the start of their long journey home. She was also saying her goodbyes to Ishraq and Lakshmi. She had a posy of flowers for Lakshmi, as a parting gift.

"Perhaps we will meet again," suggested Ishraq.

She shook her head. "You are heading a thousand miles east, while I go a thousand miles north. No, I think this is our final parting." She squeezed his hand and kissed him lightly on the brow, then did the same to Lakshmi. "Look after him," she told her.

"I have to," replied Lakshmi. "He is all I have in the world."

Edwina took something from her bag. "I have noticed how worn your pouch is," she told Ishraq. "The letter you carry is important to you and this will be a sturdy place to keep it. I bought it in the local market, as a parting gift." She presented him with a new leather pouch.

Ishraq was emotional and lost for words, tears welling. Lakshmi came to his rescue. "I will see he looks after it," she said. "Thank you."

Just then, Matty returned from his meeting with the pope and told them what happened. Edwina was incandescent, but Ishraq found it all amusing. "Attempt murder then get a plaque commemorating your goodness," he said. "It's a strange religion."

Somebody was shouting up to the boat. They went to see who it was. And there stood Lella.

Ishraq went to her. She was distraught, her clothing torn. She had been crying. He helped her on to the boat.

It was clear Lella had suffered a beating at Madame de Bruler's. Matty tended to her cuts and bruises, while Edwina gave her weak wine to drink. Ishraq fussed. No-one asked her to tell what had happened. She would tell them if, and when she was ready to do so.

Briefly, Lakshmi saw Lella as a rival for Ishraq's affections, but as she watched, her worries disappeared. Ishraq was being kind, caring, considerate, being himself. There was no desire for Lella in his eyes.

Lella remembered Matty from his time at the villa. He thanked her again for helping him escape from Erich, and she thanked him for the advice he gave to Ishraq, advice that cured her Holy Fire.

The mate came to see what was going on. "We need to take her with us," said Ishraq, almost as a command.

"Not another woman passenger. One is enough," replied the mate.

Ishraq waved his hand in the direction of the new recruits. The mate had put a new crew together but they were very young, little more than boys. "Tell me which one will cook you a decent meal? Who will sew holes in the sails? Who will tend the sick when we are at sea?"

The mate frowned. "You can do those things?" he asked Lella. She hesitated, but saw Lakshmi behind him, nodding encouragement. "Yes, I can," she said.

The mate was still unsure. "Two women?" he repeated. Like many sailors, he had a superstitious aversion to taking women on board.

The prince appeared. He had seen Lella arrive. He saw her injuries, and her beauty. "Let her come with us," he said, then disappeared back to his cabin.

Lakshmi gently pulled Lella to one side and whispered in Lella's ear. "I saw how the prince looked at you," she said. "I think you have found a new admirer, and a royal one at that." She giggled.

"He is good looking," said Lella. "A woman could do worse. What is his name?"

Lakshmi frowned. She realised she did not know the answer. "He is the prince," she said. "I don't think Ishraq even knows his name."

"Intriguing," said Lella.

"As you say, a woman could do worse, name or no name," said Lakshmi. They laughed together, then re-joined the others. "Can you tell me where we are going?" asked Lella. "Is it Baghdad?"

"I don't know," said Ishraq, frowning. "But the prince's home is to the east."

Edwina laughed. "You will get there. One day. Remember, have faith, and never give up on your dream."

Matty and Ishraq had spent some time over ale sharing memories of Rottingdean. Ishraq remembered more than Matty. It was the one area of Matty's mind that refused to come back fully to him. The blow to his head that day had wiped out the events of the battle. Now they said their goodbyes, doing what men did. A firm handshake and good luck wishes were as near as they got to an emotional parting.

All the farewells were done. There was sadness mixed with hope within the group.

Edwina and her father could go home. Ishraq and Lakshmi had found love. Lella had new companionship, though she had also lost her sons. Together, they could continue their search for a place that was safe, where they were free and that they could call home.

Part Ten

A king's Pleasure

Chapter Fifty

Noyon, Northern France, December 1378

Edwina had insisted they took this route. It was the reverse of the route she had taken to get to Avignon, following the Rhone and Saone. It was as quick as any other, and her father knew how important this was for her, so readily agreed.

He waited outside while she went into the great cathedral.

There were so few people inside that her footsteps echoed, announcing her presence.

She went straight to the side chapel Briony had taken her to months earlier. It would be a simple act, an act of homage with a quiet prayer. She had bought flowers and a single candle. She placed the flowers lovingly by the cushion that had been Briony's quiet place, then lit the candle and placed it with others that were lined up on a table.

She knelt to say a prayer for her friend. She had been rehearsing the words along the way from Avignon. She bowed her head.

"Briony. Thank you for changing my life. Without you I would never have found my father. You are ever in my thoughts. Be happy in paradise."

"I am always happy."

Edwina looked to the ceiling, expecting to see Briony in angel form. She was hearing Briony's voice from the grave. Then she felt a hand on her shoulder and turned. Briony stood there, neither angel nor ghost but a live person. Edwina took Briony's hand and got up, then hugged the young nun she had thought was dead. She felt tears flow.

"I saw you drown," said Edwina.

"No, you saw me go into the water."

"But you stayed under. You never surfaced."

"Do you remember what I told you about my childhood that I lived by a lake. I swam in the lake every day. I am an excellent swimmer."

"So why did you not jump from the boat straight away?"

"I froze. The currents looked too strong. A river is not like a lake to swim in. But when I saw your head emerge out of the water, I thought there was a chance I might survive, so took it. I owe my life to you."

"But you disappeared."

"I stayed underwater for as long as I could, to fool the pirates into thinking I was dead. It seems I also fooled you. I'm sorry. When I finally surfaced you were gone, so I made my way to the shore. I thought about continuing to Avignon, but something told me my work was done and I should come back here. I'm sorry."

"Don't be. You are alive, and I am so happy."

Edwina hugged Briony again and gave her the flowers. "I'm glad they are no longer a graveside token," she said. "They are full of life and so are you. But come, you must meet my father."

"You found him! I knew you would."

Edwina took Briony to meet her father, giving her a brief account of the events in Avignon. Briony was wide-eyed. "I went so far to find the Benedictine, yet it is he who has found me," she said.

Matty pointed to his clothing. "I don't wear a monk's clothing now and am no longer called by that name. I'm an ordinary man again. I am myself."

"I felt called to go and meet you," said Briony. "But it was Edwina I was really called to meet."

Matty could see how important this reunion was for his daughter. He wanted to press on but decided they should stay a while. "We will rest for a day or two," he said. "We need a break from our journey."

So they stayed, until it was time to move on again, and when they did, Edwina had a new spring in her step.

Chapter Fifty-One

Windsor Great Forest, February 1379

It was not snowing but the driving English rain was enough to cause misery after such a long journey. They had travelled more than seven hundred miles.

"Remember how warm it was in Avignon?" said Matty.

"I don't think we've been dry since Dover," replied Edwina.

"No. But it's good to be nearly home. Not much further now. A mile, no more."

"Do you think they will be there?"

"Each day for the last three months I've wondered, and thought *yes*, then *no*, a hundred times."

"And today?"

"Today, it has been a thousand times."

They rode the final mile in silence. Matty sat up on his horse, craning his neck, hoping to see smoke. A fire burning in the old lodge would mean people were there. But there was no smoke.

The lodge gate was open. That meant little. It was rarely kept closed. The location was remote with few casual visitors.

No children came out to greet them. That was another bad sign. They got off their horses. With immense self-discipline, Matty took his mount for a well-earned drink from the stream. His whole being wanted to burst through the lodge doors, but his horse's needs came first. Edwina did the same. She looked sideways at him. His face was gaunt with anxiety. He was expecting the worst.

They went inside the lodge. It was as Matty had left it more than a year previously. The furniture was where it had been. But there was no sign of life, and neither were there any signs of recent habitation. The larders were empty.

He explored the bedrooms looking for personal possessions that Charlotte and the children would never have left behind. There were none. Wherever Charlotte was, she was not planning to return. He sunk to his knees.

Edwina found him. She helped him up. "Let's eat," she said.

They collected water from the stream. For Edwina, memories flooded back, of times playing in the water, but also of darker days. She paused by some rocks where once she had to hide from evil men who had come to do the family harm.

In the lodge's outbuildings was firewood, stored to keep it dry. They collected a bundle and built a fire in the main hall, then ate what was left of the rations they had with them. "So, what now?" she asked him.

"They may have gone to Kent," he replied. "Charlotte's sister Olivia lives there. But I will go to see Parker. He will know where they are."

Edwina remembered what Charlotte told her about Parker, the forest warden. Charlotte said he was in a hospital in Oxford and had lost his mind. She decided to keep that to herself. Windsor was the place to go, whatever Parker's situation. "I will come with you," she said.

"Your mother needs to know you are alive and well. You should have written to her from France."

"We both know the letter would take as long to get there as it will take for me to get home. Though you are right, I must go home soon. But not until we find out what has happened to Charlotte and the children. Anyway, Windsor is in the right direction for home, so it's no delay."

"As you wish, and of course I will be glad of your company."

They sat for a while, staring into the fire. "Something occurred to me in France," said Edwina. "When we approached Noyon I thought about trying to find Briony's family to tell them what happened to her. It made me think, how would I have dealt with it if I found out you had died at Rottingdean? How would I tell Charlotte? *What* would I tell Charlotte? Is it best to know, or to stay with hope? In the end I decided Briony's family was better off not knowing."

"And then she was alive."

"Yes, thank God."

****

The following day they made their way to Windsor. The weather had improved and the sun created dappled shade in the forest. It was beautiful, but that did not lift their spirits. They both carried a sense of foreboding with them.

At the castle gates, Matty asked to see Parker. The guard gave him a quizzical look. "Parker?"

"The keeper of the forest."

A second guard intervened. "You know," he said. "The old booze hound." He pretended to stagger, mimicking a drunken man.

"Oh, him," said the first guard. "I can tell you where to find him but you'll get no sense out of him this time of day."

"Or any time of day," said the second guard, laughing.

"Just tell me where."

"Try Pesscot street."

Edwina was surprised to hear that Parker was not in the hospital.

Matty knew *Pesscot* street. It ran down from the castle towards the river. It was actually Peascod street, named because it was an area of the town dedicated to the growing of peas, but in the local accent, it became Pesscot street. And it contained half a dozen inns.

They found Parker with ease, lying outside one of the inns, just as the guard had said, drunk so early in the day. He did not recognise Matty. He probably could not remember his own name. His clothing smelled of stale vomit. His beard and hair were unkempt, and he was much thinner than he had been, the result of much ale and very little food. It was a pitiful sight. He had once been a proud and important man.

Matty and Edwina spent the rest of the morning working to sober Parker up. In return, he gave them foul language and demands for a drink. At one point, in his frustration, he became violent, but lacked the strength to cause any problems for Matty.

By mid-afternoon, Parker was finally talking some sense, mixed in with garbled nonsense. Edwina cajoled him until she managed to get him to understand who Matty was and why they had come back to Windsor. Understanding dawned.

"I remember you," said Parker. "The lodge. You lived there. You rebuilt it." He cackled. "Isabella got it for you." Then he was serious again. "The old king should never have neglected it."

"That's right, but what happened to my wife, Charlotte and my children?" asked Matty. "Where are they?"

Parker tried his best to dredge his memory for an answer, but it would not come. So he reverted to his new self. "Buy me a drink," he pleaded. "Buy me a drink." And, against his better judgement, that was all Matty could do.

So Matty and Edwina returned to the castle gates. "I need to see John of Gaunt," said Matty.

The guard, the same one as before, smirked. "And who shall I say wants to see him? A lord, or maybe a duke?" His voice was sarcastic.

Matty explained who he was and why he wanted to see the prince. The guard was unimpressed but did she job, going to report the request. He returned a little sheepish, "Prince John is not at home, but you are granted an audience with one of the king's courtiers."

The gates opened and they entered the castle. As they crossed the inner courtyard, more memories came back to Edwina, of the wedding she was invited to but never attended, the friends and enemies she made, and the young princess whose wedding she missed.

They were taken to one of the drawing rooms, with its fully panelled walls, beautiful wall hangings and sumptuous furniture. And there, sitting by the fire, was someone familiar to Edwina.

Robert de Vere, Earl of Oxford, was now aged seventeen. Accompanying him was a youth a year or two younger then himself.

It was the earl's wedding to young Princess Phillipa that Edwina should have attended last time she was at Windsor. She wondered whether he remembered her. She did not have to wait long to find out.

"We meet again, Lady Edwina," he said. "And I presume this to be your father, the archer who once saved the life of my mother-in-law."

"Yes, this is my father, Matty Cutler." Hands were shaken, "How fairs your wife?" asked Edwina.

"She is well enough," he replied. "And she sometimes speaks of you with fondness."

"She must be twelve now. Nearly an adult," said Edwina pointedly. The tender age at which the princess wed had always been a matter of distaste for her.

The earl laughed, dismissing the irony. "We have a king the same age," he said. "Some people have to grow up quickly."

"Too quickly, I think."

This earned a look of reproach from her father. They needed the earl to be on their side but Edwina was provoking him. He intervened. "We are looking for my wife and children," he said.

"A man who gets to the point," said the earl. "I like that. Well, I was with his majesty King Richard when the guard brought your request for an audience. As soon as I knew Edwina was with you, I volunteered to deal with it."

The earl introduced the young man who was in the room. "This is Gregory. He has been keeper of the parks since Parker retired. I fetched him so he could tell you what happened."

Gregory was a tall, thin, spotty teen. When he spoke, it was without confidence because he was afflicted with a stammer. No doubt he got his position because he was related to someone of importance. But he did have the information Matty needed. He addressed Edwina. "It was, it was early December," he said. "The Countess of Bedford had sent a, a letter from France telling of your visit to her."

Edwina smiled. "So she did act on our behalf, despite what she said."

362

Gregory continued. "The king read the, the letter and asked about the, the lodge. He had, he had, forgotten it was there."

The earl had little patience with Gregory's stammering, so took up the story himself. "The king was advised about the lease you held. If you were missing, presumed dead, the lease would not be renewed at the end of the year. He decided the future of the lodge should be a matter for the king's pleasure."

Matty thought that if the earl already knew what happened, Gregory need not be there "In other words, he could do what he wanted with it, regardless of how that affected my family," he said.

"Has that not always been the case? Anyway, our young king is honest and just, a patron of arts and a man of decency."

There was more than loyal respect in the earl's voice. There was a level of personal affection. Edwina was reminded that, when she was at the earl's home of Hedingham Castle, rumours had circulated about him, that he enjoyed the company of men as much as that of women. "I have known him since we were children," added the earl. "And am honoured now to be his closest advisor."

"He has evicted my family."

"Be careful and hold your tongue here. And you are wrong. The lodge is still yours to live in until such time as the king decides otherwise."

"So, where are they?"

The earl looked to Gregory. It was clear he did not know.

"Your wife, your wife got a letter herself," said Gregory. "She said she had to go, to go, away."

"Away? Where to?"

"It was a family matter. The letter was from a, from a relative. Your wife said her sister was in danger. She had to go home."

Matty and Edwina exchanged a look. He had thought Charlotte might be in Kent, but this was news. Kent was where he needed to go, but with added urgency. If Olivia was in danger, it was likely that Charlotte and the children were also.

363

"So, will you go back to the lodge?" asked the earl.

"To live there at the king's pleasure, wondering when he will come and take it from us at a minute's notice? I think not." He got up to leave. There were no more pleasantries, no invitation for Edwina to visit Phillipa at Hedingham. Just a cold ending to a formal meeting.

Outside, there was still some light left in the day. "I can make five miles before dark," said Matty. "Get yourself a room and set off home to Nottinghamshire in the morning."

She shook her head. "Your business is unfinished, which means mine is also. I'm coming with you. Home will have to wait. But this time I *will* write to my mother."

He feigned anger with her and made a weak attempt at protestation but was glad she would be going with him. She had become more than his daughter. She was his best friend and most trusted companion. They had shared more than one adventure, more than one life-threatening experience. It seemed he was heading for another, and there was no-one he would rather have by his side than Edwina.

Edwina quickly wrote her letter and left it with a castle clerk to forward to her mother. She felt no sadness that she would not yet be going home. She was living a life of her choosing. It felt good.

They set off, five miles to cover. It would take two weeks or more to get to their destination, Kent. There was no time to lose. But what would they find there? What was the danger the family faced?

Edwina had a wistful look.

"What are you thinking?" her father asked her.

"I was wondering where Ishraq is. I hope he is lying lazily in the sunshine in some lovely place, but something tells me he is more likely meeting some new danger, just as we are. Do you suppose he ever wonders where we are and what we are doing?"

"I'm sure of it. You are kindred spirits, I think."

"Yes, we are that."

Chapter Fifty-Two

The Mediterranean Sea, February 1379

Land had come into view. They had reached their destination.

For almost three months they had made little progress, hampered by unusually bad winter weather in the Mediterranean. Now, they sailed under a clear azure sky skirting the west coast of an island looking for a place to land. They could see only one other ship, out on the horizon.

A wide bay came into view, shaped like a horseshoe. They entered it. Inside, the sea was calm. It was a good, sheltered place to drop anchor.

The *Hero*'s mate patted Ishraq on the back. "At last," he said. "Finally, we have reached the island."

Ishraq knew why they had come here. The prince had explained. The island was on the maritime silk route, and the prince had long wished to find out more about the western extremity of the ancient trade route that extended for 4,000 miles.

When he first learned where they were going, Ishraq was devastated. It was west, the wrong direction for Baghdad.

Now, thinking of his wish to reach Baghdad, he went to the pouch Edwina gave him, intending just to touch, to hold his precious document. He was about to take it out when he noticed something else there, tucked in a fold. It was a small piece of vellum. On it was an address. *Lucan House Manor, near Nottingham, England.*

Edwina's address. Why was it there? It must be so he could contact her in the future. He felt happy to think he was important to her, yet sad because he was unlikely to see her again. He thought of her as a sister, the nearest thing to family he had until he met Lakshmi.

Lakshmi was now his wife. They had wed in a simple ceremony. Nothing could now dishearten him. He smiled at the mate, who thought he had gone mad.

The prince came on deck to see the island. Lella was with him. Lakshmi had been right about the glint in the prince's eye when the two first met. The relationship had developed and blossomed during the months of inactivity in Marseilles.

"Prepare yourself for excitement," said the prince excitedly. "There will be traders and wares here from all over the world, and I will strike some new deals. But first, we will relax in this beautiful bay."

"I wouldn't be so sure," said Ishraq. He pointed out to the bay entrance, then up into the hillsides.

A large ship had followed them into the bay. It carried a flag of red and yellow stripes. "It must be the one we saw earlier," said the mate.

And on the highest hillside, a beacon was lit. It was the call to arms for the people of the villages surrounding the bay.

"Let's hope they are just being cautious," said the prince. "If not, we are in for a very warm welcome."

The mate shouted orders. "Make ready. We have company."

Ishraq ushered Lakshmi and Lella to a cabin. "Do you think we will be attacked?" asked Lakshmi.

"I don't know," he replied. "But I will protect you. I promise."

"We will soon know whether our prince has made a good decision bringing them us the Kingdom of Mallorca," said Lella.

Ishraq climbed the steps to the deck. He paused to take in the air, then took out the piece of vellum Edwina gave him and spoke to it as though to her. "Are you home now, lady? Or are you on some new adventure, just as I am. Maybe our paths will cross again someday. Until I met Lakshmi, you were the nearest thing I had to a family, like a sister." He put the vellum back into the pouch, tucking it in alongside another souvenir, the lucky clover the captain of the Santa Lucia gave him. "Now, let's find out what these islanders want of us."

He took a deep breath and went to his duties with the rest of the crew, preparing to meet the islanders. He was confident now in his ability to meet new dangers, and ready to face whatever might come next.

Author's Notes

The Benedictine is my fifth book in the Matty Cutler series and the stories have followed Matty over more than thirty years of his life.

I have explained before that I am not an historian but I do try to be true to the historical events which are the context for the stories.

My main source this time has been *Avignon of the Popes, City of Exiles* by Edwin Mullins. I recommend it as a fascinating account of the time during which the papacy was in Avignon.

When I started writing about Matty, his family and friends, I never thought it would go beyond a single book, but then it became a trilogy and the trilogy became a series. I am now researching book six.

Thank you for reading *The Benedictine*. I hope you enjoyed it. I look forward to creating the next chapter in Matty's story. No doubt Edwina and Ishraq will again play central roles.

Allan Jonas

Previous books in the series are:

There's No Time to Mourn, a Matty Cutler Tale

Two Kinds of Evil

False Prophecy

The Yeoman's Daughter

Printed in Great Britain
by Amazon

11368516R00210